ENTWINED DESTINY

"You see, *chérie,* fate made us meet. Will you not believe as I do? Here we are in the most unlikely setting for two people from France, and yet we meet. I'll wager that I know why you come to this lovely spot and sit on the cliff, to look across the land beyond the water to France, *n'est-ce pas?*" Pierre asked.

"Yes, it is so." Charmaine was amazed for he understood her feelings so completely.

"I knew it," he told her and then drew her to him, pressing her against his broad chest. Slowly his mouth met hers, his lips capturing hers and her thick lashes fluttered with a curious excitement as they embraced. Such touching and caressing was new to her, but she readily responded to the wonderful sensations evoked in her.

Pierre sensed that she'd never been kissed as he was kissing her now, and he lingerly savored the sweetness of her. Rare, she was! He was determined not to lose her again. Possess her he must!

MOONLIT SPLENDOR
Wanda Owen

ZEBRA BOOKS
KENSINGTON PUBLISHING CORP.

ZEBRA BOOKS

are published by

Kensington Publishing Corp.
475 Park Avenue South
New York, NY 10016

First printing: March 1987

Printed in the United States of America

With sincere appreciation to Zebra Books, I'd like to express my thanks by dedicating this book to Roberta Grossman, president; my dear, devoted editor, Leslie Gelbman; the artist, who creates such magnificent covers and numerous members of the staff, who work on my books.

Author's Note

My story and my characters are fictitious, but the New Madrid earthquake which occurred on December 16, 1811 was very real and very devastating. Amazingly, no lives were lost because the region was so sparsely settled at that time. However, in my story, I took the liberty of having one character, White Wolf, die.

In January and February of 1812, two more earthquakes hit the same area, and their effects were felt as far away as Canada and the East Coast. Yet, out of all this devastation, a breathtaking sight was created—Reelfoot Lake. I've seen it and I can vouch for its beauty. This story was such a joy for me to write for this is the part of the country I was born and spent my childhood in.

They say this region is still seismically active. Can you imagine the untold damage that would occur if such horrendous earthquakes struck it today?

PART I

The Channel Islands

Chapter 1

Charmaine Lamoureux sat atop the rugged cliff gazing across the waters of the bay to the land beyond, the coastline of France. Only fifteen miles separated the island of Jersey from the Normandy coast but to Charmaine they might as well have been five hundred. She had a wistful look on her beautiful face as she mused that five years had gone by since she'd left France and come to Jersey to live with her aunt and uncle.

A gentle breeze caressed her, blowing her thick golden hair, as she sat in the serene splendor of the twilight. Her deep blue eyes stared across the waters as she silently vowed that someday she'd return to France, though it would not be the same now that her parents were dead.

Engrossed in her private world, she did not think about the darkness that would soon descend on her favorite spot on this lofty perch, nor did she heed her uncle's bellowing at the fine herd of milk cows grazing on thyme in the open meadows. Actually, she should have been in her Aunt Simone's kitchen helping her with the meal but she was daydreaming.

Her Uncle Angus was a hard-working farmer with a gentle, kind heart, and his wife Simone was the older sister of Charmaine's mother. The couple, whose three sons were already grown, had taken their orphan niece into their home on the island of Jersey. In the little brown granite cottage with green shutters Charmaine had been treated kindly by the Keene family. Like most of the farmers, the Keenes, spoke a patois, Norman French along with English, so Charmaine now spoke both languages.

Charmaine's moodiness had nothing to do with her aunt and uncle not being good to her. It simply came upon her from time to time, a calling and a yearning so intense she could not walk away from it.

Actually, she loved the beautiful countryside, the fertile fields, the colorful flowers, and the fruits and vegetables that grew with such abundance they supplied the family's needs and gave Angus a livelihood.

Now, as she sat at her favorite spot, she was unaware that the golden glowing twilight had darkened and the shadows of approaching night were moving in swiftly. Had she not been so bewitched by the blissful state she was in, she would have noticed that the distant shore was now obscured.

But the pretty golden-haired girl was enjoying that strange, wonderful magic which was hers alone. It was something she did not talk to anyone about, for she did not want to be thought daft.

The only person who might not laugh at her would be John, Simone's youngest son. He was little older than Charmaine, and she'd been closer to him than the others. But John was not home very often lately, not since he had his own fishing boat and went out daily into the bay seeking a catch.

Charmaine had been aware of his absence because Johnny, as she called him, was always playfully teasing her and she adored his fun-loving nature. Yes, she mused, she might just tell Johnny about this magical spot here on the cliff.

Johnny was to be at the cottage for dinner, to enjoy the catch of ormers he'd given to his mother to prepare, but caught up in her daydreaming state Charmaine had completely forgotten. Otherwise she would have been scampering to the cottage to greet Johnny and to enjoy the ormers, a special treat and very costly in the marketplace.

The lapping waters of the bay now covered the sandy beach, and there was a soft, rhythmic sound of waves slamming against the jutting cliffside reaching Charmaine's ears. It was soothing to her.

A few night birds trilled, and the contented lowing of Angus' cows filled the air. Simone moved hastily around her kitchen to see that her table was completely set now that the fish, potatoes, and bread were cooking.

Angus would be coming in from his chore of milking, and she hoped her tall, lanky son would soon be bursting through the door, a warm broad smile on his face, his unruly hair escaping from his billed cap to fall over his forehead.

But where, she wondered, was Charmaine? Not that Simone was about to complain to Angus when he came into the cottage, but it was dark and she worried about her beautiful niece who loved to stroll along the high cliffs beyond the meadowlands. Charmaine might fall if that pretty spun gold head of hers was up in the air and she was staring out in space, as Simone had caught her doing so often.

Disturbed, Simone thought of a couple of her son's friends, lads who had fishing boats over on the neighboring island of Guernsey. Simone didn't like the way they'd leered at Charmaine the last few times they'd come to visit John. Oh, she knew exactly why they eyed her niece!

Gently, she'd admonished Charmaine lately, telling the girl not to linger out by the cliffs after dark. Boats were always out in the bay, and Simone could well imagine the glorious image her niece projected up there on the cliffside.

Simone envisioned the secluded path Charmaine always

took. It trailed between two huge boulders as it headed down the cliff, on an incline, into the meadow. The isolation of that route would make it easy for the girl to be waylaid before she'd reach the open meadow.

Simone had lived long enough to know such things happened, but it was hard to impress that upon a young girl like Charmaine. She was so trusting and innocent. In fact, it had surprised Simone that Charmaine had shown so little interest in any of the young gents around the countryside or in the town of Saint Helier. *Mon Dieu,* they'd certainly ogled her the last couple of years!

That boyish, coltish figure of hers had changed drastically, and the girl's eyes had to be the most beautiful shade of blue Simone had ever seen. She was reminded of the deep purple and dark blue larkspurs in the garden when she gazed into Charmaine's eyes. Charmaine's mother had had blue eyes and so did Simone, but theirs were a different shade entirely. Actually, Simone could not see anything in Charmaine's features or expressions to remind her of herself or of her sister Suzanne.

Although Simone knew Charmaine did not wash her glorious, long, silky blond hair every day, it surely looked as though she did. It was so glossy it resembled shimmering gold.

As Simone puttered in her kitchen, letting her thoughts linger on her niece's loveliness, she became more concerned and nervous. Charmaine should have returned to the cottage. As her apprehension increased, she became vexed as she had when her boys were late returning for supper.

As she lifted the lid from one of her heavy iron pots, hot steam washed over her face, making her hastily replace the lid. She wiped her face with the end of her apron and sighed. "Maybe it was best I had boys. Girls are more worry and concern."

Behind her, a lighthearted husky chuckle sounded and she whirled around to see her son John standing there with a

14

bundle swung over his shoulder, a broad grin on his face. His brow arched up sharply in a skeptical teasing look as he inquired of Simone, "Now, you surely would not be talking about our little sweetheart Charmaine?"

"That I am! The little imp should have been here over a half-hour ago. I know she is just lingering up there on the cliff, but I do worry, John, when it gets dark and the child stays out there too long."

John tried to sound casual and he still wore a smile on his tanned face as he remarked, "Well, Momma, you know and I know she isn't a child anymore. No doubt, that is why you worry, eh?" He had been too aware of Charmaine's blossoming in the last year, but he had not dared to expose his innermost feelings about his golden-haired cousin. Indeed, they frightened him so he'd stayed more and more on his fishing boat. Yet the temptation Charmaine presented became overwhelmingly painful to him at times. She was so breathtakingly beautiful, so innocent and trusting.

"You are right, John, she is no child anymore. Terrance Heyward's young son has been coming around, and the son of the merchant over at Saint Helier is lovestruck over her. Mercy, John, I'm too old, I think sometimes, to raise a young girl, and I want to do right by Charmaine. She's real precious to me as you know."

"I know, Momma, and you're doing good. Look how you kept all us boys in line." John laughed.

Simone laughed too, recalling earlier times, but the years did make a difference and raising a young lady assuredly was not the same.

John didn't dare show Simone his own concern over Charmaine's lateness, for she was usually there to greet him when he made his appearances at the cottage and she must have known he was coming in from the pier. Trying to sound far more casual than he was feeling, he declared, "I'll go fetch the little minx. Spank her too, with your permission."

Simone waved him off and laughed, knowing he was only

15

jesting with her.

John left the cottage, and his long legs took giant strides through the meadow as he plowed across the width of it to get to the cliffs beyond. A bright full moon lit the way for him, but more than ever he agreed with his mother. This was entirely too late for Charmaine to be out on those damned cliffs alone.

There were always boats pulling into the bay below, and riffraff roamed the beaches, men into their cups from jugs of rum or whiskey. He shuddered to think what could happen to a naïve girl like Charmaine were she to meet up with a couple of those blokes. She wasn't that great a scrapper, though he knew she could wield a mighty blow on occasion when she was riled.

He began to walk much faster and his concern mounted.

Charmaine swore she'd never seen such an absolutely glorious moon as that in the evening sky, so perfectly round and gleaming, so golden. But she'd tarried far too long and she knew it. Aunt Simone had a right to be frightfully angry with her, she confessed to herself as she jumped up from the rocky ledge. Brushing down her cotton skirt and tucking her blouse neatly inside the waistline, she left the edge and headed down the sloping path which led directly into the open meadow.

Girlish whimsies still consumed the beautiful golden-haired girl as she light-heartedly strolled along. Capriciously, she swished her skirts and jauntily skipped. It seemed to Charmaine that the moon was lighting the way homeward. Oh, it was truly a wonderful night!

Some would think her silly if she told them how she felt this night, but she swore there was a magic to that big, old moon up there in the sky. By now, darkness was enfolding her, but Charmaine had no fear of missing her footing or going in the wrong direction, not with the moon to guide her.

But a pair of cold gray eyes was observing this saucy little miss who appeared in the moonlight. For a minute, their owner pondered whether he was still drunk from that afternoon's bottle of rum which he'd shared with his good buddy Jacques. Her hair, like golden moonbeams, flowed back from her face, and Pierre Renaud instinctively felt it was lovely.

This was a mermaid up from the sea. His eyes widened. But that was foolishness. He knew better. Nevertheless, she was an enchanting little creature, and he wasn't going to miss the opportunity of getting a closer look. Pierre never did, not where lovely ladies were concerned.

He leaped out of the seclusion of the tiny cove where he'd been asleep after Jacques had left him to return to his boat. The sight of the golden-haired girl had quickly sobered him, and Pierre now positioned himself at the rock gateway to which Charmaine was heading. Like a Colossus, he stood, muscled legs spread slightly apart, hands on hips.

A crooked grin etched his tanned face and his dark, tousled hair fell over one side of his forehead. His linen shirt had been snowy white and without wrinkles when he'd put it on that morning, but the front was carelessly unbuttoned now and his finely tailored pants were smudged from sitting on the ground while he caroused with Jacques.

When an awesomely tall shadow suddenly blocked the opening ahead of her, Charmaine stopped suddenly and her heart started beating erratically. This was a man . . . like the ones her dear Aunt Simone had warned her about. She realized just how casually she'd shrugged those warnings aside, smugly feeling nothing could happen to her. Now she didn't feel so smug!

She knew she couldn't just stand there and let him come farther into the tiny space between the rocks, but there was little chance a scream for help would be heard. No, she'd dare not shout. She forced her tiny feet to move forward.

Could she outsmart him, or bluff him into letting her pass?

Or would it be better to lie and tell him someone was behind him—her sweetheart, perhaps? Anything was worth trying.

A sudden surge of wild excitement pounded in Charmaine, the likes of which she'd never known. Exhilaration mingled with fear as the girl marched right up to peer into the face of the man standing before her.

"Well, pretty mermaid, you just came up from the sea?" he taunted her. Now that she was closer, Pierre again looked at the gleaming, long tresses of hair falling over her shoulders. The moonlight, reflecting down on them, made them appear more golden, and her face was more breathtakingly lovely than he'd imagined. The Frenchman experienced an overwhelming desire to kiss those lovely lips, half-parted and so alluring.

But blue eyes flashed fire as a soft voice declared in a firm, demanding tone, "Move over. I've no time to amuse you, sir!" This man had to be one of the rogues Charmaine had been warned about, but her boldness so surprised and shocked him that he broke into a gust of laughter, leaving Charmaine still unable to get around him. She let out an impatient, disgusted sigh, "Oh, you! You're disgusting! Move over!"

Still laughing, Pierre lifted her petite body upward, crushing it against his broad chest and capturing her lips with his. The sweet nectar of her lips made him greedy so he let his mouth linger, taking his fill of her divine sweetness.

Wide-eyed and breathless, Charmaine felt utterly helpless as she floundered while he held her there in the moonlight. But the gentle brushing of his lips against hers stirred a strange, wonderful sensation in her. It made her want to surrender, and she responded to his kiss.

At last, Pierre slowly released her, then sighed. "Oh, *ma petite! Ma petite,* you can't be of this earth." His voice was husky for untamed passion fired through him like a burning, searing liquid. His gray eyes devoured her as if he had to

18

satisfy himself that she was real and not a dream.

His grip on her relaxed slightly but he still held her about the waist when a loud, roaring voice broke the silence.

"Charlie! Charlie! Where the devil are you?"

At John's shouts, Charmaine broke from the strong hands clasping her, and she ran like a gazelle, away from Pierre and into the meadow.

A stunned Pierre Renaud stood frozen for a second, but Charmaine heard his deep voice calling out to her as she rushed on into the meadow, "See you, Charlie! See you real soon!" His deep laughter followed her. As she continued to rush farther away from him, she mumbled breathlessly, "Oh, no you won't!" But the heat of his lips, of his kiss, still seemed to be with her as she hurried toward John, still summoning her at the edge of the meadow.

She ran as fast as her legs would carry her, putting distance between her and the man back there in the darkness. But what a handsome devil he was!

Pierre Renaud could no longer see her spun-gold hair, which had flown wildly about as she'd rushed from his arms, nor her petite figure; the black of the night had swallowed her up. But his virile male body pulsing and aching with desire, he yearned for the mysterious little moon goddess he'd just held in his arms.

He sauntered slowly and thoughtfully along the path he'd trod hours earlier with his friend Jacques, when the sun was still high in the sky. There was no urgent hurry for Pierre to be anywhere so he ambled along, taking his time.

Who is she? he wondered. How anyone could possibly call that divine piece of loveliness Charlie, he couldn't figure out. Charlie be damned! The oaf had to be daft in the head! The soft curvy body his hands had felt and his arms had enclosed was no Charlie, and her soft rosebud lips were sweeter than honey.

Before he departed the shores of Guernsey, the neighboring island to Jersey, Pierre determined he'd find out who this golden-haired miss was. The reckless, adventuresome Frenchman had never been so enchanted by a young lady, and there had been many women in Pierre Renaud's life.

A woman was the reason he was on the Channel Island of Guernsey instead of home in France. Even the wealth of his father hadn't gotten him out of his present dilemma, although for once Pierre was not guilty of dallying with a nobleman's wife, of which he stood accused. To have proven his innocence, however, he would have had to put in jeopardy another lovely lady's reputation, the one with whom he'd spent the evening in question.

It was decided by the aristocratic Monsieur and Madame Étienne Renaud that their randy, handsome son should be sent to some faraway place. The logical choice was to the New World where Étienne's younger brother had gone two years ago to prospect for minerals in the virgin land across the vast ocean.

His period of waiting on the isle of Guernsey had been boring for Pierre, seemingly endless until this moonlit evening. Now he found himself hoping there would be more delays before the ship on which he was to sail to America arrived. He was not eager to get to his ultimate goal, some godforsaken place his uncle called Missouri Territory.

Pierre sighted his friend Jacques on the wharf as he sauntered toward the dock, and he threw up a hand to wave. Jacques waved back, cursing the other young man silently, nonetheless, for his lateness in returning to the docks. He'd planned to be back in Guernsey over an hour ago. Perhaps, he shouldn't have invited young Renaud to share the jug of rum that afternoon, he reminded himself. Old Wakefield would be angry.

Still, Jacques found it hard not to like the fun-loving Pierre. He watched the broad-shouldered Frenchman swagger toward him, shirt unbuttoned, hair tousled, and dirt smears on his pants. He looks not at all like an aristocrat's son, Jacques mused. Indeed, Pierre could have been one of the local fisherman, young, brawny, and tanned.

A fisherman or a seaman in port was what Charmaine assumed the roguish Renaud to be as she rushed breathlessly up to her cousin who had an anxious, concerned look on his face.

While he was greatly relieved to see her spritely figure dashing across the meadow toward him, John was still annoyed by her recklessness. "Are you bloody well stupid, Charlie, or do you just not care if harm comes your way?"

Well, harm had almost come her way, but she dared not tell him that. Instead, she pouted and appeared slightly shocked by his harsh tone. "How can you be so hateful, Johnny? You, of all people!" John found it impossible to stay angry with her when she had such a pained expression on her lovely face. He took her dainty hand in his and soothed her. "I was just worried about you, Charlie."

They walked along together, but Charmaine's thoughts were on the gray-eyed man she'd encountered back by the cliff. A couple of times her eyes darted in John's direction, yet it was the other man she saw. It was likely he'd haunt her dreams for many nights to come, she decided.

She prayed her cousin didn't detect her strange mood as they followed the path to the cottage. Of all the Keene family he understood her the best.

John Keene, however, was thinking of many other things at that particular moment as he held his cousin's hand in his and felt the tantalizing warmth of her young body by his side. He yearned so to kiss her lips that he ached, so he slowed his long, striding steps to lengthen the time of their moonlight walk. He wondered just how long he could court disaster like this without yielding to the temptation which grew stronger every time he was around the beautiful Charmaine.

As the bright light of the moon was reflected down on them, Charmaine happened to glance up and see the expression on John's tanned face. She innocently prodded him. "Well, I guess I'm not the only one in a strange mood tonight. You seem to be too, Johnny."

Her soft gust of laughter brought John Keene out of his private musings. "Suppose there's some strange malady going around, Charlie?" John forced himself to play the happy-go-lucky cousin Charmaine considered him to be, but he was not feeling at all like a cousin.

In response, she swung into a capricious jig and flung her golden head first to one side and then the other. Lifting her skirts slightly, she swished them back and forth. "I think, Johnny . . . I think it's moonlight magic! Maybe, it's casting a strange spell on us." Her deep blue eyes searched his face, so innocent and honest, as she asked in a more serious voice, "Do you suppose it could, Johnny?"

"Anything's possible, Charlie!" He looked at her adoringly. Lord, he loved her so much!

Chapter 2

When Angus Keene was alone with his fine Jersey cows going about his evening chore of milking, he swore it was the best time to make wise decisions. Tonight, he'd made a difficult one, but there was an ordeal ahead, convincing his good wife to go along with it.

God knows, it wasn't a matter of not liking the pretty little girl. He felt he had to do this for the girl's own good. But he knew Simone well enough to realize he'd have the devil's own time getting her to discuss the possibility of marrying Charmaine to Henry Seymour's nephew, though the young man was considered a good catch by their farmer friends.

Weeks ago, Henry had approached him about the possibility of his nephew George coming to call on Charmaine. Angus had put him off and he'd not said anything to Simone, not tried to see how she'd feel about it.

But something had happened, something Angus could not dismiss. He had not dared to say a word to Simone about it, but he was a man and he knew the signs. He knew now why his own son John was staying away from home so much.

God Almighty, he didn't like thinking about it but he knew, after watching John's eyes and face one evening a few weeks ago, that he was attracted to his beautiful cousin. Oh, yes, the fever was in his son's veins and it would explode one day. Then John would no longer be able to control it.

That possibility had never crossed Angus' mind when the thirteen-year-old French girl had come to live at their cottage, for John was almost grown and their other sons were married, living in their own homes. The truth of the matter was that he and Simone were too old to start on a new family.

But a more urgent issue was staring Angus in the face lately. He knew if something happened to him, his beloved Simone would be welcome in any of their sons' cottages. But a luscious blossom like Charmaine would not be accepted by his sons' wives, who were Charmaine's age or older by a year or two. And who could fault them for that? Not him!

It would be damning for John to get himself into such a scandalous mess, but Angus knew that would happen if something wasn't done very soon. So by the time he'd finished milking the last cow he'd decided what he must do for his family's sake. If Charmaine married some nice fellow, she'd have a home and John would forget her. Then, if he himself died, his wife would be taken care of, for she could not run this farm alone. It was, Angus thought, the only solution for everyone concerned.

The tall, lean farmer carried a pail of milk in each of his huge, weatherworn hands as he entered the cottage. The sight of his wife putting a delicious meal on the table made him aware, despite his firm decision back there in the barn, of Simone's strong, determined nature.

Suddenly she turned, giving him a quick lovely smile before she suggested, "It's going to be ready to eat, my dear, by the time you've washed up. Does it not smell good?"

"Wonderful, Simone. Just wonderful! And John . . . is he here?" Angus asked, swiping his graying hair off his forehead. There was no sign of Charmaine in the large roomy kitchen, Angus noted.

"He is here and by the time you are ready to take your seat, I'll get them to the table," Simone said, hoping she wasn't proven to be a liar. John should already have returned with Charmaine in tow, but, to Angus, she gave no hint of this.

Angus emitted a grunt of sorts and moved to do as his wife had suggested. A frown creased his rawboned features because from what Simone had just told him, the two young people were together when Charmaine should have been helping her aunt instead of strolling with John.

All the time Angus washed his hands and as he ran the brush through his thinning hair, his mind was on John and young Charmaine. Thoughtfully, he rolled down the sleeves of his faded blue shirt. He would talk to Simone tonight, after they retired to their bedroom. There was no point in delaying any longer.

Back in the kitchen, Simone had poured the last glass of milk, and a large platter of fish was on the table, along with potatoes and hot freshly baked bread. The blue crock of Simone's creamy, churned butter would soon be consumed with relish, as it always was when she served good hot bread.

Hearing the laughter of the two young people coming through the door, Simone greeted them with a delighted smile on her face, jesting gaily. "So, *mes enfants,* you smell the food, eh?"

Simone was not a beautiful woman, but she had attractive qualities. Like her son John, she had a twinkle of mischief in her eyes when she teased or cajoled, and there was a hint still of her once-voluptuous figure which had now become a little too plump. She could have worn her thick hair in a more attractive style, perhaps, but she always pulled the two long braids into a neat coil atop her head.

As the Keene family sat down to their evening meal, eating their fill of the ormers John had caught, it was Simone who was filled with troubled thoughts about the two young people she loved so dearly.

Do I dare approach Angus about my suspicions? she wondered, as she nibbled on her food. He might think her just foolish, a ridiculous old woman. But Simone knew she

25

was right. She would not close her eyes and pretend otherwise. But just how long had this gone on, and why hadn't she noticed the way John looked at Charmaine before. Dear Lord, how blind a mother could be! When she turned her experienced eyes from John and looked at Charmaine's flawless face she saw what she called a "love-struck" look. If the two young people's eyes weren't locking, Charmaine stared out at the night beyond the kitchen windows. Simone could recall how young girls sat, entranced and daydreaming. Age had not made her forget that. Twice she'd asked Charmaine some casual question and had had to repeat it.

Simone's nature was not like that of her husband Angus. He well knew she was a woman with a strong will and very stubborn, but he was about to learn that she, too, could act on impulse. So when she abruptly announced at the dinner table that she'd invited the Seymours for dinner on Sunday, Angus almost choked on the food in his mouth.

"Angus, dear, are you all right?" Simone asked her red-faced husband, who was still coughing.

All Angus could do was shake his head to try to reassure her. Charmaine was momentarily concerned for her uncle, but John was too riled by his mother's announcement to even glance his father's way. His face was tense for he knew the Seymours' American nephew would accompany them.

Anytime a stranger arrived in St. Helier the locals immediately learned of the newcomer's presence, and John had heard about the arrogant George Seymour. Not wanting to give himself away, he tried to sound very casual when he told his mother, "Set another plate for me, Mom, and I'll try to get back out here."

Simone gave her good-looking son a warm smile and nodded her head, but his reaction to her announcement heightened her suspicions about him. Under different circumstances, she would have been overjoyed that he would be coming to have dinner with them, but she sensed that jealousy was urging John to be here while the Seymours visited.

When the meal was over and the dishes were cleared away, Charmaine excused herself to seek out the seclusion of her own room. She wanted to be alone for her mind was too preoccupied to permit her to join in conversation in the parlor. Simone's talk of company for Sunday dinner had gone in one ear and out the other. Even Johnny's usually enjoyable personality didn't interest her this evening. Her thoughts were concentrated on the mysterious man with the compelling, piercing gray eyes and the devilishly handsome face. Her young heart started to pound now, hours later, when she envisioned his taunting, crooked smile. Oh, Lord, she'd never imagined a man's kiss could be so exciting and so very pleasurable.

In the last couple of years, her dear sweet aunt had spoken to her about men and about the ways of men and women when they courted. Indeed, Simone had laid down very exact rules on the proper behavior of a nice young lady when she was being courted. Certain liberties were not to be allowed, she'd said.

But in the privacy of her room, stripped of her cotton frock, Charmaine sat in her chemise and stared out at that big full moon up in the night sky. Was she one of those naughty girls her aunt had spoken about, the ones who allowed a gentleman to take liberties? The truth was she would have liked him to kiss her longer, and she could only speculate on what else would have happened if John's voice hadn't brought her back to sanity. How far would I have allowed him to go? she wondered.

Had he been as huge as she'd imagined? She remembered him as an imposing figure blocking the passageway, and when his muscled arms had enclosed her, they'd felt as firm and hard as iron. But for all his power and strength, she'd sensed a gentleness as he'd slowly lowered her back to the ground after holding her up so her lips could meet his in a

27

long, lingering kiss.

Who was this handsome stranger who'd come into her world so unexpectedly? Charmaine didn't even know his name. All she knew was that he wasn't from Jersey or she'd have seen him at some time before, yet she'd never gazed on this man before.

The thought that he'd come to the isle of Jersey from a faraway place made him more interesting, more exciting, to her.

She shut her long-lashed eyes in an attempt to try to go to sleep, but it seemed the bright full moon and the mysterious stranger were in league with each other. Swaying, dancing shadows reflected against the walls of her bedroom, and Charmaine's vivid imagination gave way to wild, wonderful fancies. She was not ready to relax and sleep.

Neither were the occupants of the other bedrooms asleep. In their own little cubicle, Angus and Simone were discussing Charmaine. Angus was relieved that it was his wife who'd brought up the subject, confessing to him her fears about the two young people under their roof.

Angus' rough, weathered hand reached out to give his wife an assuring pat, and he whispered as softly as his deep voice could manage, "We've done good by the girl, Simone. You know that and so do I. She's of marrying age—soon eighteen. We're not pushing her out or marrying her off too young."

"I know that, Angus. Besides, I've heard this young man is considered very prosperous—a tobacco farmer, Angus. To be a farmer's wife can be a happy life. I've been one," Simone giggled softly, girlishly, and patted her husband's shoulder affectionately.

"I'd want her to be happy, Simone. It's not as if her life would be so changed if she and this George would take a liking to one another, as Henry thought they might if his nephew could meet her and court her before he returned to America."

"That was my thinking, Angus. I guess we'll just have to see when they come to dinner on Sunday," she told him. Then, releasing a lazy yawn, she bid Angus good night and rolled over on her side to go to sleep.

John was not mentioned by either of them, but he was very much in their thoughts. Like Charmaine, he was of marrying age and Angus wanted him to wed some nice Saint Helier girl, as his brothers before him had done. Simone, being more sentimental, wanted to shield her youngest son from heartbreak. The practical side of her knew the mere fact John and Charmaine were cousins would not smother the passion she'd seen in her son's blue eyes this night. Only one thing would do that: Charmaine must be removed from his sight, put where he could no longer be around her.

Of all the people in the Keene cottage this night none was as tormented as Johnny Keene. After his mother's announcement at dinner, he knew old Henry was scheming with Angus to get his nephew acquainted with Charmaine. That was the conventional way things were done here in Saint Helier. Two families got together and introduced the two young people involved; then they let nature take its course.

It was torture to know he could do nothing to stop George Seymour's introduction to his beautiful little Charlie. Old Henry Seymour was no fool, and there was no lovelier miss on the isles of Jersey or Guernsey than John's golden-haired cousin. The next thing Henry would try was lining John up with his oldest daughter, Janice. Never, Johnny vowed, would that happen! He'd never settle for the likes of Janice Seymour.

John Keene tossed and turned in his bed for over three hours but his aggravation continued to mount so he got up. Slipping into his clothes, he decided that as soon as he was dressed he would go back to the docks and his fishing boat. His mood was too reckless for him to remain at the cottage with the three people he loved the most. As soon as he'd scribbled his mother a brief note saying he'd left the cottage early to go out in the bay to fish, he delayed his departure no longer.

He'd lost his heart to Charmaine when he was eighteen; nothing would ever change that, John knew. His feelings were even stronger now, three years later. No girl he'd met or been with could bring out the thrilling feeling that overwhelmed him when he was around the sweet, uncomplicated Charlie.

The problem was Charmaine Lamoureux's mother and his mother were sisters. For John, that meant he could never have the one woman he desired.

Chapter 3

The island of Guernsey is situated some sixteen miles northwest of its neighboring island of Jersey and some twenty-eight miles off the coast of France, but Guernsey is much smaller than Jersey, only eight miles long and triangular in shape. On the north are lovely picturesque beaches, and to the south are the beautiful scenic cliffs of granite.

Like Jersey, Guernsey has lush open meadows of thyme on which herds of cattle graze, and its fertile soil produces massive crops of flowers, fruits, and vegetables.

But the Renaud industry was interested in the rich deposits of blue granite on Guernsey, so a few years ago Pierre Renaud's father had sent one of his partners to the isle to establish an office in the city of St. Peter Port. Renaud ships docked in the harbor every month, and it was on one of his father's schooners that Pierre Renaud would soon be crossing the Atlantic on his voyage to America.

Old Étienne Renaud had arranged to have his good friend, Captain Martin Wakefield take his fun-loving, adventure-some son Pierre under his wing and into his home until a Renaud schooner sailed for the New World.

Martin Wakefield was not in a position to refuse his dear old friend, but he did not relish having the randy Frenchman under his roof, not with his lovely daughter Sarnia there to tempt the young rascal. From the minute Pierre had arrived, some six weeks ago, from Cherbourg, Martin's nerves had been on edge. His sleep was anything but sound.

Étienne Renaud had his greatest respect, however, and their friendship went back thirty years. Wakefield, an Englishman, and Renaud, a Frenchman, never let the war waged by their two countries affect their feelings for one another. But Martin had raised his daughter alone, and he'd groomed her to be a proper young lady. Now that she was seventeen, he'd picked out a fine young Englishman he wanted her to marry, and he wanted no brief interlude with this handsome young Frenchman to change his plans. It was only a matter of weeks before Pierre would be sailing to America, but the protective Wakefield knew that was more than enough time to ruin everything he'd planned for his pretty brown-eyed Sarnia. Étienne's son was a striking figure of a man.

Martin loved his daughter as fervently as the isle of Guernsey. That was the reason he'd named her Sarnia. Sarnia was what the ancient Romans called the island. But the clever Pierre Renaud was aware that Martin Wakefield's eagle eyes were constantly measuring him when he was around Sarnia. So he had been cautious.

True to his roguish nature, Pierre's gray eyes had given Sarnia Wakefield their usual appraising glances when he'd first settled into the captain's home, but he'd found her lacking in vivaciousness. While she had big brown eyes and warm brown hair, she was not Pierre's kind of lady. He confessed this one morning as he and Jacques Bernay sat on the docks.

"Captain Wakefield has no need to worry that I'll deflower his lovely blossom," Pierre bluntly remarked to the robust Jacques as they were loafing and talking.

The seaman threw back his curly head and roared with laughter, "*Mon ami,* I am glad to hear you say that for I

32

don't think your papa could save you from the captain's wrath if you did." Jacques couldn't help liking Pierre, though he was a little too cocky and too conceited for his own good. Being slightly older than Renaud and a bit on the wild side himself, Jacques enjoyed the camaraderie they'd shared these last weeks.

Like Pierre, Jacques had fled France a few years ago to come to Guernsey, but his reasons were different from Renaud's. His affairs with ladies were numerous and usually brief. He was restless by nature and he needed to roam from St. Peter Port, so a wife was not for him.

As on most mornings, Jacques and Pierre ambled down the long plank wharf to board the sleek-lined schooner belonging to Pierre's father. It amazed the young Renaud to think that until he'd come to Guernsey, he'd never boarded any of the Renaud ships. Everything about this fine vessel fascinated him, even Jacques' cabin, and he now felt he'd wasted a lot of time at his family's château and at their palatial mansion in Cherbourg.

He confessed to Jacques, "If I'd been here instead of Cherbourg, I might not have gotten myself into so much trouble. This is a simpler life, and I like it."

"Ah, there is trouble here, my friend. Never doubt it, for it will come right up and slap you in the face sometime when you least expect it."

Just then a roaring blast came from the old Norman fortress, the firing of the Noon Gun. It blasted daily, except on Sunday. Most of the people of St. Peter Port were used to it, but Pierre wasn't. Once again, he jerked to attention and Jacques broke into thundering laughter. Pierre gave him a good-natured grin.

"All right. You've had your fun for today. By the time I get used to it, I'll probably be shipping out. By the way, when does it look like we'll leave?"

"Can't get a thing out of Wakefield. You getting impatient, *mon ami?*"

"I'm getting damned impatient. I can't locate that delectable little golden mermaid I was telling you about. I went back to the same spot a couple of times, but there was no sign of her."

"She must have made an impression on you. Perhaps she is some farmer's wife, eh? Perhaps she is the trouble you don't need right now." Jacques' brown eyes twinkled with a hint of mischief.

"Perhaps, but I'd sure chance it," Pierre replied, failing to add that the girl's beautiful face had haunted him since the night of the full moon when he'd been on the neighboring isle of Jersey.

Jacques smiled, but did not mention to his young friend that he was going to question some of his fishermen friends. If this golden-haired lady was married, as she just might be, then his young friend would be walking into a hornet's nest.

In fact, he intended to check into her tonight when he and Renaud parted company; Renaud always went to the Wakefield house for dinner. The Cozy Cove would be his best bet because it was the gathering place of fishermen from Guernsey and from Jersey. These two factions argued endlessly as they drank their ales, each claiming their island was the best. Each group declared that the best milk was produced on their isle, the best fruits grown there, and each professed to catching the biggest fish. For certain, the subject of which isle had the prettiest girls was always hotly debated. That would provide an opportunity for a little investigating, Bernay decided; then he might have some good news to tell the love-struck Pierre. If what he learned was not favorable, he would have done his fellow Frenchman a great service.

Once they boarded the schooner, however, Bernay forgot his plans for the evening and gave his attention and energy to his usual chores. Pierre dogged his footsteps, pitched in like any of the other deckhands. His willingness to work along with Jacques impressed the seasoned seaman. Here was no

34

milksop, no obnoxious snob. Jacques would have been repulsed if he'd had to put up with that sort of young pup just to please Captain Wakefield.

While the two worked, barechested, their shirts removed as they'd both worked up a good sweat, they laughed and joked and indulged in playful fisticuffs.

Pierre found out that Jacques' huge firmly muscled arms were even stronger than he'd realized. After finally freeing himself from his friend's iron clasp, he confessed, "I want you to teach me some of your fancy technique. You're too good for me, Bernay!"

Jacques brushed his dark curly hair away from his face, and there was a smug grin on his face as he declared, "I can hold my own with most, *mon ami*. I will teach you, if you like."

Pierre hastily accepted. "I would like!" His gray eyes compared the broadness of Jacques' hairy chest to his own, and they measured the strong hands of the tanned seaman.

"Then it is settled." Jacques strutted along the deck of the schooner, his hands at the waistline of his dark duck pants.

Pierre followed him, brushing his dark hair off his damp face, but he suddenly hastened his gait in order to catch up with Jacques. A thought had struck him, and he saw no reason not to approach Jacques. Besides, he'd decided the two of them made a hell of a pair, so why not invite Jacques to accompany him to this Missouri Territory he was headed for? What would hold Jacques here?

The younger Frenchman could not have known that Jacques had already been thinking along the same line. The idea of the strange New World titillated his reckless nature, and the prospect of traveling with Pierre Renaud excited him. There was more to it, but Jacques Bernay was not ready to admit that, even to himself, because if he did, he might not have liked this young man so much. Instead, he might have bitterly resented the cruel blow fate had dealt him. In good time all would be known to him. He dared not tempt fate. No good seaman did that! Besides, Pierre could not help what another Renaud had done.

The Cozy Cove had its usual lively Friday evening gathering of fishermen from Jersey and Guernsey. The tavern's serving girls were setting tankards of ale before them, and a few of the local doxies were in evidence. A pungent aroma was already engulfing the tavern: the combined odors of tobacco, spilled liquor and ale, and fetid body sweat brought forth by a hard day's work in the bay, casting nets on the waters to catch fish.

Some of the rugged men were tallying the mackerel and herring they'd landed, and an Irish bucko was telling the three fishermen sitting at his table that he was sailing north.

The youngest of the three inquired, "Why so, Teddy? What's to be found north that we aren't catching here in the channel waters?"

Roarke laughed and taunted young John Keene. "See boys, he's still green behind the ears. Salmon and trout, young Keene. Salmon and trout in those Scottish streams, that can fill your coffers fast."

John didn't mind being teased by the fun-loving Irishman. Like most of the fishermen from Jersey and Guernsey, Teddy Roarke was friendly, and the more he drank the bigger a clown he became. When he was at the tavern, John became weak from laughter by the end of the evening. Lately, he'd needed the humor Teddy provided, and he'd tried desperately to keep up with Roarke's drinking.

Tonight, he certainly had every intention of getting drunk. He'd gone to his home today, and as he'd imagined, the obstinate, aloof American was at the cottage to call on Charmaine. As a result, John's stay had been brief, and he'd found it difficult to be civil to his mother when she'd walked him to the gate to say farewell. He could not hide his anger.

For a moment, he'd felt a tinge of hatred for her because

36

she was conspiring to promote Seymour's courtship of his beloved Charlie. So he'd headed directly to the Cozy Cove, determined to get roaring, floor-crawling drunk as old Roarke always said.

A slightly accented voice called his name and a huge hand came to rest on John's shoulder as he sat with Roarke and the others. "How was it today, *mon ami?*"

John turned, to recognize the Frenchman Jacques standing behind his chair and presenting an indomitable figure. Like Roarke, Jacques was likable, and he had a unique personality.

"Today wasn't worth a damn in more ways than one. Come on, sit down. Grab that chair over there. No one's using it." John pointed toward the empty table beside them.

John and Jacques talked for the next hour and they drank. The jollity of the crowd was becoming more boisterous. Two men, just tipsy enough, began to fight. John was getting well into his cups, Jacques noticed, when he turned to him to comment, "It has to be an argument over a woman."

"A woman! The damnation to the souls of men—God love them," John mumbled.

Jacques laughed at his drunk friend from Jersey. *"Cherchez la femme . . . oui?"* Jacques gave him a brotherly pat on the shoulder. "Always look for the woman to do the man in, my young friend? Tell Jacques, has one played you false?" Maybe he'd get young Keene to talk so he wouldn't drink so much.

"No, I can't say she has played me false. Fate played me false."

Jacques laughed good naturedly. Perhaps he was at a lucky stage of his life. It would seem, now that he was in his thirties, he could better handle affairs of the heart better than his two young friends who were in their twenties.

"Well, since I can do nothing against fate to help you, maybe you can aid another young man like yourself. He is looking for the most beautiful creature he's ever seen."

Jacques gave a dramatic gesture with his huge hands. "It would seem this most charming miss has to be one of the fair maidens on Jersey or Guernsey. So good-hearted man that I am, I've promised to inquire about her, to see if I can help him with his quest. Would you know some fair-haired damsel with eyes—he swears—of the deepest blue he's ever seen?"

In his drunken stupor, John shook his head and mumbled that he knew no such girl. Jacques directed the same question to the others seated at the table there and the answer was the same. Jacques then decided that to pursue his inquiry in the tavern was rather foolish, for most of the crowd was too drunk to think before responding.

Better he get back to his cabin in the schooner, Jacques decided, for he must rise early. So he bid his carousing friends good night and rose to leave.

As he was going through the tavern door, he heard staggering footsteps behind him and turned to see the swaying figure of John Keene following him. Together they went out into the night air, so fresh-smelling after the smoky maze of the tavern, John gave Jacques a pat on the shoulder and said good night. "Hope your friend finds his lady."

"So do I, John."

"Tell you something, Jacques, your friend hasn't seen the most beautiful girl around here. The loveliest girl on both of the islands has long hair that looks like spun gold, and her eyes are as violet as amethysts or maybe the blue fire of a sapphire. That's my sweet Charlie," John boasted.

"Oh, this Charlie—she is the girl giving you the problems of the heart, eh?" Jacques said, observing the look on John's face.

"No." John struggled to lie. "Charlie is my cousin, Charmaine Lamoureux."

"Ooooh, I see. Your cousin, *mon ami,*" Jacques Bernay responded slowly and thoughtfully. He felt sorry for the young man beside him. Instinct told him this cousin was the same young lady his friend Pierre had briefly encountered and had lost his heart to.

Jacques found himself most curious about this ravishing creature who had obviously captured the hearts of two handsome young men. She must be *fantastique!*

The wily Frenchman had not been fooled by young Keene. Cousin or not, this Charmaine was the one he was mooning over!

Chapter 4

Charmaine slipped the sprigged muslin gown over her head. It was her prettiest frock, trimmed at the sleeves and neckline with frosty white lace, and its deep blue color enhanced Charmaine's eyes, so her aunt said. The scooped neckline was most flattering. Indeed, it made Charmaine's satiny flesh and firm, rounded breasts quite alluring. A tiny gold cross hung suspended from a chain around her neck. It was the only piece of jewelry she owned; her parents had given it to her on her tenth birthday.

Now, as she stood in her chemise and gave the gown a firm shake to rid it of any wrinkles, she realized it was obvious why her Aunt Simone had insisted she wear this frock for the Seymours' visit. She'd thought her aunt had fussed over her appearance more than usual. Heavens' sakes, Aunt Simone was trying to match her with that George Seymour.

She grimaced, recalling him. So stern-faced and dull he'd seemed. Why his face had looked as though it would crack if he tried to give just one nice warm smile. Now that she thought about it, he must be middle aged! Surely her aunt wasn't serious. She must have misunderstood her intention because she knew her happiness was important to Simone, who had been gentle and kind all these years. The same could be said for her Uncle Angus.

Charmaine crawled between the sheets and gave no more thought to the silly notion that Aunt Simone was trying to push the tall, lanky Seymour at her.

Her sleep was deep and sound, and the next morning she reluctantly awoke to a voice echoing in her ear. She gave a startled jerk. For a moment she didn't grasp her aunt's impatient shaking of her shoulder.

"Come on, dear. We've . . . we've got company," Simone said. "That nice Mr. Seymour has come over."

"Wha-what's that got to do with me, Aunt Simone?" Charmaine mumbled in a faltering voice, her long thick lashes fluttering with the lazy languor still washing over her.

A sly smile came to her aunt's face as she replied, "Why, Charmaine, you must know it isn't Angus he really wants to see. Having your uncle show him our cows is just the young man's excuse to see you again."

"You are talking about George then, not Mr. Seymour?" Charmaine stared up at her aunt wide-eyed as she propped herself up on the pillows.

"Of course, *ma petite*. I thought you knew it was George I was talking about. I think he thinks you're very pretty."

Charmaine said nothing, for she truly didn't care whether the American thought she was pretty or not. She certainly didn't think he was handsome! But she noticed her aunt bustling around her room, gathering up one article of clothing and then another.

"Please, Aunt Simone! You don't have to do that. My goodness, just because George Seymour happened to drop by we don't have to get into such a frenzy."

Simone straightened up, an astonished look on her face. Brushing a stray hair away from her face, she declared, "Dear, it is a compliment to you and to us that Henry's nephew has come to call. Don't you realize that, Charmaine?"

"I—I guess I didn't, Aunt Simone," Charmaine replied, a little perplexed. "I'll get dressed and be along soon. You get on with whatever you need to be doing," she urged her aunt, not wanting her fluttering around the room as she was dressing. By now, she'd swung her legs over the side of the bed and had stood up.

"Do hurry, Charmaine." Simone started to leave her room, but before going out the door, she turned to give her niece a broad smile, which Charmaine weakly returned.

It was the first time since she'd come to the Keenes' cottage that Charmaine was out of patience and was displeased with her dear aunt. But the woman's gushy excitement over young Seymour, in whom Charmaine had no interest, was disturbing to the seventeen-year-old girl.

Since it was only a weekday and no special occasion, Charmaine did not put on her nicest gown. Instead, she picked the sturdy, dark brown one with the simple white collar. She ran the brush through her hair, letting it flow free and loose without even a ribbon as an adornment.

Nor did she use one drop of the precious jasmine water Johnny had brought her from St. Helier. That is for special times or festive occasions, she thought as she ambled through her bedroom door.

When she walked into her aunt's parlor, she heard the men's voices coming from the small front porch. She recognized George's coarse voice telling Angus, "No, Mr. Keene, my harvest time is due anytime now. Tobacco has to be at just the right maturity if you want the right quality."

"I see. Don't know a thing about growing tobacco. Don't smoke that cheroot you speak about. I'm a pipe man myself."

Charmaine heard George respond with the shrill chuckle she found so irritating. Then she saw his lean body rise suddenly whereas her Uncle Angus remained seated and there was no sign of Aunt Simone.

George stammered that he'd best be on his way back to his Uncle Henry's place. "You might tell Miss Charmaine I'm sorry I missed seeing her though. Perhaps . . . perhaps I might come by this evening to see her? I'm to leave before too long. I sail the last day of this month."

Charmaine heaved a sigh of delight, figuring she would slip by the door and get to the kitchen without being seen for she badly needed a cup of hot chocolate.

When she was almost at the door, she heard her aunt urge George to wait just a minute. "Don't know what's keeping her. She was— She will want to say hello to you too, Mr. Seymour. I know she will."

Charmaine moaned. How could Simone lie so? What was possessing her aunt this morning. So riled she was seething, Charmaine proceeded to the kitchen for her hot chocolate, and she was filling her cup when her aunt entered, calling out her name.

"Yes, Aunt Simone," she replied as she took a sip of the chocolate.

Her aggravation reflected on her round face, Simone said sharply, "I thought you knew we were waiting for you, Charmaine! Where are your manners this morning?"

The harshness in her aunt's voice was new to Charmaine and it hurt her. She forced herself to abstain from telling Simone she was being ridiculous, and merely mumbled that she didn't realize she was rude in seekng a cup of hot chocolate upon arising. However, she couldn't resist adding, "I consider it is rude of George Seymour to come calling so early in the morning."

"Sssssh, child! He wanted to see your uncle's cows."

"Then my presence isn't necessary. I'm not a cow!"

"Lord, Charmaine, we must have a talk later, but for heaven's sake will you come with me now?" The older woman sorely tempted to swat the younger one on the rump. Instead, she heaved a deep sigh as she motioned her headstrong niece to accompany her out to the porch.

When Charmaine went out the door, she found Angus still sitting on the porch whereas George was standing. Hesitating to depart, he was speaking about his tobacco farm,

44

explaining the steps in the curing of the leaves. His expressionless eyes darted up to Charmaine, and he managed a weak smile of greeting.

Charmaine, in turn, told him good morning, but she could not resist darting a glance at her aunt. It seemed to her that her aunt was calmer now, and pleased.

George Seymour observed Charmaine carefully. He was beginning to think his uncle was probably right about Charmaine Lamoureux being a suitable wife to take back to Virginia. Oh, it went without saying that she was a pretty, little thing with a fine figure, but George figured she was young and healthy. He wanted a woman who could give him some fine sons—sons who'd help him farm his tobacco land.

But the impressive thing about Charmaine this morning was her simple, unadorned frock. George wanted no fancy little filly who'd expect him to spend his hard-earned money on a lot of expensive gowns and such. So he guessed he'd have to give his Uncle Henry credit for considering his welfare by suggesting he get acquainted with the Keenes' niece.

Nonetheless George found Angus' sharp, piercing eyes a little disconcerting and he decided he'd take his leave for now. Better to come back this evening when he might have some time alone with Charmaine. He turned first to Simone Keene and addressed her, "Nice to see you again, ma'am. Glad I didn't miss seeing you this morning, Miss Charmaine." George couldn't hide the slight blush coming to his cheeks when he looked at her. "I've asked your uncle if I might visit you this evening. I hope you don't mind?"

"Uh . . . if my aunt and uncle approve," Charmaine replied in what George took for a timid tone of voice. This also made George think her the right choice for him. He wanted a meek docile girl. No uppity, high-handed woman would live under his roof.

There was nothing meek or mild about Charmaine's private thoughts, however, but she did not know how to refuse him in front of her aunt and uncle. She was already in trouble with her aunt.

Giving a bow to the two ladies standing on the porch, George extended his hand to give Angus a farewell shake. "You've got one fine herd of cattle, sir. Wish I had at least a couple of those milk cows in Virginia. I appreciate your taking the time to show them to me."

As his long legs moved backward, he awkwardly caught the heel of a boot between the stepping stones of the walk. Giving out an embarrassed chuckle, he said his final goodbye and turned to depart. Charmaine thought he was a clod and she gladly watched him go, saying nothing. Simone directed her words to Angus. "Fine young man, that one. Don't you think so, Angus?"

"Appears so. No fancy dandy, that's for sure. Hard worker, I'd say." He stood up and wiped the seat of his pants, declaring, "Speaking of work, I've got some chores to do."

"Come on, Charmaine," Simone urged. "We've got some work to do too. You'll most likely be wishing to be through early so you can wash that pretty hair of yours." She gave Charmaine a sly, teasing smile.

"I wasn't planning on doing that. Don't you remember I washed my hair just yesterday, Aunt Simone."

"But I just thou—"

Charmaine interrupted her with a teasing remark of her own. "Why I do believe you're trying to play Cupid, Auntie!"

Simone's round face became flushed, and she nervously swiped at her apron as she went on into the kitchen. "I was just doing what any parent does when a daughter reaches your age, Charmaine. I do want you to marry a nice, good man. You've not many chances to meet men, except for the fishermen John knows. I'd want none of them to be a suitor."

"Maybe I've yet to meet the man I shall marry," Charmaine retorted light-heartedly.

"Oh, *chérie,* you must realize that romantic dreams are fine but life rarely turns out that way. No, dear, I think it's a grand opportunity to have a prosperous man like George

46

Seymour court you. Most likely he wants to take a wife back to his home in Virginia. That is what Henry told Angus."

"But I might not want to be that lady. I might not want that at all." Charmaine's eyes sparked blue fire. It irked her that her feelings seemed of no importance.

Simone giggled uneasily, "Well, dear, it's too early to say that. Once you have a chance to know George Seymour you might just find he possesses certain qualities you'd like."

Charmaine had spent her adolescence with the woman talking to her, and she'd always respected her Aunt Simone and her Uncle Angus, but her heart would not believe that she could ever find George Seymour interesting or attractive. His face was ugly, and he had plain, sharp features and expressionless eyes. His tall body looked thin and gaunt. No. It was obvious that he was not the sort of man she should marry.

Honesty demanded that she bluntly inquire of her aunt, "Are you saying it is your wish I allow George to court me, Aunt Simone?"

"My goodness, Charmaine, you—you make me sound so very—well, I don't really know what to say. I am not pushing you, child. You should know that. It's just that I want you to consider George before you thoughtlessly refuse his attentions. At least, his are honorable. Many a man's won't be, Charmaine."

Charmaine excused herself immediately, intending to get busy on her chores and, more urgently, wishing to hear no more of George. As she left the room, she told her aunt, "I will think about what you've said, Aunt Simone."

With an authoritative tone in her voice, Simone remarked, "Marriage is not a festive party, and a dapper gent with a smooth tongue and winning ways isn't the best of husbands. It's day-to-day living, Charmaine. A hard-working man proves to be more sensible and dependable."

Charmaine jauntily walked away, her golden curls bouncing against her back. Her indignation was pouring forth as she walked with her head high, lips held tight, and eyes sparkling. She could not accept her aunt's concept of life and marriage. Her own mother and father had been loving with one another, she remembered that. Was it because they'd been younger than Aunt Simone and Uncle Angus? Was that why they touched and kissed one another? Perhaps that was the reason they seemed to be so much gayer, and she recalled the ring of laughter when she lived in France, when they were alive.

As the afternoon progressed, Charmaine often thought about her Aunt Simone's advice, but her mind dwelt on memories of the years she'd spent with her mother and father. Amidst these preoccupations, she recalled the man whose divine eyes had adored her ever so briefly and whose lips had caressed her, evoking such wild ecstasy she flushed at recalling those rapturous moments.

She could never settle for someone as lifeless and wearisome as George Seymour, despite her aunt's wishes.

When it was twilight, Charmaine knew exactly what she must do. Tonight, she'd be the dutiful niece and comply with her aunt's wishes, but she was also determined to discourage George's attention. This one night would be the last time she'd endure his boring company.

More than ever, she yearned to be back at the little house where she was born—back in France.

She yearned desperately to rush to her cliff instead of going to her room to straighten herself up. But the hands of the clock showed her that was not possible.

Tomorrow night I will go, she promised herself!

Tomorrow night she would do what she wished to do instead of appeasing her aunt. After all, it was her life. She must live it according to her own desires, and she certainly had no desire for George Seymour!

Chapter 5

The weather did not brighten Charmaine's miserable mood, for a heavy fog had moved in on the island of Jersey during the early morning hours. The unwelcome, awesome sight greeted her eyes when she woke up the next morning, and the first thought to rush through her pretty, tousled head as she raised it from her pillow was that the gruesome presence of George was still with her.

George! She didn't even like his name, and the preceding evening had convinced her that she did not agree with Aunt Simone's taste in men.

She thought she'd surely wilt away when Aunt Simone had suggested she and Seymour stroll in the garden after dinner. There had certainly been no moon magic last night, no magic to his touch either when he'd sought to hold her arm and then her hand. Oh, she'd allowed it, but she could not help thinking what she'd have done had he been bold enough to have tried to kiss her as the man on the cliff had. Thank the dear Lord, he hadn't!

As she prepared to start this new day, Charmaine was perplexed by the puzzling manner of her cousin when he'd dropped by the cottage last night. Johnny had hardly spoken to her or George. Indeed, she'd been devastated by his cold, offhanded attitude when he'd met them in the yard.

What had she done to rile him? she'd wondered after he'd taken his hasty leave. As she'd watched her aunt walk to the front gate with her son, she'd noticed that he looked like a thunderhead. She knew Johnny well enough to know when his temper was boiling.

A quietness had settled over Simone after he'd gone. What was this thing that was suddenly hanging over the Keene cottage? Charmaine had no inkling that it involved her.

Sadly, Charmaine found the day didn't improve. Heavy rains replaced the thick fog as morning slipped into afternoon, there was most assuredly a tense atmosphere in the cottage. To Charmaine, it seemed that her aunt and uncle were at odds. He was confined to the house because of the weather.

When she inquired about John, she regretted doing so for Simone was quite sharp with her. But Charmaine didn't drop the subject. Instead, she proceeded, "But John acted so mad at me, and I can't think of a thing I've said or done, Aunt Simone."

Simone knew exactly what had been gnawing at her son when he'd arrived at the cottage to find George Seymour strolling with Charmaine, his hand holding her arm. But she sought to disillusion her niece by saying, "Oh, Charmaine, don't be troubled by John's disgruntled mood. He'd most likely come from seeing his girl friend. They'd had a little lover's spat, I'd venture to say."

With wide-eyed innocence, Charmaine candidly disagreed with her aunt. "But Johnny doesn't have a girl friend, Aunt Simone. I'm almost sure of that."

Simone forced a smug smile. She knew what Charmaine said was probably true, but she just refused to believe that John had no interest in any girl except the cousin with whom he was infatuated—Charmaine.

"Oh, *ma petite,* that is where you are so very wrong. John doesn't tell any more than he tells his papa and me. Excuse me, dear. I've my bread to check," she lied, turning her eyes from Charmaine's searching blue gaze. It pained her to mislead her niece and she had small qualms about promoting George Seymour, but the possibility of a serious dilemma demanded it of her. She justified what she was doing by considering it necessary because of her love for the two of them: John and her niece. This was what she told her husband, Angus when he later voiced some misgivings about this match.

"Are we doing right, Simone?"

"Oh, dear lord, Angus! You know the reason we must do this thing. We've talked about it, and I thought you agreed with me. You saw for yourself John's monstrous jealousy. I thought he might just punch poor Mr. Seymour in the nose for a minute there."

"I suppose you are right, but I also saw that Charmaine can hardly endure the man."

"Sometimes, it takes time for a young girl like Charmaine to come to respect a man like George. She's like my sister, whose heart was lost to the first handsome man she met. Suzanne thought with her heart, not her head. I fear Charmaine takes after her."

Angus gave her a nod, for he knew what she was saying was the truth. Of the two sisters, his beloved Simone was the practical one.

As if to reassure himself, he muttered, "I hope you're right, dear."

"So do I, Angus. I've reason to believe that our John will not be coming home for a while. I think he is miserable today. He certainly was last night. I just hope he doesn't act foolishly."

According to Simone Keene's code, John was being very foolhardy, for he was sauntering down the dark fishing wharf, occasionally stumbling and swaying due to having had too much to drink.

Ambling along the same wharf, another tall figure approached him. The man puffed on a cheroot as he aimlessly walked by John, and with a light-hearted, jesting air called out, "Good evening and good luck, *mon ami.*" Pierre emitted a deep throaty chuckle for he knew the condition of the fellow he'd just passed. He'd been in the same boat many a time. He wished him good luck.

Although they were two strangers passing at a late hour, they shared a common bond: Pierre and John Keene were both thinking about Charlie. Pierre had welcomed the solace of a late night walk after his tedious evening meal as the guest of Captain Wakefield and his promiscuous, clutching daughter Sarnia. Christ, she'd put him in a precarious spot during the evening! The bitch couldn't seem to understand that he had no interest in her, and besides, Wakefield was watching him like a hawk. He'd done that ever since Pierre had arrived at the two-story house.

The young Frenchman wanted no part of Wakefield's wrath, or of Sarnia with her flirting dark eyes. Oh, there was no question in Pierre's mind that he could get her in his bed anytime he desired her, but he found Sarnia a curious example of femininity: a sweet, proper maiden around her father, but an outrageous flirt when the man wasn't around.

He'd known that she'd cleverly plotted going down the long winding stairway before the dinner hour when he was leaving his own room to join the captain for a drink as was their custom. Of course, he had been most courteous, greeting her and taking her arm as they descended the steps.

Naturally, his male eyes had noticed her low-cut neckline, and he'd appreciated the display of cleavage. But Sarnia had caught him staring at her, and she'd sought to play on that. Wickedly, she'd swayed her hips closer, and she'd pressed against him so that his arm could feel the fullness of her breasts.

When Pierre had given her a slow, sly smile, she'd boldly prodded him. "You like my new gown, Pierre?"

"It is very lovely, Sarnia." He'd purposely loosened his hold of her arm for he'd noticed the captain at the foot of the stairway, glaring up at them.

Throughout dinner Sarnia had flaunted herself, but Pierre had determined that he'd not let the little wanton get him in a kettle of hot water. He would be under the roof of his father's old, trusted friend only a short time before leaving to join his uncle in America. If he could only find the golden-haired girl he yearned to take with him, he'd sail from Guernsey at any time.

It was she he ached to hold in his arms, not Sarnia Wakefield. She kindled the wild fire of passion, and he couldn't forget the night he'd met her, although many nights had come and gone.

As soon as the meal was over and he could graciously excuse himself, he'd left the Wakefield home. He didn't have to look at Sarnia to know she was pouting.

Captain Wakefield didn't miss the displeasure on Sarnia's face, and it only heightened his misgivings about having young Renaud under the same roof with his daughter. When he inquired about his daughter's young English suitor, she exhibited instant and utter disinterest, and her reply was most disturbing.

"Oh, him! I think he is coming tomorrow night, Papa. I'm not sure." She shrugged.

Captain Wakefield played nervously with his mustache, then declared, "Nice young man, good family too, Sarnia my darling."

She muttered a disinterested reply as she swished the skirt of her lavender silk gown upon leaving the dining room. She was wondering just where Pierre was heading. Had he rushed off to enjoy the pleasures of some tavern trollop? Or was he seeking out some St. Peter Port girl?

Well, I am not without resources, Sarnia told herself! There was Bernay. Her father had assigned him to watch over Pierre, and she knew they'd spent a lot of time together

53

since Pierre had come to stay at the Wakefields'. She'd approach him and insist on knowing what Pierre did in the evenings, she promised herself as she angrily marched upstairs to her room after refusing her father's invitation to play a game of chess.

It was Jacques Bernay Pierre was hoping to run into after he left the Wakefield house, but when he'd walked down the wharf, he'd encountered the drunken John Keene. Ironically, John had just said good night to Jacques a short time ago outside the Cozy Cove.

After Pierre boarded the schooner he took the liberty of going into Jacques' small cabin, even though Jacques didn't answer his knock. He made himself comfortable on the bunk, then helped himself to a snifter of Jacques' brandy.

Shortly thereafter, the muscular Bernay arrived. He laughed good-naturedly when he spied the young Frenchman sprawled on his bunk, relaxed and sipping his brandy. "Well, I see you've made yourself right at home, *oui?*"

"*Oui!* Damned good brandy you serve, Jacques," Pierre said, flashing a broad grin. "Didn't think you'd mind."

"Not at all. In fact, it pleases me to see you. You see, I, Jacques Bernay, think I have news which will delight your ears." He struck a dramatic pose.

"News? What kind of news do you speak of? Are we getting ready to sail? Wakefield mentioned nothing tonight."

"No, *mon ami,* not that. Something far more exciting, I think, from the way you were talking." Jacques laughed.

"Come on, Jacques. What are you talking about?"

"I speak about the golden-haired lady. I think I've found out her name. That is what you wanted. *N'est-ces pas?*"

"You're not just jesting, are you, Jacques?" Pierre sat up in the bunk, so excited that he was not cautious about the overhanging wooden edge above his head. Wincing from the stab of pain he felt when his brow struck it, he insisted

54

impatiently, "Tell me, damn it?"

"Mind you, I can't be certain, but your description sounds like a lady by the name of Mademoiselle Charmaine Lamoureux."

"God!" Pierre sighed, then flashed his pearly white teeth and softly repeated the name. "Beautiful! A fitting name for the beautiful maiden I met there by the sea. Isn't it, Jacques?"

Jacques smiled as he looked upon his friend's love-struck, handsome face. It made him wish he weren't so old or so hardened by life to know again the zest of romance. He wondered when it had left him, this youth.

"Beautiful, Pierre, and French too," Jacques replied.

"She is beautiful. But I met her over on Jersey. I wonder if she, too, came from France."

"Slow down, my young friend. You can't be sure it is the right girl until you see her. There are many golden-haired lovelies on these two little islands."

"Something tells me she is the one. Right here, it says so," he told Bernay, pointing to his heart, and when Jacques told him the source of his information—John Keene—Renaud declared, "Tomorrow, I will go to Jersey and find the Keenes' house."

Then, like a bolt of lightning, he heard the male voice that had summoned her away from his strong arms that moonlit night. "Charlie," the man had called before she'd fled swiftly down the slope and into the meadow, her golden mane flowing in the bright moonlight as she ran. God, what a glorious sight! He had to find her again. His heart would not rest until he did!

Chapter 6

It took a stubborn, determined Jacques Bernay to do battle with an equally hardheaded, impatient Pierre Renaud the next day as heavy rain and fog prevented them from crossing the waters dividing the two Channel Islands.

The formidable Bernay would not be swayed by Renaud so Pierre, who had come to respect highly Jacques' skill and knowledge of sailing and ships, as he knew Captain Wakefield did, finally bowed to his wisdom.

As the downpour detained Pierre on Guernsey, it kept Charmaine confined to her cottage on Jersey.

Yet that turn of fate happened to play to George Seymour's advantage because he returned to the Keenes' cottage to pay a call on Charmaine. She could not help feeling somewhat impressed that he'd dared to journey through such rain to see her. Perhaps, that was why she was more cordial when she greeted the drenched young man at the door. He did present a rather pathetic sight!

"My goodness, George, you're wet to the skin!" she exclaimed, urging him to get on inside. It was the first time she'd addressed him so casually.

He gave her an awkward smile, and in a bolder manner than he'd ever spoken to her before, he admitted, "Wanted to see you as often as I could before having to leave, Miss Charmaine."

"Oh, for mercy sakes, George, call me Charmaine," she declared as she observed the damp, wet hair falling over his forehead and the small rivulets of water dripping down his face. Something about his demeanor on this damp, dreary day mellowed her attitude. He hardly looked that much older than she at this moment, nor did he seem so serious and harsh.

"May I call you Charmaine?" he falteringly inquired.

"I'll be mad if you don't." She softly laughed as she guided him toward the heat of her aunt's cookstove. As if she were a mother ordering her son to take off his wet shoes and socks, Charmaine took full charge of the situation.

After she'd brewed him a hot cup of tea and George sat with his bare feet baking, sipping the steaming liquid, Charmaine suddenly realized that he wasn't so hard to chat with. She secretly confessed to herself that her aunt could have been partially right.

Since he had finally opened up and was willing to talk, Charmaine wished to keep their conversation going. "That seems like a tremendous amount of acres of land—five hundred!"

Her genuine interest thrilled George. "Oh, ma'am, there's some that've got a thousand or more. But I guess I could say I'm mighty proud of what I've done in the last five years, how much of the timberland has been cleared and planted to yield me a crop." He laughed. "Wasn't too easy I can tell you."

Charmaine had to agree with something else her aunt had pointed out to her earlier, and that was that George wasn't lazy. No, he was obviously a hard worker.

George Seymour was rather startled himself after they'd sat there talking for almost an hour, for he wasn't an outgoing talkative man at all. Once, he'd started, however, it seemed he couldn't stop. Maybe the beautiful Charmaine Lamoureux brought out this strange, new side of him. If that was so, then he certainly would find her the perfect choice for his wife.

A surge of exaltation pounded within him. He couldn't recall feeling so bold or sure of himself around a woman before. Usually, he was so uncertain his words seemed to stick in his throat. Actually, that was why he'd preferred laboring on his land to courting any of the neighboring farmers' daughters.

He suddenly heard himself telling Charmaine how he'd built most of his house himself. "It's nice too, if I do say so myself. About twice as big as your aunt's house here."

"Really?" Charmaine declared, finding herself impressed.

"Course, it hasn't had a woman's touch put to it. It's sorta hard for a fellow like me to know how to do things like curtains and stuff—if you know what I mean?"

Charmaine nodded her head and suggested, "Maybe one of your neighbors' wives might lend you a hand."

George shook his head and quickly asserted his opinion. "No, ma'am—not my house. It should be my wife that does that."

"I see."

"Miss Charmaine—I mean, Charmaine—I was thinking, or at least I've been hoping that maybe that was something you'd get interested in being after I met you. My wife, I mean." An anxious uneasiness flooded over him as he spoke.

With fluttering eyelashes and gaping mouth, Charmaine found herself speechless. "Married? Me and you? I—I—"

"I've taken you by surprise, I suppose? I figured that you must have guessed. Course, a beautiful girl like you has to have gents coming all the time. I—I don't doubt that for one minute." Wooing a young lady could be taxing, he was finding. Charmaine offered no comment, just a sweet coy little smile.

"Well, I can only say I think most highly of you, Charmaine, and I can offer you marriage, a nice home, and a good life. Country living much like you have here in Jersey actually."

"I appreciate your offer, George. I just don't know what to

say right now." Charmaine wouldn't have thought twice yesterday about flatly refusing his offer of marriage, but for some unknown reason, she now did not wish to hurt his feelings.

"I have a few more days, Charmaine. Just sleep on it, if you'd like." In a light-hearted, jesting manner unusual for him, George Seymour added, "The offer won't be withdrawn. It will still stand a day or two from now."

Waking up from her afternoon nap, Simone came upon the two young people sitting in her kitchen, and she could hardly believe what she was seeing. They seemed to be enjoying each other's company. Later, after George had left it was a changed Charmaine she spoke with, and Simone did not know what miracle had occurred during her lengthy nap, but she was pleased. Any misgivings she had were swept away, and she felt rather smug that she'd been right after all. She could not wait to tell Angus about this new turn of events.

The inexperienced Charmaine now questioned at just what point a young, romantic girl like herself put fantasy behind her and allowed reality to take over. Having had a vivid imagination all her life, she now questioned whether she'd actually met such a man up there in the cliffs on the moonlit night. Maybe she'd only wished that it had happened.

Daydream or not, the handsome man had not returned, and the man asking her to be his wife was the American planter. This afternoon, she realized she'd allowed herself to get to know him just a little. That had happened because she'd let the sweet memory of the tall, handsome stranger fade for that short span of time.

It seemed this rainy day was to be one of surprises and revelations for the seventeen-year-old miss. By the time she undressed to retire for the night she'd decided that she would give George Seymour a chance, at least. She would see him for the short time he had left here on Jersey. Certainly, Aunt Simone's mood had certainly been warmer since she'd found them in her kitchen, Charmaine thought with amusement.

With her long gown on and barefooted, Charmaine gave way to the impulse to tiptoe down the stairs for a glass of milk, for it seemed the dinner hour was a long time ago.

She cautiously walked by the door of her aunt's and uncle's bedroom, down the narrow hallway from her own room. All was quiet and they were obviously already asleep. She maneuvered her way through the dark cottage, then helped herself to a glass of milk without bumping into a wall or any of the furnishings. Only when she was again in the upstairs hallway did her toe tangle with the little rug on the plank floor, causing her to do a juggling act to keep from spilling her milk or dropping the glass to retain her balance. Muttering a curse word she'd heard Johnny say once when he was angry, she stood frozen in the spot for a mere second, but in that moment she was privy to what her aunt was saying to her Uncle Angus.

What she heard mesmerized Charmaine to the spot. Her aunt's statement was startling. "You know John will come to visit more often, Angus, once he doesn't have to be around Charmaine," Simone was saying.

Johnny—her cousin, Johnny? He did not wish to come to the cottage because of her? Charmaine was perplexed. It could not be so! She found that impossible to accept. So she continued to listen for she wanted to hear what her uncle said.

"Funny that we never gave any thought that our son, being a robust healthy lad with the natural desires of any man, would become infatuated with his pretty cousin, Simone. If he'd had a sister it would have not have been so, but a cousin—well, a cousin is farther removed and a young man can easily forget that she is kin. How could we foresee that young girl would become the stunning beauty she is today?"

"That's just it, Angus, we couldn't. John used to look on her as a bit of a pest, an adorable little nuisance," Simone recalled.

It was hard for Charmaine to absorb everything they were saying but what was obvious to her was they wished her gone from the cottage.

She was too stunned to move on, yet she wished to hear no more of this disturbing talk. Finally, her aunt made everything perfectly clear when she told Angus, "Well, Angus, we'll just have to pray John will fall in love with some other girl when he accepts the fact that he can't have Charmaine. Now I've no doubt his love is blinding him to the fact that they are cousins."

Charmaine muzzled her mouth to keep a gasp from escaping, and her tiny body bent to give way to the tightening in her belly from the shock she'd just experienced. She felt as though someone had given her a sharp blow in the gut.

As she finally managed to walk on to her room and close the door, Charmaine's eyes filled with tears. Those things her aunt had said about Johnny—how could that be? How could she have not seen it? Was she such a naïve simpleton? After what she'd heard tonight, it was obvious that she was. All her eyes had seen in Johnny was goodness and kindness. She'd considered his feeling for her a kindred warmth.

Dear God, if Johnny was in love with her, that explained why he'd acted the way he did when he'd come to the cottage and found George Seymour with her. Now, she realized that what she'd thought was anger was jealous rage.

She suddenly understood why her aunt had pushed her toward George Seymour, and that awareness soothed the hurt from feeling that her uncle and aunt didn't love or care for her as they had seemed to. They were deeply concerned about what might happen.

She mumbled to the emptiness of her darkened bedroom.

"Well, I must ease their concern and cause them no more worry. I owe them that much."

As Charmaine saw it, knowing what she knew now, there was only one solution. She'd marry George and go to this place, Virginia, in America. The Keenes would then not be deprived of their son in the last years of their life. They had been well beyond middle age when Charmaine had come from France, and she did not question that she owed them a debt of gratitude. Somehow that decision wasn't so repulsive to her now.

She shut her eyes to sleep. Tomorrow, she'd proceed with her plan to tell George she'd marry him. After that, her aunt and uncle could breathe easier.

At least, she told herself as she relaxed between the sheets, she'd be realizing one of her daydreams. She would be going to a faraway place across the ocean—a strange, new country.

Chapter 7

A brisk breeze swept in from the bay this morning, and the lingering dampness from the rains the day before added to the chill of the October day. Charmaine's dark striped challis skirt whipped around her legs as she walked along the road leading into St. Helier, intending to purchase some goods for her Aunt Simone. Her brown knit vest felt good over her long sleeved blouse, but she was wishing that she'd flung the light wool shawl around her shoulders as Aunt Simone had suggested before she'd rushed out the cottage door.

She sashayed jauntily along the dirt road glancing every now and then at the pearl ring on her finger, George had presented to her after she'd told him she'd accept his proposal of marriage. It should have been exciting to her to have a ring with twinkling little diamonds on either side of the pearl, especially since she'd never owned one. Charmaine kept telling herself that, but merely felt it was a nice ring. She wondered if she was ungrateful.

Her heart was gladdened by the high spirits her aunt was in since she'd announced her plans to marry George, and her mission in St. Helier was to secure material and sewing articles so she and Simone might start sewing on the new frocks her aunt had insisted she must have for her wedding.

The town was bustling with carts and people by the time

Charmaine got to the outskirts. It was Friday, and the marketplace would be alive with the vendors selling buckets of flowers or the fruits and vegetables which the fertile soil of Jersey grew in such abundance.

The smell of fish would be there too, for fishermen like John did well when people flocked to the marketplace. Charmaine hoped she would not run into Johnny today for she was now uncertain how to act with him. The camaraderie they'd shared for five years was forever gone; she knew it. This made her sad for she'd always had a special fondness for Johnny Keene in a special way, though certainly not in the way Aunt Simone was talking about.

Soon, Charmaine was mingling with the people going up and down the busy street in a constant stream, and it became necessary to place her basket over her arm so she might get around the clusters of farmers chatting and visiting with each other. On market day everyone learned the news and gossip of the countryside for usually they were confined to their farms for days or weeks at a time.

Charmaine's pretty golden head turned from one side of the street to the other as she took in the people and the sights. She was now glad Aunt Simone had sent her on this errand.

She passed one of the stalls utterly covered with buckets of colorful, autumn flowers, their various fragrances were sheer delight. Delicate pinks and whites blended with lavender and purple-hued blossoms. The vivid reds and blues alongside rich golds and bright yellows made a glorious display of color. Charmaine could not imagine anything more beautiful to behold than flowers, any perfume more intoxicating than their scent.

The hunchbacked lady with a plaid shawl thrown over her shoulders beckoned Charmaine over to her stall. "Here, dearie! Take it!" She held out a lovely bright red posy to Charmaine. "For your pretty hair, dear. Stick it by your ear, eh."

Charmaine smiled sweetly at the wrinkled woman. "I thank you, ma'am. It's beautiful!" She took the blossom and placed it to the side of her thick, loose hair. "There—is that all right?"

"Just beautiful, miss. And so are you."

The old flower vendor's gesture and her compliment brightened the day for Charmaine. She thanked the woman again before moving back into the busy crowd, on her way to Gorey's for the articles her aunt wished her to purchase. But she'd walked only a short distance when she heard someone calling out to her. "Charmaine! Hold up—wait a minute. Charmaine!"

She turned to see tall, willowy Janice Seymour back in the crowd, waving her hands frantically. She stopped thinking suddenly that she and Janice would be kin when she married George. Another thought was a little more tormenting to Charmaine: George and Janice were cousins like she and John. It had struck her abruptly, making her even more aware of John's romantic feelings for her. Why, John? Why? she mused sadly. She felt some resentment toward him for allowing such feelings to grow.

"My word, Charmaine, you look absolutely radiant this morning, and what a beautiful flower in your hair," Janice declared, although she was slightly out of breath from rushing through the crowd. Taking Charmaine's arm as they began to walk on down the street she added, "Guess love and romance does that to a person. Makes me anxious for it to happen to me."

Charmaine smiled as Janice went on to say that the whole Seymour family was delighted when George had returned with the news that Charmaine had accepted his offer of marriage. "Well, you were our family's first choice for my bachelor cousin. Honestly, we told him that Charmaine Lamoureux was the most beautiful girl in the Channel Islands. You are too."

"Well, thank you, Janice. That's very kind of your family," Charmaine told her.

"'Course, I don't think I have to tell you who I think the

handsomest young man is, but I must confess he's a hard man to get acquainted with," Janice rambled on.

"You mean Johnny?"

"Yes, that's who I mean. Funny too, for his brothers are so friendly."

Charmaine could not tell her the truth, that Johnny didn't care for her forwardness so he shied away when the Seymours paid a visit. Neither could she say that Johnny's heart belonged to another girl—her. So she casually shrugged the subject aside by saying, "Oh, I think Johnny is just moody, Janice."

"Well, he doesn't seem that way around you, Charmaine."

"He's so used to me being around all the time, Janice. I'm just like an old piece of furniture in the house." She forced a laugh.

"Guess that does make a difference," Janice flippantly replied, accepting Charmaine's statement.

"Of course, it does. Oh, here we are. I've got to go in here, Janice," Charmaine announced, turning toward the entrance of Gorey's Shop.

Across the way, two fine-figured gentlemen elbowed their way through the Friday-market crowd. For a minute, Pierre's heart almost stopped beating, and he tensed with excitement, certain he'd spied the golden-haired beauty he was seeking. But when he pointed toward where he thought he'd seen her and urged Jacques to look, Bernay strained to see, then replied, "I see no fair-haired miss, *mon ami*. I see a frazzled old hag, some gents, and a few ladies. None are like the one you described."

"I could have sworn I saw her until some tall wench blocked my view. I wasn't imagining it, Jacques." Pierre's gray eyes sparked bright as he scanned the crowd.

"You want to see her so badly, Pierre. Confess it. Your trip here has not been fruitful, and you received news you did not wish to hear at the Keene's house, *oui?* The woman there said it could not be her niece you seek when she informed you she was not at home. The woman must be the mother of my friend, John Keene."

"Well, I'm not so sure I believe the lady. She was too eager to be rid of me. I sensed it. Perhaps, the girl was at the house."

"Oh, Pierre, listen to yourself. You are not making sense at all. If that were so, then who is the apparition you were just trying to draw my attention to?" Jacques broke into a gale of laughter and patted his friend on the back.

Disgruntled, Pierre barked, "Oh, all right. So your friend's mother told me the truth, we'll say. She didn't invite me to wait, did she?"

"Of course not. She is probably not accustomed to inviting strangers into her home. Now, my lovesick pup, shall we sail back to Guernsey?"

Pierre's gray eyes were busy looking over the crowd, however, and Jacques had to repeat his inquiry. When Pierre did answer it was in a strong, determined tone Bernay recognized. It told him not to try to persuade Renaud to leave. "I'm not going back with you, Bernay. I'm going to stay in St. Helier tonight."

"You're what? Wakefield will be furious, Renaud. You know that."

"Let him! There's nothing he can do about it once you get back. He won't order you to return until daylight. Believe me, my friend, it will be all right. I've got to satisfy myself about this girl. Tonight. I won't fail, I feel it!"

Jacques shrugged his broad shoulders in a hopeless gesture and mumbled, "If this is what you wish, *mon ami.*"

"It is what I wish." A broad grin came on Pierre's face and he assured Jacques, "I will be at the dock in the morning. You'll see."

There was nothing more to be said so Bernay turned to go down the sidestreet which led to the berth where his boat was docked.

With a wave of his hand, Pierre turned to amble on down

69

the street. He passed Gorey's where Charmaine was shopping with Janice, and but for a matter of a few minutes, he would have encountered her when she left, her basket filled with purchases of sewing goods. But fortune did not smile on him and make it happen that way. Their paths took them in different directions.

Charmaine traveled down the dirt road that led from the town to her uncle's farm a mile away, and Pierre sought to quench his thirst in a nearby tavern.

Once he'd sought a secluded corner table and ordered his ale, he sank into a quiet, thoughtful mood which made him ignore the efforts of the buxom girl serving him.

Such a handsome bucko he is to be so shy, she thought to herself because he made no move to pat or pinch her hips as most of the patrons did, nor did he lustily ogle her overflowing breasts displayed by her lowcut blouse.

Realizing her efforts to flirt with him were of no avail, she busied herself with chores and allowed Pierre to drink his ale in peace.

He was, indeed, in a reflective mood, and he realized he was feeling strange. What was this consuming force that drove him to desire one little female. He was Pierre Renaud, the elusive bachelor more than one beautiful French lady had sought to charm and win for her lover back in Cherbourg. Now, he was on this small island in the English Channel, banished from France by his own father because of a so-called love affair that never took place.

He had been in the loving arms of a lady named Colette on that fateful night. Indeed, his refusal to accept the invitation of the aristocratic Daphne Delacroix had provoked the noble lady's scorn and wrath, and she'd accused him of trying to ravage her while her husband was away from their country estate just outside Cherbourg.

The gorgeous Colette was also married, and on the night he'd spent with her, her husband was away on a hunting trip. Pierre had no way to clear himself of the charges without divulging the name of the fair lady he *was* with.

Pierre sought from women only moments of pleasure. He never gave them a second thought. Like a butterfly, he went casually from one to another, enjoying the sweet nectar he found before seeking some other beautiful blossom of femininity. No woman had whetted the interest of the Frenchman except that tiny slip of a girl he'd met for one brief, but spellbinding moment. He couldn't understand why, but he knew he'd not rest until he found her again.

Before the sun came up the next day and before this night was over, he was going back to the cliffside where he'd seen the maiden with the delicately featured face and long golden tresses streaming down her back. Brief though their meeting was, Pierre recalled the little minx's dainty figure, her tiny waist his hands could encircle, and the spirited look on her lovely face. Oh, yes, he also recalled the glowing fire in her deep violet eyes, and her lips whose taste was sweeter than honey.

He'd find her, he promised himself, as he rose to leave the tavern.

Chapter 8

Charmaine was repulsed by the vision of herself the full-length mirror offered as she turned first to one side and then the other. Why had she put her long, thick hair in that coil atop her head as Aunt Simone did? Already, she looked like a dowdy farmer's wife, she thought, in her simple muslin frock, her hair in that severe style, and she suddenly felt old and drab.

The entire evening she'd sat sewing, and as she'd worked on her new frock, she'd thought of what marriage to George was going to be like. When, finally, her aunt had suggested they call it a night Charmaine had readily agreed. Her eyes were as tired as her fingers, for although she had accepted her fate, she could not make herself feel eager or excited about her future or the frock.

In her bedroom, as she'd started to remove her clothes before retiring, she'd taken note of herself in the mirror. Her image filled her with utter distaste. It also inspired an insistent need to go to her peaceful cliff.

A strong, gusting wind was blowing in from the channel. Charmaine had only to glance out the window to see the trees bending from its force, but that did not matter to her. She took the black woollen shawl hanging on the peg behind her door, and left her bedroom.

The night's blackness was lit by bright beams of moonlight so she did not concern herself about finding her way across the meadows and up to the path which would take her to her favorite spot. The Normandy coast was obscured, but she knew it was there.

If she married George would she have to forsake her dream of returning to France? More than likely.

Lately her girlish dreams were being swept away. Since this was so, she was going to indulge herself, give way to her foolish fancies while she still had time.

As she hastily rushed from the brownstone cottage, her romantic heart felt light and gay. With the old black shawl tucked securely around her shoulders and her hands holding it tightly because of the breezy winds, she skipped across the quiet, peaceful meadows like a wood nymph.

By the time she'd left the meadow and scrambled up the incline to go through the natural passageway between the boulders, the future no longer occupied her thoughts. For the moment, she was a young girl, feeling capriciously gay and romantic.

Pierre stood by the horse he'd obtained from the livery in town, feeling rewarded by the glorious sight of her. He had been right to stay the night on Jersey. Securing the reins of the jet black mare, he began to approach the beautiful girl he'd been seeking. He knew she existed, that she was not just a product of fantasy. He'd kissed the most luscious of lips, gazed into the most glorious pair of amethyst eyes, eyes he felt he could drown in. She was here, only a few feet away from him, and soon his arms intended to claim her.

He yanked his jacket around to fasten it but he could do nothing about the strong wind assaulting his dark hair, which cascaded over his forehead. Nor could he control the firmness in his tight-fitting trousers of brown wool, for his entire being had come alive the minute his black eyes had caught sight of the girl.

He chuckled, amused to find desire firing in him. His long

strides had almost taken him to the cliffside where Charmaine was already seated before she turned to face the intruder approaching her. She opened her mouth to speak, but no words came forth, so she sat, wide-eyed and silent.

"You look surprised, *chérie?* You remember I told you I'd see you again," Renaud told her, a handsome grin on his face. She was enchantingly lovely, as he'd remembered. It wasn't just his imagination.

Charmaine was awestruck. She, too, was musing, about the handsome devil standing before her. Here was no god she'd dreamed up. Had she not heard him speak just now? This was no ghost or imagined fantasy.

Calmly yet boldly, she told him, "I remember the night and—and you." And her eyes locked into his, for she was like one hypnotized. For this was what she'd secretly yearned to have happen.

He sank down on the ground beside her, his face was close to hers. She could see that his features were as she'd remembered, especially his sensuous lips and the wispy curls of jet black hair that seemed to caress his ears and tease the collar of his jacket. He smelled of lime and spice, as well as tobacco and leather. When he smiled at her, his teeth flashed pearly white.

"I'm glad you remember the night, *ma petite.* I remember that you ran away from me because some bloody fool called out to you—Charlie, isn't it?"

"Yes, Charlie!" She stiffened and quickly added, "But it was not a fool, *monsieur!*"

She started to move away from his side, but Renaud's hand restrained her, the strength in it suggestive of the power in his muscular body. She relented, letting him draw her back to him so that their sides pressed together. His arm snaked around her back and his hand clenched her waist.

"To me, he is a fool for the name does not suit you, *mademoiselle.* Tell me, what is your real name?"

Charmaine found it gratifying to be embraced by him. "I

am Charmaine Lamoureux," she replied.

The way she said that and turned to look up at Pierre revealed a certain haughty pride in this little slip of a girl. He liked that about her.

"Charmaine . . . that's beautiful just like you. Yes, I like that. I like that very much. It's right for you." He bent to caress her ear with a featherlike kiss, softly murmuring her name meanwhile. "So you are French too? We have something in common. So am I," Pierre proudly declared.

"And am I to know your name, *monsieur?*" She turned and the motion of her body caused her leg to touch his. Pierre drew her closer to him for the feel of her flesh against him had fired his desire.

"My name is Pierre Renaud and I come from Cherbourg. May I ask why a gorgeous French belle is here in the Channel Islands?"

"My parents both died, and I came to live with my Aunt Simone, my mother's sister."

"You see, *chérie,* fate made us meet—did it not?—in this most unlikely setting for two people from France. I'll wager I know why you come to this lovely spot and sit on the cliff, to look across to the land beyond the water—to France. *N'est-ce pas?"*

"Yes, it is so." Amazed that he understood so completely her feelings, Charmaine gazed at him in wonderment, her thick long lashes fluttering with a curious excitement, as they sat in their intimate embrace. Dear God, this is how it should be between a man and a woman, she thought to herself. She could never feel so affected by George Seymour—never!

"I knew it," he told her and at the same moment he drew her to him, pressing her against his broad chest. His heart was pounding so hard she could feel it pulse against her breasts. Slowly his mouth met hers, capturing her lips, and when his tongue sought entry to her mouth, she opened it. Its touch,
its caress was new to her, but she readily responded to these stimulating sensations.

76

Renaud knew she'd never been kissed before, not as he was now kissing her, and he let his mouth linger and savor the sweetness of her. Rare, she was! And he was all the more determined that he'd never lose her again, that he would possess her.

When his lips released hers, he murmured her name in a way Charmaine had never heard it spoken. His deep voice seemed almost to be singing it, as if it were a romantic ballad. She made no move to free herself from his warm embrace, and for a moment they looked into one another's eyes as if each was seeking out what the other was thinking.

Only then did Charmaine become aware that his nimble fingers had released the huge coil of her hair and its thick golden mass fell over her shoulders. "You should never wear that beautiful mane of spun gold up like that." His hands played with the long strands, and the mere touch of his fingers stirred a reckless wildness in Charmaine she didn't understand. She only knew she'd never felt such exhilaration before.

Because of the spellbinding madness engulfing her, she made no protest when his hands slipped under her hips and he then cradled her in his strong arms, his huge body rising from the ground. She cared not where he was carrying her as his long strides took them away from the cliff. When she heard the sounds of the moving waters lapping at the sandy shore, she turned to see walls of natural stone and she knew they were in the secluded shelter of one of the many coves.

Pierre removed his wool jacket, and set her down upon it, her shawl draped around her shoulders still. But she was not cold, for the heat of his male body had warmed her. As he sank down beside her, his two hands caressed her face in a loving gesture, and he let his eyes dance slowly, adoringly, from the top of her head down to her throat as he pleaded, "Tonight, let us pretend we are back in France. Will you dare to dream with me, *chérie,* as I've dreamed about you so many nights since that time we met?"

She did not answer him with her lips, but her body moved toward him, drawn by natural instinct and reckless desire. Pierre needed no other response, and as she swayed toward him, his lips took hers in a flaming kiss that left both of them breathless.

When his searing caress trailed down her throat and then explored the supple, satiny mounds of her breasts, she did nothing to deny him what he wanted. As his lips took the rosy tip of one of her breasts, his tongue teasing the taut tip, she couldn't restrain a soft moan of delight. This, too, was a pleasure she'd never before experienced.

Pierre throbbed with surging desire, but he urged himself to control his need and to lavish on her the love he yearned to give her. He wanted this to be a night of remembered rapture, not one of regret. His experienced hands sensed the sensitive places of her soft flesh, and he felt her tremble as he tenderly teased her. Charmaine moaned his name softly as her body undulated against his.

Pierre was very knowledgeable about undressing ladies, and his magic had so blinded Charmaine that she wasn't aware that practically all of her clothing had been removed until she felt his bare chest burning into her naked flesh. But that mattered not to her now, for shamelessly, she wanted nothing more than to absorb the tantalizing feel of his flesh. Such stimulating titillation was new to her.

Only when he sought to kick off his pants did he raise himself from her, for his strong will was hastily waning. As he lowered himself back down onto her, Charmaine felt a liquid fire flood through her body when his pulsing hardness touched her thigh. His hand sought her velvet softness, so warm and inviting, and he regretted that he must hurt her to bring them the ultimate joy they both eagerly desired.

"Chérie, I will be gentle . . . gentle as possible," he whispered soothingly in her ear. "One small moment of hurt before I give you pleasure you've never known. Trust me, my sweet Charmaine." His fingers caressed and gentled her as his lips sought to assure her.

She tensed when he made his forceful stroke, but her arms still clung to his neck. Then his magnificent maleness filled her, and for one brief moment he let her warmth devour him. When he felt she was ready, slowly and sensuously he swayed his powerful body, his excitement mounting as she gave out a new moan of pleasure, then began to respond to this hitherto unknown ecstasy he was bringing her.

His fierce male body reminded her of the coming tide that invaded the shore, and she arched her body to absorb his powerful, thrusting wave.

Each new wave was more forceful, more furious, and she found herself gasping with passion. When, at last, his body shuddered and the seed poured from him, he collapsed atop her, releasing his own husky moan of delight, and Charmaine held him very close.

After a moment, he rose from her and sank down by her side, still enclosing her in his arms. Then they lay snuggled close together, both wishing they could remain in the cove all night long. But that could not be; they knew it.

His voice still warm with passion, Pierre finally spoke, his lips moved against her damp cheek meanwhile. "A goddess of love—that is what you are, Charmaine Lamoureux. My goddess. No one else's. Tell me it is so."

"No one else's, Pierre." Her voice was but a whisper. It was true. Even if she married George, her heart would belong to Pierre Renaud.

"So you are not sorry then?" He clutched her closer against him.

"No, I am not sorry. I'll never be sorry." At that moment, she could not possibly tell him her thoughts. She did not want to put a blight on this moonlit night.

"God, that makes me happy, *chérie*. I tried to be so careful. I knew you were a virgin, and I didn't want the first time to be bad for you. I didn't want that because I plan to spend a lifetime loving you, *ma petite*." He swiped his unruly hair away from the side of his face.

"You were gentle, Pierre, and I wanted you to make love to me, just as you did," Charmaine confessed without an ounce of shame.

"To think I thought you were a figment of my imagination. A little golden mermaid who'd risen from the sea to haunt and bedevil a poor seaman. Dear God, I wanted you to exist, and now that I know you do and I've loved that sweet body of yours, I'll never doubt myself again or any of my wild imaginings. He gave out a husky laugh. Charmaine adored the boyish look on his tanned face, and she rose slightly to kiss his cheek. But Pierre moved her face so that their lips met.

"Love me one more time before we must go our separate ways, *chérie*. Love me and promise me you'll be here tomorrow night. I'll have exciting plans to tell you then. Promise me, Charmaine."

Charmaine would have promised Pierre anything at that moment, and she, too, was eager to make love.

Another hour passed before the moonlight lovers forced themselves to leave their bower in the cove. Their parting was not so painful because they anticipated their rendezvous tomorrow night, and the heat of their parting kiss was enough to make the young lovers light of heart.

Charmaine swore the stars were gleaming brighter. Indeed, she felt she was soaring to their lofty heights for she was intoxicated with love.

Chapter 9

The witty, sharp Jacques Bernay was not surprised by
Captain Wakefield's reaction displayed when he told him
that young Renaud had not returned with him from the
island of Jersey. The older man's outburst of salty curse
words was anticipated. The cocky Frenchman had been
privy to such scenes many times during the years he'd
worked for Wakefield Fleetlines.

Indeed, Jacques admired the Englishman's spirit and his
iron will, much as he admired those qualities in the young
Renaud, his fellow Frenchman. What annoyed Bernay was
the spot Renaud had put him in where his boss was
concerned. Wakefield accepted no excuse when he issued an
order. Men who didn't comply with his commands didn't
last long at Wakefield lines.

Renaud was his responsibility, but he couldn't have
dragged him back on the boat without slugging him and that
would not have pleased the captain either. So Jacques was
damned if he did and damned if he didn't, he figured.

When a man was as randy and fevered as Pierre over a
woman, there was no talking sense to him. Jacques recalled
the times he himself had been in such a state.

Now, as he stood in the cozy library of the Wakefield's
large imposing mansion awaiting the captain's return,

Bernay relaxed somewhat. At least, when Wakefield returned to the room his temper would have had a chance to cool, Bernay hoped. He'd welcomed the butler's summoning the captain out into the hall, for though it was no secret that Wakefield was a volatile man, exploding easily, his hot temper didn't last long.

Jacques paced in front of the huge stone fireplace instead of sitting in one of the oversize leather chairs. The brisk winds and the chill of the night air made the huge mansion drafty, and warmth given off by the crackling log in the fireplace felt good to him. He had also taken the liberty of replenishing his glass with some of the brandy in the cut-glass decanter resting upon the liquor cabinet.

It is a fine home the captain has, Jacques thought to himself as he scrutinized the furnishings and the rich wood paneling of the walls. The miniature ships lining the long mantel above the fireplace were Wakefield's prized possessions, as well as his hobby. But the captain's most prized possession was depicted in the portrait hanging above these—Sarnia, Wakefield's dark-headed, black-eyed daughter.

He took a deep gulp from his glass and sighed with relief, glad that Renaud hadn't messed around with that little piece of fluff. Then there would have been real hell to pay.

He couldn't explain why, but the first time he'd encountered Sarnia Wakefield, he'd felt an instant aversion for her. She was so smug and haughty he'd wanted to slap her. At least, it hadn't been his lot to be around her too often during the years he'd worked for her father.

Nonetheless Jacques was appraising her portrait when the captain's deep, gruff voice announced his return. "Sorry, Bernay. No rest for the wicked, as they say," Wakefield remarked, in a more mellow tone than Bernay had hoped for.

"Quite all right, sir. Been enjoying the comfort of this nice room of yours. It's really quite something."

This pleased Wakefield, but then he always found Bernay

a most likable chap. He could never fault him as a worker, and he'd realized in the brief space of time he'd been out of the room that it was that bloody son of Étienne's who deserved his anger. Jacques could hardly be expected to keep a reckless fellow like Pierre within certain boundaries. The lad's own father hadn't been able to do it or Pierre wouldn't be here on Guernsey. He did agree that Étienne had come up with the best medicine for the young rooster, sending him to the New World where it was still unsettled and primitive. Maybe that would take some of the ginger out of him, tame him down.

"Bernay, pick the young scoundrel up in the morning as he requested. I'll talk to him when he returns. You've put in a long enough day due to him already."

"Yes, sir. Thank you, Captain Wakefield. I'll sail back over to Jersey at daybreak." Jacques flashed a broad smile, tipped his cap to the captain, and jauntily walked out the door.

He swaggered down the long hallway and out the front door, thinking to himself he was glad everything was smoothed out with his captain. Even though he'd made a point of keeping his own life uncluttered by troublesome females, he wasn't immune to the problems they caused, but at least, this little episode was resolved.

He took in a deep breath of cool night air, his dark sweater expanding with his robust chest. Then jauntily tilting his cap atop his curly dark head, he started to whistle a sea chantey as he skipped down the stone walkway leading from the Wakefield mansion to the street.

He was headed toward the harbor, wanting the serene comfort of his bunk for in the morning he had to get an early start for Jersey and St. Helier.

"Jacques, Jacques Bernay!" a feminine voice called out to him. He turned to see Sarnia Wakefield coming from behind a long row of rose bushes. An ecru shawl was draped over her dark hair, and she clutched it around her shoulders.

"Mademoiselle Wakefield? Is that you out in the cool night air?" He knew it was, and he instinctively sensed that she was seeking information when she inconvenienced herself so much—about Pierre and his absence from the house tonight.

"Yes, Jacques," she said in a syrupy tone. He knew she would expect this sweetness to be rewarded. "I need your help. I was going to try to catch you before you left the house, but one of the stupid servant girls delayed me. You see, Jacques, I—I want to give Pierre a nice party before he departs from St. Peter Port, and I consider you to be the one to tell me whom I might invite that evening. Who here on Guernsey, or on our neighbor Jersey over at St. Helier, would I invite, Jacques?" She prattled on, thinking she was being clever, but Jacques could hardly mask his amusement.

"I have no one but you to help me in this, Jacques. But I've heard at dinner about the many hours you and he have spent out on St. Brelade's Bay, and Petit Bot and Fermain. He often mentioned going to Jersey with you." She smiled sweetly, anticipating his answer.

There was a bit of the clown in Jacques, and some of the practical joker, so he gave out a perplexed frown and shook his head. "I am ashamed to say I'm going to be of no help to you, *mademoiselle*. It's just been me and him on all those outings. Now, isn't that something! It surely pains me that I can't assist you."

Sarnia knew the Frenchman was lying. She just knew it! It riled her so that she whirled around, hissed something Jacques couldn't hear, and stomped back across the grounds. But Jacques had seen the fire sparking in her dark eyes, and he could not contain the gust of laughter that erupted as he headed down the long narrow, cobbled street.

He'd suspected the captain's spoiled daughter was a conniving little wench. Now he knew it for sure. Renaud had better beware, for she'd go far to get her way with him.

As he headed back to where the schooner was moored, his laughter faded, along with his amusement. Because Sarnia's trickery hadn't worked, she wouldn't quit inquiring around until she found out the name of the beautiful girl Jacques had remained in Jersey to seek out.

God help that poor little innocent when she came up against the wiles of Sarnia Wakefield!

When Sarnia returned to the house her anger had become a raging tempest. She knew it was best she not show this trait to her doting father, so she temporarily set aside her scheme for revenge on the lying Bernay, as well as on Pierre.

How dare Bernay have the audacity to defy her by concealing the information she'd requested of him! He, a lowly seaman working for her father, should have some loyalty to the Wakefield family. Well, the cocky Bernay would rue his behavior when she got through waging her little campaign with her father in the morning. She smirked as she marched up the steps.

And Pierre Renaud would regret shrugging her aside for some little village minx over in St. Helier. Whoever she was, she could not be as beautiful as Sarnia Wakefield. He was merely gratifying his animal lust in some farmer's haystack because the restrictions of a mansion filled with servants cramped his style. Her father was always present at the dinner table every night.

Yes, that could be the only possible answer, the vain Sarnia firmly decided, to Pierre's restrained behavior toward her. It wasn't always such a privilege to be born into wealth and to have to be the proper young lady. More than once she'd yearned for the freedom of the poor, lowly born maidens she'd seen wandering around the streets of St. Peter Port.

While she removed her gown and jewels, she reviewed her

85

plan to belittle Bernay in her father's eyes. She knew she could do so, though she was aware that he put great trust in the Frenchman. Long ago, Sarnia had learned that Wakefield had a blind spot where she was concerned. He'd never believe her capable of conjuring up such a lie.

As she freed the two huge coils of her dark hair, angrily tossing the pins on the fancy gilt dressing table, she almost wished she had summoned her maid to assist her. She'd wanted to be alone and to think, but she'd not realized how many pins Rose had stuck in her hair when she'd put it up. When the last pin was out, she gave her head a couple of shakes to make her hair fall freely over her shoulders. Then she disgustedly thought about the waste of enduring such a special toilette again this evening for Pierre's benefit when he might not return to the house.

When she crawled in between the sheets of her frilly canopied bed, she muttered to herself and to the empty room, "Actually, Daddy dear, we want the same thing for little old me. Dear Lord, a prestigious marriage is what I want too. Marriage to a very wealthy man who can give me all the things I'm accustomed to, a man as devilishly handsome as Pierre." Renaud could offer her all that, more than Francis Neville, her present English suitor of whom her father heartily approved.

No lady in her right mind would want to settle for Francis Neville when there was the slightest hope of having Pierre Renaud as a husband.

Just thinking about the young Frenchman made hot liquid fire surge through her, and she tossed and turned in the bed, awash with discontent and frustration. Her plight made her all the more determined to do anything she must to have her way.

When Sarnia's dark eyes finally closed in sleep, she was confident about her scheme for destroying Bernay's future with the Wakefield Lines, nor did the tiniest pang of conscience disturb her sleep. The wicked little miss was far too self-centered to concern herself about anything or anyone except herself.

While Bernay lay in his bunk he anticipated that Sarnia might just brew up something, he never dreamed of how far the vicious vixen was prepared to go with her contemptible lies.

Chapter 10

As Charmaine silently entered the stone cottage and made her way cautiously to her room, she knew the dawn would soon be coming, but she was so gloriously happy the knowledge that she'd get little sleep didn't bother her. As she hastily undressed and crawled into her bed, her lover's name echoed in her mind like a magnificent ballad. She smiled, snuggling herself, and said it aloud. "Pierre Renaud! Pierre Renaud! Oh, how I love you, Pierre."

She recalled every precious moment of their togetherness, and her flesh tingled at the memory of his sensuous caresses. A flush went through her. Just to know she would meet with him tonight was enough to make Charmaine eager for the dawn to come.

The future? Her reckless heart didn't care about the future. If she dared to worry about the days to come, that could put a blight on this rapturous interlude, and she would not allow anything to deprive her of this glorious bliss. These moments were all, and Charmaine intended to lock them away in a secret place in her heart.

She was reminded of the time when she and Johnny had had a special secret they'd told no one—a fuzzy little kitten they'd hidden away in an obscure corner of the barn to keep Angus from knowing about. The two of them would sneak out of the house with milk for the kitten, and for many weeks, their intrigue had gone on. But one night when they'd slipped out to the barn, the kitten had been gone and she'd been devastated. Johnny had put his arm around her and had soothed her tears away by pointing to a small hole in the wood siding of the barn and convincing her the kitten had wanted to wander.

Johnny—her dear, sweet Johnny! Regardless of what she now knew, she had a special love for him, and always would. But she regretted the hurt and pain his feelings for her had caused him. Dear Lord, she'd never meant that to happen! If she hadn't been so naïve, she might have realized what was going on.

More than ever after being with Pierre, Charmaine realized how simple and inexperienced she was. Aunt Simone had not really prepared her to deal with men, but she felt that her mother would have. Suzanne was not the prude that her aunt was. That was becoming more and more obvious to Charmaine.

She wondered if her aunt's attitude was partly Angus' fault. He'd had a very strict upbringing, whereas her father, Phillippe Lamoureux, had had such a different nature, demonstrative and amorous. Would she become like her Aunt Simone if she married George Séymour who was not at all like her own father?

I will not, she vowed. Having done that, she surrendered to her weariness.

With a basket of foodstuff in her lap, Simone perched on the seat of Angus' wagon as they prepared to travel the two miles over to visit an ailing neighbor.

"I figured you'd have gotten Charmaine up, Simone. She could have gotten a couple of hours work done while you're paying your call on Tessie," Angus grumbled, reining his team into action.

"She worked late last night on her new dress, Angus, and she was sleeping like a baby when I looked in on her so I just didn't have the heart to. She's a good child, Angus."

"Never said she wasn't, did I? I just want you to make it easier on yourself, my dear. She's young and full of spice."

Simone pretended indignation and playfully taunted her gray-haired husband by saying, "Are you telling me, Angus Keene, I've got no spice anymore?"

Angus broke into a slow smile. "Never would I say that. I just don't want you using it all up. We've gotten to an age when we should be a little kinder to ourselves, wouldn't you say?"

"We have, dear, and especially you, Angus." Simone gave her husband a warm smile. He'd looked very tired the last few weeks. She'd never given much thought to the ten years' difference in their ages until recently, but Angus' fifty-ninth birthday was quickly approaching.

Was it any wonder that the pace of his long days on the farm tired him? She herself was wearier after the dinner hour and glad to seek the comfort of her bed. She promised herself as they traveled down the country road to Tessie's that she was going to insist that Angus make his work days shorter.

Back at the Keene cottage, a constant rapping on the door woke Charmaine and she stumbled around her room trying to find her wrapper. So insistent was the rapping that she rushed down the steps in her bare feet. Her rumpled blond hair fell carelessly over her face, and she brushed it back with her fingers just before she got to the front door.

If George was calling so early in the morning, he might as well be prepared for the shock of her not being dressed, she thought to herself as she turned the knob of the door.

But it wasn't the tall, lanky George standing before her. The caller was a very impressive young woman, fashionably dressed in a wine-colored morning suit with a short fitted jacket trimmed in black braid. On her head was a saucy bonnet with a black plume that swished back and forth in the gentle morning breeze. From one of her wrists, a black velvet reticule hung, and covering her hands were matching black gloves. The lady was absolutely stunning.

Before the young woman announced herself, Charmaine decided that her unexpected visitor's carriage had broken down.

In a very assured voice, the stranger inquired, "Is this the Keene cottage?"

"It is," Charmaine replied, a questioning look on her face as her thick-lashed eyes stared at the elegant miss. Secretly, she envied this young lady her grand clothes. It must be absolutely marvelous to have such exquisite things to wear, she thought to herself.

"May I please come in then? I am assuming you must be Charmaine Lamoureux?"

"I am," Charmaine slowly declared, hesitation lacing her voice.

"Then Miss Lamoureux—I guess I should say Mademoiselle Lamoureux—we have a matter to discuss."

Something in this woman's tone of voice, the hint of a slur when she uttered Charmaine's name, brought forth an instant dislike. The young lady's haughtiness aroused a cocky arrogance in Charmaine, and she let her deep blue eyes lock with Sarnia's dark ones as she curtly remarked, "I can't imagine what we would have to discuss. I've never seen you before in my life. Since you seem to know my name, may I inquire who you are?"

"I am Sarnia Wakefield," the intruder declared with an uppity air, as though Charmaine should recognize the name immediately.

As Charmaine ushered her into the small parlor, she was still at a loss as to what they had to discuss. "May I offer you a cup of tea?"

"No, I won't be here that long," Sarnia retorted, fidgeting with her gloves. "Let me get to the point of my visit, Mademoiselle Lamoureux. It will save us both any prolonged embarrassment." Her dark eyes carefully surveyed the face and figure of this golden-haired girl who'd attracted Pierre.

"Embarrassment? I'm sorry, Miss Wakefield, I don't understand any of this."

"Well, in that case I am doing you a favor too. I . . . I have to admit that it has taxed my dignity sorely. That rascal should be admonished severely for what he's done." Sarnia gave a twittering little laugh, and pointing her gloved finger in a dramatic gesture, she added, "I do intend to give him a piece of my mind, too."

"I'm . . . I'm still unclear as to what and who you are speaking about," Charmaine said, a frown on her lovely face.

"My betrothed, *mademoiselle*. That naughty boy, Pierre. He should not have come over here to Jersey and dallied with you just because he was impatient and couldn't sully me before our wedding day," Sarnia said, a smug look on her face.

"Your . . . your betrothed, you said?"

"That's right, my dear. Now you see why I came to see you. As I said, I am doing you a favor by putting myself out to do so." Sarnia rose immediately, for the girl's startled face told her that her mission was a success. Charmaine sat speechless for a moment or two. A feeling of exaltation swept over Sarnia as she watched the gullible girl's expression. How naïve she was and how easily she'd swallowed the concocted story. Sarnia was as delighted as she'd been that morning when she'd manipulated her father and had blackened Bernay's name.

But she had no need to linger on Jersey, so she gave Charmaine a sympathetic look as she ambled toward the front door. "I see, my dear, that I've distressed you, and for that, I'm sorry. As I said that naughty boy should be spanked, but he's such a big devil I'm afraid neither you or I could manage that." Sarnia laughed softly.

By now Charmaine had managed to get some control of herself. "Don't give it a thought, Miss Wakefield, really. Pierre Renaud means nothing to me. I, too, am to be married—to a very nice American gentleman." With difficulty she managed to smile. In her own way she was as proud as Sarnia Wakefield.

"Oh? Well, congratulations, my dear," Sarnia replied, a little taken aback by Charmaine's remark.

"Thank you. The same to you and . . . and Pierre." Charmaine was amazed, she'd never guessed that she had the talent to be such an actress, and a liar.

"Good day, *mademoiselle.*"

When Sarnia left the cottage, Charmaine hastily closed the door, knowing as she slowly walked back into her aunt's parlor that she must also close the door on any foolish ideas she'd harbored about the handsome Renaud.

But how could he possibly have loved her so ardently last night in their little bower if his heart belonged to this Sarnia Wakefield? She couldn't understand such a love. Was it different for a woman? she asked herself.

Thoughtfully, she walked back to her room, not trying to stop the tears from flowing. When she was inside her bedroom, she looked at herself in the mirror, and it wasn't hard to see why a man like Pierre would prefer such an elegant, sophisticated lady like Sarnia to be his wife. She looked at her tousled blond hair and her wrinkled cotton wrapper, comparing it to her visitor's exquisite gown. What an utter fool she'd been to think that such a man would want a simple, little farm girl for anything other than a moment's pleasure.

As Miss Wakefield had said he wouldn't dare soil his bride-to-be—she was special and to be respected—but he'd not cared that he'd taken her voraciously, deflowering her unceremoniously in the cove.

George Seymour would be getting no pure, innocent virgin when they married. Perhaps, he'd refuse to allow her to go to America after their wedding night, she thought to herself. He might just desert her. She yanked the wrapper away from her body and jerked the gown up, pulling it over her head. Standing there naked, she scrutinized herself for a long time. Her nude body showed no signs of Renaud's caresses. It looked exactly as it had before last night. Yet deep within her she would never be the same again, for his fingers had caused her to tingle and his lips had taunted and teased her unmercifully, evoking sensations her supple body had never known before. When his hot-passioned body had invaded hers, they were for that one moment in time joined. But none of this showed.

Charmaine knew that a part of Pierre Renaud would forever be implanted in her, even when she was married to George.

She cursed him for that!

Chapter 11

Captain Martin Wakefield was a man who liked and insisted upon an orderly routine life, but there were days, like this one, which taxed his patience to extremes. His housekeeper was ailing this morning and one of the servant girls was filling in for her. His porridge and cream, and his kippers, were miserable, provoking him to roar like an angry lion. The poor servant girl trembled with fright as she scurried away, fearing he might just hurl the bowl of porridge at her.

By the time his daughter appeared downstairs and joined him at the long dining table, his disgruntled mood had not improved. But as she sat sipping her tea, the sight of her mellowed him as it usually did.

Noticing her unusually quiet, withdrawn manner, however, he questioned her. "Something bothering you, my darling?"

This was exactly what Sarnia had wanted him to do. Putting on a demure act, she tried to pass off her mood as nothing for him to be disturbed about, but Wakefield would have no part of that. He was now primed for Sarnia to tell him the outrageous lie she'd concocted about Jacques.

"Why I couldn't believe the audacity of the man. He was so bold right here in our own home, Father. I firmly put him in his place. I . . . I know you think highly of him as a seaman, but I could do no less," she declared.

She watched him clench his teeth and knew he was restraining his rage. His huge hands tapped nervously on the table. "You did exactly right," he said proudly. He planned to do a lot more, but he wasn't going to burn her pretty ears with his plans for Bernay. The bloody Frenchman must have taken leave of his senses, Wakefield thought. Still, Bernay had come in and out of this house so many times the captain couldn't understand why he'd suddenly forgotten his station and had pulled such a foolish stunt. But Martin Wakefield didn't ponder that too long. After Sarnia excused herself to go on an errand, he decided it was the influence of his fellow Frenchman, Pierre. That was the only possible explanation since such a thing had never happened before and the two of them were together constantly.

Wakefield decided he'd not wait another fortnight for word of the situation in the ports in America. There was a salty old American sea captain in port now. He'd known Jim Garrett for many a year. Garrett owed him a favor or two and he might as well collect. That way he could rid himself of Pierre Renaud and at the same time dole out a just punishment to the man who'd dared to take liberties with his precious daughter. In fact, this resolution of his problems was so devilishly clever Martin's face creased in a smug smile as he reached into the teakwood box on his desk to get one of his cheroots.

Without a moment's hesitation, he began to write a message to be delivered immediately to Captain Jim Garrett aboard his schooner moored out in Cobo Bay on Guernsey's west coast.

A few hours later the inscrutable, rugged-looking Garrett was marching into Martin's study to greet him with his usual enthusiastic, firm handshake. Martin never failed to be impressed by the striking image old Jim presented. The man had a huge frame and sharp features with a hawklike nose, and his deep-set piercing eyes, black as coal, were framed with bushy black brows.

His appearance was enough to demand a certain amount of respect from any man, but when he spoke there was a tone of authority in his deep bass voice.

"Good to see you again, old friend," Martin said, gesturing toward one of the large leather chairs over by the fireplace. "What's your pleasure, Jim?"

Martin knew it would be some of his good whiskey, so he was already sauntering toward his liquor cabinet. As he did so, he inquired, "How long are you here for this time, Jim?"

"Leaving tonight, Martin. Can't dally around to waste good sailing time, if you know what I mean and I know you do. Never know from one day to another when commerce will be banned again and the ports will be closed."

"Bloody mess as far as I'm concerned, Jim. Makes it damned hard on us in shipping. Pure hell!!"

"That damned embargo cost us all, believe me. Right now ships are leaving port constantly with their holds packed full. That's what I'm doing, I can tell you."

They sat and drank their liquor, talking business for almost an hour before Martin made his request known to Jim Garrett.

The blunt earthy American laughed boisterously. "So you want to dump two horny Frenchmen on me, Martin? Damn! You English are a greedy lot! You think you own the seas, and now you ask me to take your rascals back to Savannah with me!"

It was said in good humor, and Martin roared with laughter too for he and Garrett had been comrades years ago when they were sailing the seas as young hellions.

Martin knew his friend would not refuse him. He was just having his jest. Martin Wakefield had been generous on occasion to Garrett since they'd first crossed paths in the East Indies waters in the 1780s.

Drawing on their experiences of yesteryear, they put their

99

two graying heads together and laid their plans for shanghaiing Pierre Renaud and his pal, Jacques Bernay, that night. Both aging sea captains were without scruples about the deed they were about to do. Indeed, they were enjoying themselves, for what they were about reminded them of their randy younger days.

When Sarnia returned from the ferry trip she'd taken to Jersey, she heard the uproar of laughter behind the heavy oak doors of her father's study. Curious as to who it was with her father, she gave a soft rap on the door.

Martin was displeased to see her standing there when he opened the door, for he didn't wish her to know what he had in store for Renaud, nor did he wish to expose her to the lusty presence of Captain Garrett. Wakefield had always managed to isolate Sarnia from the side of his life Garrett represented.

But a smooth sway of her shapely body had the determined Sarnia through the door and staring at the mountain of man Garrett was. She'd never before seen the likes of him. He looked like some fierce pirate who roamed the seas. His garb left no doubt that he was a seafaring man, nor did his rugged face, weathered and tanned. As he ogled her, a salacious grin on his face, she felt that those huge hands of his would love to rip her fancy gown off so he could lustily stare at her nakedness.

"This is my daughter, Sarnia." Martin came to stand by her side, and he put a protective arm around her.

"Nice to meet you, miss. A pretty daughter you have, Martin."

"And the dearest thing in my life." He wanted her there no longer, but Sarnia's curiosity wasn't satisfied yet.

She teasingly pointed out to her tense father, "But I wasn't told this gentleman's name. Shame on you."

"This is Captain Garrett, Sarnia, my dear," he declared in a brusque tone, for she was trying his patience right then.

"Captain Garrett." She gave the huge man a smile and a

nod of her head. Privately, she decided he was one of those crude Americans.

When she seemed to make no effort to leave, Martin insisted she must excuse them, and in a fatherly manner he urged her toward the door. "The captain is pressed for time and we've business to discuss, sweetheart. I'm sure you understand." He gently, but firmly, nudged her toward the door.

Sarnia Wakefield went to her room, unaware of the fact that the wheels were already in motion to secure her the vengeance she sought. Only this time she had outfoxed herself!

Her revenge on Jacques Bernay would deprive her of the man she wanted more than anything else in the world. For the first time in her pampered life, she would not have her way.

Her trip to Jersey to see Charmaine Lamoureux was of no consequence, but she spent the rest of the day maliciously gloating about it.

Not suspecting any foul play was in the making, Pierre and Jacques accepted Martin Wakefield's invitation to accompany him out on Cobo Bay late that afternoon. Renaud figured he'd have more than enough time to get back to Guernsey to keep his late rendezvous with the enchanting little temptress who'd be waiting for him. God, he'd thought of her and of their hours together every minute of the day, and he eagerly anticipated their reunion.

Tonight, he'd ask her to marry him and accompany him to America when he sailed. To seal his vow of love, he planned to insist she wear his gold ring since he had no other to present to her. At least, she could wear it on a ribbon around her beautiful throat, letting it dangle snugly between her breasts.

Jacques was amazed at the cordial hospitality Wakefield

displayed but he didn't question it. Besides, he was anxious to tour the trim-lined American schooner he'd seen moored out in the bay for days. Never had he imagined he'd be privileged to board it.

Martin and Garrett found the two young men easy to hoodwink. The jolly American sea captain was so entertaining as he recounted tales of his adventures that Pierre and Jacques freely imbibed the good Jamaican rum he offered. In the midst of the laughter and gaiety, neither Renaud or Bernay noticed that when the jug was passed neither Martin nor Jim availed themselves of its contents. The ribaldry, rum drinking, and reveling had reached a peak after a couple of hours. But the young men did not notice that the late afternoon sun was now down over the water and darkness was deepening outside the captain's cabin. By now, neither of them cared. The sly Martin Wakefield exchanged a glance and a smile with Garrett. By the time sea chanteys were resounding in the cabin, Martin got ready to take his leave for he knew he'd never be missed and the stiff breeze wafting through the porthole told him Jim would be unfurling the sails of the schooner and heaving anchor before the midnight hour rolled around.

When Bernay's curly head slumped down on the bunk, Captain Garrett gave Martin the sign to depart for he knew Pierre would soon be as out of it as his friend.

At the cabin door, Garrett chuckled. "Well, they're off to Savannah. As far as I'm concerned, old friend, I'm goin' to be as innocent as a babe in the woods when these two come back to the livin'. Far as I knew, they'd been told they were going to be sailin' with me, eh?"

"Whatever you do, I couldn't care less, Jim. I'm just bloody glad to have them out of my hair and home," Martin said in a lowered voice.

"Guess a pretty daughter can prove to be a problem, eh Martin?" Garrett grinned. His friend said nothing in reply, but headed up the steps to the deck above.

By the time Martin reached the wharf, Garrett's schooner was plowing through the water, away from Guernsey. A broad grin lit the pudgy Captain Wakefield's face. He felt no qualms about the way he'd treated the son of his old friend Étienne. After all, there were some things a man could not jeopardize even for an old friend.

A grand feeling of self-satisfaction engulfed Wakefield as he entered his house and prepared to mount the winding stairway to go to his bedroom. But he had just entered his room and was about to close the door, thinking to himself he was going to have the best night's sleep he'd had in a long time, when Sarnia's voice called to him. She stood before him, in a pout.

"You left me to dine all by myself tonight. Fanny said you had an engagement elsewhere."

"And I did, Sarnia, but it wasn't for dinner."

"Oh?" she drawled, a questioning look on her face.

"I had a matter to attend, which I did, quite cleverly I think. I ridded us of Jacques Bernay," Martin declared, removing his coat.

A glint sparked in Sarnia's dark eyes as she ambled up behind him and placed her hands on his shoulders. "Really? How, Father? Tell me?"

"Well, you met Captain Garrett? He sailed for America this evening. In fact, they'll make very good time with the stiff winds out there, I'd say."

Sarnia laughed delightedly. "Good enough for that cocky rooster Bernay."

"I thought it fitting." Martin laughed with her. "I'm sure we'll both have a very good night's sleep, won't we, Sarnia dear?"

"Oh, a divine one." She sighed, regretting that Bernay would not know it was she who was responsible for his departure from Guernsey. "Was he put in chains to get him aboard, Father?"

"No, dear. He was helplessly drunk. Most likely, it will be

morning before he knows he's out in the Atlantic."

Her eyes twinkled with amused delight as she exclaimed, "Oh, what fun it would be to see the look on his face! I'd also like to be around when you tell Pierre that his pal Bernay is gone."

"Renaud won't have to be told, Sarnia. He's with him right now. He, too, is on his way to Savannah."

Her pretty rosebud mouth gaped and her long-lashed eyes went wide with disbelief. She was too numb to utter a word before she fainted, collapsing onto the carpeted floor.

"Dear God!" Martin gasped, trembling with concern as he knelt beside her on the floor. He'd not contemplated this reaction from Sarnia.

There was no smug smile on Martin Wakefield's face now as he sat by his daughter, holding her limp hand in his and patting it.

Just before the wave of blackness consumed Sarnia, she was engulfed by such anger and hatred for her grinning father she wanted to kill him. Her head felt as though it were exploding as fury consumed her.

Chapter 12

Charmaine was glad that she'd been alone at the cottage when Sarnia Wakefield had made her unannounced visit. She'd been able to go to her room and cry herself out. When she had no more tears to shed, she rose from the bed. Washing her eyes and face, she promptly dressed to go downstairs and do her chores.

Her face an expressionless mask, she moved vigorously around the cottage as though determined to sweep away her deep hurt and pain.

She realized that she'd been a lovesick, silly fool. Luckily, however, no one knew it but her—and, of course, Pierre Renaud. One thing was certain; he'd not find her there on the cliffs tonight, waiting eagerly to rush into his treacherous arms.

She almost felt sorry for the girl he was supposed to marry. What a despicable cur he was to be so unfaithful to her! Charmaine's simple, honest nature could not understand a scoundrel who could whisper words of love to one woman when he was betrothed to another.

As she busily wiped the dust cloth over her aunt's table in the parlor, she gave vent to the venom she was feeling and almost knocked a little vase onto the floor. "Not tonight, Pierre Renaud . . . not tonight," she angrily muttered.

She would be better off marying good, dependable George Seymour—being a farmer's wife with her own little cottage to putter around in—than ending up with a worthless rogue like Renaud.

When Simone and Angus returned to the cottage and set the empty basket down on the kitchen table, Simone was pleasantly amazed to see how sparkling clean her kitchen looked. She tossed the few remaining crumbs from the baked goods she'd taken to her sick friend out the back door for the birds to feed on.

"She is a good girl, Angus, I'll swear! See how busy she's been while we've been gone. I'm glad now I did allow her to sleep. Bless her dear heart!"

Angus hung up his hat and took the old one he wore for work from the peg by the back door. "Charmaine has always been a fairly good girl, Simone. I've nothing to fault her about, as I've told you before."

When Angus went out to the meadow, Charmaine came into the kitchen to join her aunt. She said nothing about her visitor, however, and the two of them spent the rest of the day attending to the usual housekeeping chores and chatting as they worked.

During these hours it dawned on Simone that she was going to miss Charmaine, that this cottage was going to be lonely once her niece left for Virginia. If only things had not turned out so badly, Charmaine could have had a suitor here on Jersey, she thought. But she reminded herself that if Charmaine had married some local boy and lived close by, John's yearnings would persist. Nonetheless Simone wished Charmaine could be near.

Noticing her aunt's sudden quietly, thoughtful air, she inquired, "Are you all right, Aunt Simone?"

A wan smile appeared on Simone Keene's round face, and she brushed back a straying wisp of her hair. "I was just thinking how I'm going to miss you when you leave, *ma petite*. With the days going by so fast and your wedding drawing nearer all the time, you and George will be sailing for America soon."

Charmaine was touched at hearing her aunt speak so sincerely. It was good to be loved. She walked over and gave Simone a tender hug. "It makes me so very happy to hear you say that, and I will miss you terribly too."

"I . . . I just wish we could have afforded more for you as a daughter. Somehow, boys don't seem to need certain things. If only we'd had more wealth, we could have opened more doors for you, Charmaine, given you an opportunity to meet more young men."

After seeing Sarnia Wakefield in all her expensive clothes, Charmaine realized what her aunt meant. She could imagine all the balls and parties that young woman must attend, the eligible young bachelors she met. Heavens, Sarnia had probably had her pick of a dozen men before she decided on Pierre Renaud.

But Charmaine wanted to soothe her aunt's apprehensions and lighten her spirits so she flippantly remarked, "Why, you won't be rid of me, Auntie! I'll bet you we'll be back here for a visit a year or so from now. You'll see!"

Simone's face brightened at that thought. She and Angus would never travel far from home, but it was possible George would bring Charmaine back from Virginia to visit the Keenes and his uncle's family on Jersey. "Ah, that is something to keep in mind, isn't it? I might even have another one to see in a year's time too . . . a wee one, eh?" Her blue eyes twinkled in anticipation.

The effect of her aunt's statement was overpowering for Charmaine had never given that possibility a thought. Now it stuck in her mind, haunting her the rest of that evening. It was, indeed, a possibility that she was carrying Pierre Renaud's child within her at this very moment.

What would she do? What could she do but marry George and pray he'd never know it wasn't his?

The fear that plagued Charmaine, that the night of

abandoned lovemaking might have left her pregnant, also bedeviled Pierre when he roused from the bunk aboard the American schooner and learned he was miles at sea.

It was his pal Jacques who'd awakened first, with a splitting headache and a foul taste in his mouth from the sweet rum. Suddenly leaping off the narrow bunk he'd been lying on, he'd frozen for a second before moving to the small porthole to peer out at the endless span of sea. Laboriously, he'd struggled from the cabin and up the steps to the deck above, intending to seek out the captain.

Weakness prevented Bernay from being his normally cocksure self, but he intended to get an explanation as to why he and Pierre were on board. This was a foul turn, his instinct told him.

He had sauntered only a short distance on deck when he heard a jolly voice yelling, "Hey, matie, is it me you're lookin' for?"

Bernay turned to see the grinning, ugly face of Jim Garrett. The big man strode up to him. "You French boys like your rum, I found out. A head on you, I'll wager."

"What the devil is this all about, Captain Garrett? What's . . . Where are we? Why were we not taken off, even if we were dead drunk last night?"

"Son, that rum did parch your brain, I'm thinkin'. You aren't makin' much sense this mornin', and after we all had such a jolly good time last night too. Hell, you act upset," Jim said, solemn-faced and all sincerity.

"Upset . . . hell! Why wouldn't I be? I had no intention of shipping out with you, and most assuredly my companion Renaud is going to be a madman when he wakes up."

The towering captain placed a huge hand on Bernay's shoulder, and even though Bernay was a muscular, robust man he was dwarfed by the formidable Garrett. "Well, now . . . I've dealt with a few buckos in my life, as I'm sure you can figure, and I've no doubt I'll deal with a few more. If your man Renaud is mad he's goin' to have to be mad at someone other than me. I don't invite guests or passengers on my ship. I was instructed to carry you two with me and that's what I'm doing. I damned sure ain't turnin' this ship around for you or your friend. So I'd say you two best be congenial like you were last night."

Bernay got the man's meaning, and he was not fool enough to try to fight a losing battle with the likes of him. Pierre had better control his hot temper too, for this American allowed no quarter. But he could not resist saying as he turned away to go back to the cabin, "Didn't realize Wakefield wanted us gone from St. Peter Port that badly."

Behind him, Jim Garrett, a broad grin on his face, yelled out in his deep roaring voice, "See you later, Jack. Give your friend Pete a good mornin' for me!"

"I'll do that, Captain," Bernay replied. Under his breath he called him a sonofabitch, then he headed toward the cabin to see about Renaud. Thinking over the things Garrett had said to him, he came to the conclusion that the wily bastard was in league with Wakefield, sure as the devil. But for the life of him he couldn't figure out why Martin wanted to be rid of him so badly he'd have him shanghaied. At this point that really didn't matter though, for whether he liked it or not he was in the middle of the ocean, on his way to a strange country. Whether Renaud liked it or not, so was he, and they'd both have to accept it for aboard this ship Captain Jim Garrett was in charge. He had to convince Pierre of that paramount fact!

Bernay watched Pierre raise himself slowly on the bunk, rubbing his eyes and head, a puzzled look on his face. He was not startled to hear the curse words pour from the Frenchman when he enlightened him about their where-abouts and Pierre became aware of the movement of the vessel.

Venting his wild rage, Pierre kicked at the walls and slammed his clenched fists angrily against them. When his fury was finally spent, he sank down on the bunk, heaving a deep sigh of his utter dismay. Jacques didn't have to tell him they were helpless, surrounded by water. For many days and nights they must endure their penance for carousing with that untrustworthy pair.

But the day would come when he'd taste sweet revenge, Pierre promised himself. He would make a point of informing his father of the insult Wakefield had bestowed on the Renaud family. Some friend to Étienne Renaud Martin Wakefield had proved to be. Pierre knew more about Wakefield than the English captain realized because his mother had told him some things before he'd left France to come to Guernsey.

By God, Renaud money had financed the Wakefield Lines many years ago, according to what his mother Eugenia had told him. It might just be Renaud money that destroyed the man.

When Jacques proceeded to lecture him, in an almost fatherly fashion beseeching him not to let his hot temper get the best of him, Pierre laughed, "Oh, *mon ami,* never fear. In fact, I plan to become a good pal to the old American. Yes, Garrett and I are going to get along famously before this voyage is over."

Giving his younger friend a skeptical look, Bernay prodded, "Just what have you got on your mind, eh?"

"Well, we know he's a sly old fox and a greedy one, for there obviously was money involved in this little favor he's doing for Wakefield. So perhaps my money can buy us a favor from the salty old dog. I aim to even the score with Martin Wakefield—the son of a bitch."

A slow smile came to Bernay's face as he appreciated the cunning of his friend. He wholeheartedly approved of his plan. "I applaud you, *mon ami.* I am glad I am joining you on this venture after all, even though our departure wasn't exactly as I would have expected it to be," he said, giving a chuckle.

"I'm glad you're along too, Jacques, but my heart is heavy

because of the one I had to leave behind and for that Martin Wakefield will pay dearly before I'm through with him." Pierre did not say to his friend that his beautiful lady would think he'd deserted her and she could have been left with his seed in her.

Yet he was pondering the possibility that Charmaine was pregnant as he traveled farther and farther away from her, unable to do anything about his situation. It was a hellish torment!

His vindictive soul would know no peace until Martin Wakefield dwelled in his own hell!

Chapter 13

Having lived over fifty-odd years and having dealt with all kinds of fellows as he'd roamed the world, Jim Garrett had credited himself with knowing people fairly well. But he had to admit that he'd been dead wrong about Pierre Renaud, or Pete as he called him.

On their first encounter on deck after the night of reveling in his cabin, he was taken by surprise by Renaud's nonchalant attitude toward being on this ship. When the happy-go-lucky Frenchman had sauntered up to him, a grin on his face, Garrett had assumed the young rascal was still feeling the effects of his drinking bout.

But Renaud had shrugged his broad shoulders and flippantly remarked, "Makes little difference to me. I was bound for America anyway, so why not aboard your ship, eh?"

Shocked for a second, Jim found his voice to reply, "Glad you feel that way, Pete my boy. Besides, this honey of a schooner sets a fair pace, as you'll see if the weather holds."

Renaud put himself in Garrett's good graces instantly by generously admiring the trim lines of his ship and saying he envied him the carefree life a sea captain must enjoy. That left an opening for Garrett to speak endlessly as the two wandered around the deck of the ship.

The deckhands going about their duties naturally assumed the Frenchman was a friend of their captain because of their camaraderie. Bernay stared in disbelief when he came topside for a breath of air. Pierre and Garrett were ambling along like the best of friends. It merely confirmed his former opinion that Pierre was able to charm the devil himself. Though Wakefield hadn't been charmed, he told himself.

Bernay walked over to the railing and stood there alone, for it was obvious that Renaud was wasting no time in getting started on his scheme. Jacques certainly didn't want to cramp his style, not when the cunning Pierre was working his spell on Garrett.

Later, he was to find out from an amused Pierre that that was exactly what he'd been doing, and he told Jacques, "We're invited to dine with him tonight in his cabin. I've got him taking the first nibble, *mon ami.*"

"My cap's off to you then." Jacques gave his friend a comradely pat on the shoulders.

"I promise you, by the time we leave this ship I'll have made myself a deal to have Wakefield taken care of in a proper fashion by Garrett."

"Hope you aren't counting your chickens before they're hatched, *mon ami,* but you seem so sure of yourself I have to believe you."

"I've known a few Captain Garretts in my life. They come in all sizes and are found in all stations. His only loyalty is to himself. That is why he'll jump at the chance to enrich his coffers with my gold," Pierre declared, giving Jacques a wink.

The two of them broke into a gale of laughter, then playfully cavorted around the small cabin doing a jig.

Most of the servants in the Wakefield mansion had felt the sting of Sarnia's waspish mood, which had been brought on by her father's shocking revelation that Pierre had sailed for the New World. Fanny Bronson, long in the service for Martin Wakefield, had endured the ill-tempered miss since Sarnia was a baby. But her duties as the housekeeper did not include tolerating the childish tantrums she'd suffered the last couple of days, so she sought an audience with Wakefield himself by the end of the second day. Besides, she wanted to inform him that one of the servant girls had flung off her apron in disgust and had left when Sarnia had thrown a cup of hot tea at her. But poor Martin Wakefield was as frustrated as his housekeeper, and as unprepared to deal with his daughter.

The usually masterful Wakefield was mortified when Francis Neville came to call and Sarnia flatly refused to see him. He'd been forced to return to the parlor and to announce to young Neville that his daughter wasn't up to seeing him.

Somehow, Francis found Martin's manner questionable, and he left the house convinced that Sarnia was seeking to shun him because she preferred the company of the Frenchman who was staying with the Wakefields. His ego wounded, he drove off in his carriage, not aware that Renaud was gone and that many miles separated him from Sarnia Wakefield.

From her bedroom window, Sarnia watched Neville march down the walkway to his waiting carriage. A smirk appeared on her face, for she could tell by the way he slammed the carriage door that he was irate. She was delighted, and she hoped Francis would not woo her anymore.

In fact, she had very definite plans for her life, now that her father had ruined everything by sending Renaud off along with Bernay. Knowing Martin Wakefield as she did, he wasn't going to approve of her choices. However, that didn't matter to her. She wanted to hurt him for he'd been the cause of her anguish.

When her maid came to her boudoir an hour later to see to

her needs should she wish to retire, Sarnia was so pleasant that the young woman left the room slightly dazed.

Moments later, she rushed through the kitchen door to exclaim, "Blessed be the saints, you won't believe it, Fanny, but I've been dismissed for the night. Miss Sarnia just told me she won't need me for the rest of the evening."

Fanny shrugged, a scowl on her weary face. "Well, aren't you the lucky one! I haven't been so lucky and certainly poor, dear Millie wasn't. I told the captain this evening just what's been going on with that uppity one and that I can't be held responsible if we lose half the help around here."

Moving her hefty figure around the square-topped table, in her arms three pots which had been cleaned and were now ready to be hung back up on the hooks, she advised the young maid, "Best you get a good night's rest. You never know what kind of monster you'll have to face come morning."

Helping herself to a fruit tart from the platter on Fanny's working table, Rose nibbled at it and thoughtfully mumbled, "I think maybe I'll do that." She moved unhurriedly toward the door to go up the backstairs.

The pretty little brown-haired maid turned back just before going through the doorway. Feeling closer to Fanny than any of the other servants in the house, she said to the good-natured housekeeper, "I hope you understand, Fanny, that I'm not trying to nose around and . . . and I'd only mention this to you, but is there something wrong around here? I mean Miss Sarnia is in such a frenzy for the last two days, and suddenly Monsieur Renaud's not around?"

"Listen, duckie, and listen good! I don't know and I don't want to know. Got all I can take care of as it is. Best you think the same," she said in a firm voice but she gave the little maid a smile. Rose was a sweet child and to be Sarnia Wakefield's personal maid was an undertaking for one so young. That the girl had lasted over four months amazed Fanny.

To her own way of thinking, which she intended to keep to

herself, something definitely was going on. She'd been privy to the captain's conversation yesterday morning when he'd told one of the men who worked for him that Bob Blakely would be replacing Jacques Bernay and that Bernay had left. This had surprised her for she'd thought of Bernay as one of the most dependable and one of the most mannerly men to come to the Wakefield home.

Like Rose, she'd been aware of Monsieur Renaud's absence, but the captain had not given her any explanation as he would normally have done. He hadn't even told her there'd be one less for the evening meal. So she'd dared not mention Renaud to him.

Now that Rose had gone, Fanny was all alone. Her chores were done for the night, but she lingered, sitting in the wooden rocker by the huge stone fireplace for a while before going to her quarters. For a moment she thought she'd seen an apparition float by the kitchen windows, but when she rushed to look out, she realized it was Sarnia, draped in a light-colored cape, darting through the back garden. She watched the fleeing figure dash across the grounds of the estate into the late night, and she pondered where in the world the young woman was off to at this late hour.

In a low voice, Fanny mumbled, "Up to no good, I'd wager. Mister Wakefield is going to have heartache over that one." She moved slowly to dim the one remaining lamp in the kitchen before leaving to go to her quarters.

Her many years in the Wakefield home had given her many chances to observe the mercurial moods of Sarnia, from the time she was a child, and Fanny was not blinded by overwhelming adoration like her father so she knew that wicked streak in Sarnia Wakefield.

She wondered what the girl's mother had been like, for she'd come to the Wakefield mansion a few weeks after that lady's death to take over the housekeeping chores.

Actually the dead Mrs. Wakefield, with her gentle ways and delicate frailness, would have been mortified had she lived to see what her precious dark-haired darling had become. Sarnia's mother was a prudent woman, gentle of soul and kind of heart. None of these traits had been inherited by Sarnia.

She was her father's daughter as Martin Wakefield was soon to realize with deep regret. Although he had successfully hidden his shady past from his daughter, his blood flowed in her veins. Had she been a son, Martin would have laughed at her traits, said his rascal of a son was just doing a little hell raising, sowing a few wild oats. But his daughter's conduct was a shattering blow to the proud English sea captain.

To seek her revenge Sarnia went to a place where Martin's men clustered to do their carousing and drinking, down by the wharves in the harbor. One night when she'd been riding with Francis Neville in his fancy carriage they'd traveled down the cobbled street where the Boar's Inn was situated, and she'd seen the drunken seamen stumbling out the door with their lady friends. So she'd decided to go there this evening, to seek the wild, exciting pleasure her father had denied her by sending Pierre Renaud away from her. She'd show him he wasn't going to set the course for her life. Only she would do that!

As she saucily walked up the street toward the tavern, she removed the shawl. Letting it rest on her shoulders, she tossed her thick black hair so it fell down her back, loose and unrestrained. She wore no fancy adornments or ribbons in her hair, and her gown was the simplest one she could find. Her fingers, neck, and wrists were without jewelry.

Just as she started through the tavern door, a deep male voice stopped her by calling out, "Hey, pretty one! Wait a minute!"

She turned to see a very good-looking young seaman grinning at her as he sauntered up to her. He wore no seaman's cap, and his mass of sandy-colored hair touched the collar of his shirt, wisps of it falling over one side of his forehead.

As they stood in the light of the entrance way, Sarnia realized he must be an inch or two over six feet as he stood surveying her with bright blue eyes.

He isn't bad to look at, she thought to herself. His plain, simple attire was clean at least. She flashed her dark eyes invitingly at him, and assuming a flirtatious air, she purred a soft hello to him.

He took her arm in a most possessive way, for she was assuredly what he'd been looking for this night. She had a beautiful face and a curvaceous body. John Keene particularly liked her gorgeous black hair which was completely different from Charmaine's spun-gold tresses. And this woman's willowy body could certainly not be compared to Charlie's petite figure.

No, this was a woman who bore no resemblance to Charmaine Lamoureux, and that was what he desired this night.

"What's your name, honey? I'm Johnny Keene," he told her, bending down to kiss her cheek and draw her closer to his side.

"Just call me Sarnia," she replied. Something stopped her from adding Wakefield. For the moment, she didn't want him to know she was a Wakefield, though she did plan to let everyone in the tavern know she was Martin Wakefield's daughter.

Before she could protest, however, she was whirled about and Johnny's strong arm guided her back down the cobbled street toward the wharf where his fishing boat was moored.

"I've a much nicer place for us to go, my beautiful Sarnia."

He had such a masterful way about him Sarnia didn't want to protest. "Wherever you say, Johnny." She giggled coquettishly and pulsed with wild anticipation of what this night with this devilishly handsome Johnny would bring.

Chapter 14

Charmaine had firmly convinced herself that her game of deception was superb. She refused to accept the various little hints her body was giving her that it was taxing her to play at the fraud. Simone had no inkling that her niece was playacting as they worked together and spoke of her wedding day, nor did George, whose nightly visits to the cottage demanded the same forced pretense of light-hearted gaiety Charmaine did not feel in her heart.

She had to admit that George was much nicer than she'd thought. He was enthusiastically trying to enlighten her about life in Virginia, she felt he was genuinely hoping to make her feel at ease about the strange place to which she would be going. For that, she felt kindly toward him.

Many times she thought it would be a blessing if she could love this ordinary, plain-looking man who was offering to share his future with her, but when she was alone in her bed at night, darkness all around her, silver-gray eyes haunted her and she moaned softly in despair, "Oh, God, please let me forget him!" But her prayer was not answered.

It seemed to Charmaine that the only balm for her agony was work. Only sheer exhaustion gave her the sleep she could not get otherwise. That was why she started helping Angus with chores around the barn, something she'd never

121

done before. While her uncle appreciated her vigorous energy, he noticed the tightness in her lovely face. As they were working together more closely, he scrutinized her tiny figure. She looked thinner to him.

When he questioned her, she flippantly shrugged queries aside. "Oh, Uncle Angus, it's just wedding nerves. All girls get them. Why, I've heard—pardon me, but I've heard some can't keep their food down."

She let out such a lilting, gay little giggle, Angus chuckled. "Guess you could be right. Being an old man I guess I wouldn't know all those things, dear."

But Angus started to watch Charmaine at mealtimes. He saw that she only nibbled at her food, and that just wasn't her normal appetite. She'd always been a hearty eater for such a wee miss. He'd often marveled at her capacity and had teased her good-naturedly. No, there was something bothering her. He was now convinced of it.

But before he could discuss his concern with his wife, a turn of events made it unnecessary. A late-night storm blew in over the island, and the fierce winds jarred one of Angus' barn doors loose. In his scramble to get some of the young calves back inside, he noticed that Charmaine was rushing around in the downpour helping him.

By the time they'd managed to get all six of the calves back into the shelter of the barn and Angus had secured the door against the fury of the wind, Charmaine slumped onto the sacks of grain, gasping for breath after her frenzied exertion in the barnyard.

Only then did Angus become aware of just how drenched they both were. He saw her gasping for breath because of the running she'd done, and he noticed that her golden hair, dripping down over her woollen shawl, looked like the cut skeins of Simone's yellow yarn, straight and limp without any hint of a curl. Her beautiful face was wan and pale, and there was no rosy blush to it.

"Charmaine, honey! You shouldn't have done this to

yourself," Angus rushed over to her, and his huge hand reached out to take her in his. He was genuinely worried about the young miss sitting there so very still and lifeless.

Her long-lashed eyes opened slowly and she let out a deep sigh. "You'd have . . . have been out there yet, Uncle Angus," she muttered in a faltering voice.

"Well, maybe I would have, but that work's too strenuous for a little slip of a girl like you. Now, as soon as you get your legs back and feel strong enough, let's get ourselves into that warm house and get dry."

Charmaine nodded her damp head and took another deep breath. While Angus had no desire to rush her, he was aware that she was chilled and trembling so he urged her to rise. Giving her his support, he helped her cover the distance between the barn and the cottage.

Simone held the door open, and upon surveying them, she gasped, "Lord, the two of you look like you fell into the bay!"

She took charge immediately, ordering Angus to get them both a swig of his brandy and then go get his wet clothes off. "I'll get Charmaine out of these," she declared. She was as concerned about Angus as she was her niece.

As she began to strip Charmaine down, making her stay by the stone fireplace, she paused long enough to wrap a towel around the girl's wet head. By the time Angus joined them by the fireplace, Simone had put one of her own flannel gowns on Charmaine and she was vigorously rubbing the girl's thick hair with the towel. When he was pleasantly warmed by the heat of the roaring fire in the fireplace, Angus helped himself to another portion of brandy and he refilled Charmaine's glass.

"One for good measure, eh little one?" He gave her a big, warm smile.

"Thank you, Uncle Angus. I'm already feeling better though," she told him with a smile, albeit a weak one.

"Good," he said. He left the room then, returning in a few

123

minutes with a pair of his heavy woollen stockings, which he slipped onto her cold feet.

The concern and care her dear aunt and uncle were showing her did Charmaine's heart good. She wondered how she could possibly have doubted them. She chided herself now for having had such foolish thoughts about these dear people.

Later, as her aunt was tucking the quilts securely over her, Charmaine realized that she could never repay them for everything they'd done for her since she'd come to their cottage.

Her eyes closed for she was weary from the night's happenings and languorous from the generous sips of her uncle's strong brandy.

Angus Keene slept deeply too, due to the brandy and the impact of his exertion on his aging body.

The gleam of bright sunshine was a welcome sight to Simone Keene as she moved around the quiet cottage the next morning. She'd had a leisurely breakfast alone and was glad to do so for she wanted her dear Angus to rest this morning, Charmaine too.

However, when she turned to see Angus, looking quite fit and rested, amble into the kitchen, she was more than pleased. She eagerly jumped up to plant a kiss on his cheek, then started to prepare him a hearty breakfast. "Didn't know but what I'd find you with a fevered cheek this morning, Angus Keene." She gave him a pleased smile.

"You see, love, I'm still not such an old man," he teased, and flipped her apron strings playfully.

They enjoyed a pleasant hour together before Angus left the cottage to attend to his chores. Then Simone got busy with the sweeping and dusting, unconcerned that Charmaine was still upstairs. Only when midday was approaching did she decide to check on her niece to see if she was still sleeping soundly.

As she opened the door to Charmaine's room, Simone was filled with an awesome feeling that all was not well. The odor of illness wafted to her nose, and she knew before she touched Charmaine's face that the young woman was burning with fever.

When she did place her hand against Charmaine's cheek, Simone found her flesh as hot as the pot of stew simmering downstairs.

Without any hesitation, she rushed to get a pan of cool water and cloths so she could administer to her niece. As she dashed out the door, Charmaine tossed back and forth on the bed, mumbling in her feverish delirium.

When Simone returned to the upstairs bedroom and applied a cloth to Charmaine's head and face, she listened to the girl's ramblings, wondering who in the world she was talking about. The names she mentioned were unknown to Simone Keene.

The kind woman tried to spoon small droplets of water between the girl's dried lips in the hope it would cool her insides just a little. To have tried broth right then would have been useless, Simone knew. She was flooded with guilt because she hadn't checked on Charmaine earlier, feeling that the fever would not be so intense and high if she'd started applications of cool cloths sooner.

After an hour, it seemed to Simone that Charmaine was resting better so she decided to go downstairs to check her stew. The broth would be good for Charmaine if she could get her to sip some of it later.

The rest of the day Simone spent time upstairs with Charmaine and then trotted downstairs to tend to her chores. By the time Angus came into the cottage, she didn't have to tell him that she was weary for her face showed it.

He insisted that he take over for her for the next few hours. But their constant vigil continued for the next twenty-four hours, during which Angus spent more time around the cottage than usual.

When George Seymour paid a call on the Keenes and

learned of Charmaine's illness, he didn't linger after Angus told him his niece just wasn't up to seeing anyone because of the fever she was still running.

Neither Simone nor Angus gave any thought to the days that passed with Charmaine so ill, and tending to her was their sole dedication.

On the fourth evening when George came to see how she was, he pointed out to Angus that their planned wedding date was only a couple of days away.

Angus shrugged aside the serious look on young Seymour's face as he bluntly retorted, "Charmaine's got to be a lot better than she is this night, young man."

There was such a stern, gruff look on Angus' weathered tired face that George said nothing more. He did not dare to inform Angus Keene that he could not deviate from his plan to sail for Virginia whether Charmaine was well enough to accompany him or not.

He was unable to delay his departure to allow her to get well enough to make the voyage even though that meant their wedding had to be postponed, for his tobacco crop did not permit him to dally around Jersey any longer. But this information, George decided, he'd convey to the gentler Simone Keene. In fact, as he bid Angus good night he made up his mind to pay an afternoon visit to the cottage in the hope that Angus would not be around.

George had accurately perceived Angus' mood. After young Seymour had left, Angus sat smoking his pipe in solitude, thoughtfully wondering just what had stirred up such a sudden flare of impatience with and revulsion for George this evening. But he had felt it.

The feeling didn't please him either, not when this was the young man Charmaine was to marry. Angus' concern for his niece had deepened during the last week. She could be the daughter he and Simone had never had, and he'd never before been so conscious of that as he now was.

Because he felt as he did about Charmaine, he planned to

126

observe Henry Seymour's nephew closely for the next few days. Angus wanted to be absolutely certain George was worthy of such a fine, sweet girl like Charmaine. That was the very least he could do for her!

However, Angus Keene would not have that opportunity because George Seymour didn't plan to be in Jersey that much longer.

He was sailing for America the day after tomorrow with or without Charmaine!

Chapter 15

As he guided his buggy along the bay road to journey into St. Helier for some supplies, Angus yanked his hat firmly to an angle so it fit his head snugger. Nothing like the early morning hours, he thought as he gazed upward to the azure blue sky with its cottony clusters of white clouds.

The countryside he'd traveled over was quite still, but as he looked over in the distance at the bay he saw the slow, graceful movement of a three-masted ship sailing out into the Channel. He watched the rippling motion of the sails as the constant flow of the breeze filled them, and it was a magnificent sight. It was no wonder they named ships after women. They had grace and charm. He wondered where that vessel was headed . . . for what part of this vast world it was destined.

He saw another ship docked at the wharves, sails still unfurled, and it, too was magnificent. He had no way of knowing that this was the vessel his niece would have been on on this day, had she been able to go through with her wedding plans.

Yesterday was gone and so were the plans for the wedding. Instead of standing by Charmaine's side this afternoon, taking vows, George was speaking with her Aunt Simone. It was working in George's favor that Angus was not at the cottage. Simone was alone, as he'd desired.

Simone listened to the young man's declaration that it was imperative he return to Virginia. In his unbending solemn manner, George went on to say, "When she's well enough for a voyage she can join me. I know you'll give your approval for such an arrangement now that you know I'm an honorable man, Mrs. Keene."

"Well, I . . . I . . . well, yes, George. Of course, if this is the way it has to be, what with your crop to get in," Simone replied, feeling she could voice no objections, not when he'd placed a heavy pouch of gold in her hand to cover the expenses of Charmaine's journey to America.

This was not as she'd have hoped it would have been, but she couldn't fault the young man for not chancing the loss of his crop. After all, tobacco was his livelihood, and it would be Charmaine's when they were married a few months from now.

Having secured Simone's accord, without so much as bending to kiss his bride-to-be who lay in her sickbed, George quickly turned to leave, and Simone Keene ushered him to the front door. Charmaine was oblivious to the plans already made for her.

As the afternoon and evening went by, Simone found no moment to tell Angus about George's visit. But when she took Charmaine a bowl of broth up in the hope of coaxing her to sip a little, she found her niece free of a fever and possessed of a voracious appetite. Gladly, Simone trotted back down the stairs for a second bowl of broth and a nice slice of crusty homemade bread.

"Ah, *ma petite* . . . what a blessing! What a divine blessing!" Simone tearfully declared as she stroked Charmaine's tangled, matted hair. Tomorrow, she'd tackle the tedious job of combing and brushing it free of the tangles, she thought to herself. Her niece should be stronger then, if

130

she continued to eat as she was eating right then.

"Broth never tasted so good." Charmaine sighed as she finished the last drop of it. She took the piece of bread and smiled at her aunt sweetly.

"Ah, you will be like a different person by this time tomorrow night with a good day's eating behind you, I know! You must regain your strength now. Oh, Angus is going to be so happy to know you're better, dear."

Simone made no mention of George Seymour and his departure from Jersey. Somehow, that just didn't seem important to her, and she was so happy about Charmaine's improved condition that she forgot to tell Angus of the arrangement when he returned from St. Helier. That evening the Keenes dined on a simple meal of stew, but for them it was a joyous occasion.

No one rejoiced more than Charmaine Lamoureux as she sat propped up on a mountain of pillows, heartily enjoying more than broth. With great relish, she ate the succulent chunks of beef and the tasty vegetables, and she found the good rich milk produced by Angus' cows delicious. For dessert Simone had made up tiny crocks of pudding from the thick, rich cream. Charmaine downed hers with dispatch.

After the meal the young woman even rose from her bed and walked over to the small dressing table to get her brush and comb. Then she sat back down upon her bed and began to give her hair leisurely, long strokes.

Her mood was thoughtful, and there was a look of serenity on her pale, but lovely face. Yet for someone who had been so ill and flushed with fever the day before, there was a bright twinkle in her deep blue eyes as she began to smile.

Was there such a thing as destiny? There had been no wedding yesterday, so tonight she was still Charmaine Lamoureux, not Charmaine Seymour.

She was totally convinced that fate had had a hand in it when, the next day, Simone told her about George Seymour's departure on the day he'd booked passage for the two of them. "He had to sail as he'd planned, dear. His crops, you know," Simone had explained to her.

Charmaine didn't wish to appear too overjoyed because her husband-to-be was gone from Jersey, but her spirits did mount.

"Oh, I can understand that George had to get home, Aunt Simone," Charmaine declared, wishing to quiet any apprehensions her aunt might have.

As Simone chattered on about the impossibility of a wedding and a long ocean voyage when her niece was so ill, a light gust of laughter erupted from Charmaine.

"Oh, I'd certainly not be up to that. I'm glad George understood and went on."

"Yes, dear. It's as I'd said from the first time I met him. He's a very nice man. You could have done worse than George Seymour for a husband."

Charmaine was just about to say aloud that all that had happened had rather changed that situation, but her aunt had turned from her to pick up the dust cloth she'd been holding. After a brief lull in her conversation, Simone began to prattle on, her next comments making Charmaine realize with startling disillusionment that her future had not really changed. It had only been delayed for a few weeks.

Sadly, she accepted her fate—to be George's wife. Not that she didn't want to scream out at her aunt and tell her that she would not board any ship and sail to America. Every fiber of her being yearned to do just that, but she could only give Johnny back to them if she was gone from Jersey, gone from the cottage. Only then would their son come to the cottage to visit them for he would not be tormented by her presence.

Yes, she had to leave and her wild, hopeful folly must be forever forgotten! That was the price she must pay for her keep the last five years.

Convincing herself to follow this course of action, she slowly improved in strength during the next week. She lost the pallor caused by her illness, and a calm air settled around her.

But, on occasion, her heart reminded her that life with George would never be the fairytale romance her dreams had depicted.

Each passing day Martin Wakefield was tormented by the promiscuous ways of his daughter. However, as distraught and disgusted as he was feeling, he was not beaten. Not even the daughter he worshipped could break him, for Martin knew the price he'd paid to build his empire and to make the name of Wakefield a prestigious and respected one.

Sarnia was fooled into thinking that the elder Wakefield was sitting by idly twiddling his thumbs and allowing her to have her way. It did appear to be that way. He knew about the young fisherman over on the island of Jersey, and that she had been secretly slipping out of the mansion to keep her rendezvous nightly with him. However, the devious Wakefield was already scheming to rid the islands of Jersey and Guernsey of one Johnny Keene in such a way that Sarnia would never guess his hands were soiled, would never know he had any part in what occurred.

Knowing he'd soon take care of Keene made Martin relax when his daughter joined him at the dinner table, and he restrained himself from lecturing her. Indeed, he began to greet her quite pleasantly.

The sudden change in his mood put Sarnia into a quandary. Her thinking being so like his, she wondered if he'd concocted some foul plot against Johnny, who had entranced her far more than she'd expected. The handsome sailor's boyish charm and generous lovemaking had awakened Sarnia in amazing, exciting ways. When John's huge, tanned hands had tenderly fondled her body she had discovered the rapture she'd imagined she'd have if Pierre had come to her bed as she'd so desperately desired.

133

Her lover's body was firm and muscular, and he'd taken her masterfully, conquering her completely. Although the first night they'd lain together in the darkness of the cabin of his fishing boat, she'd imagined it was the naked Pierre so fiercely making love to her, on the following nights, she'd had no urge or desire to pretend Johnny was Pierre Renaud.

A mere fisherman John Keene might be, but he was all man as far as Sarnia Wakefield was concerned. She was in love with him, that was all that mattered. In fact, in her state of newfound happiness with John, she no longer needed to seek revenge upon her father. But, knowing Martin Wakefield's attitude about the man she should marry, she knew he'd not find John Keene acceptable.

Therefore, one desire consumed her when she wasn't in John's strong loving arms, and that was to bring the two of them together, to have her father accept the man she loved. So Sarnia welcomed her father's gentler manner. Even his gruff voice seemed more mellow. On this particular morning, as he dined on his kippers with such relish, she wondered if she should say something to him about Johnny.

She sipped at the hot tea Fanny had just finished serving her and then nibbled at the biscuit, debating whether she should approach the subject weighing on her mind.

Martin made the decision for her by announcing, "I won't be home for dinner tonight, my dear. I . . . I have a meeting to attend."

She looked up from her plate, and it was nice not to see a scowl on his face. "Will . . . will you be here tomorrow night?"

Hesitating a moment, he replied, "Why I suppose so? Any particular reason, Sarnia?"

"I'd like to have a friend for dinner," she said, her dark eyes measuring the look on his face.

"This has always been your home, Sarnia, and you're to invite any of your friends to dinner. I will plan on being here if you wish me to, whatever my previous plans." Martin brought his napkin up to his mouth. He was now the one curious.

"Yes, I would like you to be here," she remarked, a little amazed that she had suddenly put into motion her scheme to bring her father and her lover together. It had been far more simple than she'd expected; he'd not even questioned her as to who the friend was.

Seeing that he was preparing to leave the table without inquiring about the guest she was to invite, Sarnia breathed a deep sigh of relief. Only when Martin had walked out into the hallway to fetch his hat and walking cane did he break into a grin.

If all went according to his plans, and he intended to make certain it did, her so-called "guest" would be sitting at no one's dining table tomorrow night. He knew who she was inviting; there was no reason for him to inquire.

As repulsive as it was to him, he satisfied himself with the secret thought that this would be the last night she would be in that bastard's arms. That common fisherman was tarnishing his daughter, sickening to Martin when he'd made every effort to groom her to be a proper young lady of quality.

When he climbed inside his carriage and instructed his driver to take him to Barney's Warehouse, Martin was ready to order the ruffians to strike. For some time, he'd monitored his daughter's nightly routine so he knew when she'd be safely back at the house and John Keene would be exhaustedly sleeping in his bunk—alone.

The valise he'd carried out of the house and had placed on the floor of the carriage beside his feet was heavy with gold. But this deed was worth the cost to Martin if it preserved the name of Wakefield. Dear God, he mused, it had cost him much more than this to make his name prominent! He was now a man of distinction and not even his daughter was going to take that away from him!

Chapter 16

Strong, swift winds and clear blue skies sent the three-masted American schooner speeding across the Atlantic. Captain Garrett could not have asked for more perfect weather for his crossing, but the wily old sea captain knew in another six or eight weeks there would be an abrupt change. He wouldn't have to fret, however, because he'd be in Savannah and his *Sweet Sally* would be moored in the harbor by that time.

It had been a good voyage, thanks to the unexpected profit he'd made due to his old friend Martin. Jim was pleased. His bounty from the journey was enough to keep him in fine shape for many months to come. Let a new embargo be put on, he thought to himself! I'll not be hurt, he was happy to say.

And some good things had come out of what could have been a bad scene, the salty old sailor had concluded after spending some time with the two fun-loving Frenchmen. He damned well liked both of them. They were the daring, devilish kind of men Jim found interesting. The nights of the long, lonely crossing had been more entertaining and far less dull because of the two young men, Garrett had to admit. Their jovial wits and keen senses of humor had filled his nights with laughter as the trio had sat drinking ale.

During those nightly discussions Jim had learned many things about the young Frenchmen. It was little wonder that Pierre Renaud was so sharp and clever for he had a rich father who could hire the best tutors in France for his only son. And Bernay might not be a wealthy man's son, but Jim appreciated his quick wit and glib tongue. He'd surmised from Jacques' talk that Bernay had lived a rather full and eventful life as a seaman.

After being around these two men for a time, he began to figure Martin was a bloody fool to have played such an underhanded trick on the likes of this pair. Oh, they'd not said anything to him, but they'd not forget what Wakefield had pulled on them. Hell, he couldn't blame them!

Down the passageway from Garrett's cabin was the quarters assigned to Pierre and Bernay. In that cabin were a different-looking Renaud and Bernay. Both men now had beards and their hair touched the collars of the faded blue shirts they'd borrowed from members of Garrett's crew.

This was not the first time Jacques Bernay had grown a beard, but Pierre had always kept himself clean-shaven. His face had taken on a darker shade of tan due to the time he spent on deck with the salty sea breeze whipping his face. He found his new image diverting, and he could not help thinking what his father and mother would think if they could see him now.

He'd light-heartedly jested with Bernay about their appearance. "We look like a fierce pair, don't you agree?"

"I'd say if we but had ourselves a fine ship like Garrett we could become pirates and sail the seas to gather ourselves bounty, then live quite handsomely." Bernay laughed.

Pierre peered into the small looking glass to survey himself again. So dark was his skin that his gray eyes had a piercing, silvery gleam about them. He grabbed his old red neck scarf and tied it around his head. "You're right, *mon ami*. Perhaps, this place where my uncle lives in Missouri Territory still has some Indians roaming the countryside and

138

we'll be taken for one of them."

Light conversation and jesting or playing cards helped them pass the long evenings after they'd dined with the captain. By now, both were impatient and bored with life aboard the ship.

Unless he drank generously of Garrett's whiskey, Pierre found he was restless most nights. He might lie awake for hours, thinking of the beautiful golden-haired girl so far away, or he might sleep, only to dream about her, then to wake up in a cold sweat or a heated flush, aching for the touch of her.

His frustration mounted with each day and night for he was in limbo, unable to return to her as he yearned to do. He could do nothing until he was off this damned ship on land. He fumed with impatience, and it was at these times he hated Martin Wakefield with every fiber of his being.

At least, he'd accomplished what he'd set out to do at the beginning of this sea voyage. He'd found out the thing Jim Garrett wanted more than anything was to own the *Sweet Sally* free and clear, for the captain still owed a tremendous sum to creditors. With this, Pierre would bait him in helping him settle his score with Martin Wakefield.

This had to be a waiting game, however. Pierre preferred that Garrett not know the funds he carried on him until he and Jacques were safely on land. Only then would he make the man an offer that, Pierre knew, the American captain would surely take.

Jacques was in complete agreement with Pierre on this plan.

As Pierre was anxiously counting the days until he'd get his first glimpse of the shores of America, Charmaine was counting the days until she'd be sailing from her home.

It was obvious that nothing could prevent that. She was completely well, and Angus had already traveled into St.

Helier to buy her passage with the funds left for that purpose by George Seymour.

She had hoped that her leaving would be delayed when poor Johnny's misfortune had forced her injured cousin to return to the cottage. She'd wanted to help with his nursing and care, but Simone had taken full charge of that, leaving all the household chores to Charmaine.

Tension had engulfed the stone cottage since the night Johnny's two fishing buddies had brought him home, his hands badly burned, his face and body bruised.

Terry Roarke told her aunt and uncle, "There's no doubt his boat was torched, sir. No doubt at all."

"But why would someone want to do that to John?" Angus asked John's friend. "Why, everyone always liked our John. He had no enemies ever since he was a little tad."

A solemn-faced Roarke remarked, "He had one, sir. One who was hellbent on destroying him—maybe killing him."

Angus shuddered at the seaman's blunt words, but he could not argue with the young Irishman. He felt that Roarke spoke the truth.

After John's friends took their leave, as Angus sat quietly in the parlor, Charmaine came to serve him a cup of hot tea, then she took a seat. She was feeling helpless because Simone had insisted that she go back downstairs and keep Angus company.

"I . . . I wish I could do something. He looked so bad, Uncle Angus. He will be all right, won't he?" Her face was etched with concern for her cousin.

"I think so, Charmaine. John's a robust, strong lad." He gave her hand a consoling pat. "Simone has certainly always had a healing hand or else we'd never have raised all these sons of ours."

"Oh, I know that. But how . . . who . . . could have wanted to burn Johnny's boat? Another fisherman, Uncle Angus?"

140

Angus shook his lion's mane of graying hair and replied, "Oh, I hardly think that, Charmaine. For years and years, the fishermen of these Channel Islands have shared these waters and the bounty of fish in them. I'd find that very hard to believe. There's no call for any of them to be greedy."

Charmaine arched her brow, a questioning look on her face. "Then this was done to harm Johnny? Is that what you think, Uncle Angus?"

"Yes, Charmaine. I think someone must hate John very much!"

Neither Angus nor Charmaine had heard the soft footsteps of Simone. "Angus Keene, what are you saying?" His wife's shocked voice called out from the parlor door. She moved on into the room where they were sitting and took a seat. As she swiped the straying wisps of hair away from her forehead, she inquired again of Angus what he was talking about. She could not believe that anyone hated John that much.

In a firm, stern tone, Angus declared, "We'll speak of that later. Right now, tell me how our son is?"

"Not as bad as I feared. Thank the lord he was quickly rescued by his good friends." As she gave her husband a detailed account of John's injuries a startling realization hit her. Once she'd cleaned away the smudges and dried blood from her dear son's face, she'd seen definite signs of the brutal beating John's face had taken. The burns on his hands were not too serious.

"Then, my dear Simone, let us just be grateful," Angus told her as he rose from his chair to give her a warm hug. Sensing all that had happened had taken a toll on her, he insisted that she go lie down for a while.

Though Simone immediately protested, Angus ignored her. She might be a determined, stubborn lady, but there were times when he could be indomitably stubborn too.

After Simone excused herself to go to the bedroom to rest,

141

Angus accepted Charmaine's offer to prepare their evening meal while he sat with John. A calm then fell over the Keene cottage.

At daybreak Charmaine was awakened by a thunderous rapping on the door, and holding it slightly ajar, she recognized the deep bass voice of John's oldest brother, Jason. He'd obviously received word about his brother's tragic misfortune.

After Angus and Jason spoke a while in low voices which Charmaine could not hear distinctly, she saw Jason's heavyset figure mount the stairs and she quickly closed her door. Jason was a robust man with rugged features like Angus', and something about his movements told Charmaine there was a rage boiling in him.

Hastily, she put on her morning gown and gave her hair a few quick strokes with her brush. Maybe, if she got to the kitchen ahead of Simone, she could prepare breakfast for the family. She'd not heard Simone greet Jason, and she suspected Angus was the only one up.

As she was about to descend the steps, however, she heard the two brothers' voices from within John's corner bedroom. Because the door was open just a bit, without either of them noticing her, she paused in the hope of getting a glimpse of John.

The last time she'd seen him he'd looked pathetic. His face had been bloodied, his hands raw, as his two friends had carried him up to his room the day before. Her dear, sweet Johnny had looked like a poor, whipped puppy who'd taken the worst of a beating.

But now as she quietly peered in at him Johnny was sitting up in his bed and he looked much improved. Oh, there were ugly red scars etched across his face, but he was able to speak to his brother, who was at his bedside. The sight of him brought a pleased smile to Charmaine's beautiful face and

142

she sighed gratefully.

Her expression changed, though, when she heard Jason's next words and Johnny's answer. There was no gentleness in Jason's irate words to his youngest brother, yet Charmaine knew of his deep devotion to John. Ironically, Jason and John were the closest of the Keene brothers, Charmaine knew.

"That kind of woman is never anything but trouble, and you should have known that, boyo," Jason's gruff voice barked.

"Didn't know that was who it was, Jas. Swear it!"

"Oh, hell! It could never be proven, but down by the wharves rumors are flying around. Your friend Roarke brought me word as Pa asked him to, and we talked and shared a few drinks. He said you'd been rather busy lately. None of the fellows had seen you at the Cozy Cove in the evenings. Seems you've been busy at night with a certain lady friend, aboard your boat. Gossip has it she leaves just before dawn."

Angrily, John jerked up in the bed. "Suppose you tell me just who the hell has been so goddamn nosy?"

"Come on, John. You know the hour some of the fishermen leave to go out in the bay. You're not foolish enough to think an attractive lady walking down a wharf isn't going to be noticed, especially Sarnia Wakefield!"

"*Sarnia Wakefield?* You aren't telling me she's that old reprobate Martin Wakefield's daughter?"

"I'm telling you exactly that. Are you saying you didn't know it?" Jason had a skeptical look on his rugged face.

"Hell, no. I'm not a complete fool, Jason."

"Then she lied to you, little brother."

John shook his head and replied, "No, Jason . . . no, she never lied. She just told me to call her Sarnia and never mentioned her last name. I really didn't care at the time."

Jason got up and stretched his long legs, admonishing his brother firmly, "Well, you should have. She's cost you one

143

fine fishing boat and your livelihood."

Charmaine walked down the steps, a name ringing in her ear. Sarnia Wakefield! Dear God, what had Sarnia Wakefield cost her? Charmaine wondered.

Had she not come to the cottage and told Charmaine that she was to marry Pierre Renaud, the rendezvous at the cove would have been kept.

Instead, Charmaine had remained at the cottage. Had Pierre been there as he'd promised? Now, she'd never know!

Chapter 17

Charmaine's mood was pensive the rest of the morning, and Angus noticed it as she prepared their breakfast. Simone was far too concerned about her son to do so. Later, when Jason had come downstairs to visit with his mother and father for a while before taking his leave, he told them in his straightforward way what he suspected, declaring that John had helped confirm it. It was Martin Wakefield who was responsible for the torching.

Jason, too, was so occupied with family problems that he gave his quiet cousin little more than a fleeting glance. Apart from those gathered together around the kitchen table, Charmaine moved about the room doing chores, but all the time her mind was on Sarnia Wakefield.

That one person had it in her power to change the whole course of another's life was frightening, she realized suddenly. Yet, God knows, this young lady had done that with devastating ease and swiftness.

What a foolish country girl Charmaine felt. But she promised herself she'd be wiser from now on, not so vulnerable the next time. She tossed her golden hair back over her shoulders in a defiant gesture as she silently lectured herself, and when her chores were finished, she quietly left the kitchen without interrupting the conversation of the

Keene family.

She'd not thought about John's door being open or that he could see her as she started to go past his room to her own. But his voice called out to her. "Charlie, aren't you going to come in and see me?"

With her folded apron still in her hand, she turned and smiled at him. "I . . . I didn't want to bother you, Johnny. I thought you might be resting," she lied.

But John knew her better than anyone, knew her long-lashed eyes always fluttered nervously when she was lying as she was doing now. His own eyes were devouring her, for he'd forgotten just how gorgeous those deep blue eyes of hers were. For the last few weeks, he had gazed into the dark, mysterious eyes of Sarnia. But consuming all of Charmaine's golden loveliness now, he surged with a renewed fire he knew he could never put out. It was hopeless! As long as he lived he'd never love another as he loved Charlie.

"Are you feeling better, Johnny? You certainly look as if you do," she said, a warm smile on her lips. Taking a seat near the bed, she gave away her nervousness to the all-knowing Johnny by playing with one of the wee wisps of hair by her temple. Why is she suddenly shy with me? John wondered. It was not at all like Charmaine to be ill at ease around him.

"How could I not be better with that mother of mine nursing me and feeding me that all-healing broth she swears by." He laughed.

In a sudden move, his hand reached over to take hers. It was a natural gesture for John, and at one time Charmaine would have thought nothing about it. But now she awkwardly jerked her hand from his.

A hurt, pained look clouded John's face, and his bright blue eyes flashed with shock. "Charlie? Holy Christ! You're acting like I'm a leper."

She didn't know what to say to him so she sighed in anguish. "Oh, Johnny! Johnny!"

"Honey, what in the world is it? This is not my Charlie, but I'm still your Johnny. Now come on, tell me?"

She couldn't tell him she could never be his Charlie again, not as she once was. So what could she say to him?

"I'm just upset, I guess, Johnny. I was so worried about you," she told him. At least, this was not a lie. Again, John's hand reached out for hers, and this time she let him clasp it. His eyes warmed with feeling as he murmured softly, "Thank you, Charlie for worrying about me and caring enough to do so. I . . . I'm afraid I'm not worthy of it though. You see, I was very foolish."

As it had always been with them, John confided in her about his interlude with Sarnia. The only thing he didn't tell her was that he was desperately trying to erase sweet visions of her from his thoughts.

"Do you love her, Johnny? And her . . . what about her? Does she care for you?" Charmaine inquired in a low, faltering voice.

"I don't know how to answer you honestly, Charlie. Really I don't." He let his eyes dance slowly over her face, so lovely and so curious. "Have I shocked you, Charlie?"

"No . . . no, you haven't shocked me. Why should I be shocked about you and some lady, Johnny. My goodness, I imagine you've had many lady friends."

With a crooked grin on his face, he shook his head and laughed, "I've not had all that many lady friends, as you call them, Charlie." His finger tilted her chin, and with a jesting air, he told her, "Don't you know you're my Charlie girl, eh?"

Charmaine was spared a reply but not embarrassment when Simone entered the room. Her voice was sharp and Charmaine realized her aunt was very displeased to see her with John.

Ignorant of his mother's feelings and suspicions, John did not help the situation by his chipper remark. "Ah, Mother, Charlie's the best tonic I've had yet. I feel much better. Now, I'm not saying your broth wasn't a big help too."

147

Her son's happy, jolly mood would have been a source of great delight to Simone Keene if she hadn't found Charmaine sitting so close to his bed. She wished Charmaine's departure date was tomorrow.

With a forced smile on her face, she declared, "You've obviously made a miraculous recovery, my dear. The ones we must truly thank are your friends who rescued you from that blazing boat of yours, don't you think?"

"Good friends they are, and believe me, I'm beholden to them forever," John agreed.

The chill in Simone's eyes when they darted in Charmaine's direction urged the young woman to excuse herself from John's room, and she did just that. But John's voice echoed in her ear as she went through the doorway, "Don't stay away so long, Charlie."

She dared not turn around for she had no wish to see the accusing look in Simone's blue eyes, cold as the winter wind that blew across the Channel.

The following days were strained and tense for Charmaine. John was always beckoning her to spend time with him, and Simone's unspoken disapproval was obvious. Sadly, Angus watched, but he knew of no way to ease the situation in his home.

Never would Charmaine have expected to eagerly mark off the days remaining before she was to leave the island of Jersey. However, she now wished to be on her way to America. Whatever awaited her there, it could be no worse than this, she told herself.

The endless days did finally pass, and the departure of the packet ship *Sea Witch* was due the next morning. It was decided that Angus would see her to the vessel and make certain she was safely inside the cabin she was to share with another lady sailing to America.

The last evening she spent at the stone cottage was a strange one for Charmaine, as it was for Simone Keene. In her motherly fashion, Simone was giving her niece last-minute advice and warnings. She urged Charmaine to be sure not to lose George's letter with its multitude of instructions and the list of his friends in the city of Norfolk, people Charmaine could turn to in case something prevented him from being at the harbor when her ship docked.

"Oh, I do wish George had delayed his departure so the two of you could have been married and left together. I don't like having you travel so far all alone," Simone declared now that the final moments were upon them, only too aware that her niece would be leaving at dawn.

"I have to confess I am a little apprehensive about my first long voyage. It's . . . it's not exactly like the crossing from France to Jersey. So many, many days!" Charmaine admitted.

Looking at the girl, Simone was engulfed with sorrow. She thought of Charmaine's sweet innocence and of the small cloistered world she'd known here on their farm, and she was almost persuaded to pull the girl into her arms and plead with her not to go.

She did love Charmaine, and her sincere concern for her niece's welfare made her realize that Charmaine should go. John would be living at the cottage for weeks, even months. His boat was gone, and he would be forced to hire out to another fisherman when he was well enough to work.

"You will be fine, Charmaine," Simone comforted her. "You've always been a smart girl, and a level-headed one, so I've no doubt that your common sense will guide you."

A skeptical look came to Charmaine's face as she thoughtfully remarked, "I hope so."

"Let's get ourselves to bed, young lady, eh? You've got to get up awfully early for your uncle to get you to the wharf." Simone was too near tears to linger any longer.

Charmaine rose up from her chair to follow her aunt up the stairway on this her last night in the Keene cottage, but she could not allow the night to pass without telling her aunt what was on her mind. "I know you've always done what was right for me, Aunt Simone and . . . and I just wanted to tell you that it is best I go to America to marry George."

Nothing could hold back Simone's tears now, and she clasped Charmaine in a tender embrace. The two of them stood together, both crying.

There was no mention of John, and there was no need for it because they understood each other. For Simone, what Charmaine had said made her leaving easier to bear and it lightened her worries about her young niece's ability to take care of herself until she was reunited with George. The girl was far smarter than she'd realized.

They said good night to one another and quietly closed the doors to their respective rooms. With the dawn, Charmaine would be gone.

It was hard for Angus to be jolly, but it was not his nature to shed tears either. He'd not anticipated how badly he'd feel when he stood by the rail of the packet ship and said farewell to Charmaine. But it was comforting to know that a nice lady would be sharing her small cabin for the long sea voyage, a lady who was older than Charmaine.

In those last few minutes, as he held her gloved hands in his rough, wrinkled ones and declared, "You've always been a joy in our home, dear," there was a mist in his deep-set eyes.

Charmaine was trying to be brave, pretending to be light-hearted for she genuinely loved Angus. Considering it a favor to both of them if she eased their agony, she kissed his cheek and urged, "Now that you've got me all cozy let's say goodbye so you can get back home. I . . . I love you, Uncle Angus, and please tell Aunt Simone and Johnny I love them too." Giving him a playful pat she teased, "Now, be off with you. Your breakfast will be waiting for you and it will get cold."

A big grin lit up Angus' face though he saw right through her act of bravado. "God be with you, child!" he said, turning quickly to leave.

The rugged, robust man walking down the wharf drew stares from those passing by. He hardly looked the sort to cry, but Angus Keene cried without shame, not caring that people saw him as he walked to his buggy.

PART II

A Strange New World

Chapter 18

Wide-eyed, Charmaine Lamoureux stood entranced by this strange, new experience of being aboard a ship. It was very exciting to watch the seamen scurrying around the deck of the three-masted vessel. Their hands expertly worked at the ropes as they called to one another. Like busy bees they worked as teams, Charmaine thought.

The mass of canvas billowed with the gusting winds that churned the water lapping at the hull of the ship. One prominent figure of a man caught Charmaine's deep blue eyes and she knew instinctively that he must be the ship's captain.

The movement of the ship as it slowly plowed through the water was noticeable to her as she stood by the rail, allowing the wind to blow her hair and whip at her cape. It felt glorious! She was titillated by excitement and by a wonder she'd never known, but then she'd never been aboard a large ship like this one.

Suddenly, she was glad she was going to see the new world George had described to her, and consumed by the sights around her, she forgot the sadness in her heart. She paid no heed to the light mist of spray that caressed her rosy cheeks, and while she was admiring the magnificence of the sea, she caught the eye of the captain who'd had only a fleeting glimpse of her as his packet had gotten underway.

She was a striking young lady, and he could not help admiring her. All his other passengers appeared to have taken refuge in their quarters, but she stood by the rail exhilarated, the excited flush on her lovely face telling him she was enjoying their departure.

It is obvious she loves the sea, Captain Fleming reasoned, for he had no way of knowing that Charmaine had never been to sea before. In his eyes this little beauty was a golden sea goddess if ever there was one, but she seemed very young to be traveling alone and unescorted. Such a gorgeous creature could be an overpowering temptation to any lusty man.

The truth was, he was having a few lusty thoughts himself at the moment, although this young woman also elicited a feeling of protectiveness from the captain for she was such a pretty young thing. His eyes beheld her blossoming femininity as her dark blue cape swept back to expose her breasts molded by her blue merino frock. The clear morning sunlight enhanced her flowing long hair, so glossy and golden. Fleming was already planning on monopolizing a fair share of his lovely passenger's time.

His spirits mounted in anticipation of a very pleasant crossing. This would be his last one for a few months, for all too soon the rough weather would settle in over the Atlantic, making it too treacherous.

In fact, Fleming's years as a mate and as captain of the *Sea Witch* made him aware that he was pressing his luck by sailing for Virginia this late. He'd had to lay over in England ten extra days. That had proven costly and could prove more costly yet.

He pulled his eyes away from the lovely Charmaine to observe the full billowing sails above him. With good luck, days filled with bright blue skies, and strong stiff breezes he could make a record run.

And with luck of another kind, Captain Fleming might

make a conquest of the lady fair who stirred his wildest desires.

Charmaine was pleased with the woman with whom she'd share many hours on the voyage. Her cabinmate was older than Charmaine by a few years, and she seemed glad to have Charmaine's companionship for the long trip.

"It's a bit scary for me. I've never been anywhere in my whole life." She gave a nervous little laugh. "You will certainly be a comfort . . . Charmaine, is it?"

"Yes, Charmaine Lamoureux and you said your name was Natasha Weer?"

"Isn't that the oddest combination of names. They don't sound as though they belong together. My father was English and my mother was Russian. But please, Charmaine, please call me Tasha. That's what all my friends call me."

"Oh, that's a beautiful name—Tasha. I feel we're going to be friends by the time our journey is over."

It was a tremendous comfort to the young French girl to learn that the older lady was to reside in Norfolk, Virginia, and that she would be living with her brother, whose wife had died, leaving him with three motherless youngsters.

"Sad it was, indeed," Tasha told her. "It seemed just when good fortune was finally coming their way Jacob's dear wife was taken from him and the tots. God love their little hearts—just babies really. Five, four, and two."

"Well, he is lucky to have a sister such as you, Tasha. Very lucky indeed!" Charmaine declared.

"Well, Charmaine, it may be that I'm the lucky one, for I'll have a very good home and security under my brother's roof. That means a lot to me. I'm not a pretty lady as you can see, and I've never had beaus beating a path to my door as you probably have."

It was true. Tasha's features were sharp rather than

157

delicate, and her figure was more square than curved. But Charmaine saw a warm gentleness in this woman's big black eyes, and she noticed that her new friend was blessed with beautiful black curly hair. The olive hue of Tasha's complexion was flawless, except for a mole at the side of one of her eyes. However, Charmaine found the mole rather interesting.

She admonished her cabinmate tenderly, "You're far too hard on yourself, Tasha. I've certainly not had many suitors, as you said. I lived on a farm with my aunt and uncle, and that sort of life doesn't allow much time for social affairs."

"Then all I can say is the young men where you live must be blind, Charmaine. Surely, your mirror must tell you how absolutely stunning your face and figure are. Your hair looks like silken gold."

"I guess I have to thank my dear mother for that." Charmaine laughed lightheartedly. "I was always told I had my mother's looks and my father's temperament."

"Well, you are a most beautiful girl, and I already know you are nice. Yes, I think you and I will be good friends, Charmaine Lamoureux."

The next few days the two ladies were rarely apart. They chatted incessantly during their strolls and in the evenings before retiring. Each day, Captain Kip Fleming became more irritated by the sight of the tiny black-haired woman, who was always at the pretty Mademoiselle Lamoureux's side.

Fleming wasn't known for his patience, especially when he was anxious to become acquainted with an attractive woman. Charmaine had no inkling that she was being admired as she and Tasha strolled the ship in the afternoons, and when the young cabin boy came to their quarters to extend an invitation to dine with Captain Fleming the poor lad innocently included Tasha. When the captain had dispatched him with the message to be delivered to the women's cabin he'd assumed his captain meant it for both occupants, not just one.

When the boy rushed back out, Charmaine and Tasha exchanged glances. "Well, that is very gracious of our captain, isn't it?" Tasha remarked. It would seem he was as well mannered a man as he was fine looking, for Tasha had noticed him often as they'd roamed around the deck. While he seemed rather aloof, she imagined that sort of manner was required of a ship's captain.

In a jovial mood, Tasha jested, "Shall we dress fancy? After all, we're dining with the captain."

The two women broke into a gale of laughter.

"I'd love to dress fancy, but I hardly have such a gown, I'm afraid, Tasha." Charmaine recalled the exquisite ensemble Sarnia Wakefield had worn on the morning she'd paid a visit to the cottage. Simple, ordinary frocks were all she possessed, however.

Tasha was already going through her things and she pulled forth a rose-colored silk gown, with a short, soft wool cape of the same color. She gave it a firm shake before spreading it out on one of the bunks. Saying nothing as she continued to fling other articles of clothing to one side, she lifted another garment out of her luggage. This gown, a vivid shade of purple, was splashed with frosty white lace. When she let it unfold in front of Charmaine's eyes, it brought forth a sigh of admiration from her friend.

"It's magnificent, Tasha. The most gorgeous gown I do believe I've ever seen," Charmaine exclaimed, fingering the material of the purple gown and letting her fingers trail up to the lace trim of the scooped neckline.

"My mistress gave me some of her castoffs when I left or I never would own such gowns as these. Try the purple one on. It would be much more flattering on you. The rose-colored one is more my style." She turned once again to reach for something, and this time she held forth a white shawl, beautifully embroidered along the bottom. "This will keep the chill off your shoulders Charmaine."

"Oh, Tasha! Tasha!" Charmaine was overcome by her friend's generous offer, and she could only shake her head in disbelief. A childlike excitement bubbled inside her and she could not wait to get dressed and go to the captain's cabin for dinner.

While she wasn't as excited as her young friend, Tasha derived pleasure from Charmaine's glowing radiance as she slipped into the vivid purple gown. The low neckline so flattering on Charmaine exhibited just enough cleavage to tantalize any man, and Tasha wondered what the sight of her friend would do to the manly captain.

She had been wise to pick the rose gown, with its high neckline, for herself. Lord knows, her flat chest would not have enhanced the appearance of the purple one. No, that was the style for Charmaine. Tasha knew she was not the kind of woman who made men turn around when they passed her on the street.

Should she ever draw a man's attention it would not be for the beauty of her face or for the comeliness of her figure. This knowledge had made her decision simple when her brother's letter had come. The thought of crossing a vast ocean had petrified her at first. The job she had was pleasant enough, and her mistress was good to her and generous. But there was the future to consider.

Charmaine complimented her on the rose-colored frock, but secretly, she yearned to tell her friend to free her hair because the severe coils made her look older. Instead, just before they started to leave the cabin, Charmaine pulled her cherished little bottle of jasmine water out of her reticule and dabbed some behind her ears and at her throat. Then she insisted Tasha use some of it.

As they strolled toward the captain's quarters, each in a fancy gown, they exchanged smiles when the deckhands ogled them as they passed.

"We must look very fetching, Tasha. You see how they stare at us?" Charmaine nudged her friend.

Wearing a gorgeous gown gave her confidence, Charmaine had to admit to herself as they drew near to the captain's quarters, and by the time the door slowly opened, her face was glowing. She seemed very self-assured to the eager captain who greeted her with a smile on his strong-featured face. He made a most striking figure in his white ruffled shirt and blue pants, which were perfectly molded to his muscled thighs and legs. But his greeting puzzled Charmaine.

"Good evening, *mademoiselle* . . . uhh, ladies." Kip Fleming was exuberant, then stammering as he struggled to maintain control when his eyes went beyond the gorgeous vision in purple to the black-haired lady right behind her.

The full impact of his expression was not seen by Tasha, but Charmaine quickly glanced down the front of her to see if something was showing that should not be because she'd never worn such a low-cut bodice before. Her saucy self-confidence was quickly crumbling as they stood there while the captain was acting so strange.

After all, he had invited them, hadn't he? Yet he now looked like someone who'd been intruded upon. Strange behavior, she thought.

Although he urged them to come inside, Charmaine sensed that he was indignant, and she could not figure out why since it had been his idea to invite them. What kind of a man was this Captain Fleming? She was beginning to realize that there were many types of men. They are complex creatures, she mused.

As annoyance stabbed at Kip Fleming, he swore to have the young cabin boy's hide before this night was over for making such a mistake. He cursed the little bounder for saddling him with this black-haired wench for the evening, but he was forced to play the gentleman if he hoped to gain what he wanted from the golden-haired miss. Exerting his will power, he forced a pleased look onto his face and commented, "Such a lovely sight before my door is a rarity,

161

ladies. Please forgive me if I was so startled I forgot my manners." With the gallantry of a perfect gentleman, he directed each of the young ladies to a chair but his eyes admired only Charmaine. As he stood behind her when she was seated he noted the softness of the skin at the back of her neck and the daintiness of her shoulders. He ached to caress her.

"It was thoughtful of you to invite us to dinner, Captain Fleming," Tasha said, since Charmaine appeared so quiet and shy. Tasha thought that the girl might be intimidated by the arrogant captain, who she judged to be in his thirties.

"My pleasure . . . Miss Weer, isn't it?" Fleming replied.

"Yes, Captain. I'm Miss Weer and this is Miss Lamoureux." She turned to Charmaine smiling.

"My pleasure to meet you, Miss Lamoureux. I apologize for my duties have prevented me from becoming acquainted with you. I hope you are finding your journey on the *Sea Witch* pleasant?"

Charmaine finally broke her silence to respond. "I find the sea and your ship all very exciting, Captain Fleming." Her eyes sparkled with glowing blue fire as she spoke, and Kip found himself entranced. He stared openly at her, a pleased smile on his good-looking face.

"It is exciting—the sea!" He silently thought to himself, so are you. Swelling with desire, he offered his guests a glass of wine, but more than ever, he resented the presence of Tasha Weer.

When their dinner was served by the galley cook and the cabin boy Colin, the captain's piercing eyes let the lad know he was displeased about something, leaving poor Colin in a quandary. Fleming's mood didn't bother old Harry that much. He shrugged it aside for he'd been with Fleming as cook for the last five years.

When they scurried back down the passageway, Harry soothed Colin's worried mind by trying to tell him all would be well. "After all, laddie, one woman is a handful and two can be sheer havoc. Captain's got two in there tonight."

Young Colin froze in his tracks and gasped, "Do you suppose, Harry, he meant me to invite only one of the ladies? Lord save me if I made a mistake."

"If so, he should have told you which one. Laddie, you are too serious for one so young," Harry declared.

But Colin's fears didn't ease as he walked back to the galley.

Chapter 19

Captain Kip Fleming could have told no one what he ate for dinner, but he did imbibe generously on the wine. Even that did not dull the agonizing ache in his groin caused by the tantalizing vision of Charmaine Lamoureux across the table.

The candlelight heightened her radiant beauty and bewitched him more. After a few glasses of wine, she became more relaxed and vivacious. Her soft lilting laughter was like music to his ears, and he was delighted to know she was having such a gay time.

What an unforgettable night it could have been if only Charmaine and he were in the cabin, he dejectedly thought to himself.

Both his guests praised old Harry's meal and sipped the wine with enjoyment. Charmaine knew she'd overindulged herself by the tight feel of Tasha's purple gown, and Tasha noticed that Charmaine had had quite enough wine for she was unusually light-hearted.

So the older woman graciously thanked the captain for a delightful dinner and a pleasant evening before turning to her friend. "We must say good night now, don't you think Charmaine?"

"Oh, yes—yes, we must. My goodness, time has escaped

me, I am having such a nice time," she said, giving the captain a lovely smile.

"So am I, ladies," he told them as he rose from his chair. He helped them on with their light wraps, then said, "I'll escort you to your cabin."

As they started down the passageway the clever captain managed to make Tasha walk ahead of them while he took Charmaine's arm and strolled by her side. She sensed the strength of him as his hand clasped her arm. When they reached the door of the ladies' cabin, Tasha voiced another brief thank you, and Charmaine was about to do the same thing when Kip grasped the opportunity for one stolen moment with her by suggesting, "If you aren't too tired, as your friend seems to be, I'd like to suggest a stroll above to view the most beautiful starlit night we've had in a long time. There are a million diamonds up there in the heavens, and the biggest, brightest moon you've ever seen."

Charmaine wondered if the moon really was as big and bright as the ones she'd seen from her cliffside perch, and because she'd had such a wonderful time in her beautiful borrowed gown, she wanted to capture the magic of the moonlight she'd loved back on Jersey.

"Oh, I'm not the least bit tired, Captain, and I'd very much enjoy a stroll after that wonderful meal." Without taking much notice of the look on Tasha's face, she told her friend she'd be back shortly, and then she took the captain's proffered arm.

Kip Fleming was more than pleased that he was finally going to have some time alone with her. At long last, Tasha's shadow was not going to haunt him. But, when the door closed behind her, Tasha paced the cabin aimlessly, realizing she should have known all along that the good-looking American sea captain was attracted to the beautiful Charmaine. She had been included in the invitation only to insure that Charmaine would accept.

She would wager that he was finally reaping the pleasure

166

he'd anticipated all evening. She smiled, seeing the humor of the situation.

Fleming and Charmaine strolled leisurely along the deck to the secluded spot by the rail Fleming had had in mind. Her head hardly reached his broad shoulders even though she wore heeled slippers. A tiny slip of a miss she was, and he became more aware of that with each passing moment.

Charmaine was so quiet that he wondered about it at first, then he realized she was thoroughly enjoying the moonlight stroll when he noticed the enchanting smile on her face.

"You are very lovely with the moonlight shining on you, Charmaine," he told her, his hand moving from her arm to clasp her small hand. She accepted his touch without flinching, which pleased Fleming.

She seemed not to hear his compliment and exclaimed with girlish enthusiasm, "Oh, it is a gorgeous night, Captain Fleming. Thank you for inviting me along." Her eyes glanced over toward him, and rose to meet his admiring ones.

"It is I, who should be thanking you, my dear young lady. I don't have the honor of enjoying the company of such a beautiful woman often. Indeed, there are times when life at sea is very lonely."

"I can understand that, I think, but I'm sure it must be exciting too," she replied.

He chuckled softly, and there was a teasing twinkle in his eyes. "Something tells me you like the sea, and I'd venture to add you love to stroll barefoot on a sandy beach and to pick up shells along the way. Am I right?"

"You are." She laughed. "But how . . . what made you think that?"

"A particular look . . . the brilliant sparkle in your eyes . . . the relaxed serenity of your face. It is obvious to me you like the sea by the way you come alive when you are around it." Kip Fleming dared to become bolder by confessing, "It is that quality which attracted me to you, along with your other many charms."

As she gazed up into his handsome face, Charmaine was reminded of another handsome man who had looked at her in much the same way. Suddenly, she was filled with apprehension about what he might do next because they were alone in a dark deserted part of the ship.

Now she realized she'd been too eager to accept his invitation for a night stroll. She should have insisted that Tasha come along. Fleming was a very experienced man— he had to be traveling the world as he did—and he probably had pretty ladies in every port where his ship docked.

His arrogant, self-assured air made that likely, and he was older than she was by ten years or so. Charmaine's experience with Pierre Renaud had taught her a lesson about the winning way of worldly, experienced gentlemen. *Mon Dieu,* he'd charmed her out of her senses, and made her forget all of her aunt's warnings about the proper conduct of a nice young lady.

Kip noted her slightly tense air and sought to tease her. "Now, I wasn't too bold for you, was I? I didn't intend to offend you. I'm . . . I'm a rather straightforward man as you'll learn if we spend any time together—and I hope we shall."

She dared not seem like a trembling country bumpkin so she assumed the most sophisticated image she could conjure up. She forced a soft flurry of laughter and in a voice she hardly recognized as her own said, "I am hardly offended to hear you say you were attracted to me."

But as soon as she'd uttered the words she wanted to bite her tongue, for she realized she sounded far too bold. She saw the glint in Kip's eyes as he bent closer to murmur in her ear, "Ah, good! Can't stand squeamish females." His laughter was deep, throaty. "Knew you couldn't be one of those, though. Everything about you says otherwise. You're

168

a woman of spirit and fire, Charmaine Lamoureux."

She cocked her head to the side, and in a coquettish way, she pointed out, "Now, Captain Fleming, you know nothing about me."

"*Ma petite mademoiselle,* I know more than you think. And by the way, call me Kip, eh?"

"I do not know you that well, sir." Charmaine was not aware that her manner seemed a challenge to Kip. The American sea captain considered her twinkling eyes to be daringly flirtatious, and he felt that her disarming smile was encouraging him to kiss her rosebud lips.

He murmured as he started to pull her close to him, "Well, I'll remedy that right now." His mouth pressed down on hers with fierce urgency for his desire had been smoldering all evening.

Charmaine felt helpless as his strong powerful arms enfolded her and his demanding lips held hers captive. When he finally released her, she stood for a moment, breathless and unable to say a word. She realized he wanted to make love to her.

"I . . . I couldn't help myself, Charmaine," he gasped, slightly breathless himself.

Her arms free now, Charmaine swung one hand at his flushed face, dealing him an amazingly sharp blow for one so small. Shocked by her unexpected reaction to his amorous caress, Fleming stared at her. Her indignant, beautiful face reflected her aversion to the liberty he'd taken, and fire sparked in her deep blue eyes, making them seem as purple as the gown she had on.

"I just couldn't help myself either, *Kip!*" She quickly dashed away from him, fleeing across the deck of his ship like a gazelle.

As he watched her hurry across the deck, Kip Fleming remained in a state of wonder at her vicious wallop. Then a smug grin came slowly to his face. He was right about her, he knew it now. She was a spirited little vixen, full of spice and fire!

He didn't give a bloody damn that she'd slapped him, for he was certain that his kiss was enjoyed. If it hadn't been, she would have protested sooner while they were lingering in their cozy enclosure.

As Charmaine darted past two young sailors in her mad dash away from Kip Fleming, they grinned at her. Had they witnessed the intimate episode between her and their captain? Lord, she'd be embarrassed to stroll around the deck with Tasha now! She'd allowed herself to get mixed up in another mess.

Why had she not just politely turned down Fleming's invitation and gone on into the cabin with Tasha? She could almost hear Aunt Simone saying, "A proper young lady wouldn't have put herself in that position in the first place."

Was there a streak of wildness in her? Maybe, a little of the wanton too? The tall captain's kiss had given her a moment of pleasure, and under the persuading warmth of his lips she had almost yielded to his demanding touch. I cannot deny it, she admonished herself as she rushed on toward her quarters.

Lord, let Tasha be asleep, she silently prayed as she approached the door of their cabin. She'd been foolish, but she didn't want to confess it to Tasha.

Her motions slow and cautious, she entered the cabin not questioning why it wasn't secured but glad of her luck. Tasha's voice didn't call out to her, and she was greatly relieved to see her covered figure turned toward the wall.

With much nervous fumbling, she slipped out of her gown and undergarments, placing them on the nearby chair. Then she sighed, grateful that she'd not roused Tasha, and she crawled into the bunk unaware that Tasha's protective attitude had made her investigate Charmaine's long absence from the cabin. When Tasha had mounted the steps to go on deck, however, she'd seen Charmaine rushing toward her.

Hastily, Tasha had returned to their quarters so Charmaine would never know that she'd sought to check on her. She certainly didn't want her friend to resent that gesture.

Now, poor Tasha lay with all her clothing still on, the coverlet pulled up to her chin. In misery, she waited until she was certain Charmaine was fast asleep. Then she slipped out of her bunk and quietly undressed.

When she'd finally managed to slip on her nightgown and get back into the bunk, she lay awake for a period of time, thinking that she should caution Charmaine about a man such as Captain Fleming whose motives were probably not honorable. He was so virile looking and he wandered the seas, seeking some pretty maiden in every port.

Tasha found herself feeling like the older sister of her new friend, Charmaine, and she could not idly stand by and do nothing.

When she heard Charmaine stir in her bunk she sat up to listen, much as a mother heeds a restless child.

Charmaine was dreaming. At first, she'd had visions of Captain Kip Fleming, but his face had suddenly changed to that of the devilishly handsome Pierre Renaud, who spoke words of endearment in French as he had in the cove.

She started to slap his face as she had Kip Fleming's, but instead her hand reached up and caressed his cheek. Then she started to flee from him as she had from the captain. However, she did not do so. She remained in his arms, willingly and eagerly.

Their lips met and his arms enclosed her. Bodies touched and thighs entwined, and Charmaine was swept into a wonderful moonlight ecstasy, but sadly, she awoke to find it was just a dream.

For a moment, she was flushed by the searing heat of her half-conscious imaginings. Maybe she'd never see Pierre again, but she knew her reckless heart would forever yearn for him and for the rapturous love he'd stirred in her. In her secret heart, she'd always be his!

Chapter 20

From the minute they docked in the busy seaport city of Savannah, Pierre Renaud was impressed by this strange new country to which his father had banished him for a year. Indeed, he was already thinking he might never want to leave if the Missouri Territory was as interesting as the city of Savannah had proven.

Ships of all sizes, schooners to frigates, moved in and out of harbor, their presence telling Pierre that the shipping trade was lively in America. And the city, with its tropical atmosphere, was unique, Pierre discovered. It was built on a walled bluff overlooking the river that bore the same name.

Savannah's fine homes with impressive fences and grilled gateways, bespoke prosperity and wealth. Pierre was reminded of some of the fine country estates in his native France as he viewed the beautifully landscaped gardens surrounding the palatial mansions he and Bernay passed on their way to seek lodgings.

By the time the two young men had bid Captain Garrett a final adieu and had hired a carriage to take them to an inn, Pierre was high in spirits for he'd made the deal with Garrett as he'd plotted doing weeks ago. Garrett had accepted Renaud's offer without a moment's hesitation, but he had been unable to refrain from asking, "But how will you know that I've carried out the act. You're putting a hell of a lot of trust in me, young man. Who's to say I'll not just take this pouch of gold you've deposited with me and not carry out the deed you've paid me for?" A devious twinkle was in his deep-set eyes.

Pierre laughed throatily before he turned the full impact of his cold gray eyes on Garrett's face. His air indomitable, he declared, "I'll give you six months to earn the bounty you've been so generously paid. I'll know whether it's done for I have sources there and in London town. If it isn't, then my good captain, a very similar deal will be made, this time for your hide."

Their eyes locked as they measured one another respect-fully. After a moment, Garrett threw his head back and roared with laughter. "You, Pierre Renaud, I like!"

Any man who'd dare to challenge him in such a way as Renaud had just done had to be worthy of his esteem. Furthermore, the American captain also appreciated the clever working of the Frenchman's mind. Renaud had disembarked from the *Sweet Sally* and was sitting with her captain in one of the many taverns near the wharf before he'd made his proposal. Yes, he is a shrewd bastard, Garrett thought.

It didn't dawn on Jim Garrett until after Bernay and Renaud had left in a carriage that they'd not mentioned where they were staying in Savannah. Perhaps, Renaud had not intended him to know their whereabouts. Yes, young Renaud was sly as a fox!

But in the late afternoon as Garrett ambled back down the wharf to his docked schooner, he knew he was a lot richer because of the pouch of gold tucked inside his worn jacket. Perhaps, he'd never cast his eyes on either of the Frenchmen again, but come tomorrow, the *Sweet Sally* would be all his.

For the life of him, he couldn't figure out his old friend Martin Wakefield's stupidity in crossing the scion of the influential Renaud empire. It was well known that the powers of the old French industrialist Étienne Renaud extended far beyond France. Of all people, Wakefield should know that.

With an offhanded shrug of his shoulders, Garrett strode along with a jaunty gait, deciding that wasn't his problem, nor was the man's fate going to be on his conscience. The pouch of gold had washed away any qualms.

The Magnolia House was an unpretentious-looking establishment on a quiet, secluded street. Its grounds were surrounded by a white picket fence, and ancient, massive magnolia trees blocked out the view of the front of the two-story building as Pierre's carriage came to a halt at the front gate. This area was quiet, unlike the busy, bustling one they'd just traveled through.

On the way they'd passed fine carriages, one horse gigs, and farmers' carts laden with produce or returning home empty. Vendors with hand-drawn carts clung to the sides of the streets, staying clear of the traffic. The varied classes and color of the people he observed caught Pierre's attention. Black women and men balanced filled baskets atop their heads, while the gentry, elegantly dressed, drove by in their fine carriages and those less fortunate strode about in coarse work clothes or simple cotton frocks.

The air was filled with the aromas of flowers, spices, and tobacco, and the inviting odors of the foodstuffs the ambling vendors were hawking. Raggedly clad, tousled-haired youngsters romped in the streets, and their presence told Pierre that all were not wealthy in this strange country. But his eyes caught sight of a young lady strolling with her parasol angled over her head, and he had to confess that there were beautiful ladies here. Bernay noticed her too, and he gave Renaud an admiring wink.

By the time they got out of the carriage to go up the walk to the inn, both men were curious about Savannah and anxious to explore more of it.

Their valises in hand, the two Frenchmen marched down the flagstone walkway and up the three steps to the front entrance. The door was opened for them by a black man in rich blue livery. He greeted them in a most elegant manner. "Welcome to the Magnolia House, gentlemen."

As a younger black man rushed to take over their luggage, Pierre quipped to Jacques, "I'm glad old Wakefield thought to toss our belongings aboard when he shanghaied us."

Jacques laughed. "Just goes to show you how neatly the old bastard had it planned. Wouldn't be worth a lot to anyone but me if mine had remained back in my cabin on the schooner. But as you say I'm glad to have them." Bernay was happy that he'd not lost his few cherished keepsakes from his past too.

As they stepped into the lobby of the inn, both men were amazed to find it elegantly furnished. Its unimpressive exterior gave no hint of the grandeur now surrounding them. Two dignified gentlemen sat over in a corner, playing backgammon at a Regency game table made of Amboina and calamander woods, and their chairs were ebonized and gilded Regency pieces.

A collection of Dutch still-lifes adorned the rich paneled walls in that particular corner of the lobby, and noticing the fine tapestries on some of the other walls, Pierre was reminded of those his own mother had hanging in their home in Cherbourg.

By the time the young Frenchmen had registered and had mounted the wide stairway leading to their suite, Pierre realized with astonishment that this new world was not as primitive or uncivilized as he'd expected. At least, Savannah didn't seem to be. The Missouri Territory might be quite different.

Now that his feet were firmly on land he had many things on his mind, and many details to attend to immediately. Foremost on his agenda was contacting a young woman named Charmaine Lamoureux, for he had no intention of departing from Savannah until he could set wheels in motion to right the wrong Wakefield had caused. Charmaine had to know that he'd not lied to her, that he did care very much about her. He'd desired more than one night of lovemaking. He'd wanted a lifetime with her and so it would have been if Martin Wakefield had not played his foul trick.

The astute, worldly-wise Étienne Renaud had not sent his son from France unprepared for the various situations he'd encounter before he arrived at his brother's home in the Missouri Territory. In Pierre's possession was a black book listing his itinerary. Along each place were names of people to seek out should he need any services.

Looking at that small book now, Pierre thought of his father with glowing admiration. Odd as it might seem, he'd had to leave the man who'd fathered him to really appreciate him. He'd never before given any thought to the fact that his father was so knowledgeable about the world or that his lifetime had been lived so fully.

During the idle hours aboard Garrett's ship, he'd perused the black book so tediously prepared by Étienne Renaud, and his chest had swelled with respect and admiration for his father. He'd never thought as he'd sat across the dining table observing Étienne's quiet manner that he was viewing such a powerful individual. How naïve he had been, how simple-minded, never to have wondered how they lived in such a luxurious state!

The always-perceptive Jacques Bernay took notice of his friend's quiet manner after they'd been left in their suite. *"Mon ami,* something bothering you suddenly?"

"I have many plans to make now that we've arrived, a lot of things to do before we can leave here. I'm probably not going to be much company this evening after dinner so don't hesitate to seek some excitement, Jacques," he said, giving Bernay a knowing wink of his eye.

"Me seek pleasure, *mon ami?* Aren't you getting the two of

us confused? A good bath, a tasty meal and a good night's sleep in that comfortable bed sounds wonderful to me. But what is going to keep you so busy, eh?"

"I, my friend, have a book of names to look over so I can be certain we go to the right people to provide us with the provisions we'll need to go to the Missouri Territory." Pierre sat down on the bed and yanked off his brown leather boots.

Jacques' dark eyes questioned Pierre, and his dark brow arched skeptically as he inquired, "You have names of people in this strange place. How so, may I ask?"

"My father supplied me with them before I left France, anticipating just such a need as we now face. He is a most thorough man. I just hope to be as smart someday."

"I see," Jacques drawled slowly as he sank down on the bed. Bernay had often wondered how different his life might have been had he known his father or had he had a father like his friend's.

However, never in his heart had he faulted his mother because he was a bastard. Indeed, he still carried cherished memories of her with him though she'd been dead for seven years. Only after her death, when he was going through her belongings before he'd departed from France, had Jacques come across the small miniature picture of the man he knew to be his father. He still wondered why she'd never shown it to him.

A few hours later when the two Frenchmen had enjoyed the luxury of a hot bath and a change of clothing, they went downstairs to the inn's dining room. Their entrance drew the curious eyes of the other guests for both were strikingly handsome. Something about their manner told the oglers these guests were new to the inn, which had a friendly atmosphere and always catered to congenial people.

By the time Jacques and Pierre had dined on creamy bisque, tender duckling cooked in a rich sauce, and tasty green vegetables, they could understand why the guests seated around them looked so content. The food was good enough to put anyone into a pleasant mood. The friends shared a bottle of a good white wine, but neither finished his portion of ripe, sweet raspberries topped with thick cream.

Although they didn't speak to any of the other guests as they took their leave, they did return smiles and nod their heads in response to friendly gestures. Only as they were going up the steps, did Jacques remark to Pierre, "They seem like a hospitable lot here in Savannah, don't they?"

"A very friendly city, I'd say," Pierre agreed. "Perhaps, you want to explore more of it?"

"I think I'll wait for your companionship, *mon ami.*" Jacques gave Pierre one of those sly smiles of his.

"Suit yourself, but my nose is going to be stuck in that book."

"Well, I've found, my young friend, that a dull evening can be a pleasant change once in a while," Jacques declared as they now approached the door of their suite. When they entered the suite, which consisted of a sitting room, and two adjoining bedrooms, Jacques retired to his room, leaving the door ajar.

"You wish me to close my door for the task you're going to be occupied with?" he called.

Pierre was already removing his coat as he answered Bernay. "No, that's not necessary."

Seeing that Renaud was most serious about being occupied for the rest of the evening, Jacques set about emptying his valise onto the bed. His belongings made quite a pile. It seemed the right time to check through them to see if old Wakefield's thugs had gathered up all his things in the cabin.

In the pile of clothing he found the letters he'd received since leaving France, the two small miniature pictures he treasured so much, and a small leather-bound book a lady friend had given him. He couldn't help thinking this wasn't much to show for thirty-odd years of living. When he'd neatly folded the clothes and had placed them, the letters,

179

and pictures back into the valise, he lay across the bed and opened the old book to read. It was a seafaring tale so, cozily propping himself up on the pillows, he read for the next hour.

It was a sleepy Bernay Pierre found when he sauntered through the doorway. He was already turning to leave when Bernay raised his half-closed eyes to mumble, "I'm not off yet. Got to reading and I almost went off. Did you finish what you were about?"

"Yes. I've two gentlemen to call on tomorrow. But what I was going to show you was a picture of my father, since I talked about him so much to you this afternoon. In fact, I've a picture of my mother and father." Renaud held in his hand two small miniatures very similar to the ones Bernay had in his possession. Jacques took one of them.

"Your parents, eh? Yes, I'd like to see them. Bet you look like your father," Bernay declared.

"No. I inherited my mother's traits in height and hair and eye color. My father is a very short man," Pierre told him.

"Beautiful lady . . . your mother. Beautiful indeed!" Jacques handed the miniature back to his friend. Then he gazed at the other miniature held out to him. The man didn't resemble Pierre, but he looked like an older version of Jacques. Hints of curly hair were at his temples, once black, now snow white. The eyes were dark like Bernay's, and Pierre's father had a thin upper lip and a full lower one like his own, Jacques noted.

This was a picture of the same man on the miniature he carried. It took all the control he could muster to maintain a calm façade for his heart was pounding.

As much as he yearned to hate his half brother for having what he was denied, he could not find it in his heart to do so. From the first, he'd liked and been mysteriously drawn to Pierre Renaud, and he knew the young man was not responsible for the sins of their father.

With great effort, Jacques forced his eyes to meet Pierre's, and he quietly remarked, "Nice family you have."

"I think so. I'm lucky."

"*Ah, oui!* Most lucky, *mon ami!* Most lucky."

When Pierre left the room after bidding him good night, Jacques silently added under his breath, "Good night, my brother." At the same moment, he vowed never to let Pierre know what he now realized. Étienne Renaud was his father too!

He, Jacques Bernay was the bastard of Étienne Renaud, the wealthy French industrialist!

Chapter 21

Thoughts of the beauteous Charmaine Lamoureux had to be put aside, for Captain Kip Fleming found it necessary to concentrate on the ominous signs of a storm. The air was oppressive as he walked his ship's deck, surveying his men as they went about their routines. He kept wishing he'd left a week or ten days earlier as planned so he'd not have to face the bad weather the next twenty-four hours would bring.

If his calculations were correct he was less than fifty miles east of Cape Henry and the port of Norfolk. How welcome the sweet sight of the Chesapeake would be with the skies looking so threatening. Fleming had lived through more than one deadly storm and he respected them. The most able captains could be overwhelmed by these gales, he well knew.

As the day wore on, his already taut nerves became more strained, and he prayed for the strong breeze to continue. He dreaded the ghostly calm that preceded a storm, the awesome quiet that smothered one—the signal that nature was ready to strike. Kip knew he wasn't the only one experiencing forebodings. Most of his sailors were well seasoned, and he sensed their tension. Yet, none made a comment. Their expressions and the looks in their wary eyes spoke for them.

When Charmaine and Tasha took their afternoon stroll

around the ship's deck, however, they were unaware of the cause of the strange feeling they sensed in the busy seamen working the ropes and rigging of the three-masted schooner.

Tasha was the first to mention the sudden changes aboard the *Sea Witch*. "Is it just me or have you noticed what a queer lot this crew has become? I don't think we've had one friendly smile since we came up to walk this afternoon."

The breeze was playing havoc with Charmaine's long, thick mane of hair so she brushed it back. "I've noticed. Perhaps, it's because the voyage is almost over and weariness is finally taking its toll. I, for one, am ready to see land. How about you?"

"Glory be, yes! I'd make no sailor. I like to walk on the good earth too much, see the glorious trees and the beautiful flowers. I find it dull to be completely surrounded by nothing but water. No, I can't say I wish to go on a voyage for a long, long time. And you, Charmaine?"

A faraway look in her blue eyes, the younger woman gave her friend a slow smile. "To sit on a lovely sandy beach, or up on a cliff, and gaze out over the horizon would delight me, but, as you said, I've no desire to be aboard another ship for such a long time. And since I'll be married to George, I'm certain I won't be."

Tasha yanked at the collar of her frock, then dejectedly sighed, "Lordy, I just pray that this place we're heading for isn't like this all the time. I wondered if this miserable weather is what we're to expect. I can hardly breathe at times. Do you feel that way too, or is it just me?"

A concerned look etched Charmaine's face as she said to her black-haired companion, "Oh, Tasha, I hope you're not going to be ill! I've had no trouble breathing, but the air seems so heavy it seems one could cut it with a knife. And in the distance, the sky looks the same. It reminds me of the thick, moist fogs that moved in over Jersey."

Charmaine was really not ready to return to the confines of the small cabin, but thinking that would probably be best for Tasha if she was feeling poorly, she suggested they end their afternoon stroll.

"I think that is a good idea. Think I may just finish that book I started a couple of evenings ago."

"And I've just created a mending job for myself." Charmaine giggled. "My heel caught on the hem of my dress."

Once they'd returned to their cabin, neither knew the skies directly above had become more threatening. Captain Fleming spoke to some of his passengers, informing an Englishman and his two teenage sons of the impending danger, but he decided to spare the two ladies as long as he could. Besides, he didn't have the time or patience to pamper two panicky females.

Charmaine and Tasha ate the evening meal in their cabin. While Charmaine had a ravenous appetite, Tasha merely drank her tea and nibbled on a fruit tart.

By eight in the evening there was a rap on their door, and when Charmaine responded she saw the giant black seaman called Timbo standing before her, a most serious look on his face. He announced that the captain requested them to remain inside their cabin for the rest of the evening and, as he was speaking, pelting raindrops beat against the portholes and brilliant streaks of lightning lit up the sky. Then thunder exploded, making the cabin vibrate. Tasha sat wide-eyed, her mouth agape.

Timbo wanted to make sure he'd impressed on the two ladies the firm order his captain had issued. "Please, miss, do stay inside. Our decks will be flowing like a river. In such hard rains, men have been swept right into that old ocean out there."

"Oh, Timbo, I promise we won't venture out of our cabin. You can assure your captain of that," Charmaine told him.

"That's jus' fine, ma'am. Jus' wouldn't want nothin' happenin' to you two nice ladies. No sir!"

When Charmaine gave him a warm smile and thanked

185

him, Timbo returned her smile. Then, nodding his head, he turned to go down the passageway, eager to report to Captain Fleming that he'd carried out his orders. Yet, he was tempted to go back to the cabin to caution the pretty golden-haired lady one more time. It would be a shame to see such flawless, satiny skin as hers bruised or cut and he should have warned her about the pitching of the ship. He knew before the night was over the *Sea Witch* was going to be tossed about. He'd mention that to Captain Fleming for the sake of those tiny fragile misses. Why they'd be tossed around like feathers in the wind!

Timbo did voice his fears to the captain, and when the weather permitted him to be absent from the wheel, Fleming went below to give the women an additional warning.

By now, Tasha and Charmaine were already aware of the swaying of the schooner, and Tasha started at each blast of thunder or bolt of lightning. Her body trembled so Charmaine felt so sorry for her, but she knew nothing she could say would ease her friend's fear. She just hoped the storm would hastily pass on over them or they'd move out of its path.

But Kip Fleming dashed such hopes when he entered the cabin. "If you could tie yourself to the post of that bunk, Miss Weer you'd be giving yourself some assurance of not being thrown about. At this point, I might as well tell you the worst is yet to come. I'll try to check on you, but I'm going to be too busy to stay with you." His eyes went searchingly to Charmaine and lingered on her for an instant.

"We'll be all right, Captain Fleming. We shall take your suggestion and secure ourselves to something solid," Charmaine declared, bracing herself against another sharp sway of the ship. Had she not have steadied herself against the wall of the cabin she would have lunged against Fleming.

Kip's huge, strong body was attuned to the swaying motion and it did not faze him, but he was very aware of the effect on Charmaine. As Timbo had said she was a wee one and he was filled with concern for her. Even though he'd tried to persuade himself he could find such a blond beauty in any port, he was devilishly attracted to her. She was something else—rare and unusual.

He broadly smiled and declared, "We'll make it just fine, ladies. Captain Fleming's never lost a ship yet." He was trying to give them courage, but he was doing the same for himself for he'd never seen a meaner sky. As he closed the door behind him he pretended a light-heartedness he did not feel. "Why, this time tomorrow we could be in Virginia, ladies. When we dock I've a date with you two for dinner, and I won't take no for an answer."

"Do . . . do you believe him, Charmaine?" Tasha asked once they were alone. Her voice was full of doubt.

"I certainly do, Tasha! He's the captain, isn't he? I'm sure this is only one of many trips for Captain Fleming." Charmaine, too, pretended a bravado she did not feel. She was standing while Tasha sat frozen on the bunk, so she could detect the mounting violence of the ship's movements, and she wasted no time looking for something to tie around her waist and Tasha's.

No longer were the pelting raindrops beating at the cabin windows. Now great sheets of water like vicious monsters tried to invade the cabin. The timbers of the three-masted ship moaned in anguish with each brutal blow, and as Tasha listened to the fierce howling sound of the wind, she was reminded of the doleful calls of the wolves on the English moors.

By the time Charmaine had managed to tie a torn sheet around Tasha's waist, as securely as she could, the ship was yawing erratically in the turbulent seas. She didn't waste any precious time, but flung the other strip of sheeting around herself and then sank down on the floor beside her cabinmate. As she finished tying the third knot in the sheet now secured around the bunk's post, the ship dove suddenly, like an impish dolphin playfully romping in the sea.

Charmaine knew that Kip Fleming had wanted to prepare them for this very thing, but he'd also tried to shield them from the seriousness of their situation.

A mighty shattering explosion occurred just above them, and she wondered what it was. Perhaps lightning had struck something on deck, she concluded. But above, on the flooded deck, there was no doubt about the cause of the deafening sound. One of the towering masts had splintered.

The fury of the storm seemed eternal to the husky Timbo who'd just lost his footing for the third or fourth time. While his faith in the captain was not wavering, the drenched seaman now doubted that the old *Sea Witch* was going to ride this one out. He was almost certain they'd been so tossed and twisted in these devil's waters they'd veered way off their charted course.

Holy Moses, he'd never seen Fleming moving so fast. The man seemed to be everywhere. Yelling out orders and pitching in to help, he lent his brute strength wherever it was needed. In the midst of the melee, Timbo wondered about the two wee ladies below. They must be filled with sheer panic. If it did come to the worst, he vowed to try to aid them.

Below, Tasha Weer swore the worst was surely upon them. She was so frightened she could not speak, and she just sat, wide-eyed, staring at her friend. Charmaine was so concerned about Tasha that she had little time to fear for her own safety, and she scarcely realized it when she was whirled into a black pit of hell. When she next became conscious of herself and Tasha, she was disoriented until the black man, Timbo, urged her, "God sakes, missy, please hold on to the timber. Can't—can't hold you both up." Charmaine came to her senses long enough to realize that she, Tasha, and Timbo were afloat on the ocean, and their life raft was a massive part of the ship's hull. Timbo's muscled arm encircled Tasha's limp figure while part of her body was flung over the floating timber. The black man's face reflected the strain of holding on to the two of them. She got out a grateful "thank you" and grasped the makeshift raft.

She'd never known such awesome darkness as that which greeted her eyes. It was obvious that the ship had not weathered the storm, though now the sea was ghostly calm.

"You doin' fine, ma'am, just fine!" Timbo encouraged. He was able to catch his wind now that Charmaine was holding onto the timbers keeping them afloat.

What about the others? Charmaine wondered. What about Captain Fleming and that nice family from England. Hopefully, they were afloat out there in that vast darkness.

"What happened to the others?" she said hesitantly.

"Lord, 'a mercy, miss, I don't know. It all happened so fast." His big black eyes looked kindly at her as he muttered, "We gonna' make it. Now you just believe Timbo 'cause I ain't lying."

Charmaine responded with a weak reassuring smile, "I know we will, Timbo. We've made it this far."

"Yes, miss." Timbo's own faith mounted at her words of confidence. The little golden-haired missy had a lot of grit!

Time seemed measureless, but after a while, Tasha came out of her state of numbness and spoke her first words. Before she could go into a frenzy because of their new dilemma, the most wonderful sight appeared on the horizon—a flock of gulls swooping and diving in the first rays of dawn.

"Look, miss . . . over there. See 'em? We're gittin' ready to see the coast of somewhere," he excitedly exclaimed.

"Oh, Tasha, look! Timbo says that could be the coast of Virginia." Charmaine giggled delightfully, and poor little Tasha even managed a weak smile.

"No, ma'am, I didn't say that was Virginia. If'n I was bettin' I'd say we might be landin' in Carolina. Think we were blown way far south of our port."

"Carolina? Where's that from Virginia?" Charmaine asked.

"Miles south of Virginia, for sure," Timbo told her.

Actually the black man had underestimated the fury of the tempest they'd survived. It was the coastline of Georgia they were soon to see.

Chapter 22

For a while Timbo questioned his own sanity. He wondered if the horrors of the last twenty-four hours had taken a toll on him. Could this be the coastline of Georgia? he asked himself as he struggled to help the women onto the beach. After he'd situated them as comfortably as he could, he walked a ways to see the lay of the land. The walled bluff was very familiar to him. He'd seen it before.

His superstitious nature took over, and he reasoned that the good Lord must have guided them here because he knew where to go for help. He had a sister living in a shack on the river if they were where he thought they'd landed. At least, those poor women on the beach could get some good warm food in their bellies and dry their clothes.

His sister Belle didn't have fine accommodations like these ladies were used to, but Timbo figured after what they'd been through his sister's shanty would look like a palace.

Nothing would be accomplished by tarrying, Timbo decided. He would leave the ladies where they were and get help. If he was right about the landmarks, he had a good five miles to walk. Along the way he'd pray that Belle was still working for that nice seamstress in the city and that she still owned a little cart and a roan mare, so he could get the ladies to the shack.

A feeling of helplessness flooded over Timbo because he had the responsibility for the ladies on his broad shoulders. If he'd had only himself to worry about, there would have been no problem.

He rushed back across the pebbled, sandy beach to tell Charmaine what his plans were. He figured she was a little more in control of her nerves than the little black-haired lady. But he was surprised to see that Tasha Weer was calm now that they'd made land.

"Ladies, I've got to leave you here alone if I'm to find help. Can you manage?" Timbo inquired of the two women sitting on the sand.

"We understand, Timbo. Yes, we'll be all right. After what we've been through, I don't think I'll be afraid of most things," Tasha said, managing a weak smile.

"Go on, Timbo. We'll be fine," Charmaine urged.

"Be back just as fast as these old legs will carry me." He gave them one of his big broad smiles, which swept away any doubts Charmaine harbored about this fierce-looking giant of a man. Timbo was kindhearted. He had risked his life to save them, and she would be forever beholden to him.

She watched him go, believing he'd do just what he'd promised. They could only sit there and wait patiently anyway. Neither woman spoke. They looked at the sea, which they now knew could be so dangerous, but the waters were deceptively calm, the sky a beautiful shade of blue. The warmth of the bright sun felt good, and the flocks of sea gulls proved entertaining as they followed a schooner slipping toward shore a few miles away.

Both young women felt serene, and no words were needed to express their feelings. They showed on their faces.

After Timbo had walked almost two miles, he knew how to get into the city. It was Georgia they were in, and Savannah was nearby. He did debate with himself over whether to head for Belle's shack or go directly to Miss Babette's Boutique. As Timbo recalled from his last visit with Belle, his sister only worked on certain days. He decided to follow his instincts and try the shack first. If he found Belle there, he could take the cart and mare, and return for the waiting ladies.

Two hours later, Timbo was thoroughly convinced God had guided him. He had found his sister at the shack as he'd hoped. Then he'd returned to the beach, set the two young women in the bed of the cart, which he'd thoughtfully covered with two old quilts, and hauled them back to his sister's.

Belle had been busy while her brother was fetching her unexpected "guests." She had a pot of chicory coffee brewed, black as coal. A simmering pot of beans was on the stove and she'd made some pan bread. Knowing Timbo was a ravenous eater, she put a pot of water on the stove so she could boil up a mountain of rice to supplement the beans.

Scurrying around the small shack, she put in order the numerous frocks she was sewing for Miss Babette. It was a strange sight, exquisite gowns hanging on pegs in Belle's meager cabin. The only luxuries in her home were the various articles the generous Babette Demoreau handed her in appreciation for her expertise and hard work. Belle cherished every little article her employer had given her for these items brightened her shack and her life.

As was her habit Belle performed her tasks speedily. When she was satisfied with the way her house looked, she helped herself to a cup of coffee and sat down to await Timbo's return. She took only one sip, however, before she heard a cart coming down the dirt road that followed the bend of the Savannah River.

By the time she set down the cup and threw the door open, Timbo was leaping down to help two pathetic-looking white ladies from her cart. They were the saddest sight to greet Belle's eyes for a long time, and she went forward to aid one

193

of the women while Timbo supported the other.

Belle was rewarded with a friendly smile as she led the petite lady up her steps and through the door. When Charmaine had been guided to one of the chairs by the stove, she thanked Timbo's tall slender sister. What a sharp contrast there was between the two of them, Charmaine thought.

"I'm Belle La Crosse, miss. Welcome to my home." Belle now saw the loveliness of her guest's face despite weariness reflected there.

"You're very kind to take us in like this. I . . . we're grateful to you and Timbo." Charmaine held out her hand to be shaken.

"Well, I'm happy Timbo's life was spared, and yours and your friend's too." Belle was already covering Charmaine with a wool blanket. "Just take the chill off while you have a few sips of my hot coffee and then we'll get you into dry clothes."

With swift motions Belle poured two cups of her chicory for the ladies, while Timbo covered Tasha by placing a blanket around her shoulders. The instant warmth of the blankets and the sips of strong chicory had a bracing effect on Charmaine and Tasha. Then Belle took charge of her guests, seeing that they stripped themselves of their damp, torn clothing.

While his sister busied herself with the ladies in the other room, Timbo helped himself to some more coffee and took one of the cakes of pan bread.

His huge body desperately needed food so he unceremoniously got a bowl from his sister's cupboard and ladled out a generous helping of the white fluffy rice, smothering it with beans, thick and rich with brown juice.

He was thoroughly enjoying his second spoonful of food when he heard Belle's harsh voice admonish him severely, "Shame on you, Timbo. You got no manners at all!"

"I'se starved, Belle. God Almighty, ain't ate nothin' in so

194

long," he declared, and the doleful look in his black eyes made Belle smile.

"Eat your fill then, but I imagine those poor ladies are just as hungry as you." She gave him a sisterly pat on his broad shoulders. "You did fine, Timbo! A fine thing! I'm proud of you."

"Thanks, Belle!" He gave her a big, broad grin before eagerly scooping up another heaping spoonful of beans and rice. Lord, it's good, Timbo thought to himself.

It was a strange scene in the small shack on the banks of the Savannah River that night, but Charmaine felt so warmed by the loving care of Belle and her brother Timbo, she knew she'd never forget them.

Tasha was enjoying the pleasant evening too. She ate so heartily of the beans and rice she was amazed. Then Timbo entertained them with his banjo and Belle sang some of the songs he played. There was laughter and gaiety in the shanty until at a late hour Belle announced that she must get some sleep since she had to deliver some sewing to Miss Babette's the next day.

Timbo, his blankets in his arms, retreated to Belle's shed to make his bed for the night. His sister intended to offer her bed to the two ladies while she made a pallet for herself on the floor, but Charmaine quickly refused.

"Belle, we've already put you to too much trouble and extra work. Besides, you've got to get some rest so you can work tomorrow. I'll take the pallet, and you and Tasha take the bed."

"Mercy, miss, I couldn't do that!" Belle's doelike eyes sparked with disbelief. Charmaine reminded her of the fragile daughters of the wealthy Georgia planters. Those young ladies frequented Miss Babette's. Now that Charmaine's face was washed, her complexion was flawless and soft like skin of the Savannah women who protected themselves with the parasols sold at the shop.

Charmaine laughed light-heartedly. "Well, I've another

solution. My Aunt Simone did this once to get three into her bed. Let me help you push that little cot over beside your bed, Belle. Then we can pile stuff on it to make it level. Three can lay across the length of a bed. I've done it."

Is this child telling me she doesn't mind sleeping with a negro? Belle wondered. Where did this sweet, innocent woman-child think she was? Up to now, Belle had considered Mademoiselle Babette the dearest, sweetest lady she'd ever known. She had a good, kind heart, but Lord, she wouldn't be caught dead sleeping in the same bed with her, Belle knew.

But the determined Mademoiselle Lamoureux was already busily pushing the cot over to Belle's bed, and Belle had to admit what she'd suggested did work for the length provided room the width didn't allow.

"Child, aren't you the clever one!" Belle giggled. Charmaine gave her an affectionate hug as she declared, "Well, you've got to admit it beats the floor. Now we'll all rest better. Neither Tasha nor I would sleep well knowing we'd deprived you of your bed. Would we, Tasha?"

"Oh, no . . . no we wouldn't." Tasha felt a bit guilty for she would not have been so considerate, and a wave of shame washed over her.

Once the shack lay in quiet darkness and the three women had retired, the divine comfort of a real bed felt absolutely wonderful to Tasha. There was a sweet fresh smell to the sheets covering her body, and the quilted woollen coverlet provided such warmth sleep came swiftly to Tasha Weer. But before she closed her eyes she vowed secretly to herself she'd never be so selfish again. She would be more like her friend Charmaine.

That night, the distance separating Pierre Renaud from the lady he loved so dearly was less than ten miles, but he had no way of knowing that.

He'd been in the shipping line's office that very day making arrangements to send a letter on the next packet leaving Savannah. Along with a letter to his beloved Charmaine, he also sent missives to England and France.

The office and the wharves were abuzz with the dismal news about the sinking of *Sea Witch* off the coast, and no one knew how many people were lost. But Pierre did not know the *Sea Witch* had carried his golden-haired enchantress.

This was a busy day for Pierre Renaud, and Jacques Bernay tagged along while his friend called at the Carlton Fleetline and then consulted a local banker.

Once again, Bernay was astounded by the many facets of Renaud's character. His encounters with influential businessmen amazed Jacques. The down-to-earth, fun-loving Renaud who'd joked and drunk with Captain Garrett had been replaced by a suave, debonair aristocrat, the epitome of a wealthy upbringing. Pierre was now a member of the *haut monde*.

For all his genuine liking for his friend, Bernay could not fight the envy welling up in him. It seemed to Jacques that Pierre had everything he himself should have had a portion of.

However, a strange thing happened late that afternoon, after Pierre had finished his business. Before they returned to the Magnolia House, they stopped at a tobacco shop so Renaud could purchase some cheroots. After the purchase was made, the two Frenchmen, jauntily puffing on their cheroots, got into their equipage, and it was easy to see that Pierre was in a good mood, satisfied with his accomplishments that day.

Leaning back against the plush seat of the carriage, Pierre gave Jacques a comradely slap on his cheek. In all seriousness, he declared to Bernay, "Wish I'd had a brother like you, Jacques. Think I got cheated being an only child. Really do!"

"Maybe not, *mon ami*. I've a solution. We'll become blood brothers. Who's to say we aren't, *oui?*"

"*Oui!* From this day forward we are brothers!"

Simultaneously, they broke into laughter, and Bernay knew that he'd never again be tormented by that devilish gnawing of envy. Pierre would not resent the fact that he was his half brother, of that Jacques felt certain!

Chapter 23

The biggest, grandest ball of the year was to be held in a fortnight and Babette Demoreau was going crazy wondering how she was ever to complete all the orders for gowns. When Belle told her about the two young ladies staying at her shack due to their misfortune, she thought it a good idea to hire Charmaine and Tasha to work at the shop.

Delighted by Mademoiselle Demoreau's offer of employment, Charmaine and Tasha were grateful for it as well. Neither of them had the funds to get from Savannah to Norfolk, and they did not like to be forced to remain at Belle's. It bothered them that they were a burden on her.

Their first week at the shack they had done the housework and prepared the meals in order to help her for she worked long hours for Babette. At least, when the weary Belle arrived back at the shack, her fingers sore from sewing, she had a clean house and warm meal awaiting her. Timbo had gotten himself a job down at the wharf. In the evenings when he returned to the shack, Charmaine and Tasha always asked if he'd heard of any other survivors from the *Sea Witch,* but when the answer was always no, a feeling of sadness engulfed them both.

On the evening Belle had come home with her news of work at the shop, Timbo came in with his ebony face all bright and smiling. "Guess what, Miss Charmaine? Heard today that a couple of men were washed ashore some forty or fifty miles north of Savannah. The description of one sorta' fit Captain Fleming. Lordy, I sure hope so. He's one fine man, the captain."

Excitedly, Charmaine declared, "Oh, I hope so, Timbo. She regretted being so harsh with Fleming when he'd been so kind except for stealing a kiss on deck that night. Pierre had stolen more than a kiss. He'd taken her virginity and had never bothered to seek her out again. He'd obviously thought her a simple farm girl, not the type of woman to become the bride of an aristocrat like Renaud. Only a lady of quality would be acceptable as his wife. Her husband had to be a man in a lower station. Someone like George Seymour was all she could expect to marry. What, she pondered, had he thought when she had not arrived? Was he heartbroken and desolate? And Tasha's brother Jacob must surely be mourning her supposed loss at sea.

At least, Timbo had brought good news. Captain Fleming might be alive. And it was also heartening that Charmaine now had a way to pay back the good-hearted Belle. The future looked brighter!

As the days passed and her life followed a certain routine at the boutique shop, Charmaine almost began to think of the shack beside the river as her home. Some days she'd sew along with Tasha and Belle, but often Mademoiselle Demoreau picked the beautiful Charmaine to make some of the deliveries to her special clients and patrons. Being a shrewd businesswoman, Babette saw the advantage in having Charmaine wear her creations when she went to make deliveries to the gentry.

One afternoon, when Charmaine returned after dropping gowns off at several mansions in the city and at a couple of the plantations on the outskirts, Babette invited her into the office. "I'd like to speak to you, *ma petite,"* she said. She had plans for this little charmer!

At first, Charmaine was apprehensive. She feared that she'd displeased the seamstress. But once she'd entered the privacy of Babette's office and removed the gorgeous velvet cape, one of Babette's new creations, she noticed a pleased smile on her employer's face so she relaxed.

The middle-aged seamstress was admiring her as well as the rich-looking russet cape with the warm fur lining the hood. Babette was a perfectionist about her ensembles for she believed every item of a lady's attire should enhance her image. She had insisted Charmaine wear a chocolate brown gown with a high neck and long fitted sleeves, her only adornment a gold lavaliere.

Charmaine accepted Mademoiselle Demoreau's offer of a cup of tea.

"I am smiling with such pleasure, Charmaine in case you're wondering. I find in you the most unique qualities, *ma petite.* Please, sit down for I'd like to talk to you," Babette requested as she went about the task of serving the tea.

Wide-eyed with wonder, Charmaine did as the forty-year-old matron requested. At least she could be thankful she'd not mishandled any of the deliveries.

"You, with your devastating looks and your stunning figure, could be a tremendous asset to my shop. Nice women like Belle and Tasha are ideal for the sewing room, but you, Charmaine, could promote my gowns."

"Me, *mademoiselle?* But I—"

"Mon Dieu, ma petite . . . don't you ever look in a mirror? Don't tell me you've not noticed the admiring stares of any gentleman within viewing distance of you?" Babette found it inconceivable that Charmaine could be that naïve. Was she actually a starry-eyed virgin, and with such a luscious body? The experienced, blasé Babette found that hard to believe, but the girl certainly seemed sincere.

"You know, I told you there was a rare quality about you.

Most young ladies are either sweet and demure or bold, flirtatious, and sensuous. You possess the qualities of both personalities. With your beautiful gold hair and your sparkling blue eyes, one man could look at you and see an innocent angel. But there is a twinkle in your eyes which gives you an air of raw sensuousness. This, *ma petite,* makes you a most bewitching temptress." Babette laughed and winked her green eyes devilishly.

Charmaine found herself mumbling Babette's words. "Raw sensuousness? I . . . I am afraid I'm lost, *mademoiselle.* I hope this is good not bad."

Babette exploded with light-hearted laughter. "Ah, *chérie,* that is very, very good. Some ladies I know would spend a fortune if it could be bought. Alas, it cannot, and that is why they pay my high prices for their gowns and buy the expensive jewels. You, Charmaine, seem to have been gifted by God." Babette decided the girl was as innocent as a babe.

"Well, I guess I must learn about this thing you say I have, *mademoiselle.* Perhaps, you will enlighten me?" Charmaine's face didn't reveal her thoughts to the seamstress, but she was wondering if this raw sensuousness of which that Mademoiselle Demoreau spoke had attracted such a man as Pierre and had driven Captain Fleming to boldly kiss her. Had it also made her dear Johnny throw common sense to the winds and care not that they were cousins? A part of her dwelled on her personal thoughts, though she was aware what Babette was saying.

"I will do my best, *chérie,* to tell you, but it is not something that is easy to put into words. Do you understand what I'm trying to say?"

"I think so."

"I do want you to think about my idea, Charmaine. Since I've gotten to know you a little better in the short time you've worked here I've gotten the impression that the gentleman you are going to marry doesn't delight you. Maybe I've misjudged the situation. If so, forget my offer. If not, this would be a way out for you. You wouldn't have to marry him."

"But I have promised. I would be breaking my vow, my word, *mademoiselle*.

"Vows are broken constantly, *ma petite*. Besides, tell me why you should marry a man you don't love. Why be miserable, little one, eh? If you tell me you love him, I will shut my mouth." The likable seamstress smiled, and Charmaine smiled in return, finding it hard to be offended by her very direct questioning. Actually, it was a tempting offer that she would think about, regardless of her declaration about keeping her vow.

In her straightforward manner, Charmaine admitted, "You are right. I don't love the man I was going to marry. But I do have an obligation to him since his money paid for my passage from Jersey."

"My dear innocent girl, work for me and repay the man whatever it was he gave to you. Think about it, Charmaine. Make no definite decision today." The vivacious boutique owner winked and flippantly remarked, "Who can say that I'm not giving you a chance to change the whole course of your life, *ma petite!* Don't hastily throw it away!"

Babette Demoreau politely dismissed the young lady and went about her duties, but she'd put Charmaine into a quandary.

Charmaine finally decided destiny had made Babette cross her path. She was a stranger in this country and surely she had been meant to meet the seamstress in Savannah instead of landing in Norfolk.

Excitedly, she told Tasha about Babette's offer, noticing that her friend was quiet a moment before she remarked, "You have a choice to make then."

Uncertainty prodded Charmaine to inquire, "Do you think I should go on to George even though I don't love him? I could be very happy working with Mademoiselle Demoreau. She's a kind woman, don't you think?"

Tasha quickly smiled and replied, "Of course. How could I not think so after she's been so good to us?" Tasha was admonishing herself for being disappointed that Charmaine would not be traveling with her on the packet which made the run from Savannah to Norfolk, for in less than two weeks' time she figured she'd have the amount she would need for the one way fare. Having to say goodbye to Charmaine instead of leaving with her, saddened Tasha. But she didn't want to let that influence Charmaine's decision. She knew she was being selfish.

"Tell me, Tasha, what do you really think? Should I stay and work for Mademoiselle Demoreau?"

Tasha's black eyes locked into Charmaine's searching blue gaze, and she said decisively, "I think you should do what will make you happy, Charmaine."

"Oh, thank you, Tasha. I think I shall!" The sparkling blue of Charmaine's eyes and the radiant glow on her face told Tasha what her decision was going to be.

She would be catching the packet alone. Charmaine would be staying in Savannah.

Two weeks later, Tasha was leaving Savannah. Almost a month later than her planned arrival, she would be reunited with her brother in Norfolk. The anticipation of seeing her beloved Jacob after so many years took some of the bitter edge off the sad farewell on the wharf before she boarded the *East Wind*. The little coastal packet would be making its regular stops at Charleston and Wilmington before docking at Norfolk.

Timbo had brought her and Charmaine to the pier in Mademoiselle Demoreau's fine carriage, and Tasha wore a new frock and cloak, a gift from Babette. With a heavy heart she said goodbye to the dear people she'd come to love. Belle had tears in her eyes when Tasha hugged her, and so did Babette when she told them she'd be forever grateful for their

204

kindness and generosity.

The giant black man had a hint of mist in his dark eyes when he said goodbye. After walking with Tasha as far as he could, he offered his huge hand for a final handshake, but Tasha clutched him about his thick waist, not caring what passersby might think of her hugging a black man.

Last of all she said goodbye to Charmaine. That was the hardest farewell. Neither tried to hold back their tears as they embraced one another. When they stepped back, Charmaine wiped her eyes and giggled nervously. In a faltering voice cracking with emotion, she declared, "This isn't our last goodbye. I'll come to Norfolk to visit you, I swear it! I'll save the money I earn and get on a packet. I promise, Tasha."

"I'm going to hold you to that, Charmaine," Tasha told her in a sobbing voice.

"I promise we'll see one another before spring is over and summer begins. There, that will give us both something to look forward to."

Somehow, that thought eased the pain of the farewell, and their tears ceased. Smiles brightened their faces as Charmaine turned to walk away.

She turned back once and called out to Tasha, "Spring isn't too far away. Goodbye for now, Tasha."

"Goodbye, Charmaine and . . . and take care of yourself." Tasha waved her gloved hand.

Chapter 24

The little miss is awfully quiet, Timbo thought as he drove the carriage back to the shop. But he noted that the look on Charmaine's lovely face was reflective, not sad. Indeed, memories consumed her.

Draped in her warm, luxurious cape of bottle green wool and the matching bottle green frock, she found it amazing that she was now dressed in the magnificent attire she'd so envied Sarnia Wakefield for having. How could one explain, much less understand, the strange circumstances that had changed her life.

Her existence had been routine and uneventful there on the farm with Angus and Simone, until that fateful night on the cliffs. Then the full moon seemed to have changed her life forever. Now, in the brief period of a few months, she had traveled the vast distance from maidenhood to womanhood. What a staggering distance it was!

To Charmaine, it seemed that one shocking blow after another had slammed into her before she had even recovered from the first. It had all started with the handsome stranger's kiss in the moonlight. Her lover, Pierre seemed to be the spark that had ignited all the strange happenings that had occurred in this brief interlude.

The next blow had been the discovery that her cousin,

whom she loved as a brother, was romantically attracted to her. That had opened Charmaine's eyes to the fact that she knew nothing about the ways of men.

While her head was still whirling over that disturbing situation, George Seymour had entered her life. But it was Pierre Renaud who had opened that door through which she could never go back. The night she'd known his all-consuming love, surrendering completely, she'd learned what it was like to love a man.

Later, through Sarnia, Charmaine had learned the pain of loving, and that had been a crushing, heartbreaking blow. Yet that pain and deep hurt had made her grow up. Now, she felt like a woman. Of course, the stark terror of the shipwreck had also matured her. Facing the possibility of death is very enlightening.

If Timbo thought her pensive mood was due to the departure of her friend Tasha, he was wrong. Charmaine Lamoureux was not sad. In fact, serenity engulfed her, and she'd never felt so self-assured about what she wanted and how she was going to live her life. The feeling was exhilarating.

She was thinking about working for the kindhearted, Mademoiselle Demoreau, about wearing her lovely clothes around the city of Savannah. That prospect appealed to her independent nature. It was certainly more exciting than being George Seymour's wife and spending her days and nights on a farm.

By the time Timbo had brought the carriage to a halt and had offered his hand to assist her down to the walkway in front of the shop, she was radiant.

Babette noticed the new serenity about her, and she asked herself why she had not noticed the changes in the girl. The sophisticated dressmaker had to confess that the transformation was due to more than her gorgeous gown. This presence had been in Charmaine all the time, lying dormant and waiting to be awakened.

It was no surprise to Babette when one of her wealthy patrons noticed Charmaine and inquired about who she was. However, when the wealthy Monsieur Lomax appeared the following day at the shop and in the privacy of Babette's office approached her about Charmaine accompanying his friend to the Grand Ball, she was stunned.

"Let me explain, Mademoiselle Demoreau. My friend is coming from Atlanta, and it would be nice if a charming young lady would accompany him to this function. I assure you it would be all very proper."

Babette knew she must choose her comments very carefully. Lomax spent most generously on gowns for his beautiful mistress. To offend him would cause her a terrible loss. Yet, she wanted no part in turning Charmaine into the hapless prey of some lecher.

"I will do whatever I can, Monsieur Lomax, but of course, you realize it is the young lady's decision to accept or refuse your kind invitation."

A sly smile broke out on Lomax's atristocratic face as he replied. "But of course, dear lady. However, I'm sure Mademoiselle Lamoureux also puts great store by your judgment, so I would appreciate your informing her of my invitation and letting me know how she responds."

Babette caught his insidious meaning, and she sought to jest. "Ah, *monsieur,* she is a free spirit with a mind and will of her own. Charmaine is a rare young lady who bends to no will—mine included."

"Ah, you make her sound most enchanting, madame. You whet my determination to see that she accompanies my friend." Lomax gave her a broad grin.

Babette forced a smile to her face, though she realized she'd most likely outfoxed herself. It had not been her intention to make Charmaine sound more exciting to the gentleman.

When Lomax left her shop she mentioned his proposal to Charmaine, and found some consolation in the young woman's excitement about the prospect of going to the Grand Ball, at least until Charmaine candidly said, "But I just happened to think about something. Why would he invite me for his friend? Monsieur Lomax is the friend of Mademoiselle Lisa Conroy, isn't he? Doesn't he come in here with her?"

"That's right. As to why he would invite you to join them, *ma petite,* it is the way it is done. When a gentleman sees a very beautiful lady he will go to amazing lengths to meet her and to try to win her favor." A skeptical frown appeared on Babette's face as she asked Charmaine, "Tell me, dear, have you never had a love affair? I don't mean to pry, but you seem so . . . so inexperienced."

"I've been in love with a man, Mademoiselle Babette if that is what you're asking me. But only one." Charmaine's pain was as hurtful as an old wound which was being jabbed.

Her declaration eased Babette's concern that she would be sending Charmaine into a "lion's den" should Lomax's friend be a randy sort. At least the young woman had had some experience with a man.

Belle styled Charmaine's golden locks into a most flattering hairdo. Masses of long curls fell down her back, like glossy rolls of gold, whereas the side tresses were swept up to meet at the back of her head in a lovely crown of smaller ringlets. Tiny, teasing wisps covered her ears, and a jeweled aigrette of deep blue and purple plumes decorated Charmaine's crown of curls. The plumes matched the glorious gown Babette had chosen to allow Charmaine to wear to the ball. It was a taffeta moire imported from France, and the material was a blending of blue and purple hues.

The full flowing skirt made a swishing sound at the slightest movement of Charmaine's body, and the deep-cut neckline was outlined by a ruffle that extended over

210

Charmaine's satiny-smooth shoulders. She was a stunning sight! A magnificent blue velvet cape lined in purple taffeta was the final touch for the gown. Babette felt Charmaine's appearance would sell a dozen or more orders of these garments. She pridefully admired her little "mannequin."

As she watched Charmaine leave in the carriage, she felt rather like a fairy godmother. Charmaine was indulging in a fantasy too, until she arrived at the palatial mansion of Leonard Lomax and was ushered into the lavish parlor.

A trio sat before her, sipping champagne. She recognized Lisa Conroy immediately. The woman was seated on the brocade settee beside Leonard Lomax. She also recognized her expensive gown adorned with seed pearls for it had been finished just a few days ago. The elegantly attired Lomax instantly rose from the settee to greet her and introduce her to the others in the room.

"Absolutely stunning, my dear! Isn't she gorgeous? I think you know Lisa, don't you, Charmaine?"

"Yes, I do, Monsieur Lomax. Good evening, Mademoiselle Conroy." She tried to keep her voice from cracking, but she yearned to flee the room as fast as her satin slippers would allow. The sight of her escort was a shock. His balding head and paunchy girth were abhorrent, his lusty eyes and smirking mouth revolting.

Lisa Conroy's greeting was curt and cool, but Lomax laughed. "Chauncey, did I not find you a lovely lady? Chauncy Bedlow, this is Mademoiselle Charmaine Lamoureux. Now, please have a seat, then you and Chauncey can get acquainted over a glass of champagne."

She wanted to scream that she wasn't about to sit down by the old fool leering at her, but she slowly took a seat and endured his hand clasp. "Charmaine . . . such a fitting name for one so very charming. French, is it not? Well, France surely has more than its share of beautiful ladies, but you are beyond description. Words fail me right now."

"You . . . you are very kind, Monsieur Bedlow," she

stammered, aching to remove her hand from his.

"Now, come, my little dear, call me Chauncey. This is too festive a night for formality, and one I'm anticipating now that I've seen you."

Charmaine managed to smile, but she was thinking she should have known the price of such an invitation. Why, this man was older than Angus, and she didn't like the way he pressed against her side the minute she sat down next to him.

She tried to think of some way to get out of her promise to accompany them to the ball. Everything about this evening was appalling to her now, and she wanted only to escape, to hurry back to Babette's shop or Belle's cozy shack. Her mind whirled, full of wild ideas for a swift exit.

She sipped on the champagne. She knew Chauncey's beady eyes were devouring her, but she didn't care, nor did she gaze his way. The conversation the three were holding was not even registering with her. Their low, monotonous drone could have been that of a hive of bees.

Suddenly, she became aware of being assisted up from the brocade settee by the obnoxious Chauncey, and she felt his hot breath against her ear as he told her, "Time to be on our way to the ball, my dear Charmaine. I'll help you with your cape."

"Oh, y-yes, Chauncey," Charmaine absent-mindedly muttered. An urgent voice within her frantically insisted that she must quickly make her move if she were to get out of this distasteful affair.

When the smiling potbellied Bedlow came through the archway, her blue cape flung over his arm, he noticed the solemn look on her face. "My dear? Charmaine? What's the matter?"

She allowed him to drape the cape around her dainty shoulders before remarking with a most distressed look on her face, "I'm so very embarrassed I could just die. I don't know how to tell you, Chauncey, I really don't." Her look of utter dismay prodded Bedlow to ask, "What can Chauncey do, my pretty little one?"

Her golden head bowed in humiliation, she softly announced, "I want to say how sorry I am, Monsieur Lomax and Mademoiselle Conroy, but I must ask to be taken home immediately. Forgive me, Chauncey, for I'm as disappointed as you, but I'm most ill—too ill to attend a ball. My stomach! I'd likely prove an embarrassment to you and I dare not chance it." Dramatically she brought her dainty lace-edged handkerchief to her mouth as if to convey she might retch.

"*Dear God!*" the disgruntled Lisa shrieked. From the first she'd resented Leonard's idea to have one of Babette Demoreau's employees join them.

Lomax was stunned by this new development, but his keen, sharp mind was used to dealing with dilemmas so he quickly suggested to Chauncey, "Lisa and I will take the other carriage. You take the one waiting at the entrance. Escort her home and then join us, eh Chauncey?"

A mumbling, perplexed Bedlow took Charmaine's arm and led her down the hallway. Within his paunchy body, he pulsed and seethed with irritation because the evening was falling apart before it had even gotten started.

When they were seated in the carriage, he noticed Charmaine sat calmly without the handkerchief to her mouth. The light of the full moon allowed just enough light inside the carriage for him to see her face. She hardly appears to be ill now, he thought to himself. Chauncey ached with his overwhelming yearning to taste the sweet nectar of her, and fired with burning desire, he decided to try a desperate measure, which could reward him with what he wanted most at this moment.

"You seem to feel a little better. Your face isn't so pale now," he told her.

"I . . . I feel just a little better, I think. Maybe the air," Charmaine told him.

Chauncey turned down a different street than the one he would have taken had he gone directly to the dress shop. He felt the little minx was faking, and if she was, he was going to teach her a lesson. He'd been subjected to the trickery of younger women before. Since he knew he was not good looking or young, he realized ladies' attentions were often inspired by his vast wealth. But Charmaine was unaware of his holdings, so Chauncey figured it was his age that had inspired her sudden illness. This riled him even more.

For a while Charmaine wasn't aware of how far out of the way Bedlow had taken her, not until she began to notice surroundings which were not familiar. "Are we on the right road?"

"You leave it to Chauncey. I'll get you home. But if we can't share the evening and the ball we can certainly share a pot of tea. That's little to ask after such a grave disappointment, I think."

Charmaine thought there was a slightly sharp edge to his words, so she nodded her head, agreeing to his suggestion.

Chauncey Bedlow was taking her to a nice tea room, but to an inn he'd frequented more than once when he visited Lomax in Savannah. There was a tavern below and there were rooms on the second floor, with a convenient back stairway.

The carriage came to a halt and he leaped to the ground, extending his hand to Charmaine. It was too dark for her to see the name of the establishment. But when he led her up the steps to the second floor, which had a roofed porch exactly like the one on the ground level, she was flooded with grave misgivings.

His hand roughly grasped her arm, and she felt he was rushing her across the porch and inside the door.

As they entered a man at the door spoke to Chauncey, and Charmaine mumbled, "You've obviously been here before, but I honestly should have gone home. I . . . I can't stay long. One cup of tea is all, Chauncey."

"One cup of tea, my dear," he echoed.

As they moved down the darkened hallway, Charmaine

214

didn't like the sounds she heard nor the foul smell that struck her nostrils. Every fiber in her body was alert to impending danger as he urged her down the hallway.

Instinctively, she sensed the powerful determination churning within Bedlow, but she didn't know how vile and evil it was!

By now, Chauncey was completely obsessed by his aching desire to possess her. Whether she would surrender to him or not was no longer of consequence. She could fight or scratch like a wildcat, but Chauncey was determined to have her.

He'd show her he wasn't too old to master her, the tiny little mite!

Chapter 25

Her golden curls were no longer fashioned in the style Belle had so expertly contrived. Now they fell askew, and Charmaine brushed a couple off her tear-stained face as she stood frozen, looking at the limp, lifeless figure of Chauncey Bedlow. The obese man's balding head was bleeding profusely.

In her trembling hand, she still held the candleholder, the brass stained with Chauncey's blood. She wished that the room had been in total darkness, but the dim light of one candle illuminated the nightmarish sight, etching the memory of his slobbering mouth and vile, lustful hands in her thoughts.

She tried to quit sobbing, and her hands fumbled to cover her exposed breast. But seeing that it was impossible—her gown was badly torn—she flung her cape around her, knowing she should listen to the voice within her and get out of this miserable place as fast as she could.

A dozen questions paraded through her dazed mind. Where was she? How far was she from the shop, from Belle's? In which direction should she head once she was outside? But her most immediate problem was how to get past the man at the door. Just go, you little fool, the voice urged to her, so she turned her back on the grotesque Bedlow and hastened out of the room.

Luckily, the man was not at the door. She scurried across the porch to the steps, and when she stepped onto the ground, she took a deep breath of night air, then tucked the cape tighter around her petite body.

Which direction should she take? Obviously, the establishment's front entrance faced the road. She glanced fleetingly at the carriage belonging to Lomax, sitting where Bedlow had left it. She dared not take it, for then she'd be a thief. It is ironic to worry about that after what I've done to Bedlow, she thought. She could have sworn he was dead from the hard blow she'd given him with the heavy brass candleholder.

A noise at the corner of the building provoked a new surge of fright. It sounded as though someone was moving toward the hitching post where some horses were tied so she dashed swiftly in the opposite direction.

Her fleeing footsteps were heard by the departing patron of the tavern, and he turned sharply to listen, then peered into the darkness. He was at the point of drawing the small pocket pistol he'd brought with him when he caught sight of the woman rushing directly toward him.

She was so busy looking behind her she had not noticed him so he prepared himself to stop her from ramming into him. Just as she was within his reach the moonlight burst through the tall oaks and he saw the gold of her hair. For a fleeting moment he felt his heart pound wildly. No, it cannot be, he reasoned.

She came to a halt as his arms caught her, and she let out a pitiful gasp of fear. "Oh, please, *monsieur!* Please hel—" Her words froze as she stared wide-eyed into a pair of disbelieving cold gray eyes.

Pierre could not speak. He simply stared down at the face which had haunted him day and night. If he was hallucinating then he wanted to keep on doing so. But she was flesh and blood. He could feel the pulsing of her little

218

body, now pressed against his. "Charmaine, it is you! It's really you!"

Charmaine felt faint, but she managed to nod her head. "Please, Pierre, take me away from here as fast as you can. I'm . . . I'm in trouble."

But for the fact that she was so very serious and scared, he would have broken into laughter, it was so exhilarating to hold her close to him. Aware of her violent trembling, however, he lifted her into his arms and carried her to his horse. Hoisting her into the saddle, he leaped up to straddle the beast.

"I must say I'm curious to hear about your trouble, Charmaine, and about why you are in a place of such ill repute," he told her as his hands and arms squeezed her tighter. He was now pondering so many tormenting possibilities that his own head was whirling. He'd last seen this golden-haired maiden on the isle of Jersey. He had fallen madly in love with her after deflowering her, and he had been determined to carry her away to America.

Now, months after he'd been unable to keep his promise to meet with her, he had found her, in a state of disarray, departing a tavern and saying that she was in trouble. Had he been mistaken about her?

If Charmaine could have read his thoughts at that moment she would not have been finding his arms so comforting. But unable to do so, as the horse cantered away from that horrid inn, she felt safe and secure. She didn't even ask where Pierre was taking her, nor did she care.

Calm now, in a soft voice, she murmured, "Yes, I'll tell you everything, Pierre."

"Everything, *ma petite?* Will you explain what you meant by trouble, Charmaine? I can't imagine it is too serious if you're the same girl I met on Jersey." He grinned.

"I . . . I think I may have killed a man."

Pierre knew she wasn't jesting. Such was not her nature. His expression became serious.

"You what? I don't believe you, Charmaine."

As she felt his muscled body tense, she turned slightly to look up at his handsome face. Quite candidly, she replied, "I am telling the truth, Pierre. I had to, if I wished not to be ravaged by the lecher."

"Then why did you put yourself in a position to invite such behavior?" he said sharply.

Now, she was the one who tensed, and her anger made her realize the reality she now faced. She couldn't return to the shop if she had killed Chauncey Bedlow. Indeed, she could seek help from no one but Pierre. But would he help her? She could only pray he would.

"Is there a place where we can talk, Pierre? I need desperately to talk to you." Charmaine's voice was emotional, pleading.

"I was just about to ask where I might take you, but I was not about to take you there just yet. I deserve a reward—a kiss—for this rescue, *chérie.*" His arms squeezed her a little tighter.

When she turned, giving him one of those sweet, lovely smiles which he found it impossible to resist, his lips met hers. So long had he yearned to taste the sweet nectar of her lips that flaming desire consumed him. Pulling up on the reins, he gasped huskily, "Damned, you bewitching little vixen, if I'm not tempted to take you right here and now!"

Charmaine could not reply, for his hungry mouth captured hers again and she pressed closer against his firm chest, wanting to absorb the heat and warmth of his closeness.

When he finally released her, she moaned breathlessly when she realized he'd turned her so that she was sitting atop his two thighs. The heat of his body was fierce!

"I'm taking you to my lodgings at the inn—a very respectable one by the way. You will be my sister, Charmaine. Understand?"

"Yes, I understand."

A mischievous grin appeared on his face as he informed her, "But I assure you, Charmaine, *ma chérie,* that I'll not treat you like a sister this night. I want you and I'll have you."

She said nothing, but her eyes locked with his. Her answer was in those deep pools of blue, so he spurred the horse into a fast gallop for he was impatient to get to the Magnolia House.

Charmaine stood in the bedroom while Pierre whispered to the man who'd peered through the door of the adjoining room. She knew Pierre was explaining her presence, and embarrassment washed over her, as well as resentment. She wondered if the man considered her some cheap trollop Pierre had picked up because he kept staring at her around Pierre's shoulder.

When the man had shut the door, Pierre turned back to her, saying, "Take off your cape, Charmaine. I'll get us some brandy." He proceeded to take some glasses and the bottle of French brandy from the chest.

When he brought the brandy to where she sat on the edge of the bed he noticed that she looked forlorn and was still draped in the blue cape. With a puzzled look on his face, he questioned her. "Are you chilled, Charmaine? This will warm you up."

She took the brandy and thanked him. "No, I'm not cold but . . . but my gown is ripped badly."

Rage ignited within Pierre at the thought of some bastard mauling Charmaine. "Let me see!" he commanded. His gray eyes gleamed like silver. She did as he'd bid, slowly removing the cape and looking up with a childlike innocence which only made his rage mount.

"Drink your brandy and we shall have our talk, *chérie.* I don't intend to wait any longer, especially now." His eyes devoured the satiny flesh so tantalizing to his eyes. When she had taken a few sips of the potent liquor, he asked her to tell him everything that had happened to her since he'd left her that night on the cliff. "I want to know everything, Charmaine," he declared.

She proceeded to do as he asked, and when she told him of her betrothal to George Seymour a displeased expression appeared on his face.

"Does he know that you still live?" Pierre asked.

"How could he know?"

"More to the point, Charmaine, I question how he could let a young, beautiful girl like you—his bride-to-be—come such a distance alone and unescorted." Pierre thought the man must be daft—certainly, he didn't deserve such a beauty—but he'd deal with that issue later. What concerned him more right now was the bastard who'd molested her.

Charmaine could not argue with him about George. She, too, had questioned Seymour's lack of concern that she'd be traveling alone across a vast ocean.

"Tell me about tonight. Just how did you happen to lower yourself to keep a rendezvous at such a place as that?"

She bristled at his lordly attitude and said so. "You were there, were you not? Are there two sets of standards, one for men and the other for ladies?" A defiant look on her face, she boldly stared at him.

"*Chérie* I was there on business, certainly not for pleasure. Now, tell me what I asked you!"

She quickly replied, "I was to have been that man's guest at the ball—that despicable man . . . Bedlow. But the sight of him sickened me so I pretended to be ill. He was supposed to be taking me home. Instead, he took me to that . . . that awful place to seduce me. When I was fighting him off, I grabbed the candleholder and hit him. I didn't intend to kill him, but I fear I did. He didn't move, and I don't think he was breathing."

He believed her story although he told himself he probably shouldn't have. "It's a good thing then you didn't return to the shop where you work. In fact, we'd best keep

222

you in seclusion until I can get you out of Savannah." While he spoke, his mind was on another subject. Much as it pained him to deny himself her charms, there was an errand he must attend to for her welfare and their future together.

"Renaud, you talk as if you're taking charge of my life," she snapped sharply, as he paced back and forth by the side of the bed and gulped the last drop of the brandy in his glass.

"God knows someone should, it seems," Pierre curtly replied. "Who knew you were with this Bedlow tonight, Charmaine?"

She told him as she continued to sip the brandy in her glass. By now she was beginning to like the taste of it, and to appreciate the calming effect it was having on her.

"Charmaine, I've got to leave you for a while but I'm leaving you in safe hands. The man in the next room is my good friend, Jacques Bernay. I'm going in there to tell him my plans, and I want you to get some rest." He approached the bed on which she sat, his handsome face mellow and compassionate. He bent down to kiss the top of her head, but that didn't satisfy him so his two hands caressed her cheeks and his lips slowly came down on hers with gentle tenderness.

That kiss became torment, for now it made it hard to leave her. But he had no choice! Without procrastinating longer, he started to move away from her. "Rest, *mademoiselle,* because when I get back I intend to collect my reward."

Without further ado, he left the room. A few moments later, there was a rap on the door and a man's voice called out to her, "Mademoiselle Lamoureux, may I come in? I'm Jacques Bernay, Pierre's friend."

"Please do," she replied, checking the torn bodice of her gown to make sure her bosom was concealed.

He gave her a warm, friendly smile and politely told her, "Nice to meet you, *mademoiselle.* Pierre asked me to check your door to be certain it was secure."

Charmaine took an instant liking to this man with the

223

twinkling eyes and friendly face. While he was older than Renaud, he was robust and stoutly built, and his jet black hair was as curly as Tasha's. He immediately made her feel at ease, and she liked and trusted him.

When Jacques was satisfied that the door was securely locked, he turned toward his own door. Just as he was about to go back into his room, he gave her another warm, friendly smile and said, "Now you can rest, and so shall I. There would be the devil to pay if my friend returned to find you were not where he'd left you. *Bonsoir, mademoiselle.*"

"Good night, Monsieur Bernay."

Jacques now knew why Pierre Renaud had fallen in love with the golden-haired girl he'd met on the isle of Jersey. He, too, could have done so, but his deep loyalty for his friend prohibited doing so.

Chapter 26

It seemed to Pierre Renaud that he was the only person moving through the darkness of the early morning hour. The city slept as he traveled down the quiet, deserted street toward the Magnolia House. He had more than one reason to be ready for the comfort of his bed this night. He needed the comfort the woman in it could give him, and by now, he needed it sorely.

He had returned to the inn from which he'd rescued Charmaine earlier, and he had found the man, Bedlow, dead as Charmaine had feared. A just punishment, Renaud thought. Like a cat, he'd slipped into the run-down shambles of a tavern and had gone to the second-floor room Charmaine had described to him. Although he had peered into a couple of rooms by mistake, the occupants were too drunk or too engrossed in their activities to notice him. The whole scene made him furious at the man who'd taken Charmaine there, and if he'd not found Bedlow dead, he would have taken a devilish delight in killing him. However, that was not necessary. His love had taken care of the bastard. He reminded himself as he rode back to the Magnolia House that he'd better remember what a wallop she packed in case she ever got really angry with him.

Having returned, he was taking long, hurried strides down

the carpeted hallway toward his room when he swore he smelled the sweet aroma of jasmine wafting to his nose.

Oh, he planned to make the little vixen pay dearly for all the trouble he'd gone through this night. But now he could rest easy for he knew there was nothing left in that room to link her to the killing of Chauncey Bedlow. Who could prove that Bedlow had not gone there alone after taking Mademoiselle Lamoureux home? he reasoned.

However, he didn't plan to linger much longer in Savannah. In fact, the sooner they left the better it would be for everyone. Charmaine would most assuredly accompany him and Jacques, even if he had to hogtie her. Damned if he'd take her to any George Seymour!

As he unlocked the door and stepped quietly inside, the intoxicating fragrance she wore greeted him and he smiled. He wondered if she was asleep or lying there waiting for him?

The heat of desire rushed over him and he quickly yanked off his coat, flinging it carelessly on the floor. By now, he could see the sensuous curves of her petite body outlined by the sheet. What a tempting sight it was, for he immediately remembered the silken feel of her skin on that night in the cove.

So quietly she lay, Pierre figured she had drifted off to sleep. He decided that was just as well because he had no intention of telling her about his mission.

While he was slipping out of his clothing, he imagined what it would be like when she awoke in his arms to find his naked body pressed against hers. Tonight they had a soft, comfortable bed to lie upon. Before, they had made love on a beach in the seclusion of a sheltering cove, but that hadn't seemed to bother her. Her long, thick hair fanned out over the pillows. It looked like spun gold.

Just before he was about to sink down on the bed, he quietly closed the drapes for he did not want the sunrise to invade the room.

When he moved back to the bed and slowly slipped

between the sheets, he was a man burning with anticipation. He felt the sweet flush of her body even before he touched her.

As the warmth of his firmly muscled thighs pressed against her, Charmaine turned lazily toward him. He rose up on one elbow, then bent to kiss her cheek, letting his lips trail over to her soft, surrendering lips. In a sleepy voice she murmured, "Pierre? Is that you?"

"It sure as the devil better be, *ma petite,*" he whispered. As his mouth claimed her rosebud lips in an urgent, demanding kiss she fitted her body to his. Her soft, supple breasts pressed against his chest, driving his passion to new heights.

His hands took delight in exploring the satin touch of her body, and it pleased him to hear her sighs of pleasure. "Oh, my Charmaine, I've yearned for you many, many nights," he moaned in a husky voice.

"And I wanted you just as much, Pierre," she confessed. Her body was undulating more fiercely now for his lips had captured one of her breasts. His tongue leisurely teased the jutting tip creating a magic madness within her.

Her fingertips pressed into his back and she cried out her pleasure. He fought his own impatience, wanting her sweet rapture to last as long as possible. But she was such a tantalizing little vixen he was in torment. So hungry for her! The mere touch of her aroused an untamed need and he was no longer master of his own will.

Charmaine was titillated with each new caress, each part of her his fingers or his sensuous lips touched responding. She cried out with excited anguish, "Oh, God . . . Pierre! Please!"

Unable to resist her urging, he moved between her silken thighs and buried himself deep within her. She arched to absorb the essence of him, letting her velvety softness enfold him.

Their bodies moved as one, each new wave of rapture building and mounting like the incoming rush of the tide invading the shore.

When each of them would have sworn no more tantalizing wave could arise, a new surge of pleasure flowed through them. Then as the swift waters of the bay struck the cliff on Jersey, exploding into rivulets of sparkling water, Pierre's passion exploded. Charmaine gasped.

She clung to him in breathless wonder, in delight, crying out his name, filled with the overwhelming love she felt for him. Could she have wished time to stand still it would be at this moment when Pierre's warmth enfolded her.

"My sweet, sweet Charmaine," he murmured softly in her ear. "I'll never let you go again. Never!"

It didn't matter to Renaud that a man in Virginia had a claim on her. He knew he'd be a fool to deliver her into other hands. Besides in Pierre's opinion, since Seymour had made such a ridiculous arrangement for her to join him in America, he did not deserve such a precious jewel as Charmaine Lamoureux.

These thoughts parading through his mind, he held her in his arms, their bodies still flushed from the heat of passion, and he said nothing about his plans. His arms encircled Charmaine possessively, and finally the fluttering caress of her long eyelashes against his cheek told him she was drifting off to sleep.

Under his breath, he bid her good night and pleasant dreams. He knew his own sleep would be peaceful and deep. Her lovely face would not haunt him tonight for he had her beside him. His dream had come true.

The next morning Charmaine slept, undisturbed and unaware of the hubbub around her. She didn't even know that Renaud left her side and got dressed. Once again, he put Bernay in charge of looking after his lady while he scouted around the city of Savannah to listen for any repercussions to last night's episode. He hoped to find out whether the body of Chauncey Bedlow had been discovered as yet.

Pierre Renaud was not the only gentleman scouring the streets of Savannah on this bright sunny morning. Monsieur Lomax was making the rounds of various haunts his friend Chauncey liked to visit when he came to Savannah. But, after a couple of stops yielded no clues to the whereabouts of Bedlow, Lomax decided to pay a call on Mademoiselle Demoreau's shop to speak to Charmaine.

However, Lomax figured that Chauncey had taken the young woman home and had then gone straight to the high-class brothel he usually frequented when he came to town. So he went first to the Riverboat, where Madame Rocha, who operated the establishment, assured him that his friend had not been there at any time last evening.

Up to this point Leonard Lomax had mixed emotions, anger and concern. After paying a visit to Mademoiselle Demoreau's shop, however, he was confused as well. He'd been unable to speak with Charmaine Lamoureux because she had not been there.

As a young woman Babette had been on the stage, and she'd drawn on that experience to feign disgust with the young lady who'd not shown up for work when, in truth, she'd feared harm had come to Charmaine. Knowing that Lomax was looking for his guest, she was now truly petrified. As soon as Lomax had left the shop after she'd calmly told him she could be of no help to him whatsoever, she rushed behind the curtain where she knew Belle had been listening.

"*Mon Dieu,* where could she be, Belle? I'll never forgive myself for putting her into such a situation."

"Oh, Lord, let's pray she's all right, Mademoiselle Babette . . . that sweet Charmaine." Belle sighed and her black eyes filled with sadness.

"But if something wasn't very wrong she would be here. I am worried, Belle. This just isn't like her at all."

As they were discussing Charmaine the little bell on the

door of the shop jingled, announcing the impressive man who entered. His piercing eyes looked first at the older woman and then at the tall, willowy black woman standing by her side.

"Mademoiselle Demoreau?" When he walked up to stand before her, his striking good looks made Babette forget momentarily about her concern for Charmaine. It had been a long, long time since her breath had almost stopped due to the effect of a man's closeness. "I am Mademoiselle Demoreau. May I be of help to you, *monsieur?*"

Pierre Renaud flashed her a broad grin. "I rather imagine you can. I need some articles for a young lady." He wanted to measure the two women Charmaine had spoken so highly about. The black woman was surely Belle, who'd taken her in after the shipwreck.

"Monsieur, I can, if I know the size of the lady and what kind of garments you wish to purchase," Babette assured him, having regained her usual sophisticated air.

Pierre described the types of garments he wanted: proper traveling attire, and comfortable, undergarments and nightgowns and robes. Then, with amazing expertise, he described the lady's measurements for Babette.

She nodded her head, exclaiming excitedly, "Ah, *monsieur* luckily I have many of the things you mentioned in that exact size." Many garments had been especially made for Charmaine to wear and display, and Babette was thinking that was now fortunate.

Pierre noticed the black woman's intense eyes measuring him, and he could hardly keep an amused smile from creasing his face.

As the two women worked, stacking the items neatly on a counter, he ambled around the shop. Finally, feeling the need to smoke one of his cheroots, he informed them he'd return shortly. "I must get some tobacco, just down the street, while my purchases are being packaged. I'll be back in a half-hour, *mademoiselle."*

When he'd gone out the door into the street, Belle turned to Babette and declared, "Mercy, some lady sure got herself a lot of man there! Ever see such a handsome one, Mademoiselle Babette?"

"Not in a long time, Belle. The sight of him recalled a wonderful time in my life. It also reminded me of how lonely and how disgustingly old I am," Babette told the devoted Belle.

"You aren't all that old now, *mademoiselle*. I won't listen to you talk so about yourself. No, ma'am."

They shared a moment of light-hearted laughter before the front door bell jingled again. Both turned, expecting to see that the handsome man had returned, but two middle-aged gentlemen entered, took their hats off, and bowed. One announced that he was the constable. He went on to say he was seeking a young lady by the name of Charmaine Lamoureux.

At this moment Pierre Renaud reentered the shop in time to hear Babette politely say, "I'm afraid I can't help you, Constable Brown. The girl no longer works here. She has just disappeared, like a ghost. We have no idea where she went, do we, Belle?"

"That's right . . . like a ghost! But what's the law looking for Mademoiselle Charmaine for?" Belle blurted out.

An indignant look on his ruddy face and a gruff tone to his voice, Brown snapped out, "Murder, gal. That's what!"

As the men marched out the door, paying no attention to Pierre, oblivious to his return, Belle mumbled, "That sweet child didn't kill no one, unless it was someone needed killin' in the first place. I know that for sure!"

Babette was as upset as Belle, and she could not help but sigh dejectedly. "If only we knew what's become of her, Belle." Suddenly, she realized her customer had returned and was overhearing their conversation. "Please, forgive us, *monsieur*. We've just had some disturbing news about a friend."

231

"Ladies . . . don't apologize. I understand. It's very admirable to care about someone. I'm sure your friend would be most happy to know of your concern."

Belle's big black eyes stared up at Pierre as she declared, "Well, I just pray she's alive, but me and Mademoiselle Babette here are the only friends she's got in Savannah. She'd have come to us if she wasn't hurt or worse."

"Belle, I can trust you, I think," Renaud said with a sly grin on his face. "Charmaine has another very good friend in Savannah. It just happens to be me. You and Mademoiselle Demoreau may rest assured she is in good hands. I'll give her your best regards when I take my purchases to her."

"You, *monsieur?*" Belle gasped.

"These things you buy are for Charmaine, *monsieur?*" Babette stammered, throwing her hands up in the air. *Mon Dieu!*"

It wasn't until Pierre had paid his bill, loaded the packages into the carriage and driven away that the women realized something.

"We didn't ask his name or where Charmaine is," a stunned Babette exclaimed.

Belle let out a gust of laughter, "Maybe that's how he wants it, but I'm not worried about the little *mademoiselle*. She's in very good hands, I'd say. Yes, ma'am, very good hands!"

Babette looked wistful for her thoughts were traveling back over the years. She'd lived a rich, full life and had known a fair share of men. *"Oui,* he did have magnificent hands. And much more!" She slyly winked at Belle.

"I just happened to think of something, Mam'selle. Suppose that was that George Seymour Charmaine was to marry?"

Babette shook her head, saying, "No, Belle, I hardly think so. In fact, I'd almost swear it wasn't."

"But maybe he got word from Norfolk and came here to Savannah to seek her out." Belle wasn't convinced that her idea wasn't feasible.

But Babette's sage wisdom made her see reason. "If the man who was here this afternoon is the one who awaited Charmaine's arrival in Virginia, she'd have eagerly accompanied Tasha, wouldn't you agree?"

"Lord o' mercy, yes! So fast it would have made our heads swim." Belle broke into a gale of laughter. "If I'd been Mademoiselle Charmaine and that was waiting for me in Virginia, I'd have started walking."

Babette laughed along with her black seamstress. While she didn't say so aloud she knew she'd have done the same.

Chapter 27

Pierre heard the echo of their laughter as he walked down the carpeted hallway, his arms laden with packages. He'd refused the help of the young black boy down in the lobby of the Magnolia House because the fewer people who saw Charmaine in Savannah, the safer it would be for her.

He was glad the witty Jacques was keeping her entertained while he was away. Now that he must consider Charmaine and her predicament, he'd had to make some changes in his plans for leaving Savannah. Overland travel would put fewer miles between them and what awaited Charmaine in Savannah if she was apprehended.

This evening he'd approach Jacques about taking the packet which left at night and circled the Keys, making stops at Mobile and finally New Orleans, where they would debark. From there they'd go straight up the Mississippi River to their destination, the Missouri Territory. Traveling on the river would afford Charmaine more comfort than the rugged overland trek. Pierre knew not what dangers faced them in this strange country, and when he'd had only himself and Jacques Bernay to consider, that had been a completely different situation.

His rap on the door brought Jacques in response. Since the packages hid most of his face, Bernay quickly reached out to relieve him of part of the load. "You must have bought out the whole store, *mon ami,*" he declared.

Only then did Pierre notice that Charmaine had helped herself to one of his white ruffled shirts in order to conceal the torn part of her gown. He grinned.

"Did you rest well, *chérie?*"

When she smiled coyly at him, he could have sworn she was blushing. Like him, she was probably recalling how ardently they'd made love. She looked impish sitting there, swallowed up in his white shirt, and he was tempted to tell Bernay to remove himself so he could make love to her, but his more practical side restrained him.

Too many pressing matters faced him, and he knew he would not rest until he got Charmaine away from Savannah. With this in mind, he handed her a couple of the huge boxes and teased her playfully, "Here, *ma petite.* You get busy trying on some new clothes. That torn gown can't be too pleasant, eh?" He couldn't deny himself one affectionate kiss, though, before turning to Jacques to say, "Come. We'll occupy ourselves in your room while Charmaine checks these things out for size."

Jacques followed Renaud through the door, and as soon as it was closed so Charmaine could not hear him, Pierre told his friend the golden-haired lady's plight.

"It has altered my set plans. I think we should leave on the first packet we can get. The man's dead, and I've learned that the law is looking for her right now."

"How . . . how did you find this out?" Bernay was alive with concern for he already liked the young woman in the next room.

"I went to the shop where Charmaine was working and I talked to the two women she'd told me about. The constable was in there making an inquiry as to her whereabouts. Obviously he wanted to question her about the man killed. I must say this Mademoiselle Demoreau handled the situation well. It's obvious she and Belle care for Charmaine. But you

236

can see why I must get her out of here fast."

"Of course, *mon ami*. I say we go too—and fast!" Jacques declared without hesitation.

"In that case, let's set the wheels in motion. Suppose you check out the next available passage we can get. I have no intention of leaving Charmaine or letting her out of this room until we depart from this place, not after what I learned this afternoon."

Bernay sensed the depth of Renaud's concern. "I'll get right on it," he said. "We'll get her out. Two crafty Frenchies like you and me can outfox them." He favored Pierre with a cocky grin.

Once again, Renaud was glad the two of them had joined forces back there on Guernsey. Bernay was a rare breed. His loyalty was priceless. It helped bolster his confidence that nothing or no one was going to whisk his beloved away from him. Certainly not as long as he had Bernay's help.

Putting his hat at a saucy angle on his curly head, Jacques announced that he was leaving to go to the wharf. "Now, you are in charge of our little *sirène*. That was what you called her, wasn't it? I remember well that night when you came back from Jersey and told me you'd met a golden little mermaid who'd bewitched you." He smiled, then went out the door, leaving Pierre staring after him, an amused look on his face.

Renaud was soon distracted, however, for Charmaine came rushing through the door in one of her new outfits. She walked with the erect carriage Babette had taught her over the last few weeks, tilting her head coquettishly. Pierre Renaud had never seen such a delectable sight as the woman standing before him, a provocative look in her deep blue-amethyst eyes. Suddenly, he realized there were many things to learn about this woman. He was going to take delight in exploring the many sides of her.

The long, gathered sleeves of the bodice were made of a soft white material, which flowed as she placed her hands on her waist and whirled around to give Pierre a full view of the gown. Its black velvet vest was laced up the front, and its long flowing black skirt was sprinkled with multicolored flowers. When she had properly displayed the gown as she had been instructed to do for the customers of the shop, she saucily asked, "Well, Monsieur Renaud . . . do you like it?"

Dear God, she is a magnificent little tease, he thought. For a moment, he said nothing, just let his eyes dance over her appraisingly.

"Yes, I think maybe we'll keep it. On second thought, I've decided I should show you just how much I like it."

Charmaine let herself drown in the quicksilver of his eyes. "Oh, but I've more to show you, *monsieur.*"

"You most assuredly have and I'm anxious to see everything."

He took a couple of giant strides toward her, letting his hands snake out and grasp her shoulders. Then his mouth found her half-parted lips. It was a lingering kiss, and when he released her she did not move, but her long lashes fluttered. Pierre noticed that she looked very pale. "I have a hell of an effect on you, don't I? Seems you just go weak in my arms," he declared light-heartedly.

With a childlike pout, Charmaine retorted, "The effect you speak of is due to hunger, Pierre, which is not to say I don't enjoy your kisses."

"Ohhhh, you've wounded my ego. But I shall feed you so you can enjoy my kisses more, eh?"

Charmaine yanked at the black vest which had ridden up as he'd held her. "Yes, that would be a good idea. While your ego heals, I can eat."

"I must have a talk with Jacques. He should have fed you while I was gone. I do apologize."

"And where is Jacques?"

"Running an errand, if you must know."

"But Jacques hasn't eaten either. He said we'd wait until you returned and then go down to the dining room," she told him.

"No," Pierre barked, more harshly than he'd intended. But he didn't dare chance that, neither did he wish to frighten her by letting her know the law was looking for her.

"And why not may I ask?" she inquired indignantly. "Jacques will take me if you won't."

Pierre raised a skeptical, angry brow. "Oh? You think so?"

"I know so!"

"Jacques is not in charge . . . of you, *ma petite!*" He glared at her defiant face. Such bold insolence he'd never seen in her before. Yes, there are many ladies in that tiny body, he thought. He was now viewing a high-spirited, independent one—with a will that he'd have to bend to his own.

"But neither are you, *Monsieur Renaud!* Neither are you," she snapped, swishing her skirt around and moving toward the door.

Hot-tempered little minx! He caught up with her instantly and jerked her around to face him. He was just about to take the first step toward taming her when Jacques rushed into the room. There was an excited look on his face and it was flushed. He'd obviously dashed back to the Magnolia House from the wharf. Renaud wondered whether something was wrong, but when Bernay took a deep breath and began to smile, his concern eased.

"I got lucky, Pierre!" Jacques exclaimed in a smug tone. "Would midnight be soon enough?"

"The sooner the better." Pierre's chuckle was throaty. He patted Bernay's shoulder to show his approval.

Excitement still ringing in his voice, Jacques declared, "It is our good fortune that a little schooner, the *Linda Lee,* which was due to sail at eight this evening had some minor repairs to be done and was delayed until midnight. I got us booked. Is that not perfect, *mon ami?"*

"Perfect, indeed!" Neither Pierre nor Jacques had noticed the dumbfounded and riled expression on Charmaine's face. They were caught up in their exchange, but she was utterly puzzled as to what they were talking about—and still hungry, which Pierre had forgotten upon Bernay's arrival.

In a sharp and snapping voice, she angrily announced, "In the meanwhile, since midnight is a few hours away, must I start screaming just to get a little food? Is dinner too much to ask, gentlemen?"

The two Frenchmen exchanged amused glances. Both thought she looked absolutely adorable with her eyes spitting fire and her hands placed on her tiny waist.

Pierre made a courtly bow. "Your wish is my command, lovely lady. Jacques, keep this spitfire company while I seek some nourishment for us all." Without further ado, he dashed out the door.

Charmaine turned to Jacques. "Now, will you please tell me what all that was about, Jacques Bernay?"

"Tickets . . . I got our tickets . . . our passage."

He suddenly realized that Pierre had not informed her of his plans for them and he'd opened his mouth when he should have let her hear the news from Pierre himself.

"Our passage?" she quizzed.

"*Oui*. We leave Savannah tonight."

"Oh, you and Pierre?" she bristled.

"Pierre, me, and you."

"This is the first I've heard of it," she told him, swishing her skirt angrily.

Scratching his head, Jacques gave a deep sigh, "That's what I was afraid of."

"What was that you said?"

Jacques hastily turned away from her glaring eyes and gave an offhanded shrug. "Nothing . . . I said nothing, Charmaine."

But she knew he had and she suspected he was only trying to protect Pierre. Even though he was lying to her, Charmaine could not stay angry at the likable Bernay, however. He was merely being loyal to the presumptuous Pierre, who'd made plans for her without even mentioning

240

them. She would deal with him when he returned.

But when he came through the door the delectable aroma of food wafted to her nose and she was so famished she forgot to be vexed. All she yearned for was food. She ate until her ravenous appetite was sated—meatpies, cheese, and little crusted fruit tarts—and then drank a generous portion of the sweet-tasting red wine Pierre had brought.

She felt quite lazy after eating so greedily. That and the effect of the wine made her give Renaud no problems when he ordered her, "Get your things together, *ma petite,* and dress warm. There's a chill outside tonight." Next, he turned his attention to Bernay. "I've already taken care of our bill so we can leave very shortly. The *Linda Lee* is the packet we'll take?"

"That's right. The mate was in charge because the captain had gone into the city. Midnight sharp, he said."

"We'll be there," Pierre declared.

Both men then saw to their own packing.

A few minutes before the midnight hour, the trio walked up the gangplank and were met by an imposing figure of a man. There was just enough light to reveal the captain's rugged face.

"Holy Christ! What the devil are you doing aboard, Garrett?"

"Well, Pete my boy, and you, jolly Jack! We meet again." Jim Garrett let out a lion's roar of laughter. Bending low to peer into Charmaine's astonished face as her eyes scrutinized him, Jim Garrett let his lusty gaze dance over her. "Well, well, well . . . what do we have here, gentlemen? A golden-haired sea siren, I'd say."

"The *Lady* is Mademoiselle Lamoureux and she is with me, Garrett," Renaud barked, clutching Charmaine possessively.

"I get your drift, Pete." He laughed again and gave Pierre a comradely pat on the shoulder.

"You never answered my question, Garrett. What are you

241

doing on the *Linda Lee*. What happened to the *Sweet Sally?*"
Pierre insisted on knowing.

"Well, that's a long tale, my lad, and later, over a tankard of ale, I'll be telling it. Now I'll have my boy show you to your quarters for I must see that we get underway." He gave Pierre a sly, devious grin.

Chapter 28

As the three passengers followed a young cabin boy down the passageway of the ship, a chilling silence engulfed Renaud. He didn't like the smell of this, the fact that Jim Garrett was in command. That old fox was capable of anything, and Pierre resented his ogling Charmaine so brazenly. That lustful old bastard is gambling with his life, Renaud muttered under his breath as he and Charmaine were ushered into a cabin. Jacques was situated across the passageway.

Renaud had already decided that as soon as he got Charmaine comfortably situated Jacques could play watchdog over her while he had a word with Garrett.

When the cabin boy asked if they required anything before he left them, Renaud quickly dismissed him. "We need nothing more now, son, but tell your captain I will be up on deck shortly to have a word with him."

"Yes, sir. I'll tell him," the lad flippantly tipped his hat.

As Charmaine gazed about the cabin she commented, "Why, he's a mere child."

"They start early sometimes. For a lot of lads it's better than living in the streets and alleys. At least they eat and have a place to sleep."

As she flung off the blue velvet cape which belonged to

243

Mademoiselle Demoreau and the woollen jacket Pierre had purchased for her, he told her he intended to speak with the captain. "Now, for God's sake, I want you to listen to me and do what I'm about to tell you. Lock this door and let no one in but me or Jacques. Is that understood, Charmaine? Trust me. It's for your own good. I'm also going to tell Jacques to keep an eye on this door while I'm gone."

"You sound so mysterious, Pierre. You sound as though I could be in danger. Why don't you let me in on what's going on? I'm not a child, you know," she pointed out.

"That, *ma petite,* is exactly why I'm telling you to lock this door and keep it that way. If you were a child instead of a tantalizing female I'd not be so worried."

"Oh, I'm thrilled to know you noticed." Charmaine grinned at him.

"I've no time to jest with you right now, but remember what I said. I'd hate to paddle your little derrière when there are pleasanter ways to occupy my hands." With a broad grin and a wink of his eye, he closed the door, lingering just long enough to see that she locked it before knocking at Jacques' cabin.

His stop in Jacques' quarters was brief for he had only one thing on his mind, to talk to Jim Garrett.

As he marched down the passageway and up the steps to the deck above, he was fired with curiosity about the tale Jim had mentioned. But when the towering Frenchman appeared on the dark deck of the schooner, he whetted the curiosity of the few deckhands in evidence.

Jim Garrett saw him approach. The old sea captain had long ago decided Renaud wasn't the sort he'd want to tangle with for he was most assuredly a man of force and power. He knew he had the Frenchman guessing, for he'd seen the stunned look in his cold gray eyes when his party had boarded the *Linda Lee.*

"Pete, old boy . . . ready for that ale, I see," he said cordially as Renaud strode up to him. Informing his mate

244

he'd be in his quarters for a while, he urged Pierre to accompany him. "This is a bloody surprise to me as well as you. Damned nice one, I must say though," Jim remarked as the two men ambled along.

"Got to admit I didn't expect to see your ugly face again," Pierre playfully declared.

Jim roared with laughter, "I like you, Renaud! Damned if I don't."

When they entered the captain's quarters, which were unkempt and cluttered, he gruffly yelled to Jakie to fetch them some ale, then changed his mind and instructed the lad to bring the bottle of Irish Whiskey he'd been saving.

Jakie returned a short time later and was dismissed before Garrett poured two glasses of whiskey. "Want to hear my tale, son? Think you're going to find it amusing."

"You don't have to ask that, Garrett. I'm all ears. Delay no longer."

"Mind you this tale is going to cost me an arm and a leg, but the truth is, Pete my boy, I like you. So here it is. An old mate of mine just happens into a tavern where I happened to be. He'd come from the Channel Islands—Guernsey to be exact. Wakefield died. Naturally, it seems. His heart, they say. His snobbish daughter Sarnia stooped low and got herself married to some common fisherman. Now ain't that a pot of beans!" Garrett began to chuckle. When Pierre didn't join him in laughter, Jim straightened up in his chair and quizzed, "Well, ain't that what you wanted? What you paid me that fine fee for?"

"Sure, I suppose so," Pierre mumbled. Now that he had Charmaine with him he no longer had the need for revenge.

"Well, I got to admit it was a fast stroke. Only thing I can't exactly take credit for it. Wakefield's death or that haughty Sarnia's marriage to that young pup over on Jersey. A lowly fisherman's wife! She won't last long at that, I'd wager. Some farmer's son by the name of Keene, my old mate told me. That wasn't exactly old Martin's plan for her, I know."

245

"Keene, did you say?" Pierre suddenly came alert. "Would that be John Keene?"

"Think maybe it might be. Do you know him?"

"You might say that." Pierre took a hefty swig of his whiskey.

"Well, Pete, I'd like to be a man of honor and tell you I'll return your money for the job you paid me to do, but the truth of the matter is I handed it over to my creditors to pay off the *Sweet Sally.*"

"Then why are you making this run up the coast on a packet? The *Sweet Sally* having repairs done?" Pierre asked.

"I sure hope so. You see, she ain't mine no more. I lost her in a card game. Old fool that I am, I should have lost her. I know better than to play poker when I'm drinking. Well after I lost my *Sweet Sally,* I hired on with Mister Fischer as the captain of the *Linda Lee.* That's my tale. But so you'll know I have a little honor I'm returning your passage. By Jesus, I can repay you that much."

Pierre was dumbfounded, and he confessed to himself he'd misjudged Garrett. The old rascal had so boggled his mind that he couldn't speak for a moment. When he regained his rattled composure, he told Jim, "Sounds like a fair deal to me. I thank you for myself and my companions. The news you've given me and our fare taken care of makes us even."

"A handshake on it?" Jim extended his huge, weathered hand to Renaud, who grasped it.

"Now, one more for a nightcap. Oh, is the pretty lady all cozy and comfortable?"

"Yes. I imagine she's already retired for the night." Pierre quickly sought to change the subject because his opinion of old Jim's lustful eyes remained the same. He didn't trust the man that much. "What is our first port, Jim?"

"It's in the Florida Keys. Key West, my boy. Then we follow the coastline up and around to Mobile. Yes sir, we've got a few nights and days to put in. I just hope it ain't too

246

rough a voyage for that little lady. She looks a bit frail to me, Pete."

Damn the old coot, Pierre thought. He just can't seem to keep his mind off Charmaine. He had a feeling his hands were going to be full just protecting Charmaine.

Nevertheless, trying to sound very casual and offhanded, Pierre assured Garrett, "Oh, I think Mademoiselle Lamoureux will weather the trip. I certainly intend to see that she is comfortable and safe, and should any of your seamen dare to molest her, I might as well warn you, Jim, I'll take care of him. Otherwise, you're the captain and the boss of this schooner. I am in charge only where's she's concerned."

Jim raised a bushy eyebrow and his tanned, bearded face creased into a slow, amused smile. "Ohhhh, I couldn't fault you about that, son. No sireee! Any red-blooded man would feel just like you do."

Pierre knew instinctively from the look on the old rascal's face that Garrett realized the remark included him.

"Jim, I'll bid you good night. I appreciate the news you told me. See you in the morning." He turned to leave the captain's quarters, feeling somewhat relieved about some of his concerns.

It was not until he stopped at Bernay's cabin to give him Garrett's news about Wakefield that a sudden thought struck him. He asked Bernay for his opinion, "You don't suppose he was setting us up for some kind of trick, do you, Jacques? The bit about returning our fare . . . I wonder if the wily old fox thought by doing that he'd get me to let my guard down?"

Jacques smiled. "You won't though, will you, *mon ami?*"

"Hardly. I'll be watching him out of the corner of my eye every minute, especially where Charmaine is concerned. Speaking of her, I wonder why I'm wasting time in here with you," he joked.

"Damned if I know," Jacques replied. The expression on his face masked the truth from Pierre. Though he'd managed

247

till now to bury his feelings for the beautiful Charmaine, he resented the fact that she was sharing the cabin across the passageway with Pierre instead of him. He knew when Pierre walked out that door and he was alone, he'd be imagining the intimate scene between the two of them. But he couldn't stop such thoughts, regardless of how tormenting they were.

He'd wanted Charmaine from the moment he'd first laid eyes on her, though he knew that could never be!

Chapter 29

Only after Pierre left her alone in the cabin did Charmaine begin to ponder the strange encounter between the two men on deck. The fierce-looking old captain named Garrett had called Pierre by another name. Why had he referred to him as Pete? What is that all about? she wondered.

She caught herself applying her dear Aunt Simone's logic to the situation. She really knew nothing about this man she'd allowed to take charge of her life, as he'd boldly taken her body back on Jersey. What was it about this strange Frenchman that made her throw all common sense away. He seemed to cast an evil spell on her. He could work his wicked wiles by just the touch of his hand. Perhaps, that made her wicked too.

She slowly went about the act of undressing, mumbling to herself that it was about time she let Pierre Renaud know a thing or two. Yes, the minute he returned she'd tell him he need not expect her to submit every time he snapped his finger. By the time she had put on her nightgown and had hung up her new traveling attire, she was slightly irritated with herself, as well as Pierre. Here she was awaiting his return, and the fine clothes she'd just hung up were purchased by him. Without one word of protest, she'd accompanied him on this schooner. That, Charmaine

Lamoureux, makes you a kept woman, she admonished herself. A whore!

When she stared at herself in the mirror, she didn't like what she saw. She felt soiled and tarnished. As soon as Pierre came back she would demand that he move across the passageway to Bernay's quarters. It should have been arranged that way in the first place.

She smiled smugly as she recalled Pierre's caution about unlocking her door. It was he who should be denied entrance!

At this moment she heard him rap on the door and call out her name. For a moment she didn't respond. Again he knocked and called out to her, his impatient hands rattling the door so fiercely she wondered whether he'd break it down if she didn't let him in.

"All right, Pierre! All right!" She slipped her wrapper over the gown and ambled unhurriedly toward the door.

Something told Renaud she hadn't been asleep for her deep blue eyes were too bright for that. The expression on her face and the saucy tilt to her head made him wonder just what was going on inside her head. Once again, he was thinking she was a complicated little minx. This wasn't the sweet smiling lady he'd left a couple of hours ago.

"You don't seem too eager to see me, *ma petite,* though I came rushing back to what I'd hoped would be your anxious arms. I'm crushed!" Renaud casually flung off his jacket, letting it land on a chair.

"Your smooth tongue will get you nowhere, Pierre," she pertly retorted.

"Ah, but your femininity and your delectable charms will get you everything," he teased, figuring she was vexed because he'd left to go to talk with Garrett. Well, he would remedy that in short order, he thought as he reached out to grab her. But she surprised him by swaying to avoid being caught in his grasping hands. This, he was not prepared to deal with. A frown etched his face and his gray eyes flashed with his mounting anger as he barked at her, "Now, what the hell are you up to? Come here, Charmaine! The hour is late and I'm in no mood for children's games. It's been a long day and a long night."

"My sentiments exactly! I'm ready to go to bed and to sleep. I suggest you get out of here so I can do that. A bunk is waiting for you in Jacques' cabin. Please go, Pierre. I'm weary!" She shrugged her shoulders and turned aside so she wouldn't have to look at his eyes which were devouring her.

"Wha— What the holy hell are you talking about? I'm going nowhere this night!" Renaud's hot-blooded temper exploded with such fury he lunged for her, caught her roughly by her arms, and yanked her against him. His lips commandeered hers and there was no gentleness in his kiss, only a forceful demand that she return his caress. His muscular arms held her in an unrelenting vise.

Charmaine felt as though she couldn't breathe, but she knew it was futile to plead for mercy. The menacing look on his face prohibited tenderness. This "Pierre" she had never faced before. She felt a strange mixture of emotions. Her own boldness amazed her for, threatening as he was, he excited her.

Renaud's male body pulsed as he released her luscious lips to gaze longingly into the gorgeous pools of her eyes. What he saw there made him want to remove the barrier of her gown, and his hands yanked at the sheer material until Charmaine stood before him nude, a most bewitching sight.

"God Almighty! You have a maddening effect on me. I want you . . . desire you as no other."

A slow smile came to Charmaine's face, and a seductive tone came into her voice as she murmured, "And I can't imagine making love with any other man as I have with you, Pierre."

Flinging his own clothes aside with impatient haste, he grinned devilishly. "Don't even indulge in that fantasy, *chérie.*"

He drew her with him as he backed up to sink down on the bunk, and she found herself spread across the front of him, taunted by his maleness. The heat of his firmly muscled thighs seared her as his hands cupped her supple mounds, caressing them. As his mouth captured one rosy tip and then the other, Charmaine's pleasure mounted to new heights. She moaned out his name and undulated her fevered body against his, making him surge with desire.

As their bodies fused, untamed passion churned furiously within them. Her face told him of the pleasure he was giving her as he arched more to fill her need. Then, in a frenzy of desire she pressed closer to him and moaned, "Oh God, Pierre!"

"I know, Charmaine! I know! I wish this could go on forever," he gasped, knowing he was fast soaring to the height of ecstasy and had no power to delay his ultimate pleasure. Charmaine's silken flesh had tantalized him beyond endurance.

She glided with him to that pinnacle of rapture, to linger for a few breathless moments before a torrent of ecstasy flooded through them like a raging river. Forgotten was her intention to insist he sleep in Bernay's quarters. She wanted him with her all night long.

His body resting beside her, that seemed right. If he'd left her to do as she'd requested earlier, Charmaine would have felt lost and lonely.

The lovers fell asleep, weary from passionate pleasure.

The light invading the small porthole of the cabin aroused Charmaine from her deep sleep. She stretched out lazily between the sheets, and a serene smile came to her face as she became alert enough to know she was still naked. She turned to find Pierre no longer at her side.

For some moments she made no move to get up, but finally she rose and slipped on the wrapper lying on the floor at her feet. One fleeting glance out the window told her this was a beautiful day. Across the water, in the distance, she could see the shoreline. The schooner was following the coast as it plowed through the waters, and she wondered just how far they'd traveled that night. The strange places Pierre had mentioned meant nothing to her for she'd never heard of any of them before.

But the beauty of the sun urged her to get dressed, and her stomach urged her to seek food. As she took the brush in her hand and began to stroke the tangles in her hair, it struck her that Pierre could have brought her a breakfast tray. After all, it was partly his fault she was so ravenously hungry. She wagered that by now wherever he was he'd eaten a hearty meal. The more she thought about food the more eager she was to go in search of it.

Dressed now, her hair tied back with a bright green ribbon, she grabbed for the woollen shawl to fling around her shoulders. A hesitant voice and a light rap at her door stopped her. "Miss, are you awake? Captain said I was to bring you a tray."

Charmaine recognized the voice of the young cabin boy, and she opened the door to let him in. She was grateful to the captain for not forgetting her as Renaud had done.

"Thank you very much . . . Jakie, isn't it?" She gave the bashful youth a friendly smile. "I'm famished. Please tell your captain thank you."

"Can . . . can I get anything else for you ma'am?" The lad found her so lovely, proximity to her made him nervous, and he fought desperately against stammering when he spoke.

"Can't think of another thing I might need." As the lad was about to rush out of the door, however, she called to him, "Oh, Jakie . . . perhaps you could tell me if you've seen Monsieur Renaud or Monsieur Bernay on deck?"

"I saw Mister Bernay topside, but no ma'am, I can't say as I've seen Mister Renaud."

"Thank you, Jakie."

"Yes, ma'am. But if you'd like to find Mister Bernay I can tell you where on the deck he was and maybe he could tell you where Mister Renaud was." After telling Charmaine precisely where Jacques was standing, he added, "He and our other lady passenger have been standing there for quite awhile talking."

"I see. Another lady passenger. All right, Jakie and thank you again."

She was most curious about the lady to whom Jacques was talking, so she hastily gulped down the hot tea and then gobbled down one of the biscuits. She wondered where Pierre was and what was occupying him for so long. She would have expected him to have returned to their quarters with a warm greeting after the intimate night they'd shared.

A pout came to her lips as she thought about his behavior. He couldn't utter enough sweet words last night, she mused, taking the last bite of the buttered biscuit. But, in the morning light, it would seem he had no time for her.

She wiped away a smear of butter from her lips, gave a swish to her skirt, and checked to see if her ribbon was tied securely. As she peered into the mirror, she gave herself a stern lecture. A first class liar is what you are, Charmaine Lamoureux, she silently told herself. What had happened last night to her claims that she'd not allow Pierre to sleep in her bed? Thirty minutes later he'd not only been in it, he'd been having his way with her. That was the pure and simple truth of it. She couldn't resist his charms and the conceited Pierre knew it!

By the time she left the cabin and mounted the steps leading to the deck, she was once again vowing to put him in his place when she faced him. As she stepped onto the planking of the deck, her look was determined and her head was held high. She strode purposely across the deck, her eyes flashing brilliantly as they searched for the curly-haired Bernay.

As she swayed along, she was a visual treat for the crew of

254

Garrett's ship. Few could resist the temptation to turn and stare, though some merely stole a glance as she passed by.

Jakie had directed her correctly. She recognized Jacques' rugged back. The Frenchman was still standing in the spot by the railing. However, his huge, robust body obscured that of the tiny lady standing beside him. When Charmaine was within fifteen feet of the pair, Jacques turned at the sound of her footsteps.

He was hardly prepared for the shriek of joy that erupted from the tiny, black-haired lady whose companionship he'd been enjoying for over an hour. At the same instant Charmaine rushed to them, her golden hair flying back in the breeze.

"Tasha! My God, Tasha! I can't believe it!" she cried out.

"Nor can I, Charmaine! Dear Lord, I think a miracle has happened!" She flung her arms around Charmaine, and they clung together in a warm embrace, leaving Bernay in a state of puzzlement. It was obvious these two had known each other well.

When the two young ladies calmed down, Charmaine turned to Jacques, a glowing smile on her face, "This is my dear friend, Tasha Weer, Bernay! Can you believe it?"

Bernay gave her one of his broad grins. He thought she'd never looked so beautiful. Excitement brought a flush to her face, and the wind was doing wild and wonderful things to her thick, long hair. "Yes, Charmaine . . . I know who she is. I just had no idea I was talking to a friend of yours."

"I had no idea either," Tasha declared. "I mean that you and Jacques were friends." She smiled at both of them, but she was wondering why Charmaine happened to be on this ship with the gentleman she'd found to be most pleasant and friendly when she'd emerged from her quarters for a stroll. Is Jacques Bernay Charmaine's suitor and protector? she pondered.

Her untimely return to Savannah from Norfolk had been disappointing for she'd hoped to see Charmaine. Mademoiselle Demoreau and Belle, however, had told her of Charmaine's unfortunate situation. They had had no inkling of where she was, but they had said she was with a very handsome man. Tasha considered Jacques a most handsome man so she concluded it was Jacques of whom they'd spoken.

"Oh, we've much to talk about, Tasha! You must tell me what's happened to you since we said farewell in Savannah weeks ago," Charmaine declared excitedly.

"I want to know all of your doings too," Tasha told her.

Suddenly, a shadowy towering figure invaded the gathering. As he was about to make his presence known, Charmaine was urging Tasha, "Well, come to my cabin and we'll catch up on one another. You don't mind, do you, Jacques?"

"Of course not, ladies. Go enjoy yourselves," he told them. Then, turning, he noticed that Renaud had joined them.

As Charmaine was tugging her friend along with her, she saw Pierre standing beside them, the look on his tanned face reflecting his confusion about the scene he'd come upon. Charmaine briefly introduced him to Tasha before the two women scurried away.

Her quick dismissal of him irked Pierre, and he raised a skeptical black brow to mutter to Bernay, "Perhaps, you can enlighten me."

"Not much, *mon ami*. The two ladies know one another and were overwhelmed with joy at being reunited." Bernay knew Pierre was riled, but he suspected he'd be even more displeased before this voyage was over. Tasha Weer would be aboard all the way to New Orleans she'd told him so earlier.

"Old friends, eh? Well, I wonder where I'm supposed to lounge while those two occupy my cabin. Did you hear that little minx telling her friend it was her cabin? Cocksure little flip she is!"

Bernay listened to his friend's grumbling a bit, then made

a suggestion. "What about sharing my cabin along with a card game and some good French brandy?"

Pierre shrugged his broad shoulders, but the angry look was still on his face as the two men ambled away from the railing. "But I'll be damned if I'll share it with you tonight!"

Bernay could not hide the amused smile that came to his face. He dared not voice his private thoughts to Renaud for the man was too riled to see the humor in the situation.

"Oh, you could find worse to share quarters with," the witty Bernay jested.

The scowl on Pierre's face slowly melted into a grin. "But tonight not to be in my cabin would be hellish torment, my friend!"

Bernay could certainly understand why. Nevertheless, that might be Pierre's fate if the charming Charmaine decided to be stubborn.

Chapter 30

Oblivious to the time, the two young ladies chattered away the whole afternoon describing what had happened to them since they'd separated there on the wharf in Savannah. Charmaine's plight stunned Tasha, who demanded a detailed account of the evening she'd been the innocent prey of the despicable Chauncey Bedlow.

"You had the right to protect yourself, Charmaine. You have no reason to feel guilt. You killed only vermin."

"I just don't find it so easy to dismiss. He was a human being."

"I question that, Charmaine. Animals are far superior to the likes of him. Oh, I'm so glad Monsieur Renaud got you out of there. Why, he saved you from God knows what kind of fate."

"I suppose he did," Charmaine replied, omitting that he had not done it without demanding his own reward. "I've had no more problems to face than you, though. I'm so very sorry to hear that your brother died. What anguish it must be not to know where your little nephews and niece were taken."

"Well, I had nothing to hold me in Norfolk upon learning that sad news so I came back to Savannah hoping to see you. When I got to the shop and heard the news about you I was utterly devastated. I guess that's why I decided to go to New Orleans to seek out some relatives of Jacob's wife. I thought they might have some word about those poor dear children."

"It was meant to be, Tasha, our meeting again. I know it! I just know it!" Charmaine had such a sincere look on her face that Tasha realized she sincerely believed what she'd said.

"Perhaps, what you say is true. In any case, I couldn't be happier to see you again," Tasha said, reaching over to pat Charmaine's hand.

"Not half as happy as I am to see you, Tasha," Charmaine declared. She was already thinking about how she would put the arrogant Frenchman in his place so she'd not be at his mercy when he wanted to have his way with her. She was going to ask Tasha if she might share her cabin, tonight, for that seemed to be the only way to keep her reckless heart from surrendering to the handsome Pierre.

Across the passageway in Bernay's cabin, Pierre Renaud had reached his limit of card playing for one afternoon, and sips of Bernay's fine French brandy had only barely soothed his ill temper. The sun was setting in the western sky, and soon the night would be upon them. An evening spent playing cards with Bernay or Jim Garrett was not exactly what he had in mind.

The more he began to think about the tricky little miss only a few feet away, the more he felt like a fool. He had never allowed any woman to play him for that before. His sudden look of displeasure told Bernay the calm was over. This time, he was not going to be able to stop the explosion.

When Pierre rose from his chair, Jacques was not taken aback by his gruff announcement. "I'll see you later. I feel the need for a change of clothes and a bath."

Jacques merely nodded his head, knowing Pierre really needed to vent his displeasure on Charmaine. Perhaps, it was just as well Charmaine learned what kind of man she was dealing with, Jacques reasoned. Womanly wiles would not work on Pierre. Jacques found it hard to believe

Charmaine capable of such games, yet he had to confess she'd surprised him a few times. She was not entirely a simple little maiden who'd lived on a farm on Jersey. No, there was much more to her than that. She had to know that Pierre Renaud had lived a very sophisticated life and had paid court to many ladies with their aristocratic backgrounds similar to his own.

What she should have realized, according to Jacques Bernay or Pierre Renaud, did not affect the attitude of Charmaine Lamoureux when Pierre stormed through his cabin door, startling the two young women.

"Ladies, I must interrupt you, I'm afraid," he declared abruptly. His expression was cold and sober, and his fathomless gray eyes glared.

Charmaine quickly explained her friendship with Tasha, but she sensed he was not really interested for he turned his back on her as she spoke. As he proceeded to remove his jacket and fling it onto a nearby chair, she wondered just what he was about. "Pierre?"

"Yes, my pet?" His eyes pierced her.

"What are you doing?" By now, he'd sat down on the chair, and was pulling off one leather boot.

"Since this is our cabin and the dinner hour is approaching, I'm preparing to undress to take a bath. I'm sure you understand, don't you, Mademoiselle Weer? Charmaine and I share these quarters."

Charmaine was mortified by his coarseness. How dare he make her feel so low and cheap in front of her dear friend. She'd never forgive him for this, she promised herself.

Tasha was embarrassed by his manner and his tone, and she noticed the pale, stunned look on Charmaine's face. But she didn't doubt that he spoke the truth. Perhaps he was just jealous of her taking up so much of Charmaine's time. She quickly sought to remove herself from the cabin, for she wished to add no fuel to their lover's quarrel. "I must be going, Charmaine. I had no idea so much time had passed. Monsieur Renaud, it was nice to meet you."

Pierre was washed by a wave of guilt, for the woman was more gracious than he deserved. It was hardly her fault that Charmaine had treated him with such cold indifference. "Nice to meet you, Mademoiselle Weer," he mumbled in a more civil manner.

But his mellower tone did not impress Charmaine. She was trembling with rage, and nothing his silver tongue could have said at that moment would have softened her heart.

She stood up, her head held defiantly and flaming contempt in her eyes. "I'll walk back to the cabin with you, Tasha dear."

"It's time you dressed for dinner, Charmaine," Pierre declared authoritatively.

"I'm not ready yet. If you're hungry, go eat, Pierre!" Without further ado, she turned to take Tasha's arm and then marched out of the cabin.

Pierre flung his boot against the wall, cursing her and her headstrong ways which he intended to tame. The taming would begin this very night, he angrily vowed as he paced the cabin and fumed.

He stomped across the bare plank deck in his stocking feet grumbling to the emptiness of the cabin like a raging bull. Suddenly, he let out a stream of curse words, then lifted up one of his feet to examine the bottom for the splinter that had stabbed him.

He sat down on his bunk and tried to yank out the troublesome wooden shard. This just wasn't his day. A small bubble of blood emerged from the spot, and as he dabbed at it with his stocking, an unruly wisp of his black hair fell over his forehead.

As Charmaine rushed through the door of the cabin to find Pierre sitting, barechested, on the bunk. He was staring off into space and looking so serious she hesitated to lash out at him as she'd intended. *He looks like a solemn little boy,* she thought.

But then he turned to her and asked in a hateful tone, "Did you escort your friend back to her quarters?"

"I did! I resent the way you spoke to her. Your crudeness was unforgivable," she admonished him sternly.

"Well, I rather resented being kept from my cabin all day."

"All day? Come now, Pierre, it was hardly all day. Nevertheless, that will be remedied." She moved busily about the cabin gathering up articles.

Pierre stood, peering out the small porthole, his back turned to her. "That's good news. I'm glad to know you realize the inconvenience you caused me." He saw then that she had articles of clothing piled up in her arms. She stood by the open door, ready to dash out. "I'm going to go to Tasha's quarters so you won't be inconvenienced anymore." She slammed the door with a thunderous bang and ran swiftly down the passageway.

Pierre absorbed her words. Realizing what her intentions were, he, too, made for the doorway. "That damned little vixen is going to get the spanking she deserves—right now!"

Blinded by his rage, he rammed into the robust Jacques Bernay, who'd emerged from his cabin at the same moment.

"Mon Dieu! What kind of madness is going on here?" The crash of their firm, muscled bodies made them stumble and weave against the walls of the passage as they tried to regain balance.

In a husky breathless voice Pierre declared to his friend, "I think perhaps you've hit on it, Jacques. I think that little golden-haired witch has driven me slightly mad! It was her I was after, for I fully intended to turn her over my lap and whip her little behind."

"Mon ami! Come now!"

"She deserves it, Jacques. She's acting like a child."

"She's little more than a child if you think about it. Compare her age to our years, Renaud. Perhaps, you are too harsh and impatient, eh?"

"Harsh and impatient? I've been more generous and devoted to her than to any woman I've ever loved!"

Jacques couldn't resist cajoling him. "So you do love her?"

Tight-lipped, Pierre barked, "Yes, damn it, I love her and that comes as no surprise to you. Why else would I be so angry because she's gone to Tasha's quarters instead of staying with me?"

"For the time being maybe it's best that you both cool off. Let her have her way. What good would it do to force her to remain with you if she doesn't desire to? No, *mon ami,* you would not want her that way."

Pierre knew his friend was right. He wanted Charmaine to yield to him willingly and eagerly as she had the night before. A broad grin came to his face as he agreed. "You're right, Bernay. Tell me how you came to be so smart where ladies are concerned?"

"A simple fact. I'm older and have had more experience than you. Maybe you'll catch up someday." Jacques laughed and gave Renaud a comradely pat on the shoulders.

To Pierre's chagrin, he did end up spending the evening with Bernay instead of Charmaine.

Chapter 31

Charmaine persistently denied that she wanted to return to Renaud's quarters, but Tasha was not convinced. She knew her friend was utterly miserable, that she longed for the handsome Renaud. How very stubborn the two young lovers were being!

Yesterday when she'd gone for a stroll alone, she'd chanced to encounter Bernay on deck. He, too, was alone and so they'd talked for a while. Naturally, the two people they genuinely cared about provided the topic of their conversation.

"I trust your friend Pierre doesn't think I encouraged this, Jacques. I didn't. I know Charmaine's miserable and unhappy, and I wish she'd go back to him. I hate seeing her this way." Tasha's declaration was sincere.

Jacques gave her hand a friendly pat. "I hate seeing him the way he is, too. He's not an easy man to be around right now because he, too, is unhappy."

Tasha thoughtfully commented, "Then they are allowing their foolish pride to rob them of precious moments."

The tiny black-haired lady with matching black eyes was no ravishing beauty but Bernay's eyes beheld something more long lasting in her. She was unselfish and good hearted, with a capacity to love completely. And she was wise. Suddenly and surprisingly, he was attracted to Tasha Weer.

"I think Charmaine is lucky to have a friend like you," he said. "I think you are a most charming lady if you don't think I'm being too bold."

"Your kind thoughts please me very much, and I think your friend is as lucky as mine," Tasha murmured softly. She found Jacques Bernay a most dashing figure of a man. While she knew such a man would not find her appealing, she could dream.

Jacques' next comment gave her hope, however. "I'm not a man to mince words," he said, "and it's more than kind thoughts I'm feeling for you. I'm very attracted to you so if I've got no chance with you I guess you'd better tell me right now."

Tasha was so overcome with emotion she could not speak. When she finally found her voice she could only murmur, "Oh, Jacques!"

The glowing warmth in her lovely dark eyes invited Bernay to take her in his arms. He kissed her with consuming tenderness and she responded. For Tasha and Bernay, that moment was as compelling as Renaud's and Charmaine's furious desire. Both were shaken to the cores of their beings, even the more experienced Bernay who'd had many women in various ports around the world.

Tasha's spirit seemed to blend with his. For Tasha, the gift of Jacques Bernay's love was something she'd never hoped to have. She absorbed the wonderful feel of his arms and was content to say nothing.

She knew this man possessed a rare tenderness and gentleness. His rugged appearance did not reflect this, but his manner and their talks had revealed it.

Jacques was content just to hold her close without uttering a word. After their kiss, he was convinced that he had been right about Tasha Weer. Now he prayed he'd win her gentle heart. She was unique, and now as he lovingly gazed upon

266

her face, seeing it glow with the radiance of love, he felt an exaltation he could not explain to himself. But he did know he would take great delight in bringing a radiant splendor to that little face and to those jet black eyes, if she'd allow him.

When the silence was finally broken, it was Jacques who spoke first. "I . . . I don't know what to say, Tasha. It is the first time in my life I've ever been speechless." He laughed nervously. If he was wrong and she didn't feel as he did, he knew he would be shattered.

She looked up and her eyes locked with his. In her straightforward way she asked, "Could it be you're as overwhelmed as I by this thing that's happened to us, my dear Jacques?"

He was a man soaring to the heavens, and oblivious of anyone on deck, he drew her close to him and planted another kiss on her flushed cheek. "God, Tasha, I hoped you'd say something like that! I love you, Tasha Weer!"

With a look of teasing mischief in her black eyes, she replied, "And I'm pretty certain I love you, Jacques Bernay!"

By now, Jacques had recovered his clever wit so he playfully teased her. "Well, I think Tasha Bernay sounds much better than Tasha Weer. Be honest, don't you, *ma petite?*"

"I certainly do! And if this is your way, Jacques Bernay, of asking me to be your wife, I'll accept right now before you change your mind. I heard all about you fickle, frivolous Frenchmen when I lived in England."

"Ah, my sweet Tasha, all Frenchmen aren't philanderers. You are looking at a man who's had his day at that. Now I'm, ready to spend the rest of my life with one lady—you!"

They stood by the rail of the schooner, lingering in the bliss of their newly discovered love, talking about everything and anything.

Finally, Tasha turned to Bernay, a serious look on her face. "I am so happy, Jacques, but you and I must help our friends to recapture the happiness I'm sure they once enjoyed. What they're doing to one another is terrible. Promise me that we'll never hurt each other that way."

"Never is a hard word to live up to, Tasha. I will try never to hurt you, but perhaps I'm not as prideful a man as Renaud. I've been humbled more than he has. You see, while we are good friends, our backgrounds are drastically different."

She squeezed his hand affectionately. "It will be fun to learn all about you."

He smiled down on her eager face. "So you shall, Tasha, as time goes by. I do agree with you about our two friends, and we'll do our best to help them."

With one more kiss they sealed their agreement to help Charmaine and Pierre patch up their lovers' quarrel, then they reluctantly left their place by the rail. When Charmaine next encountered her little black-haired friend, she realized that something mysteriously exhilarating had happened to them, but neither imagined that they were attracted to one another.

Charmaine did not think Jacques Bernay's nature and his glib tongue would meet Tasha's approval. She always pictured Tasha as shy around men, and especially men like the carefree, fun-loving Jacques.

But when a vivacious Tasha came into the cabin, a glowing smile on her face, Charmaine could not miss the strange transformation in her friend. "I don't have to ask if you've enjoyed your afternoon stroll. You are absolutely glowing. I think I'd better do the same thing if I can get the same results."

"I can heartily recommend it, Charmaine," Tasha replied saucily.

"Well?" The impish look on Tasha's face prompted Charmaine to prod her.

"Well, what?" Tasha coyly asked.

"Well, are you going to stand there like the cat who's swallowed the canary or are you going to tell me what happened, Tasha Weer?" Charmaine said, impatience and curiosity gnawing furiously at her. She couldn't imagine much happening on a stroll around Captain Garrett's ship.

Tasha couldn't decide whether to tell her friend or to let Charmaine see for herself the next time she saw Tasha with Bernay.

"Tasha, for God's sake, my curiosity is killing me."

"Oh, all right, Charmaine! I guess I couldn't hold out anyway. I'm too happy! Do you believe in miracles?"

"Of course, I do! Look how we met here on this ship only a few days ago. Now come on, tell me about this miracle."

Charmaine had never seen Tasha's black eyes shine so brightly and her olive complexion had a rosy glow. Why, she actually is far more lovely than I've realized, Charmaine mused.

"My miracle is Jacques Bernay, Charmaine. He actually cares for me—loves me. Can you believe it?"

Charmaine was so stunned she could not speak for a second, and when she did she stammered. "Jacques—you and Jacques Bernay? Dear God, you and Jacques Bernay! Forgive my befuddled state, but you've got to admit your news is a little staggering."

"Not half as staggering for you as it was for me, yet it is the most wonderful thing that's ever happened to me. You see, I've found him dashing and handsome since I first laid eyes on him. I admit that the first day I thought you and he . . . well, I thought he was enamored of you and how I envied you," Tasha confessed.

Charmaine gave her friend a warm embrace, then giggled. "Never anything but friends, Tasha. Jacques is a very dear friend to me."

"Oh, I knew that, Charmaine, as soon as I saw you around Pierre, but at first I assumed you might be involved with Jacques."

Her mention of Pierre opened a painful wound in Charmaine. God knows, she'd fought to keep him out of her

269

mind. She just wished Tasha had not mentioned his name.

"Renaud—that—that conceited oaf!" she spit his name out as if it were a foul taste in her mouth.

"Oh, Charmaine. You know you don't really see him that way. You're hurt and angry because of the spat you had, but that doesn't change how you feel about the man or how he feels about you."

"We had more than a spat, Tasha," Charmaine grumbled.

"No man does for a woman what he did for you unless he sincerely cares for her. You must know that," Tasha remarked, taking her shawl from her shoulders. "I think he's pouting just like you are and I think you are both miserable."

"You make me sound very childish, Tasha. If I didn't like you so much I would resent your remarks."

"I hope you won't, Charmaine for I care about you too much. I hate to see you as unhappy as you've been lately."

"I know you're a good friend, Tasha—I don't question that for a minute—but you don't know Pierre Renaud. He is so overbearing if he doesn't get his way," Charmaine declared.

"I fear we all possess that trait. I guess it's just more prominent in some of us."

What is this all-knowing attitude? Charmaine thought. She seems to be giving her approval and her loyalty to Renaud. Perhaps, I should enlighten her as to what Pierre Renaud demanded of me. If I tell her I'm his mistress, perhaps she won't find him such an admirable gentleman.

Charmaine cocked her head to the side, and her face etched with indignation, she pointedly asked her friend, "What would you think if I told you he expects me to be his mistress and share his bed, Tasha?" She waited, prepared for her friend to be shocked.

"Charmaine, such a ravishingly beautiful girl as you can hardly be surprised that a man desires her. My goodness, such a handsome man as Pierre would rarely be refused. As to what I think, my dear Charmaine, I would have to say this

270

certainly doesn't surprise me. Pierre is healthy and virile."
The dark-eyed Tasha tilted her head to one side and
playfully teased her little friend. "But I am sure you've found
that out for yourself."

A rosy blush crept to Charmaine's cheeks and her long
lashes fluttered nervously as she stared at her smiling friend
whose eyes gleamed with amused mischief. It might have
been her intention to shock Tasha, but it was she who'd
received the shock.

She'd always thought of Tasha Weer as a shy, violet.
Obviously, that wasn't the case.

Love does strange things to people!

Chapter 32

It was no reflection on Jacques Bernay's company that Pierre welcomed the solitude of his cabin this afternoon. It had become tiring to constantly pretend to be lighthearted, and he didn't admire himself very much when his façade slipped and he snapped at the innocent Bernay. It was Charmaine Lamoureux he wanted to lash out at, not his companion. Damn her and the frustration she'd caused him.

He looked up from the thick journal his father had given him. It was the first time he'd referred to it since the night they'd left Savannah, and he did so because Garrett had informed him that they would be making their first port call the next day.

Much information and many names were in the journal, and now Pierre understood why his father had been gone so long from Cherbourg when he'd traveled to America. The young Renaud knew he would never be the dedicated businessman his industrialist father was and expected him to become, but the more he perused this journal, the more he wondered if his father's reasons for sending him away were what they'd seemed.

Pierre looked back to the spring and summer when Étienne Renaud was gone from Cherbourg to check out the prospects of mining minerals in America. At that time Pierre had been pursuing various aristocratic ladies from Cherbourg society. Upon his father's return home, Étienne had frowned upon his son's behavior.

Now as he sat in the cabin of Garrett's schooner, on his way to that godforsaken back country called the Missouri Territory, he was starting to suspect that he'd been the victim of a coup planned by Monsieur Étienne Renaud, that sly mastermind.

As he weighed the facts Pierre concluded that his dilemma back in Cherbourg was not so drastic or dangerous to his well-being that his father could not have arranged to clear the Renaud name of scandal.

No. The elder Renaud had decided to test the spunk of his only son, the heir to his vast estate someday. Étienne wanted him to be capable of handling such a responsibility. That, Pierre suddenly realized, was why he'd been sent on this wild-goose chase. He had to prove he was a man, not a social dandy! Étienne would abhor that in his son!

Now that the floodgates of his mind had swung open and things were clear, he wondered why he had not seen it for himself before he'd left France. The answer was quite simple, and Pierre smiled with amusement. He had a long way to go to measure up to his clever father.

His serene easygoing mother must have known what Étienne was plotting. That had been the reason for her cool indifference toward her husband during the weeks before Pierre sailed from France. She had not approved of what her husband had in mind for their only son.

Pierre had a serious look on his fine-chiseled face. Perhaps, Étienne's scheme was going to backfire on him. Pierre might not return to France. He might want to build his own little empire right here in America. The prospect of taking over his father's iron industry was not as challenging as starting something on his own, as his father had done when he was a young man.

There was a sly grin on his face as he thought that his

father had not given him credit for his independent spirit, nor for the impulsiveness Étienne swore he'd inherited from his lovely mother.

Pierre closed the journal and rose from the chair to stretch his long legs. As he picked up one of his cheroots and lit it, he realized just how long his friend Bernay had been gone. Something else dawned on him as well. He'd spent the whole afternoon without thinking of his golden-haired lady.

To add to his enjoyment of the pungent cheroot, Renaud treated himself to a glass of brandy, and there was a satisfied look on his face when Jacques came through the door. Bernay was delighted that Pierre was out of his black mood, for his own spirits were soaring.

"It is a most wonderful day and I'm surprised to find you still in the cabin," Jacques remarked, as he flung aside his cap and ran his fingers through his thick mass of curly hair.

"Come. Have a brandy with me, Jacques. What have you been up to that has you feeling so fit and fine? Did you win a tidy sum from the deckhands in a card game? If we were on land, I'd swear you'd just won the favor of some lovely lady, but alas, our surroundings prevent that."

Bernay erupted with laughter. "Ah, but that is where you are wrong. It is a most beautiful lady that has my heart fluttering.

Bernay's statement made Pierre jerk up in his chair, an angry scowl on his face. The man wouldn't dare trifle with Charmaine Lamoureux—not Bernay! But what other beautiful woman could he be talking about?

The devious Bernay noticed the sudden change in Pierre's demeanor and instantly realized what he must be thinking. Why not taunt him just a little? the fun-loving Frenchman thought.

"I know of no lady aboard except Charmaine. Perhaps, you can enlighten me, Bernay? Have I missed something in all these days on this ship?"

"You might have. Every man has his own personal

275

conception of beauty," Bernay said matter-of-factly, trying not to allow a grin to come to his face.

"Damn it, Bernay! What—who in the hell are you talking about? I know you're not stupid enough to ply your so-called 'charms' on my lady." Renaud's gray eyes were sparking and Bernay was well aware that he couldn't play his game much longer.

"But it was my understanding you had had your fill of the lovely Charmaine and that your patience was at an end."

Pierre rose up from his chair. With a menacing look on his face, he smashed the cheroot into the saucer lying on the table; then he set down his brandy.

By now, Bernay's eyes twinkled with mischief, and he quickly announced the truth to Pierre. "It is Tasha Weer who's stolen my heart. I find her absolutely charming, and to my delight, the feeling is mutual."

"*Tasha Weer?*" The little lady with all that black hair—Charmaine's old friend? You and Tasha?" Pierre mumbled as confusion claimed him.

"*Oui! Ma petite* Tasha is a most unusual lady with a kind and good heart. Today I discovered she is very smart too. Something a man does not often find in pretty ladies who are always absorbed in their looks or in frilly gowns. You see, my young friend, over the years I've had my share of pretty women, but I've rarely met a real lady."

He was serious, Pierre realized. The fun-loving, carousing Bernay was not clowning at all. Pierre was at a loss for words, so he just stood there, an astonished look on his face, saying nothing.

"I surprise you, *mon ami?*" Bernay laughed.

"You bloody well surprise me!"

"You have such a lady too, and I suggest you not let her get away from you. If you love her, you must not be too proud to tell her so."

Pierre took a couple of strides over to the window, then looked out over the churning water. "Telling her is not the problem. Convincing a woman as stubborn as Charmaine is the hard part."

"Perhaps, Pierre, you expect too much from one so young. She is little more than a child. My Tasha is older," Jacques pointed out.

"Aren't you lucky?"

"*Oui*, I think so! Nevertheless, you might try to be a little more understanding and patient."

"What is this, Jacques? I fail to understand your attitude. Are you trying to tell me that I'm wrong and Charmaine is right?"

"Oh, come now Pierre! You and I were friends long before the little Charmaine came into your life. All I'm saying is I recall the night you first met her. You were smitten by her bewitching charms and by her guileless innocence. Yet you can be a very intimidating man. Perhaps you frighten the little sparrow, *n'est-ce pas?*"

"You think so, Jacques?" Pierre looked directly at his friend.

"I do. Such a petite, fragile maiden to do battle against one like you . . ." Jacques' tone of voice and his gestures were dramatic. He knew he was baiting his friend, but he was doing it for a worthy cause so he had no qualms. He felt as Tasha did: the two young people were meant for one another, but their foolish pride was setting up a barrier which would become insurmountable.

"Maybe, you are right, Bernay. I am much more experienced, older," Renaud agreed. He knew he had been the first man in her life, and he would always take great gratification in knowing that. No man had laid claim to the sweet nectar he'd first tasted! Listening to Bernay, he was beginning to feel like a cur.

Everything about Charmaine excited his male senses and he found himself aching for just the sight of her lovely face. He envisioned the deep blue of her eyes, richer and more exquisite than the sapphires his father had brought to his mother from the Orient. Oh, the soft, silken flesh of her yielding body. It was a joy to caress it. He ached to touch her, but he was here with Bernay.

With these sensuous memories gnawing at him, he knew he must seek their source—Charmaine! Bernay had been right about one thing: pride. To hell with pride! Pride could not sate his hunger. Only one woman could do that. He wanted her so desperately he pulsed with need. Bernay sensed that desperation so he wasn't surprised when Renaud abruptly declared, "I'll see you later, Jacques. Think I'll get a little fresh air. I've been in this cabin all afternoon."

"A good idea, Renaud!" Bernay sympathetically agreed. "Nothing like a little fresh air to clear a man's head."

He watched Pierre's hasty departure, then flung himself on the bunk, satisfied that what he and Tasha had planned to get the two young lovers back together was going to work. Because he was happy, he wanted Pierre to be happy.

Tasha's confession of her newly discovered love for Jacques Bernay only enhanced Charmaine's loneliness. Like Pierre, she had a desperate need to leave the cabin she was sharing with Tasha, to be alone with her misery. She made a hasty exit, using the exact same excuse as Pierre, the need of fresh air, and she felt that she would surely smother if she didn't get out of that cabin immediately.

It was only after she'd closed the door to the cabin and had started to walk down the darkened passageway that she heaved a deep sigh of relief. Away from Tasha's prying eyes, she began to relax. As she mounted the steps to the deck a calmness came over her.

She wanted to stand by the rail and look out over the churning waters of the Atlantic much as she'd sat on her cliff in Jersey and looked toward the distant shore of France, hoping that she'd find the answer to the problem prodding her heart and soul. There has to be an answer, she told herself. Tasha found an answer in the brief span of an afternoon. Why couldn't she?

Let there be starlight and the magic of the moon. Let this be like that glorious night in Jersey, she prayed. If so, she knew she'd find her answer.

In that secret place in her heart, she wished for Pierre to come to her, to hold her lovingly, as only he could, to assure her that he loved her as devotedly as she loved him.

As she ambled across the deck toward the rail, her eyes looked upward toward the heavens. A million stars twinkled in the sky and a full golden moon shone down on her. Charmaine knew that Pierre would come to her as she stood in the moonlight. Before the night was over, ecstasy would be hers once again!

Chapter 33

The stars and the moon made her heart cry out more fiercely that she loved Pierre Renaud. The sea breeze whipped at her long, loose hair, and Charmaine's petite body felt the impact of its strong gusts. The shawl gave her little protection against the chill that had intensified since sunset.

But she was not about to return to the cabin just yet. So, unable to stop the trembling of her body, she clutched the light woollen shawl around her.

By now she was questioning her romantic, reckless heart. Perhaps, she should stop doing the impulsive things it demanded of her. Perhaps, she should start doing what her head told her, instead. Listening to her heart brought torment. Maybe, that was what her Aunt Simone had tried to teach her back on Jersey.

God knows, she'd been foolish enough the last few months and she'd paid for it with heartbreak! But her heartbreak had only increased when she had dared to stand up to Renaud.

She glanced up and saw someone ambling toward her across the darkened deck. It looked like the broad-shouldered grizzly old captain. She cringed everytime he ogled her for she felt that he was undressing her. She wished to heaven she'd not picked such a secluded spot, though it did provide shelter from the gusting winds.

The closer the figure came the more certain she was it was Jim Garrett, for she could make out a mane of hair tousled by the breeze. She realized there was no way she could avoid an encounter with the rugged old captain.

It was Pierre Renaud, not Garrett, who was ambling along, wishing he'd put a cap on his unruly head. He'd not yet glanced up to see the tiny figure directly before him. Only when the aroma of jasmine was wafted to his nose did he raise his head. Then he beheld her standing there as if she'd been waiting for him to come to her.

"Charmaine!" he spread his arm wide, and without another word being spoken she rushed to be enfolded in them. His lips whispered softly and lovingly in her ear, "You silly little fool! You're trembling, *chérie!*"

"I'm cold, Pierre! So very cold!" she said in a soft voice.

"And so am I. I've been cold, Charmaine Lamoureux, since you moved from my bed, and there has been no warmth in my heart and soul." He swept her tiny body into his arms and pressed her against his broad chest. She could feel the wild pounding of his heart, and it stirred her desire.

"Pierre?" she murmured, her eyes gazing into his.

"Hhhmmm?" He walked at a hurried pace. "What, my precious?"

"Where are you carrying me?"

"To our cabin. It's been lonely without you there, Charmaine," he confessed.

She raised her half-parted lips to invite him to kiss her and he eagerly obliged. "I've missed the sweet taste of those lips more than you know."

"I've missed you too, Pierre," she admitted.

"Then I'll see that you don't miss me anymore." He gave her one of his handsome crooked grins.

The moonlight made her so lovely he couldn't resist kissing her again. He throbbed with overwhelming desire, his hands caressing her rounded hips as he carried her. Anticipation was already consuming him, and a fever mounted in his blood at the thought of her satiny naked flesh once he undressed her in the seclusion of his cabin. God, he'd yearned for her on so many long, lonely nights. Now, soon, very soon, his dream would finally come true. He lengthened his strides.

When he finally crossed the threshold, he reminded himself not to let his overeagerness drive her away from him. But his will power was going to be sorely tested, he knew.

"This is the right place for you, Charmaine Lamoureux. You surely know it just as I do." He set her down so she could stand on the floor while he secured the door.

"Do you really feel that way, Pierre? I mean . . . it's not just—"

"It never was just one brief moment of pleasure, if that's what you're asking me, *chérie*." His gray eyes met hers and their sincere gleam bespoke honesty.

"I want to believe you, Pierre," she told him, boldly placing her hands on either side of his cheeks and arching upward so his lips could capture hers in a long, lingering kiss. His strong hands pressed at her back, and she found herself crushed against the front of him, his hardened manhood rubbing against her and displaying the potency of his desire.

"Now you know, imp, what you do to me." As he teased her, his hands were already removing her shawl and beginning to unfasten the front of her bodice. "It is only fair that I find out what I do to you, eh?"

"You know darned well what you do to me, Pierre Renaud," she retorted. His long, slender fingers worked expertly at removing her gown and she helped him accomplish the task more quickly. When the bodice lay limp around her waistline, Pierre could not deny himself the nectar of her tantalizing breasts. He kissed one and then the other, his sensuous lips and his tongue teasing them with sweetly tormenting strokes.

She moaned with pleasure, knowing too well how she'd missed his caresses. "Don't stop Pierre. Please don't. It feels so good."

"It's going to feel even better, my pet, in just a minute," he vowed, as he forcefully removed the rest of her clothing and his own.

The feel of her heated, flushed flesh undulating temptingly against him pleased him, for he knew she was starved for him and his love. This delighted him.

A wave of passion surged through him so he guided Charmaine over to the bunk. No longer able to endure the aching of his male body, he drew her down onto the bunk.

His thighs encased her, and his hands and lips roamed over her silken flesh, feeling her quiver wherever his caresses seared her. He moaned with delighted anguish when her honeyed lips kissed him, and as the crescendo of their swaying, thrusting bodies built, he felt her dainty hands pressing on him in an attempt to absorb all of his forceful being. In a husky voice he told her how very much she delighted him.

"Oh, Pierre, come to me now or I'll surely die," she gasped breathlessly. As he burrowed himself between her soft thighs penetrating her velvety softness and letting himself drown in the liquid heat of her untamed passion, she embraced him as if she would surely stop breathing if he were to leave her.

In their sensual paradise they swayed and danced to the tempo dictated by passion, their accompaniment, moans of pleasure. When Pierre's firm, muscled body shuddered, Charmaine gasped and then she, too, was flooded with rapture.

Then, content and sated, they lay in one another's arms. It was glorious!

Both dwelled in a private world of languorous dreams. Renaud was thinking about the future with Charmaine by his side. He decided he'd build his own little empire, just as his own father had. It would be all his own doing.

Rightly or wrongly, Charmaine blessed the day she'd not

boarded that packet to accompany Tasha to Norfolk, for if she had, she'd be George Seymour's wife and this wonderful night with Renaud would have been denied her.

The words of love Pierre had murmured in her ear, the sweet memory of his touch and his caress were etched in her heart and soul.

There, in the dark cabin, as she lay quietly by his side, she knew she'd love him until the end of time!

No one would have laughed more boisterously than lusty Jim Garrett if he'd known about the romantic aura hovering around his old schooner this night. He would have been envious too, for no voluptuous woman filled his bed.

When neither Renaud nor Bernay came by his quarters for the usual nightly card games and when he found neither of the young Frenchmen roaming the deck of his ship, he sequestered himself in his cabin and drank his fill of some good Cuban rum.

Renaud was not the only man enjoying the company of a lady. Bernay had known when Pierre had mentioned his need of some fresh air that it was Charmaine he was going to seek. An hour later, Bernay felt certain his friend had found his lady and they were together. Lonely in the cabin, he'd had an urge to see Tasha. As he'd run the brush through his curly hair, he'd thought it would have been nice to take her a beautiful bouquet of flowers, but that was impossible. He wished for some little trinket, some token of his affection. Staring into the mirror to check the sides of his hair, he thought to himself that he had little to offer such a sweet, deserving lady as Tasha.

Would he be selfish and ask her to share his life? What could he actually promise her? The Missouri Territory might provide only a very bleak existence for such a fragile-looking lady.

Suddenly, the thirty-year-old Bernay dug into his old

worn valise with boyish exuberance. Excitedly, he tossed articles onto the floor, seeking the wee box that contained his mother's ring. He did have a token to present to Tasha after all.

When he finally came upon the object he sought, he smiled and sat down on the floor to open the box. When he did he was pleased to find it a worthy gift for the lady he loved. Oh, the opal stone in the gold band wasn't large, but it was brilliant. Bernay leaped up and placed the ring in his pocket.

He was now ready to call on Tasha Weer. Jacques could have been a youth going to court the young lady with whom he was infatuated. There was a sprightly air about him as he strode down the narrow passageway toward Tasha's cabin. His spirit was younger than springtime.

As he'd hoped, she greeted him with a warm, inviting smile, and she was alone. In her straightforward way she remarked, "Jacques, you must surely be able to read my mind. I was thinking about you."

"Oh, I can, *ma petite*. That is why I rushed to you," he said, a grin on his face.

"Good! Charmaine has been gone for some time now and I'm hoping that she and Pierre have patched up their differences. Do you suppose they have?"

"I think that is possible, for Pierre has been gone a long time too." He took her hand in his and brought it to his lips to kiss. Then, leading her over to the bed, he urged her to sit down and he sank down beside her. His voice was husky with emotion as he confessed, "I hope they stay occupied for a long time so I can be alone with you, Tasha, my love."

"You're so sweet, Jacques."

Her adoring words made Bernay's broad chest swell with pride. Perhaps, it was her openness that made him want to be sincere with her. "I am a man in love Tasha. It's as simple as that. I've had many women in my thirty years of roaming around, but I've never really been in love until now."

Tasha flung herself into his arms, declaring that she'd

286

never been in love before either, and when Jacques lips captured hers their kiss was far different from the earlier one on deck. His lips seared hers, telling of his passion. When she responded eagerly, he realized she was a woman of fire and passion. She had only needed the right man to ignite it.

When Jacques finally released her, he took the ring from his pocket. Holding her hand in his, he slipped it on her slender finger, vowing, "It's all I have to give you right now, but it binds us if you wish. Will you be mine, Tasha?"

"Oh yes, Jacques. I'll be yours forever," she whispered, and when a misty tear crept down her cheek Jacques quickly kissed it away.

Theirs was a night of discovery. Like Charmaine and Pierre, they remained enclosed in one another's arms long after their ecstasy had turned to peaceful sharing, and Jacques had no desire to return to his lonely cabin.

Chapter 34

The captain of the packet did not know about the new arrangements regarding quarters, but he was very aware that there'd been no card games for over a week, and no late-night drinking with the two Frenchmen. He had noticed, too, how the four passengers had paired off when they'd gone ashore in Mobile during the layover there.

No one was more amazed than Tasha Weer about the transformation in her life and herself. Since that magical moment when Bernay had given her his mother's ring, she'd spent the nights with him without shame or regret. She completely trusted Jacques and she believed they would marry when it was possible. While she did not flaunt the relationship, she did not attempt to hide her feeling for the man she loved. Despite her dignified air, she reserved nothing where Jacques was concerned. He adored the free way she surrendered herself to him. He'd been delightfully pleased to discover his little Tasha was a very sensuous lady.

Like his friend Bernay, Renaud was feasting on days and nights spent with his golden goddess. Because he was so happy to have wooed her back to his cabin, he did not notice the telltale signs of Charmaine's discontent. She concealed them from Pierre quite cleverly, and from Tasha most of the time.

But there one afternoon when the two ladies were alone, Charmaine's moody manner was obvious to Tasha. Wondering if her friend was not feeling well, she asked, "Has something upset you, Charmaine? You and Pierre are not disagreeing again, are you?"

"No, Tasha—on both accounts." She forced a smile.

"Then what is troubling you?"

"Would you believe me if I told you I don't really know," Charmaine remarked.

In part, that was the truth, for she wasn't quite certain what was causing her discontent. Pierre was a devoted lover, sweet and tender. When they'd gone ashore in Mobile he had been most generous and extravagant, buying her an exquisite gold bracelet and a gold velvet reticule she'd spied in a shop window. Indeed, when the schooner had plowed out into Mobile Bay to continue the voyage into the Gulf of Mexico, he'd told her when they got to New Orleans he was going to take her on the most outrageous shopping spree she'd ever been on. She had giggled girlishly, "You've bought me enough already, Pierre."

But his lavish gifts made her feel like the courtesans she'd heard about, and she was haunted by Sarnia Wakefield's remark that Pierre was an aristocrat, the son of a wealthy Frenchman. Sarnia had smugly pointed out that his kind didn't marry common little farm girls.

During all their tempestuous love affair, Pierre had never once mentioned marriage, though Tasha had told her Jacques had. Her nature was not like Tasha's, and she found it impossible to put her life completely in the hands of Pierre Renaud. Yet, he made her feel safe and secure when he held her or walked at her side.

On the dock in Mobile when a fierce-looking swarthy man in uniform had stopped them and had spoken to Pierre, Renaud had responded in his assured, arrogant way. After they'd walked away, Charmaine had inquired, "What language did you both speak?"

"Spanish, *ma petite*. The Spanish officers are still in authority here."

"But this is America," she'd remarked, a confused look on her upturned face.

"You are right, and the United States has claimed Mobile since 1803, but the treaties were never clear. Spain still claims that Mobile is in Florida, not Louisiana. Louisiana is where we are heading next, Charmaine. The mouth of the Mississippi River is in the city of New Orleans, and we'll travel up that wide river to the Missouri Territory, where my uncle has settled."

"It sounds so far, so many miles away," she had muttered. Were it not for Pierre, she would have been apprehensive about such a venture.

To her, it seemed that Pierre Renaud knew everything, and more and more she realized how naïve she was. He was intimidating for she already knew him to be formidable when he was denied his way.

Knowing her weakness for him, Charmaine was determined not to let Pierre dominate her completely. Much as she loved Pierre, she would not allow that to happen.

With her thoughts on Renaud, she was paying little attention to what Tasha was prattling about until Tasha's insistent voice prodded her. "Charmaine, you are a million miles away this afternoon!"

"I guess I am. Please forgive me. I think I need to set foot on land. My spirits will rise when we arrive in this place Pierre calls New Orleans."

Her words seemed to satisfy Tasha who decided Charmaine was bored due to their long trip aboard the packet. "Did I tell you that Jacques is going to help me try to locate my niece and my nephews while we are there. We'll have a few days, for Pierre must arrange the last part of this odyssey we've been on." She laughed softly.

"No, you hadn't told me, Tasha. I'm certain Jacques will do everything he can to help you locate them. He's a good man."

"Charmaine, I can't tell you how completely happy I am about how everything's turned out. Why, if I died tomorrow—God forbid—I would die happy. I never expected to know such bliss. You probably dreamed bigger dreams than I did. Mine were simple because I thought I was ugly until Jacques Bernay made me feel beautiful."

"Oh, Tasha." Charmaine sighed.

"You know something? I look in the mirror now and I feel a little more attractive." Tasha laughed gaily.

Her light-heartedness affected Charmaine, and she sought to tease her little black-haired friend. "I know one thing, Tasha Weer, you're not the shy little violet I thought you were when we met on that ship leaving Jersey, I can tell you that!"

"No, I'm not and I'm glad I'm not. It was my good fortune to meet you, Charmaine Lamoureux, and then Jacques Bernay. I thank God for both of you!"

Charmaine gave her friend a warm embrace and thanked her for her gracious tribute. When she departed Tasha's cabin to return to her own, her spirits had lifted.

The packet did not linger long at the wharf in Biloxi for Captain Garrett carried only a small amount of cargo to be delivered there and he took on none. In recent years Morgan Fleetlines handled most of Biloxi's shipping. Garrett knew this and he always charted his course so his schooner made port late at night. At that hour the port was for the most part deserted and idle, but Garrett could get on his way to New Orleans sooner.

New Orleans was a different matter, however, and he'd be taking on a lot of cargo there. Besides, this was the liveliest, gayest port he'd ever made. There were lovely dark-eyed Creole ladies, numerous gambling halls, and brothels. To Garrett, every street corner breathed life and spirit, and a million wonderful aromas tempted passers-by on the bustling streets.

Such a mixture of faces was to be seen on New Orleans' streets. Garrett had never forgotten one exquisitely lovely woman who'd sauntered past him. Her black, almond-shaped eyes had stared straight ahead never glancing his way, but his had gazed after her long after she'd gone on her way, carrying the wicker basket atop her head with such perfect grace. Her head was tied in a turbanlike kerchief of colored calico, the same material as her frock, which was draped over the most perfectly shaped figure he'd ever seen. He'd fantasized many a time afterward about how her satiny, golden skin would look bared to his eyes.

Oh, he'd admired many lovely mulattos he'd seen in New Orleans, but this one was a light-skinned quadroon. He had seen her for only a moment, but he'd always felt he'd recognize her if he saw her again. That was incentive enough to make him eager to travel to New Orleans.

If the stiff, strong breeze held, another day and night would get the schooner to the Louisiana coast.

Once again, he'd be saying farewell to his French friends, Renaud and Bernay. For a moment, Garrett wished he were going to travel up the Mississippi River on one of those large keel boats Pierre was telling him about. He had no more knowledge of the Missouri Territory than Pierre Renaud for he had never been that far west or north. But the keel boat intrigued him for his sailing experience had been confined to the two- and three-masted schooners.

It would seem strange not to be propelled by sails, Garrett thought. He knew he'd not make the trip, and he'd probably never see the pair or their lady companions again once they'd said goodbye at the pier in New Orleans. However, he'd learned a long time ago never to say never.

He leaned over to dim the lantern hanging over his cluttered desk, intending to turn in for the night and get some sleep. Biloxi was a good ten miles behind, and the ship was moving at a good clip. His capable mate was at the helm, so he could sleep well.

He might not be as young and randy as he once was. However, he wasn't so old that he couldn't dream, and tonight he would dream about New Orleans. He was long overdue for a long night of carousing. He'd been sorely tempted by the gorgeous Charmaine Lamoureux for many nights. The sight of her whetted his appetite for a woman.

But Renaud's menacing eyes had warned him not to try anything with her!

PART III

Delta Moonlight

Chapter 35

Charmaine stood at the mirror, trying to tie the bow at the right angle so her bonnet would look the way she desired, but the wide green velvet band was proving to be stubborn. It kept causing the bonnet to twist, so she fumed and fussed until she made the puffy bow the right size.

"Well, finally." She sighed wearily as she turned first one way and then another to absorb the whole effect of her outfit. She was pleased by her image. The rich, luxurious deep green velvet was becoming.

She knew that part of her struggle to tie the bow was due to sheer excitement for Pierre had dashed into the cabin to relate the news that she was to get herself dressed and her things gathered together. "Captain Garrett says we'll be arriving in another hour, Charmaine," he had added, before rushing back out of the cabin.

That had been more than a half-hour ago. In the interim she had scurried around the cabin, churning with excitement as she'd packed and dressed hastily. Only the velvet bonnet had slowed her pace.

Her spirits had soared because they were finally going to dock. She would be off the schooner she was beginning to detest. And she was happy because she and Pierre had enjoyed a quiet, intimate night in their cabin, eating their dinner off trays. He had told her many things about his life. His descriptions of his boyish pranks had made her laugh, and he had spoken of his mother and father. She now felt a new bond of closeness with this handsome man she loved.

They might have been husband and wife enjoying a quiet evening at home, she thought. How nice it would be to have a home again.

Whatever had caused her happiness she wished it would last forever. Her moodiness of yesterday had not returned.

She heard a sudden burst of activity up on the deck, and at that same instant, Pierre came in the door. A broad grin on his face, he announced, "We're there, ma *chérie!* You ready?"

She gave him a radiant smile, "I am!"

When she took his arm, he couldn't resist kissing her on the cheek. Then he escorted her up on deck, to join the trio assembled at the rail. Captain Garrett was pointing out to Bernay and Tasha the small outline across the water, was telling them it was the city of New Orleans.

Already, the busy activity in the harbor could be seen. Two- and three-masted schooners and frigates were coming and going, and the numerous white dots in the sky above them were sea gulls. Garrett told them that these birds followed the shrimp boats into the harbor.

"Best damn shrimp in the world are caught right here off the Louisiana coast. I can swear to that, my friends," Garrett declared to the two couples.

High above their heads the huge sails expanded as the stiff breeze invaded them, and the schooner plowed through the waters at a faster pace.

All the while Garrett kept up a conversation with Pierre and Jacques. He teased the two of them by saying, "Why you two will feel like you're back in your native France when you get to New Orleans. The French influence touches every-thing in that city." Leaning closer so the two ladies wouldn't hear his comment, he tried to whisper low, "Wait till you see those pretty French Creole ladies! Never saw so many in one place in my whole blooming life." He chuckled lustily, and both Charmaine and Tasha looked in his direction, wondering what was so amusing.

By this time the schooner was near enough to the wharves to enable them to see the people on the piers. The crowd reminded Charmaine of the marketplace back in St. Helier, and the varied skin colors fascinated her and Tasha. The women busily scanned the throng, too engrossed in it to listen to the men's conversation.

"Look, Charmaine—look at that huge black man! How could he possibly balance such a huge basket on his hat. It looks like it would fall off for sure," Tasha excitedly exclaimed.

But Charmaine's eyes were glued to a little monkey with a wee hat atop its head. The creature was performing for a gathering of people as its owner propelled his vending cart along the wharf. Whenever the man stopped while someone purchased flowers, the monkey went into his antics.

Before the schooner came to a halt and the ropes were secured, Charmaine caught the aroma of exotic spices. They were being sold there in baskets, separated according to kind.

As a black man chanted from his flat-bedded wagon, calling out his wares as if he were singing a song, Charmaine decided there was something magical about this strange city of New Orleans. It was fascinating and exciting.

When her blue eyes caught sight of a tall gentleman who wore a hat made of fur pelts, her gaze remained upon him. She'd never seen any man wear the buckskin garb which was molded to this man's powerful body, and there was a fierceness about him. His face was so bronzed, she asked Pierre if he was one of the Indians he'd talked about.

He chuckled. "No, *ma petite*. He is not an Indian. He is an American—probably a woodsman or a frontiersman, I would say."

He noticed that the gangplank was now lowered and he urged her to take his arm so they could proceed down it. Jacques and Tasha were already heading toward the plank wharf.

As the two couples descended the gangplank, two finely attired gentlemen wearing diamond stickpins and carrying fancy-handled walking canes scrutinized these new arrivals to their city. The focus of their attention was the gorgeous golden-haired lovely on the arm of the tall, dark gentleman. But Pierre Renaud was a striking figure of a man, who did not fail to make an impression on them.

The dark green velvet bonnet which framed her face enhanced Charmaine's delicate features, and its multicolored plumes swayed as she moved along beside Pierre, her expression reflecting her excitement.

She was alive and vivacious, and the two gentlemen admiring her weren't the only ones aware of this. Pierre felt her petite body brush his side and he turned to smile at her, sensing the spice and ginger of her mood on this bright sunshiny winter day.

It was hard to believe it was late winter for the weather was so mild. Pierre recalled the cutting chill in Guernsey when they'd departed some weeks ago. To see the vendor selling winter-blooming flowers was amazing.

Charmaine was such a bewitching sight he swelled with pride. He did not notice the two men eyeing him enviously. If he had, he would not have been smiling.

As they walked down the wharf, Pierre accepted the first offer of carriage service. He did not notice that the two debonair gentlemen were boarding a carriage with the intent of following his equipage.

When Pierre instructed the carriage driver to take them to the Royale Hotel, the man tipped his tall, black hat. "Yes, *monsieur*. The Royale it is."

As the carriage rolled up the cobbled stone street, heading toward the center of the city, another followed it, carrying

Henri Gervais and his friend Adrien Bayard. They were wastrels. Offspring of prominent French Creole families, they had too much time on their hands, and they indulged in wild sprees both in the city and in the countryside around New Orleans. The victims of their sudden impulses might be men or women. That mattered not to Henri and Adrien for they were sure no one would dare to be out of favor with the Gervais or Bayard families. Up to now that had been the case.

Charmaine's golden loveliness had caught their lustful eyes, and so they intended to find out just who this ravishing beauty and her male companion were.

This was their mission as they trailed behind the carriage carrying Pierre Renaud and Charmaine, Bernay and Tasha.

The four in the carriage, being newcomers to the city, were completely engrossed in the picturesque streets they were riding through. However, Pierre was a little more prepared for what he was seeing because he'd read his father's description.

When the carriage finally came to a stop in the front of the Royale Hotel with its lavishly trimmed grill work and overhanging balcony, Henri and Adrien watched the two couples emerge from the carriage and enter the hotel.

"They obviously like the best, Henri." Adrien smirked.

Henri's expressionless face looked straight ahead. His sharp aquiline features did not reveal that he'd heard what Adrien had said. Only when Adrien repeated his statement did Henri turn in his direction to mumble an answer.

A few minutes after the Renaud entourage had gone inside, Henri Gervais prodded his friend to get out of the carriage.

"We are going inside?" Adrien asked.

Gervais, irritated with his dull friend, pointed out, "How else are we going to find out who they are, especially that little beauty."

"I see."

301

"Come on, Adrien. They should be gone from the lobby by now."

Having timed his move Henri marched into the lobby. With his usual authoritative air, he spoke to the bespectacled young man behind the desk, knowing the clerk would not dare to deny his request. When he'd secured out the information he sought, he turned sharply away and summoned Adrien to follow him.

"Where are we off to now, Henri?" Adrien tagged along, like an obedient puppy, at the heels of Gervais.

Slapping his gloves against the palm of his hand, Henri Gervais addressed him as if he were an irritating child. "Just shut up and come on!"

Once they were back inside Henri's fine carriage, he instructed his driver to take them to his father's plantation just outside the city.

Having no knowledge of the devious web being spun to entrap her, Charmaine was enjoying her first afternoon in the city of New Orleans. Later, with her three companions she tasted the delights the hotel's dining room offered. She'd never tasted such delectable fare and she found it to her liking.

Captain Garrett had certainly spoken the truth about the shrimp. She ate them so ravenously, Pierre teased her. "For one so little, you have a tremendous appetite, chérie."

She adored everything about the evening, especially the attention Pierre showered on her. He bought her a lovely blood-red rose when a woman selling flowers approached their table. Jacques picked out a yellow one for Tasha.

It was a romantic evening, and anyone viewing the two couples would have known they were lovers for their actions and their expressions made it obvious.

Pierre was as reluctant as the rest of his party to end the evening, but he knew he must attend to many details before they could hope to be on the final lap of their journey. In addition to his own affairs, he had to deliver a document

302

personally to his father's friend, Robert Gervais. When Étienne had placed the thick envelope into Pierre's hand, he'd firmly cautioned his son to give this only to a Monsieur Robert Gervais and to no one else.

In order to carry out this mission for his father, he must leave Charmaine on her own and this didn't please him. He planned to take off part of the next day so he could show her the city and let her shop to her heart's content. Most likely, she'd be deprived of fine shops once they arrived in Missouri Territory.

When Jacques announced his plans for the next day, Pierre was in a quandary. "I promised Tasha I'd help her try to locate her sister-in-law's family. We don't have much time here so we must make every minute count," he'd declared.

"I understand, Jacques." He turned his adoring eyes on Charmaine. "But what am I going to do with you while I'm gone? I can't chance having you roam about alone, not in New Orleans."

She smiled up at him. "I'm not exactly a baby, Pierre. I will wait for the three of you to finish your business."

"But, sweet, I could be gone all day, and so could Jacques and Tasha," Renaud informed her.

"Then I'll sleep late and just make myself beautiful while the rest of you are busy." She giggled.

He could have been her father sternly warning her when he next spoke. "I'm not jesting, Charmaine, about you daring to venture outside this hotel door. If your appetite gets the best of you, I suppose it's safe to go down to eat, but not a step farther."

"When you talk like that, you frighten me, Pierre!" She became serious and stared at him wide-eyed. "What is this, a city of barbarians?"

"It is a very busy port city which attracts a lot of scoundrels. A beautiful lady like you is a beacon for them. I wish no harm to come to you, *ma petite.*" His hand clasped hers tightly and held it.

"Nor do I, Pierre. My experience in Savannah was enough to last me for a lifetime. I never want to go through that again."

As she looked at him with her deep blue eyes, he had an overwhelming desire to know how she'd looked as a child. What he was feeling, however, was directed at a woman, a sensuous, sometimes baffling, bewitching woman.

At moments like this, she made him feel ancient because he realized how much more he'd seen of life than this guileless farm girl from the isle of Jersey. A part of him took selfish delight in that, for he wanted to teach her everything she needed to know. He wanted her untouched by any other man. He wanted her to be his and his alone.

But tonight he'd decided not to be too serious or too demanding, for she was so gay, so excited. She was a vision of loveliness in her blue velvet gown, her golden hair caressing her soft shoulders. His only regret, as he looked across the table at her, the candlelight flickering on her face, was that he didn't have some of the magnificent Renaud jewels to present to her. If they were at his family's fine mansion or the country estate, he would have been introducing her to his parents as the young lady he'd chosen for his bride, and it would have been his right and pleasure to have gifted her with a family heirloom.

But he was here in a strange, new world—a country he knew little about. Maybe this was their destiny. Maybe he and Charmaine would explore this land together, build something more magnificent than anything he could have attained if he'd not left Cherbourg. That must surely be so for if he'd not left Cherbourg, he'd never have met Charmaine Lamoureux.

Chapter 36

Nothing had gone right on this late winter day. Tasha
Weer was bone weary and she envied Charmaine who was
back in the comfort of the hotel where they'd spent the night.
While Charmaine had slept late as she'd planned, Tasha and
Jacques had breakfasted on coffee and buttered croissants in
the hotel dining room before starting out to try to locate
Jacob's dead wife's relatives.

Their search had been more time consuming than Tasha
had expected, for there were four families in New Orleans
with the same surname. Tasha wondered why she'd ever
labored under the false impression that her brother's wife
had ever come from the gentry, for such was not the case
when she and Jacques had finally tracked down Jacob's
wife's mother, who was a widow living on the outskirts of
New Orleans. Tasha was dismayed and disillusioned after
their brief visit to the woman's humble home for she now felt
she could possibly not possibly locate Jacob's orphans. The
poor old lady knew nothing of their whereabouts.

Tasha and Jacques boarded the carriage they'd hired for
the day, and as the sun was setting over the levee, they started
back to the city of New Orleans. As Jacques' strong arm
went around her shoulder, Tasha realized how utterly futile
her idea to come to New Orleans had been. What if she'd

arrived in this city all alone, if she'd not met up with Charmaine or her beloved Jacques? She'd have been in a miserable dilemma! God forbid, she'd not know what to do here where she knew no one!

As if Jacques could read her mind, he pressed her closer to him. Despite his rugged exterior, he had the gentle soul of a poet. His voice soothed and comforted her. "You can do no more now, Tasha. You must know that, *chérie.*"

"I know, Jacques, but it makes me very sad."

"Let me try to make you happy for the rest of your life. Marry me, right here in New Orleans. Then we'll travel to this Missouri Territory as husband and wife. Nothing could make me prouder or happier."

She flung her arms around his neck and pulled his curly head close so she could kiss him. "Oh, Jacques Bernay, fortune smiled on me the day I met you! You are so sweet and good."

"No, Tasha, it is you, who are sweet and good! I have nothing to offer you and I know not what awaits us in this Missouri Territory I've promised to follow Renaud to, but I want you to share my life. I'll work my fingers to the bone if necessary, Tasha. I've worked hard all my life whether on land or sea. I've never starved, and God knows, I'd not let you starve. I'd steal first."

She laughed light-heartedly. "You're not talking to a young lass who's been petted or pampered, Jacques Bernay. I've worked hard all my life. I'll work with you and we'll make out just fine."

"*Oui,* when the bad times come, *ma petite* Tasha, they will make us enjoy the good times all the more. Is that not so?"

"It is so!" She arched to meet Jacques' lips in a long and lingering kiss.

When they reached the hotel, they did not seek the company of their friends for they wanted to be alone in their lovers' bliss.

* * *

When Pierre rapped on Bernay's door and got no response, he shrugged his shoulders, knowing he could not tarry any longer. He'd intended to tell Jacques that he and Charmaine were invited to dinner this evening out at the Gervais plantation, but it seemed Jacques and Tasha were already out. That was just as well. The invitation did not include the two of them anyway. He was tired and weary, sorely in need of a bath and a change of clothing, and Charmaine was waspish after being alone all day. At least, he was happy to know she'd been bored for that meant she'd obeyed his orders and remained in the room. She'd even had a light lunch served there.

He dashed back down the carpeted hallway hoping to find her preparing her toilette, instead of pouting and vowing she'd not go with him. The stubborn little minx!

The day had been a taxing one for Pierre. But he had arranged for their passage on a keel boat and he'd dickered with a bastard which had riled him to the limits. Something about the rawboned pilot of the keel boat had impressed Pierre. He felt the buckskin-clad man was capable and would know the river. As Pierre had listened to him talk he'd been convinced this pilot knew every crook and bend in the Mississippi, that he was aware of the sand bars and snags that could ground a large keel boat. After they'd talked and bantered for over two hours, Renaud had made his deal with the man called Morrow. Instinct had guided Renaud. It had told him this young man was trustworthy. Cocky and arrogant, yes, but he knew the river they'd be traveling to reach Missouri Territory.

That part of his busy day had gone the way he'd wanted it to and he'd felt gratified. He'd stopped in one of the local coffee houses for a light repast; then he'd headed for the outskirts of New Orleans to carry out the mission for his father.

The Gervais estate was impressive as Pierre had galloped up the long drive on the black stallion he'd secured from the livery. He'd noticed that here they called landed estates "plantations" and as he'd ridden through the white gateway to the drive, he'd noted that the name of the plantation was Gervais' Glen. Pierre had been told by his father that his friend Robert had married an Irish lass before going to America to settle and raise his family.

As Pierre galloped past the boxwood shrubs lining the long, winding drive, he thought, What a combination—a Frenchman and an Irish lady!

But once he'd entered the fine old mansion and met his charming host and hostess he found them a charming couple. He was pleasantly reminded of his own parents. Even the surroundings were similar to those of his home in France. The only difference was that here the house servants were all black. But the graces and charm of France was here; Pierre felt right at home. Old Garrett had been right about New Orleans making him feel he was back in France. The French influence was obvious!

He'd enjoyed a most pleasant hour with the hospitable Robert Gervais and his wife, who Pierre had assumed to be about the age of his own parents. When he'd prepared to leave, they had insisted he remain for dinner, but Pierre had refused, telling him his bride-to-be and her companion awaited him at the Royale.

Then Madame Gervais had quickly exclaimed, "Why that is wonderful, isn't it, Robert? We'd be delighted to meet your young lady. I know Robert has been thrilled to talk with you, Pierre—Étienne's son. I only saw your father a couple of years ago, but his friendship with my husband goes back over the years."

Robert Gervais had made it almost impossible for Pierre to refuse by declaring, "Our house would be honored. I know if our son Henri was in Cherbourg that father of yours would insist he sit at the dining table at least one evening."

So in the end, Pierre had agreed to return for dinner in a few hours. However, he had conjured up the excuse that Charmaine's companion was feeling poorly so he rather doubted that she'd be able to accompany them.

"Then our carriage will arrive at the Royale at a quarter of seven, *oui?*" Madame Gervais had suggested.

Now that was the deadline he faced as he hurriedly returned to his room to dress. Arguing with Charmaine had taken up precious time, so he'd decided to let her fume while he had a brief talk with Bernay, to tell him where they were going for the evening and to let him know he'd obtained passage on a keel boat. But that futile attempt had only wasted more time.

At least, when he dashed back into his own suite of rooms, the sounds he heard in the next room told him Charmaine was doing what he'd told her to do. He could hear the splashing of water in the bronze tub. Did he dare hope to see a smile on her lovely face, instead of a frown?

He stopped short of walking through the door of the little dressing room adjacent to their boudoir for if he did, he told himself, they'd never make it down to the lobby to board the Gervais' carriage. *Mon Dieu,* he'd be lost if he saw her silken flesh.

Instead, he took out one of his fresh white linen shirts, finely tailored black pants, and a coat. Knowing how long she lingered in her scented bath water, he figured he'd be dressed by the time she came out. He'd also be ready to help her into a gown with the usual complicated fastenings. He grinned, wondering if the little imp was plotting to persuade him to stay here instead of going out to the Gervais' plantation. Well, he wouldn't step into her trap if that was the case!

Charmaine had set no trap for Pierre, but she felt trapped. She feared she might prove an embarrassment to the man she loved when she met his aristocratic friends, the Gervais family.

As she'd sat quietly and thoughtfully in the tub, she asked herself a dozen questions. How would she know what to say to them? What gown would be suitable for the occasion? What if there were many other guests besides the Gervais family? Oh, I feel so ill at ease, she muttered. While her

309

sophisticated Pierre would be doing all the right things she envisioned herself doing something so gauche he'd look at her with contempt.

Oh, if he did she would surely wither away and die, especially after the wonderful interlude they'd just enjoyed. Worst of all, she was haunted by Sarnia's warning that Pierre was destined to marry a lady of quality. What if such a young lady was present at dinner? Would he compare the two of them? These were longtime friends of his fathers, he'd told her hastily before he'd left a few minutes ago. When she could no longer delay getting out of the tub, she stepped out and went through the motions of drying herself off. She actually felt giddy as she did so, for her temples throbbed due to all her troubled thoughts.

When she went from the dressing room into the lavish bedroom, Pierre's gray eyes surveyed her with astonishment. He stopped pulling on his highly polished black boots, then stared at her for a moment, waiting for her to speak to him.

She appeared to be in a daze, but when he was about to call out to her, she said softly, "Oh, Pierre . . . I didn't hear you come in."

"Are you all right, Charmaine?" If this was an act she should play London's Theatre Royal for she was damned good.

Dejectedly, she shrugged her dainty shoulders and declared, "I don't know what I should wear to your friends' dinner." There was such a helpless, desolate look in her blue eyes he was convinced she wasn't faking.

He went to her, kissing her still-damp cheek. "Is that the cause of your forlorn look, *ma chérie?*"

"That just one of many things," she mumbled.

"Well, let's take care of that first, and I'll help you struggle with all the others." He led her over to help her select a gown, and as his arm lay upon her shoulders, he knew there was nothing under that draped towel but her sensuous, petite body. That knowledge was enough to drive him crazy with

310

desire, but he had to resist temptation.

He made himself put aside his sexual desire, and he concentrated on choosing a gown which would flatter her fair loveliness.

"This one, *ma petite.*" He lifted out the cream-colored satin which reminded him of her soft skin. An overlay of delicate cream-colored lace enhanced the skirt of the gown. It was trimmed with blue and pink rosettes, and the cut of the neckline was low enough to be interesting but not revealing. Ah, yes, he thought to himself, she will look divine in that.

Like a connoisseur, he picked up the satin slipper she'd worn when they'd dined in the hotel, and he draped a cream-colored cape across the bed. Then he laughed, *"Voila!* The rest is for you to do, but I am here to help if you need me, sweet. Please, Charmaine, do hurry. The Gervais carriage will be here shortly."

He fetched one of his cheroots from his gold case and made a last-minute adjustment to his white ruffled shirt, then he left so Charmaine could attend to her toilette.

She went about the task of putting herself together like an obedient child. It was a night she must go through, for there was no way she was going to get out of it. When she had finished brushing her hair it glistened like spun gold. To comply with Pierre's request that she hurry, she left it down, letting it fall over her shoulders in soft, silky waves. After dabbing jasmine fragrance at her throat and temples, she announced that she was ready.

When Renaud's eyes viewed her, he both admired and approved of the glorious vision he beheld. She was the picture of delicacy. For a brief second, she took his breath away, she was so stunning.

"Magnifique! That's all I can say!" He sighed, offering her his arm. "Come, Mademoiselle Lamoureux—shall we be on our way."

As they left the room, their light-hearted laughter rang down the carpeted hallway.

Chapter 37

After spending a pleasant evening in the cordial company of Robert Gervais and his charming wife, Charmaine wondered why she'd been frightened or so unsure of herself. It wasn't even necessary for Pierre to tell her that they'd accepted her. From the minute she and Pierre had arrived at the fine old plantation she'd felt their warmth and had begun to relax.

They might be Pierre's friends, but she was thoroughly enjoying herself, and by the time she said good night, Charmaine felt the Gervaises were her friends too.

That evening swept away her doubts that she could stand by Pierre Renaud's side with her head held high. This meant a great deal to Charmaine Lamoureux, the Jersey farm girl. It gave her confidence.

Pierre was very aware of her changed attitude. The helpless little waif he'd seen before they'd left the hotel for the Gervais' plantation and the pert, saucy miss who'd returned with him were as different as day and night. Ah, Charmaine's complexity fascinated him. She whet his interest! He wanted to know all the various women in that petite body and soul of hers. Each new side of her character seemed to have an effect on him, drawing him closer to her with each day that passed.

Another's man's eyes had found Charmaine irresistible that night, but Charmaine did not know his black, evil eyes were ogling her. For his own depraved reasons, Henri Gervais did not announce his presence or make an appearance in the parlor of his home.

In fact, no one was more stunned than Henri when he spied the couple he and Adrien had followed from the wharf sitting with his own mother and father.

Because of what he and Adrien had plotted, he had no intention of becoming known to the pair. The genteel Robert Gervais and his gentle wife had no inkling of the plans in Henri's perverted mind. Had they, they'd have been shocked. There was no rational explanation for Henri's distorted character, not when he'd been sired by Robert Gervais and born of a woman like Madame Gervais.

This pair deserved a more honorable heir than the despicable Henri who had inherited none of the character traits that had endeared his parents to their neighbors and friends. Nor had he been blessed with the dignified good looks of his parents. Henri's expressionless face was plain and ugly. His diabolic ways had evolved because he was not capable of loving or caring for anyone but himself. He had no scruples about hurting someone else. No one mattered to the self-centered Henri.

Robert Gervais and his dear wife dwelled in blissful ignorance. They did not know what a villain their son was.

Upon seeing the golden-haired lady in his own home, Henri concealed himself from sight, titillated now and eager to carry out his evil plan with the help of the faithful Adrien Bayard. His frenzied excitement mounted as he watched the unsuspecting couples in the parlor, and he finally stole from his home to go the Bayards' Cypress Cove Plantation to seek out Adrien. Now that he'd seen her again, his obsession was overwhelming. As he rode through the night at demonlike speed, the voice urged him to do it tomorrow—tomorrow! He could wait no longer.

Charmaine had no hint of danger the next morning. Quite the contrary, her spirits were high even after Pierre left her to see to last-minute arrangements for their passage up the Mississippi River. She did not feel neglected or deserted at midmorning when Jacques and Tasha dropped in to pay her a brief visit before going out on a short jaunt around the city.

Charmaine noted the radiant glow on their faces and that delighted her. She still wondered what magic touch had linked the two of them. They were such opposites. Jacques, with his sharp wit and glib tongue, was always so carefree and a fun-loving man whereas Tasha had always impressed her as being almost prudish. At least, until she'd become involved with Jacques. What a totally different woman she was now.

While the early morning sky had been overcast, at mid-day the sun shone. Charmaine looked out the window, viewing the street below. Seeing it alive with people, she wanted to leave the confining hotel room and join in the activity on the street. She realized she'd promised Pierre she'd not venture out without him, but he had promised her they'd take a jaunt around the city that afternoon. He'd planned to complete his business arrangements by lunchtime.

He'd named the tearoom in which they'd have lunch, then they were to go to a couple of shops, after which they'd make a sightseeing tour of the city.

For almost an hour, she waited, dressed and eager for him to return. When the noon hour arrived and he didn't appear, she paced and fidgeted. Several times she'd picked up the wide-brimmed bonnet and had put it atop her pretty head, only to remove it. She told herself to be more patient, but in the next moment a voice within her said nothing could happen to her on such a busy street full of passers-by. Hadn't she walked from Uncle Angus' farm into the town of St. Helier alone?

She argued with herself for another half-hour. The clock's

hands now stood at one P.M. What does Pierre expect of me? she wondered. She went to the window to see if he was coming, but he was not about. However, she saw something which caught her attention and held it. On the corner a black boy was tapping his feet and dancing while an elderly black man played the banjo. People were clapping their hands with delight at the show the black boy was putting on for them. Charmaine wanted to join that cheerful crowd. She reasoned that Pierre could not possibly miss her if he did return. She would be so close to the hotel entrance she could not miss seeing him either. She grabbed her bonnet and dashed out the door.

She walked at a frisky pace through the plushly carpeted lobby, anxious to get through the door so she'd not miss the show going on outside. She took no notice of the people sitting in the lobby or standing by the huge columns that graced the entrance to the adjacent dining room. Her eyes were straight ahead, and her quick steps made her round hips sway tantalizingly.

Henri noticed. He had been scrutinizing the lobby for hours, ever since Renaud had left without Charmaine. Henri knew she was in the hotel alone, without protection. Although he had two separate schemes in mind in case one didn't work out, her sudden appearance made his plans simpler. He immediately sent Adrien to bring up the carriage; then he hurried out the door, in hot pursuit of Charmaine.

The milling crowd and the sounds of applause and gay laughter were in his favor, he concluded delightedly. His dark, malevolent eyes saw her halt to listen to the young performer, and he turned to see if Adrien was bringing the carriage to an advantageous spot. Henri wanted to be able to depart as soon as he grabbed the petite, frail-looking maiden and hoisted her into the carriage. With Adrien assisting him, they'd have her inside faster than one could bat an eyelash. Then his driver would take them out of the city, to the secluded shack down in the bayou. In this secluded spot Henri played his sadistic games.

Charmaine tapped her foot and clapped her hands to the tempo of the music. She smiled at a couple of people standing next to her, thinking how friendly everyone seemed, and she was glad she'd decided to leave her room.

In the midst of the festivities, she suddenly felt her nostrils flare as if some predatory animal were breathing on her neck, but by then the "animal" had a viselike grip on both her arms. It all happened with such devastating haste. She felt herself being pushed roughly, and then lifted upward. By the time she opened her mouth to cry out for help, a gloved hand was drowning out her plea for help. Her eyes were wide with fear and shock as she gazed into a man's face and heard his maniacal laughter.

A few hundred feet down the street, Pierre reined in the gig he'd rented for the afternoon of fun he'd promised Charmaine. His spirits were high, for all was in readiness for their departure. While some things about the buckskin-clad pilot of the keel boat rubbed him the wrong way, Pierre was convinced Morrow was a capable boatman. To the French Renaud, his garb was no stranger than his name. Renaud had to restrain a show of amusement when the man had said he was called Cat Morrow. But when they'd talked, Morrow had had a simple explanation for that. He loved to eat and catch catfish.

Now, Renaud was ready to squire his beautiful lady around the city, and Cat Morrow was outfitting on his seventy-foot keel boat with their provisions.

He spied the crowd gathered in front of the Royale, but a flash of golden hair as a fancy-dressed gentleman hoisted a doll-like miss into a waiting carriage brought him to life. Like a lightning bolt shooting through him, it registered that the man was forcing Charmaine into that carriage. He urged the mare to move faster.

By the time he reached the spot where the incident had taken place, the carriage he pursued was rounding the corner up ahead. Renaud let out a stream of curse words!

He reproached himself for leaving Charmaine alone, especially in a city like this one. Had she blatantly disobeyed his warnings and ventured out of the hotel? Or perhaps some scoundrel lurking in the lobby had seen her go down to the dining room to eat lunch and had preyed on her? How she'd been abducted from a street in New Orleans in broad daylight really didn't matter to him now, he decided. All that mattered was to rescue her from the vile bastard who'd shoved her into that carriage. That was no cheap rig. It was a fine carriage, one which belonged to a person of wealth.

Pierre whipped the mare unmercifully, for he was driven by a primitive instinct. He was going to save the woman he loved, and nothing was going to stop him from avenging her.

His eyes strained to sight the carriage as he turned the corner. He caught a fleeting glimpse of it as it veered sharply out of the path of another equipage rolling leisurely down the street, then took another turn down a side street. Renaud sensed that the occupants, who had Charmaine as their captive, were heading to the outskirts of the city.

Pierre had learned the layout of New Orleans, and he knew if he followed the levee, he'd cut the distance between him and the other carriage so he reined his gig to go toward the levee.

His maneuver paid off because as his gig moved around the bend of the road he traveled only a short distance before he caught sight of the fine carriage turning into the road leading into the lane which trailed along the bayou.

Quiet and desolation surrounded Pierre as his gig rolled along the rutted road overshadowed by the giant cypress trees that lined the banks of the bayou. Spanish moss hung in shrouds almost to the ground, and the lonely shrieks of birds echoed over the swampy waters just beyond. Renaud charged onward, knowing that before this day was over justice would be done.

He had faith in his two strong hands, which would gladly

fight to the death for his darling Charmaine, but he was glad he had Cat Morrow's gift, an awesome knife, tucked in his belt. Pierre had had fencing lessons and he'd worked with an epée. He'd seen magnificent collections of daggers, but never anything like this impressive weapon. It was fierce and he knew instinctively he would soon try his skill with it. The two men he could now see in the back seat of that plush carriage would surely feel its blade. Strange as it might seem, he felt beholden to that rawboned man in buckskin—the man with the strange name of Cat Morrow!

His heart beat erratically and the palms of his hands were wet with sweat as he urged the mare to close the distance between his gig and the carriage. It bothered him that he'd not seen Charmaine's golden head. Where was she? Lying on the floor at the feet of those bastards, feeling degraded and debased?

He had to know she was unharmed. As long as she was alive, he'd ease her pain and hurt if that took a lifetime. Dear God, she had to be alive! That was his fervent prayer as his gig passed the carriage, then blocked its way on the narrow, rutted dirt road, compelling it to stop.

The answer to his prayers came when he saw her wide-eyed, tear-stained face peer out the window. Although the odds were against him, he leaped out of the gig. The black driver had only been carrying out the orders of his master. He'd let him live, but those milksop dandies would surely die! Cat's knife would slit their no-good throats!

Chapter 38

Still in a foggy daze, Charmaine didn't understand what had the foppish young man called Adrien so frightened as she lay on the carriage floor with the other man's feet pressing down on her. She thought she'd heard Adrien call him Henri. She was as baffled as she had been when this whole thing had started. As to how much time she'd been in the carriage she had no inkling. It seemed like hours, but she knew it was not more than a half-hour. She knew also that she saw raw panic on this Adrien's face.

In a high tenor shriek, he warned Henri, "That gig is going to catch up with us—sure as hell! That son of a bitch must have pulled up as we were leaving with her."

"Let him. There's only one of him and there are three of us, counting Bass up there. That black bastard is strong," Henri muttered, a cocky look on his face.

"Well, I can tell you we aren't going to come out of this without some marks on us. I'm scared, Henri," Adrien admitted in a quaking voice.

"You sound like some whining woman, Adrien!" Gervais' fierce eyes glanced down at Charmaine with contempt. "Quit your wiggling, slut."

Charmaine riled him all the more by continuing to arch and twist her body against his restraining feet. "Scum like

321

you calling me such a name! I think you're daft." She now knew that someone was following them. If it wasn't Renaud, it had to be Jacques. There was even a remote possibility that some gallant gentleman had seen her abducted and had leaped into his buggy to rush to her rescue. At that moment, she didn't care who rescued her from this despicable pair.

Henri's boot pressed cruelly into her hip, but the folds of her gown and her petticoats provided some protection for her soft flesh. She suspected she was spared additional pain by the fact that Adrien had screamed out, diverting Henri's attention. Her ears detected the movement of another carriage close beside them, and her excitement mounted. Soon she'd be free and out of the clutches of these two, no matter what they had in mind for her. Under her breath, she blessed her "knight in shining armor" whoever he might be.

"See, Henri! He's blocking us!"

"I have eyes, Adrien," Henri barked, trying to sound much braver than he was feeling. His courage was wavering, but he dared not let his weak, frightened friend know that. Adrien Bayard was ready to crumble into a million pieces, and Henri knew it.

This turn of events Henri had not figured on, but he'd gotten a fleeting glimpse of his enemy and knew he was about to face an indomitable man. This newcomer to New Orleans, this Pierre Renaud, did not seem concerned that it was a Gervais he was interfering with. No one had ever challenged Henri before.

As Bass was forced to pull up on the reins of the thoroughbreds drawing the Gervais carriage, Henri let out an angry hiss. "You know what you must do, Bass. You've got that club under the seat, haven't you?"

"Sho do, massa! Sho do!" Bass hastily replied, and he nodded his frizzy head. But Bass was having some private thoughts which Henri Gervais could not control although he dominated every other aspect of the black man's life. That was one big angry man leaping out of that gig. Bass recognized the fury of the man. He even appreciated it. He'd once had his woman snatched from him. He understood this man's rage. Henri Gervais had taken his golden-haired lady. She was as beautiful as the golden roses in Madame Gervais' rose garden so it was no wonder the man's blood boiled like a cauldron of water. Perhaps, it was remembering what had happened to his own woman, but Bass decided that he was not going to fight to the death for the likes of the two useless rascals in the carriage.

From where he sat on his perch seat, Bass watched their pursuer remove his coat. This man was hellbent on sweet revenge. The firm muscles of his legs and arms were taut and tense, Bass could tell from the way he'd leaped down and strode over to the carriage that he was as dangerous as one of those devil storms that hit the Louisiana coast sometimes. His broad chest heaved in and out with his raging fury.

In a deep, demanding voice Pierre ordered, "Get down. black man, and run for your life into that swamp. I have no quarrel with you, but if you want your life spared you'd better flee so you'll not be able to tell the tale of what's about to happen."

Bass dared not deny him and he raced off, heedless of Henri's calls for him to come back. He ran as fast as he could, and he never looked back.

As the huge black man was swallowed up by the swamp, Renaud yanked open the door of the carriage, and when he saw Charmaine lying on the floor, his course of action was irreversible.

His quicksilver eyes were as cold as death when they pierced those two pathetic excuses for men. Only when they darted in Charmaine's direction did they mellow.

"Can you make it over to my buggy, *chérie?*"

"I can make it, Pierre," she stammered. She shifted her hips along the floor until her legs were at the door opening. Then Pierre effortlessly pulled her all the way out so that her feet rested on the ground.

"Listen to me, *ma petite*. Shut your eyes and your ears so you'll not have to hear these squealing pigs, eh?"

She did not answer him for she did not have to. By now her eyes had caught the silvery gleam of his blade. It was the biggest, fiercest knife she'd ever seen. She knew what Pierre intended to do, but the look on his face told her that even her pleas would not be heard by him.

She obeyed him explicitly, but she still heard sounds and the muffled voices of Adrien and the obnoxious Henri. She knew without asking when Pierre had carried out the revenge he deemed proper and fitting. But the look on his face as he slowly ambled toward the gig was more frightening than his rage when he'd pulled her out of the carriage. He looked stunned and shaken!

Silently he joined her in the gig and took her in his arms, holding her close to his throbbing chest. His lips captured hers in a long, tender kiss, and only then did he reach for the reins to urge the mare into action.

Charmaine could not stand his puzzling silence. If he'd not kissed her so ardently, she'd have sworn he was angry with her. But it wasn't that, she was certain.

"Pierre, what is it? What's bothering you so much? You make me nervous and God knows, I don't need anything to do that, not after what's just happened."

"Nor do I, Charmaine," he muttered, tight-lipped.

"Dear God, I'll be glad to leave this city, beautiful as it is. Those horrible men! I still can't understand it all, Pierre," she declared, emotion lacing her voice. Her eyes questioning turned to him.

"Well, don't worry, because we'll be leaving just as soon as we can—sooner than I'd planned!" There was a snap to his words, and his eyes looked straight ahead as he whipped the mare's rump to make her go faster.

"Because of me and what happened back there near the bayou?" She could not bring herself to say because he'd killed those men, she was certain he had.

"Not because of you, because of what those two tried to do to you." He turned to look at her, and he could read her thoughts. "Yes, Charmaine, I killed them both and I have no regrets about that. They deserved to die. My only regret is that one of those bastards was Gervais' son Henri. That grieves me very much."

She gasped and muzzled her mouth with her hands. All she could say was, "Oh, my God Pierre!" For a few moments she sat in stunned silence; then fear consumed her. What would happen to Pierre if someone found out what he'd done.

When she voiced her fear, he had a quick reply, "That, *chérie,* is why we're leaving as soon as we get back at the hotel, gather up our belongings, and contact Jacques and Tasha. I just hope Cat Morrow's gotten the supplies and his men are ready to start up that river and away from here. I don't think anyone could connect me with Henri Gervais, but someone might remember you."

So the despicable rascal responsible for her brief, unpleasant encounter had been the son of the very nice people she'd dined with only last night. That didn't enlighten her as to why he'd wish to do what he'd done. Why me? Charmaine asked herself, as they sped through the country-side toward the city? Why had Gervais decided to harm her?

Pierre was preoccupied with his thoughts. He was hoping he'd find Jacques and Tasha at the hotel so there'd be no delay. The sooner he and his party were afloat on the muddy Mississippi, the better he'd feel, he mused. And the better it would be for Charmaine.

The crowd gathered in front of the Royale Hotel had long since gone their separate ways and the little black boy and the banjo player had disappeared. In their place was a flower vendor selling blossoms to midafternoon strollers.

But Renaud paid no heed to his call to buy the pretty lady a posy. He guided Charmaine through the door of the hotel and across the lobby, then directly to their room. Before going to seek Jacques, he said, "You know what to do, so get on with it, Charmaine."

She made no reply, but turned to carry out his request. He quickly left to inform Jacques of the change of plan. To his delight, he found the pair he sought in Jacques' room, and his manner was enough to tell his friend that something had gone awry. Pierre's deep voice was so blunt and sharp, Bernay knew this problem was serious.

As Charmaine had done, Tasha set about packing without asking any questions.

By five in the afternoon, the entourage arrived at the levee bag and baggage. A rather befuddled Morrow greeted them. He searched his memory about their agreed time of departure, convinced he was not mistaken, he wondered what the Frenchman was about bringing these people down to the dock fourteen or fifteen hours ahead of time. He'd been feeling very smug about being ahead of schedule. The supplies had been bought, and the last of them had been carried aboard about a half-hour ago. But the cabins were yet to be cleaned. He had planned on assigning that task to a couple of the boys this evening so they'd be ready in the morning for his passengers.

Pierre could tell by the look on Morrow's face that their appearance puzzled him, so he proceeded on ahead of his companions, figuring Morrow might object to their presence.

Cat didn't disappoint him when he barked out, "You what? How the holy hell do you expect me to do that?"

"I don't care how, but it's got to be, Cat. You'll understand when I've had a chance to speak with you in private when we're on our way. Now, instead of us wasting more time, I leave it to your hands to get the boat underway." Renaud suggested.

"Ah, hell, Renaud, I'm shy two men. I'd planned to line them up this evening, but I can't just yank them out of the damned sky," Cat grumbled.

"My friend Bernay and I will fill that gap for you," the

326

Frenchman volunteered.

"Come now, Renaud! What do you and your friend know about working a keel boat?" Cat had an amused grin on his tanned, weathered face.

"We have backs for pulling on the ropes or using the poles, and my friend Bernay was a skilled seaman."

"A seaman? On an ocean-going vessel?"

"Yes. So you are no longer short on crew. Come on, Morrow, no more delays. Just tell me where I can take the two ladies, eh?"

Cat scratched his head, then glanced beyond Renaud to where the two ladies stood with his friend. The man was certainly muscular. It could just work out, Cat supposed. But where to quarter the women was a problem, for the cabins were pig sties. Nonetheless, Renaud was determined to have his way. He had a menacing look in his eyes, Cat thought.

"The little ladies could be taken to my cabin until the boy can clean up their quarters, if that's all right?" He turned around and roared like a lion to one of the crew across the way. "Donnie, take Mister Renaud and his party to my cabin, will ya?"

Donnie eagerly nodded, delighted that Morrow had picked him to escort the party to the captain's quarters for that chore gave him an opportunity to get an eyeful of the beautiful fair-haired lady. He could hardly take his eyes off her until he chanced to see the man with silver-gray eyes giving him a warning glance.

Donnie stared no more in Charmaine's direction, and when he'd opened the door and invited them to enter Morrow's cabin, he quickly excused himself.

As he walked back across the deck of the boat, he cautioned himself to watch his wandering eyes during this trip. If he didn't, he might not be able to watch anything in the future.

He had no desire to tangle with the one called Renaud! The man could be dangerous. Donnie was not a fool!

Chapter 39

Cat Morrow stood on the deck of his keel boat yelling his orders, directing one of his crew with the lead rope. Two trappers he'd known over the years rowed alongside of his boat in their bateaux. They were coming into the city to sell their wares after many weeks of working the woods and swamps surrounding New Orleans.

It was not customary for Morrow to be leaving in the late afternoon. Early dawn, just as the sun was breaking, was his usual departure time, and most of his friends knew this.

His keel boat moved amid the numerous skiffs at the edge of the river. A few slick-lined schooners were in port, and some frigates, but then New Orleans' harbor was busy at almost any time.

Few men had the capacity to sway Morrow as Renaud had so skillfully done this very afternoon. As he'd gotten his boat underway, the Frenchman had helped his party get settled, and Cat had had time to think about his maneuver.

To say the least, he and Renaud had nothing in common, judging by outward appearances; Morrow wore crude buckskin garb, Renaud finely tailored attire. But Cat had his own rules and he measured a man in his own special way. He had the distinct impression that despite Renaud's fancy garb the man could be a deadly force if the occasion called for it.

Perhaps, Cat confessed privately as he ambled along the deck, that was why he hadn't wished to challenge the Frenchman earlier.

Before they reached New Madrid district in the Missouri Territory, he'd find out more about his man for Renaud fascinated him and made him curious.

Morrow had lived a rugged, vagabond's existence, traveling up and down the river most of his life. He'd been a trapper, a hunter, a guide. Now he was a boatman. On the Mississippi River there was a constant demand for the services he had to offer. He carried produce and goods to the markets in New Orleans and St. Louis, and the muddy Mississippi was the navigation route for many settlers. Morrow had found his keel boat a good way to feather his nest with money, and the life of a boatman was far more comfortable than that of a trapper or hunter.

And Morrow was just as curious about Renaud's golden-haired companion. But he was a little shrewder than his young crewman, Donnie. He would not have dared to let Renaud see his eyes survey every sensuous curve of the woman's body. Nevertheless, he'd managed to absorb every tantalizing wiggle of her cute little hips when Renaud's back was turned. Oh yes, he'd enjoyed every minute as she'd walked away from him. From the back, her golden curls bouncing down her back and over her shoulders, she was so wee she could be mistaken for a child, but never when she was facing you.

No, the luscious full bloom of her breasts completely negated such an error.

Cat Morrow smiled, thinking to himself that he'd know a lot more once this first night aboard his keel boat was over and morning came. If the two Frenchmen quartered together and the two ladies shared a cabin, then he was dead wrong. But he would wager everything he owned that it would not be that way. The golden-haired one would be sharing Renaud's bed, if Renaud was half the man he figured

330

him to be.

Another thing was gnawing at Morrow, for having been raised in the swampy bayou, he had learned at an early age to survive by getting the jump on danger. He wanted to know what had happened back in New Orleans, why it had been imperative for Renaud to leave that city hours ahead of their original departure time. Morrow knew there had to be a reason for Renaud's haste. In a brief period of three or four hours, something had happened! But what?

He yanked his old woollen cap down so it fit more snugly over his ears, for when the sun began to set it sank fast at this time of the year. Without its warmth the breeze on the water was chill, and the flat land on both sides of the river offered no buffer against it.

Morrow had taken Renaud out of New Orleans, but now he ordered the keel boat secured for the night, whether the Frenchman liked it or not.

Though an expert boatman, he could not see his way in the black of night, and he damned well wasn't going to chance hitting a sand bar or snag. He was a stubborn man too.

Whatever had urged Renaud to get out of New Orleans hastily, Cat had accomplished that. The city was miles away. At least a dozen such keel boats were going in the same direction as his, and all would be stopped and secured for the night.

Besides, Morrow's day had been a long one and he was tired. He yelled to his mate, ordering him to tie the ropes to the sturdy cypress trunks. He hoped to find his own quarters empty by now, if the boy had done the job he'd assigned him and prepared the cabins for Renaud and his party.

The river pilot was more than ready for a healthy swig of whiskey and some of the fish chowder his cook was preparing for him.

Morrow was not disappointed when he entered his cabin. The only hint of its previous occupants was an aroma that reminded him of the exotic blooming flowers he often smelled on summer nights as he drifted down the river. It was the fragrance of the wild jasmine which bloomed profusely along the banks.

Jacques and Tasha had not found the right moment to tell Charmaine and Pierre that they'd been married by a parish priest on their last day in New Orleans. Too much had happened after they'd returned to the hotel from the little chapel where they'd become man and wife. Indeed, in their fast departure from the Royale, Tasha had regretfully left behind the treasured little nosegay Jacques had bought for her from a street vendor.

When she'd finally gotten settled in the cabin which was to be theirs for the seven- or eight-day boat trip, she asked Jacques when they were going to announce their marriage.

"Tomorrow, *ma petite*. Tomorrow, we'll tell them our grand news," he said, kissing her tenderly.

"Oh, Jacques, I've never been so very happy. Your wife! How wonderful that sounds!" she told him, hugging his broad chest.

"And I'm the happiest man in the whole world, Tasha!"

The serene contentment Jacques and Tasha felt was absent from the next cabin. Aware of Pierre's tossing and turning restlessly, Charmaine said nothing. She decided it was better not to prod him when he was in such a mood.

He had been withdrawn since that afternoon when they'd ridden back to the city in the buggy. She, too, had felt that a dismal shroud hung over her, so she could understand Pierre's somber mood.

But the events of that afternoon were not all that occupied Pierre's thoughts, although they were enough to keep him from being jubilant. His feeling for Charmaine Lamoureux was confusing him. Such love was overwhelming.

She brought out traits he'd not known he possessed, and he asked himself if this golden-haired enchantress was some kind of witch. Certainly, his life had taken on a different dimension since he'd fallen in love with her back on those cliffs of Jersey. He'd never considered himself a man who'd experience all-consuming love. He'd always enjoyed life, taken his pleasure whenever he chose. Now all that had changed!

He was shaken to the core of his being because he'd killed two men this afternoon because of the lady he loved. He lay abed now, not feeling a qualm over that for they'd had the vilest intentions. He knew his deeds were justified. But it bothered him that he'd had a vicious urge to slam his fist into the face of the young boatman who'd focused his eyes on Charmaine.

Jealousy was taking hold of him, and he didn't like it one bloody bit! A woman like Charmaine drew male eyes wherever she went, yet he could have sworn she hadn't been aware that young man, Donnie, was staring at her so longingly as they'd proceeded to the captain's cabin.

Seven or eight days and nights aboard this keel boat could prove very taxing, he thought to himself, as he lay beside Charmaine's warm body. She was so still he suspected she'd drifted off to sleep. Her day had been wearing too.

But once they arrived in the New Madrid district and were settled in his uncle's home, Pierre decided he'd best get himself married to this little minx. He knew beyond a shadow of a doubt no other woman could possibly be his wife, but Charmaine. Yes, he quietly mused, the sooner the better for all concerned!

It was his intention to tell her of his plan when he awakened the next morning, but when he opened his eyes to find her side of the bed empty, he leaped up angrily, wondering just where the little vixen had scampered off to.

He stumbled around the room, grabbing up his own clothing and brushing back his hair, which was tousled and unruly. "Now, where in the hell could she have gone?" he muttered to the empty cabin.

333

She had no damned business roaming about a keel boat swarming with men. She must know that. Dressing took him longer than it usually did because of his mounting anger about the impetuous Charmaine's behavior. By God, he intended to lay down some rules to that irresponsible miss immediately.

Finally he got his pants and shirt on, then yanked on boots, forgetting about his rumpled hair. So riled was Renaud, he gave the cabin door a thundering slam before marching, like a soldier into battle, toward the deck of the keel boat.

The scenery had changed since he'd gone into the cabin the night before. Now the riverbanks were lined with thick woods, and he saw a great blue heron swoop down to light on an old cypress log near the water's edge. Renaud didn't have to take many more steps before his eyes fell on Charmaine, watching the men straining their muscled arms to push the poles that made the boat move forward.

An excited flush on her lovely face, she clutched her ecru shawl tightly around her shoulders. The folds of her sprigged muslin frock swayed around her legs in the gentle breeze, and her hair blew freely for she wore no bonnet.

Pierre suddenly checked his fast stride, and he stood for a moment, admiring her. She was as refreshing as the sunshiny day.

She was not alone, but in the company of Bernay and Tasha, who were finding the navigation of the seventy-foot keel boat an interesting experience. He felt very foolish. But he loved her so damned much!

Shamefaced, he walked forward to join them, and when Charmaine saw him she broke into a radiant smile, enthusiastically declaring, "Oh, Pierre, we've had fun! I'm glad you finally woke up, you old sleepyhead!" Linking an arm through his, she snuggled closer to him, then looked up at his solemn face and smiled again. He was glad she couldn't read his thoughts at that moment, for he was still feeling foolish for having jumped to the wrong conclusion about her. Love certainly had a strange effect on him.

He dared not open his mouth to say anything, but he couldn't resist bending down to plant a kiss on her glowing cheek to express the tender loving feeling flooding through him.

But when she expressed her feelings, Pierre swelled with pleasure. "I love you, Pierre Renaud!" she softly murmured.

God knows, I love you too, he thought, but he remained silent, letting his charming smile satisfy her. That alone separated her from most of the ladies he'd known in his past life, for they had demanded constant praise.

Ah yes, Charmaine was different, and that was what made her so intriguing! That was what made her rare!

Chapter 40

After three days aboard the keel boat, Pierre developed a tremendous appreciation for the pilot skills of Captain Cat Morrow. The Mississippi River was like a monster snake constantly weaving and winding. So far, Morrow's knowledge of it had kept them from getting into shallow water or from hitting a snag or a sand bar. A couple of keel boats heading in the same direction had been less fortunate.

Furthermore Pierre had noticed the skiffs coming alongside the keel boat so their owners could chat with the likable Cat. It was obvious to him that Morrow was popular with the boatmen.

As Pierre had worked beside Morrow as he'd promised he and Bernay would, he had learned things about the rugged, tan man and his past. Morrow's humble beginnings were different from his own, but that made Pierre admire him even more. To Renaud, the buckskin clothing the pilot wore seemed fitting when Morrow told him he was what Americans called a half-breed.

"My mother was an Indian, the daughter of a Sac chief from upland. I never knew her though," he told Renaud. "She died when I was no bigger than a tadpole, and my father raised me. He was a trapper, so I was wandering the woods along this river from the time I took my first steps.

Amazing how a kid can survive if he has to."

Renaud smiled. "Well I suppose you are right, Morrow." What else could he say? He'd had such luxuries as a nurse and tutors, and he'd grown up in Cherbourg in a fine townhouse and on a country estate.

"Always figured God looked after kids and the little creatures out in those woods and swamps, else none of us would last a day or two." Morrow laughed. "It's a treacherous place out there. I respect it. A man can get lost in one of those swamps and never be heard of again."

As Renaud listened, he learned many things. Morrow pointed out trees along the way: black walnut and pecan, ash and sugar maple. And when Morrow told him, "To cordelle a boat upstream ain't the easiest task in the world," Renaud believed him.

What Pierre did not know was that in the three days he'd come to admire Cat Morrow, the captain had also gained respect for standing shoulder to shoulder, sometimes bared to the waist, and working the poles and the ropes with his crew. His friend Bernay had worked just as diligently. Renaud was a man of his word! Cat appreciated that.

The only problem plaguing Cat was the awful fever in his blood for the gorgeous Charmaine Lamoureux. Hell, he fought it, but every primitive need in him cried out a protest.

The strange effect this woman had on him was most disturbing. He hoped to break the fever when he'd tied up at Natchez for a couple of hours. He went to a brothel he'd frequented on many occasions on his runs up and down the river, but that did not quench his thirst for the beautiful Mademoiselle Lamoureux. Even worse, when he returned in the skiff—he'd told Renaud he'd been ashore on business— she was the first person he encountered. The day was mild and she had no need of a cape or a shawl as she stood there to greet him, so he felt the full impact of her wasplike waist and her full breasts. Her eyes were very blue, but he saw them as mysteriously deep. A man could surely drown in those deep, blue pools and he'd just love to but for the threat of Renaud, he thought to himself. He tipped his hat to her and greeted her casually, giving no hint to his true feelings. "Good afternoon, Miss Lamoureux. Having a stroll I see."

"It would seem that way, Captain. Everyone is working on something but me. Pierre is helping one of your men untangle some rope, and my friend Tasha is mending a rip in Jacques' pants. I'm the only one idle. I feel rather useless actually."

"Useless? You, ma'am?" Morrow was grateful for the canvas bag he was carrying for he expected his amorous feelings were reflected in his skin-tight buckskins, and when he had just come from sweet Betsy's bed at the Natchez brothel. Dear God, this woman had one hell of an impact on him!

He noticed that her mouth was set in a pout; then she gave him a smile, which made him want to melt. He just stood there, feeling embarrassed, as she said, "Yes, I do feel useless, Captain. Is there something I could do to help?"

If only she knew, he declared to himself. If only she knew! Holy Christ, he'd give an arm and a leg to be with her.

He felt like an awkward oaf, but he could think of nothing else to say to her except that he, too, would enjoy a stroll and a little conversation. "You see, miss, I don't often have an opportunity to talk to such a fine lady like yourself. For a backwoods boatman like myself, this is a rare treat."

Charmaine found the rugged keel boat captain almost boyishly shy and that amused her. It was the last thing she'd ever expected from the rawboned man. In a strange way, she found Cat Morrow appealing.

She suddenly realized that he was about Pierre's age and probably looked older because of the life he'd lived.

"If you would enjoy my conversation, then I've nothing better to do." She smiled up at him. In her usual candid, straightforward manner, she gave a soft little giggle, tilting her head slightly, "You surprise me, Captain Morrow."

"How so, miss?" He paused to linger in a more secluded spot because he saw some of his crew across the deck, and Renaud might be with them. He'd just as soon not come face to face with him right now. To stand this close to Mademoiselle Lamoureux and look down at that pretty face gave him a pleasure he'd not enjoy if Renaud's piercing gray eyes were scrutinizing him.

As her soft voice explained how he'd surprised her, Cat was thinking to himself that Charmaine's fair beauty must rival the dark loveliness of his own mother. Cat had no memory of her, but his father had vividly described her. Her Indian name had been Moonbeam, and Charmaine's should surely be Sunshine, he thought, for such golden loveliness he had never seen before.

The interlude would have lasted longer if Cat had had his way, but Folsom, his mate, rushed forward to ask, "Want me to get us underway for Greenville, Captain?"

Before Morrow could answer Folsom, Charmaine quickly excused herself, feeling that she might be distracting the captain from his duties. The frown on Cat's face was not due to her distraction but to the deprivation of a few extra minutes at her side.

But at least he had a brief time with her.

Charmaine found traveling on the keel boat enjoyable. The varied sights along the river banks were preferable to the monotony of endless churning water when she'd crossed the Atlantic. The stream of canoes and skiffs plying up and down the river provided further diversion.

It also pleased Charmaine to look across the keel boat and see Pierre working along with Morrow's men. Never had she found him so virile-looking, so masculine, as when, chest bared, he was straining at the poles or the ropes. It excited her to watch the rippling muscles of his strong arms, she waited expectantly for him to glance her way and give her one of his broad, crooked grins or a wink.

These last few days had been good ones. She hoped as they went farther up the Mississippi they would be as happy. She kept telling herself it didn't matter that they weren't married like Jacques and Tasha, but that couple's announcement had startled her.

When Tasha had expressed remorse that they'd selfishly left her alone that fateful afternoon so they could get married, Charmaine had been quick to assure her what happened wasn't their fault. Though she would have never admitted it in Pierre's presence, she did tell Tasha if she'd stayed inside the Royale as Pierre had requested those scoundrels couldn't have whisked her away in their carriage. That had seemed to soothe Tasha, which had been Charmaine's intention.

But in calming her friend, she'd raised a "prodding thorn" in her own mind. Had everything not seemed so perfect between her and Renaud, she would have brooded about it more. She couldn't have asked for a more devoted lover, but if he loved her—if he loved her as Bernay loved Tasha—then why did he not make her his wife instead of his mistress?

As quickly as this thought came to her, she dismissed it.

Now, after hastily departing from Captain Morrow, she went directly to Renaud's cabin, but he was not there. Since the mate had asked Morrow if they were to be on their way, she figured Pierre was again working with the crew, for the slow motion of the keel boat told her they were once again plowing through those dark, muddy waters.

With time on her hands and nothing in particular she wanted to do, she stretched out across the bed, giving way to the languor rushing over her. Sleep overtook her almost instantly.

Two hours passed before she roused and sat up in the bed. She was startled to realize she'd slept right through the dinner hour, and to find Pierre still absent from their quarters.

When she'd arisen, she gave her gown a shake to straighten out the wrinkles and then applied a brush to her hair before she dashed out of her cabin. But as she was about to knock on Tasha's and Jacques' cabin door, she heard the soft moans of their lovemaking, so she quickly restrained herself.

Where is Renaud, she asked herself. It was obvious where Bernay was!

Wherever he was, she'd wager he'd filled his belly, but hers was growling from hunger! She decided to seek out the cook and see what she could get at this late hour.

When she arrived at the galley, the man in charge had a look of disbelief on his black-bearded face. His round cheeks shook as he spoke. "My good supper you not getting any of? How that happen, tell me?" He waddled around the table, his pot belly draped with an apron. "Best panchouse I ever make! Fresh caught today and I cook tonight."

"Well, I slept right through it." Charmaine sighed dejectedly, knowing how well the old French Acadian could cook the fish caught in the river daily by one or another of the crew. Cajun's fresh-water fish stew was constantly praised.

"You won't starve, little one. No—no, Cajun won't did that." He scurried to the cabinet and looked over his cluttered table. "Plenty of hot coffee . . . a cornbread cake. Ah, a slam of ham, maybe?" A twinkle lit up his jet-black eyes as he dramatically drew out a small crock as if he'd been harboring it for some special occasion. "For you, little one, my custard made with the freshest eggs and thick rich cream. Worthy of no one's tasting but yours, eh?" He chuckled gaily, hands holding his pot belly which vibrated with his gusts of laughter.

"I think I love you, Cajun!" She planted a light kiss on his bearded cheek.

"Ah, la belle! La belle! You are something, Cajun thinks! Come sit down! Eat, and a glass of wine I'll have," the hefty Acadian insisted. Charmaine agreed and nodded her pretty

head, taking the seat he offered her most gallantly.

"Forget the coffee, Cajun. May I join you in a glass of wine?" Charmaine asked, giving him a lovely smile. The devil with Pierre! Let him wait for her!

The broadest smile etched the cook's bearded face as he excitedly reached for another glass instead of a cup. *"Ah, mademoiselle*—a pleasure it would be for me!"

She lifted her glass to him after he'd poured the wine and handed it to her, declaring, "A pleasure it is for me too, Cajun!"

"For you, *mademoiselle,* I fix my special crawfish, *oui?* Tomorrow, I fix you my crawfish and my rice and red beans."

Charmaine could not know it, but Cajun was paying her his highest tribute. He took great pride in the way he prepared his crawfish and his red beans and rice.

"Cajun, I'll look forward to tomorrow," she said smiling so sweetly at the Acadian that his heart mellowed and he vowed to himself that his crawfish would never taste as good as they would tomorrow.

Chapter 41

It could have been midnight from the way his tired, weary body felt, but Pierre knew it was much earlier because Cat Morrow had a very definite rule about not pushing his keel boat too long after darkness descended on the treacherous river. He agreed that it wasn't worth the gamble to get stuck on a sandbar for two or three days to make those extra miles after dark.

They'd stretched it an hour tonight because of the stop in Natchez, and Pierre had put in many more hours than he usually did since one of Morrow's men had fallen ill during the morning. His muscles were aching tonight, telling him how strained they were from the extra work. Never had he been so glad to hear Morrow order the boat secured. When he'd put the long pole aside while some of Morrow's men had gone ashore to tie the ropes to trees, he had only one thing on his mind—his comfortable bed. Even the alluring charms of Charmaine could not liven his exhausted body, at least he didn't think so as he slowly ambled across the deck. She was probably already asleep anyway, and that was all right with him for he had no desire to indulge in idle conversation. He just wanted to rid himself of his clothes and crawl into bed. As he neared the cabin door, he was bare chested, his faded blue shirt flung over his shoulder. His dark hair was damp with his own sweat and an unruly wisp fell over his forehead.

No light came from Bernay's cabin and he thought how lucky the bastard was to have enjoyed the night with his lady.

Renaud would be the first to admit that this keel-boat journey had been fascinating. He'd certainly not forget Cat Morrow. In the last few days he'd learned a great deal about this part of the country from him. That would be advantageous once he arrived at his uncle's home. The man in buckskin was a fountain of information, and Renaud genuinely liked and admired him.

Perhaps, his father had known what vistas he was opening up for him when he'd sent him to the new land. If so, Pierre thought him wise. He could never have experienced such things in Cherbourg.

He opened the door to his darkened cabin and quietly moved into the room hoping not to waken Charmaine. Having removed his pants and boots with the utmost care, naked, he made his way to the side of the bed and sank slowly down onto the edge. Hoisting his weary legs up and stretching out full length between the sheets, he sighed contentedly. He could not remember ever being so tired.

It took a second or two for him to realize that something about the bed didn't feel right. His fingers trailed along the sheet seeking warmth on the other side. It was not there. The damned bed was empty except for him!

He jerked to attention and slapped at the sheets in disbelief. "What the bloody hell?"

Irate and puzzled, he lit the lantern to assure himself he wasn't dreaming. By God, he wasn't! Charmaine was not in the cabin! Where was the little vixen?

He yanked up his pants and pulled on his boots, all the while uttering every curse word he knew.

Where was his nocturnal nymph, who seemed to come alive and blossom when the moon was high? Hadn't he first met her in the moonlight?

He dashed out of the cabin intending to find her and drag

346

her back to his bed, by the hair if necessary. It seemed to him that Charmaine was the most unpredictable female he had ever met.

His face was stern and serious, his eyes flashed fire, as he strode along the passageway. Every tired muscle in his male body was taut and tense. His teeth were clenched, as were his fists.

Charmaine was just ending her enjoyable rendezvous with Cajun when Pierre arrived at their cabin. She'd thoroughly enjoyed her repast and her hunger was sated. Three generous glasses of Cajun's tasty wine had left her light and gay, so she cheerfully thanked the cook for such a delectable meal. She raved about his cream custard, telling him it was sheer ambrosia. That comment endeared her to Cajun. Such a tribute was welcomed by the French Acadian cook, who'd not had such a pleasant time in many a night!

"For you, I cook anything—anytime, *ma petite* Charmaine!" he told her as she prepared to leave. He put his fingers to his lips in an affectionate gesture.

"*Ah, merci, Cajun!* I enjoyed the time I spent with you. *Bonsoir,* my friend." She smiled warmly, then waved her hand before going out the door.

"*Bonsoir, ma belle Charmaine.*" The hefty cook returned her farewell wave. He then set about tidying up his kitchen, thinking how radiant and bright her presence had made it. She'd brought life and spirit into the dull cubicle where he spent his days and nights. He'd not been so cheerful for a long, long time.

Charmaine had found the short, chubby Acadian jovial. He had been entertaining and the meal he'd provided had been far more than a snack.

As she now strolled at an unhurried pace down the moonlit deck of the keel boat, she was happy and contented. Nothing in particular occupied her thoughts as the mild night breeze caressed her cheeks.

A male voice interrupted her solitude, startling her until

she recognized the young man standing in the darkness. She had seen him on her various strolls around the keel boat, and he'd always given her a big friendly smile.

"Nice out isn't it?" he remarked, ambling over from the corner where he'd been standing as he watched her make her way in his direction. Since she was alone, he'd decided to approach her. He'd wanted to do that since that first afternoon she'd come aboard the keel boat.

"Oh, yes," she replied, as she noticed he was now walking at her side.

"Listen to that nightbird over there in one of those trees on the bank. He's calling to his mate to come to him," Donnie told her.

Charmaine couldn't put her finger on what it was that made her uneasy, his nearness or the tone of his voice, or her awareness that his eyes were devouring her. When he took her arm, causing her to sway slightly against him, she was about to protest, but he quickly explained his action.

"Water there on the deck and I didn't want you to step in it and slip."

"I see," she said in a faltering voice. "I thank you . . . Donnie, isn't it?"

"That's right—Donnie, miss," he replied. Charmaine was very aware that his hand still held her arm and it was no longer necessary.

He chuckled, becoming a little bolder now that she'd allowed him to continue to walk with her. There wasn't one hint of indignation in her manner. Maybe she wasn't the sole property of Renaud as the whole crew had assumed.

"You're a tiny little lady, I must say. A fellow like me could pick you up with one hand," he declared.

"Oh now, I'm a little bigger than that." She laughed nervously then moved her arm, indicating that she wished to be free of his hand. But Donnie was too besotted with her beauty to notice the gesture.

"Well, I think we'd better say good night now, Donnie.

My cabin's just around this corner a little way." She started to remove his hand from her arm.

In the dark, images can be vastly distorted, and to the raging Renaud who was rushing around the corner in search of Charmaine, it appeared that the young man was trying to restrain her. Fury erupted in him, and he lunged for the boatman, seizing his throat in his powerful hands. The force of Pierre's assault caused Donnie to fall to the deck, the Frenchman atop him.

"Stop it, Pierre! What's the matter with you?" Charmaine shrieked, but he turned a deaf ear to her. His fist was already clenched, and he was about to slam it into Donnie's face. The young crewman had a startled look of confusion on his face as he stared into the eyes of what he thought was a madman.

Charmaine could not believe what she was witnessing. This was a Pierre Renaud she'd never known. Dear God, this was the same man who'd so tenderly kissed her, whose hands could caress her so gently. How many sides were there to this man's character? she asked herself. As she saw brute force unleashed in him, she had to confess she knew nothing about Pierre at all, and she realized how simple her life had been before he'd come into it.

Each day had been the same on Uncle Angus' farm. She'd known what to expect. There nothing exciting happened. She'd never experienced the wild exhilaration she'd found with Renaud, but this part of him frightened her.

She heard Donnie's moan of anguish and Pierre's warning. A menacing look in his gray eyes, he said, "Next time, you'll not be so lucky, you understand? This woman is mine and she'll not be touched by any other man!"

He rose up off his haunches and his bare chest heaved as he took a deep breath. His strong muscled body was tensed as he towered over the boatman sprawled on the floor of the keel boat. Then, slowly, he turned his gaze on the wide-eyed Charmaine. She stood frozen, not knowing quite what to expect of this volatile man to whom she'd given her heart and

349

her love these many weeks.

Before she recovered her wits, she felt herself being yanked by the hand, led away. There was no gentleness in Pierre's touch, and she sensed the fury churning within him. The heat of him permeated her and something else, something wild and exciting, as he practically dragged her to the cabin they shared.

Fiercely, he slammed the door once they were inside. Then, his silence so cold she trembled, he sat down on the chair to remove his boots. No words were spoken between them as he rose and removed his pants. She merely watched him, fidgeting with her hands nervously.

His black hair fell over his forehead, and he pushed it back. His eyes cast their silvery glints in her direction, but the expression on his face was fathomless and perplexing. Had she not known of his conceit and arrogance, she might have taken it for hurt instead of anger, but in the self-assured Pierre Renaud, this had to be anger, and anger at her. Well, damn him! Just who did he think he was? She'd done nothing wrong this night. How dare he expect her to wait in the cabin like the dutiful lapdog until he chose to appear. She would not do it.

She'd enjoyed the time she'd spent with the jolly Cajun, and there was certainly nothing wrong with that. And her innocent walk on the deck with the young man named Donnie had violated no bond between her and Pierre. So how dare he look at her with reproach!

"Well, are you going to stand there all night, Charmaine? I'm tired from putting in the extra hours on the poles and then fighting for your honor when I'd planned to be in bed."

Blue fire sparked in Charmaine's eyes and her temper flared. Hoisting a shapely leg, she lifted a slipper from her foot and flung it at him. "I could have taken care of my honor, as you called it, quite nicely, Pierre Renaud." Before he'd recovered from dodging the first slipper, the second sailed toward his head. By now she was unfastening the top of her bodice in a provocative fashion. "When in bloody hell did you concern yourself about my honor? You stole my innocence on the cliffs of Jersey without a care, and without the comfort of a bed. Oh, yes, Pierre, you honored me! I could have been left with your child, but thank God, I wasn't because you left Jersey and I didn't even know where you were." By now, she was stumbling out of her skirt while Pierre sat as one in a trance for in truth he'd never seen so much fire in a woman and he was enthralled by her.

When she had stripped to her undergarments, she lashed out at him anew. "What do you call honor, Pierre? Jacques honors Tasha, but you, wish only to possess me! I'll tell you something: you'll never own me! No man will!"

Wisps of spun-gold hair fell over her face and she stroked it aside. Her deep breaths made her breasts swell, as if they would overflow her undergarments, yet she had no inkling of the agony or the ecstasy she was stirring in Renaud.

When he sensed that she was gasping for breath after all her ranting and raving, he asked in a quiet husky voice, "Are you through, Charmaine?" He rose up from the chair where he'd been sitting, and moving like a predatory cat, his quicksilver eyes piercing hers, he came to her.

Something about him made her speechless and she stood frozen as he took her in his arms to hold her. He felt her body tremble as he held her close to him, and his hand tilted her chin so her face was directed upward. After taking a long, leisurely look at her loveliness, he murmured softly, "I understand how you feel, *chérie*. I'll make it all up to you as soon as we get to my uncle's. I thought my love was enough. I know now it isn't."

"I've not even known I had your love, Pierre. Sharing your bed does not necessarily mean I have your love." Charmaine looked into his eyes, searching those deep silver pools.

"Then I've much to prove to you, *oui?* I'd best get started for it might take the rest of my life, when I'm dealing with a hard-headed little vixen like you."

Slowly and determinedly he captured her half-parted lips, and she felt a searing heat the moment they kissed. Her body sought to mold itself to his, for she could not resist the sweet persuasion of his mouth.

Pierre forgot his weariness and his aching muscles as passion consumed him, and he ached to make love to the woman he held in his arms. When her body arched, pressing urgently against him, his desire mounted.

Eagerly he released her pulsing breasts from the chemise, and his mouth trailed down from her lips to take the tip of one while his other hand sought to cup her firm, round buttocks only to encounter the restraining folds of petticoats which denied him the touch of her smooth flesh.

Quickly, he separated himself from her so he might undo the tie at the waist of her petticoat. Then a hasty yank disposed of that obstacle, and he scooped her up, carrying her to the bed.

Now she was as he desired, tantalizingly nude—a feast for his eyes. He devoured her, letting his gaze slowly and adoringly absorb the hills and valleys of her velvet softness.

"Pierre," she purred, raising her hands to encircle his neck. She yearned for more than teasing eyes. The sight of his masculine body towering over her was intoxicating.

"But if I come to you, *ma petite*, I might dishonor you. Remember you questioned my honor?" He played with her for a brief moment.

"Pierre, honor isn't what I have on my mind right now." She arched her body provocatively and unable to resist, he sank down onto her.

Their bodies met, the fire of their passion wild and wonderful. "Oh, God, Pierre! Oh, God!" she gasped.

He chuckled, pleased about the pleasure he knew she was feeling. "Am I proving my love, *chérie?*"

"Yes . . . yes!" Her hands dug into his back, pressing him even closer.

As his powerful thrusts surged deeper, Charmaine felt she was soaring into the starlit sky. Together, they were swept to higher and loftier pinnacles until the mighty quivering of Pierre's body brought release and the stillness which follows it. Exhaustedly, he lay beside her, and she was content to have his body touching hers.

Chapter 42

Donnie Farrell had been involved in his share of fights with the boatmen who traveled up and down the Mississippi River. He'd had his nose bloodied and his ribs bruised, but he'd never figured himself to be a coward. However, the incident last night had shaken him. He didn't want to tangle again with that wild Frenchman. He'd thought a goddamned wildcat had jumped him.

Renaud's quicksilver eyes had had a deadly glint in them. Hell, the man had wanted to kill him and Donnie knew it. Mademoiselle Lamoureux's pleas were probably what had calmed him, but not even she had stopped him from pounding Donnie's face.

When the young man had staggered back to his quarters, he'd gathered up his few belongings. He was getting off at Greenville. He didn't have to look in the mirror to know that he had a lip twice the size of what it should be. A pounding pain made the right side of his face throb, and his forehead hurt.

Unceremoniously, he slipped over the side of the long keel boat just before dawn, saying nothing to Morrow or anyone else aboard the craft. He had only a short distance to swim since the keel boat was tied to the trees on the bank, and if his knowledge of the bends in the river was correct, it was not too far upstream to the small hamlet of Greenville.

He couldn't care less that he'd leave Cat speculating about his disappearance. River boatmen were not the most responsible lot anyway. It was not uncommon to lose a crewman at a stop along the way. Indeed, the cities along the river thrived on the drinking, gambling, and carousing of the boatmen. He knew Morrow wouldn't fret for long.

Donnie Farrell swore one thing as he plunged into the muddy waters of the river: he'd not put his life on the line again by getting giddy-headed over some fluff of femininity. It wasn't worth the pain. He hadn't even been rewarded with a kiss.

Cat Morrow did fume about being shy a good hand, for Farrell was one of his best men. But he figured when he got to Memphis he'd hire on one of the men milling around the wharf looking for some work.

It was Jacques Bernay who enlightened Pierre about Farrell's disappearance as he and Tasha, along with Pierre and Charmaine took an evening stroll on the deck of the keel boat.

"Gone, is he?" Renaud remarked, his expression never changing. He dared not look down at Charmaine though he could feel her deep blue eyes piercing him.

"Yes. Cat said sometime during the night he must have jumped over the side and swam to the bank. Greenville was nearby, and Cat figured that was where he headed."

"Morrow tell you when we'll make Memphis?"

"He figures tomorrow, *mon ami*. How much farther do we go then to reach your uncle's?" Jacques asked.

"I'd say another couple of days and we should be there, judging by the charts in my father's journal and the way we've been traveling thus far."

"That soon?" Charmaine suddenly realized in just two days she would be facing members of Pierre's family. A surge of panic shot through her. How would they respond to her, and how did Pierre intend to present her to them? Jacques and Tasha had no call for embarrassment, but what about her? What title would she use when they arrived?

"What is it, *ma petite?* Do you want to go on to Saint Louis?" Pierre laughed and hugged her closer to him.

"No, I didn't mean that," she said quickly. He could not see the apprehension on her face, but Tasha noticed the sudden change in her demeanor and she wondered what was troubling her friend.

Tasha saw a forlorn young woman beside her. She owed much to Charmaine, whose vivacious, friendly nature had cheered her when they were crossing the Atlantic, and she could not stand to see her unhappy.

Tasha recalled how frightened she'd been at the prospect of crossing the ocean all alone. Meeting that warm and outgoing Charmaine had been very helpful to the shy and reserved Tasha Weer.

Indeed, she credited Charmaine with all the good things which had come to pass in the days that followed. Perhaps, she and her beloved Jacques would not even have found each other had it not been for Charmaine.

She nudged Jacques' muscular arm and told him, "Charmaine and I are going to our cabin, Jacques. I need her advice on how to alter one of my gowns. You and Pierre will know where to find us when you wish."

He gave her an affectionate peck on her nose, and as if he understood that she wanted some private time with her lady friend, he urged, "Go, ma petite. We will join you later."

Tasha gave her husband a wink before asking Charmaine to join her. Then the two women made their way to the Bernays' quarters.

Tasha removed her shawl once they were inside the cabin and then casually invited Charmaine to join her in a glass of wine. "That Frenchman of mine is teaching me bad habits, I fear. But I must confess, I love every moment of the lessons."

Charmaine was still amazed at the change in the prim, little black-haired lady she'd met aboard the *Sea Witch*. It never ceased to amaze her and tonight was a prime example. Tasha moved her body differently and the look in her eyes had changed. Charmaine had sensed from the first that Jacques Bernay was a sensual man. He wore a commoner's clothes but he might well have had an aristocratic background.

"Tasha, you never cease to amaze me. I am so happy for you, but then I think I've told you that a dozen times. Yes, I will be delighted to share a glass of wine with you."

Tasha was already pouring a glass for her, but she turned to look at Charmaine. "But for you, it would not have happened, Charmaine."

Sipping the wine, Charmaine stared up at her, puzzlement reflected on her face. "I fear I don't understand, Tasha."

"Believe me, Charmaine, I owe you much. I now wish to help you find the same happiness Jacques and I share because of what you did for me, my friend. Tell me what I can do. What is troubling you? Please let me help you."

Charmaine knew Tasha was sincere but she did not know what to tell her. For a moment her long-lashed eyes went down to her lap and she said nothing.

In a faltering voice, she finally declared, "I don't think you, Jacques, or anyone can help. That must come from Pierre. Oh, we are lovers, but beyond that I have nothing to hope for—nothing to feel secure about. Jacques was honest with you. He made you his wife, but Pierre has not felt the need to do so with me. Now, in two days, I must face members of his very esteemed family, and what am I to be? You tell me. Am I a trollop . . . a whore . . . or his mistress?" Tears gleamed in the deep blue pools of her eyes.

Compassion welled in Tasha, and she rushed to Charmaine to embrace her. "Don't let me hear you say such a thing again, Charmaine Lamoureux! Ever! Pierre is just different from my Jacques. That is all. From what Jacques has told me, Pierre was bewitched by you the first night he laid eyes on you. He loves you! Oh, Charmaine, he has to from what Jacques said. He went to the island of Jersey in search of you."

Charmaine wiped her eyes with her hand, then the other. "Then why has he never said he wants to marry me, Tasha? You and I know that wanting to make love to a woman doesn't signify a man loves you. Dear God, that despicable Chauncey Bedlow wanted to make love to me! That is sheer lust—hardly love!"

Tasha patted her shoulder understandingly. "No, that's not love at all."

"That's my point. I admit Renaud is most affectionate when we are in bed, but I want more than that. I've learned a lot in the last few months. I can have that relationship with any man I desire just by crooking my little finger, but I feel so much more for him and I want him to feel as deeply for me. Do you understand what I'm saying?"

"Of course, and I agree. As I see it, Charmaine, you must let him know all this, and if you can not have him the way you want him, then he can not have what he wants from you. You see what I mean?"

"I think I do, Tasha. But it is impossible for me to refuse him when he kisses or touches me."

"Then you must exert more will power. If you want him to marry you, you will do anything you must to get your way. Believe me, I know!"

Charmaine gave out a soft lilting gusto of laughter. "I've said it before and I'll say it again, Tasha, you utterly amaze me!"

"Oh, not half as much as I've amazed myself, Charmaine. If I dared to confess the startling things I've learned about myself in these last weeks and months, we'd both be shocked so I wouldn't dare."

Two giggling ladies were what Jacques and Pierre encountered when they entered the Bernays' quarters, and they would have sworn the two women had indulged in too many glasses of wine, which was hardly the case.

But then, when two virile Frenchmen find two vivacious ladies smiling at them they would be fools not to take advantage of such an inviting situation. Neither man cared if Tasha and Charmaine had had one or four glasses of wine, but because each lady occupied a particular place in the heart of the man observing her, both men were indulging in pleasant musings.

In the secret abyss of his mind, Pierre was seeing Charmaine as the woman he'd always imagined her: a goddess of love . . . a siren . . . an enchantress. Yet this same woman would be his wife and the mother of his children. He had decided he would settle for no less, else he would never marry and commit himself to just one woman. But in Charmaine, he felt he had found the woman who suited him, but a reluctant part of him had prevented him from doing what Jacques had done with Tasha.

But Pierre knew if Charmaine ever left him he would be lost. No other woman could take her place. *Mon Dieu,* he knew that beyond the shadow of doubt!

The eyes of the older Bernay saw his lady differently than Renaud was yet ready to see in his love. In Tasha, he saw the lady he was ready to grow old with, but before that time there would be children and the sharing of their lives. Should they not have any offspring of their own, then their love for one another would be enough.

Tasha was no enchantress! He'd not been attracted to her for that reason. No. His feeling for her was much deeper, as was hers for him. Tasha would always be there if he needed her, and he would be there for her. She was a sustaining force. Until Tasha had come into his life Bernay had not known he craved such a thing.

If he hated Étienne Renaud for anything, it had to be for that, but it was through knowing Étienne's legitimate son, that he'd found his heart's desire, Tasha. An odd situation.

But he had no regrets! He had no desire for revenge. What he'd been denied earlier, he'd received tenfold from one tiny little lady with dark eyes. Bernay was the happiest of men!

So each man stood, admiring the lady of his choice in a different light, yet they had much in common. One knew what bound them; the other one didn't.

When the two Frenchmen exchanged glances, the same smile appeared on their faces. It was the smile of another Frenchman who'd sired both of them—Étienne Renaud!

Chapter 43

What caprice is she now indulging in? Pierre wondered, trying to measure Charmaine's change of mood after they'd returned to their cabin. His golden-haired Charmaine had been gay and light-hearted when he and Jacques had joined their ladies. What had piqued her, he didn't know. Surely it was nothing he'd done or said, of that he was convinced.

Charmaine was finding it devilishly difficult to follow Tasha's sage advice and to deny him her affection if he would not offer her marriage. When she'd looked up at his face after responding coolly to his kiss, she'd seen hurt reflected there. To slip from his arms to sit down and remove her slippers took a lot of will power.

"Heavens . . . I'm sleepy," she mumbled. "I'll surely go to sleep as soon as my head hits the pillow." She turned around on the stool so her lying eyes would not give her away.

"That wine you and Tasha were drinking must have hit you all of a sudden," he grumbled, pulling off his boots. "You weren't the least bit sleepy at their cabin."

"Must have been." She sighed, yawned, and gave him a weak, hasty smile.

"You want me to help you get out of that dress?"

"Would you just get those hooks at the back for me?"

"Come here then," he suggested.

As she moved toward him she wondered if she'd made a

mistake now for as soon as she presented her back to him, she felt the touch of his fingertips against her flesh and she knew it would take little effort on his part to destroy all her honorable intentions.

To keep from surrendering to him she quickly moved away from the heated nearness of his body.

"Think I'll go on deck for a while to smoke a cheroot. I don't want to keep you from going to sleep since you're ready to retire," he told her as she prepared to slip out of her frock.

"Of course, Pierre. Go ahead," she answered calmly, though she had been taken by surprise by his announcement. She slipped into her nightgown and dimmed the lantern before crawling into the bed.

Somehow, it didn't seem right to shut her eyes and go to sleep without his good-night kiss or his warmth at her side. She moaned softly. "Oh, Tasha, I don't know if I can do this!"

A cheroot was the last thing Pierre wanted, but if he'd stood there while she slipped out of her dress, inviting curves of her body would have driven him to insist they make love. So he'd taken the easy way out. When he returned she'd be in bed, possibly already asleep, and he'd slip in beside her. That would be just as tormenting for he could not reach for her as he always did.

Tossing the remainder of his cheroot in the water, he went back to his cabin, entering quietly so he wouldn't awaken her.

Charmaine was as wide-eyed as she'd been when he left. But she gave him no inkling of this, nor did she acknowledge that she felt the weight of his muscled arm when it snaked around her waist. To lie so still and not snuggle up to him was a torment for her.

Was what she wanted worth the price she was paying? Yes, she thought. So she endured the tense, endless time until her eyes closed in sleep.

*　　*　　*

After a couple of days had gone by, Charmaine was weakening. In the morning when she roused up from sleep, Pierre was always gone from their cabin. He and Jacques were helping to fill in because the crew was three men short since Donnie Farrell had gone over the side.

In the late afternoon or in the evening, he returned to their cabin so completely exhausted he gave her no more than a grunt for a greeting. Later, he went through the ritual of eating the evening meal from a tray, but when she tried to chat with him, he hardly listened to what she was saying.

After three nights of withholding her affections, Charmaine had decided to tell Tasha her idea might have been a wise one, but she was ready to scream. In the morning when she went on deck to find Pierre, she encountered Cat Morrow and he pointed to the bluffs above the muddy Mississippi. "They're called the Chickasaw Bluffs."

"What a very odd name, Captain," she exclaimed, looking at the precipitous banks which jutted up more than fifty feet above the flowing stream.

"An Indian name, *mademoiselle*. This country was the home of the Chickasaw Indians until the white man pushed them out. Very soon you will be able to see a fort built by your countrymen, the French."

In her straightforward way, Charmaine declared, "That hardly seems fair if this was the Chickasaws' home, Captain."

"I agree with you, but you must know that what's fair or right has little to do with the way this world is run."

"That still doesn't make it right." Her deep blue eyes darkened.

A couple of pirogues were afloat beside the keel boat, and the men in them yelled to Cat. One had a long black braid hanging down his back. Charmaine asked Cat about him and he told her, "Oh that grinning ape is called Laughing Bear. He's a scout and a trapper. In case, you've never seen one before, Mademoiselle Lamoureux, he's an Indian."

"So that is what an Indian looks like," she replied.

Recalling the big black man called Timbo who'd saved her and Tasha when the *Sea Witch* had been wrecked, she added, "But I expected them to be red of skin."

"Oh, there's a big variety in their coloring. Some are dark and some as light as the mulattoes back in New Orleans." Cat was thinking about the lovely Indian maiden he'd met not far from there—a Quapaw.

"I've much to learn about this strange new country, I guess, Captain. It's all very exciting and interesting."

"That it is, *mademoiselle*. It's good you are so young and full of spirit; it helps to endure this place. Guess I have to be honest with you, ma'am, when I saw you come aboard my boat I says to myself this'll be a miserable trip 'cause she'll be complaining about the discomforts." He chuckled. "I saw you in a fancy parlor in gowns of silk and lace, and God forbid, this here boat sure ain't that."

Charmaine laughed. "So I fooled you, Captain Morrow?"

"You sure as hell did! Oh, I beg your pardon, ma'am."

The tall rawboned man flushed with embarrassment, but Charmaine quickly eased his apprehensions about cursing.

"Captain, you must know I'm no sheltered child. After all, Renaud and Bernay are not priests." When she gave him one of her radiant smiles Cat felt himself go weak. That son of a bitch Renaud is one lucky bastard, he thought.

"May I be so bold as to ask you, miss, are you and Pierre betrothed?" Cat ventured. If he'd had eyes in the back of his head he'd never have dared to pose such a question for a barefooted Pierre Renaud had ambled quietly toward them from his station on the keel boat.

Charmaine had seen him approaching, but for her own reasons she'd sought to keep Cat Morrow engaged in conversation. She'd let her eyes dart over Cat's shoulder a couple of times to indulge in the magnificent sight of him. His firm muscular legs were molded in the faded duck pants as he walked toward them with a swaggering gait. Pierre was obviously irate, and she was enjoying the fact that he was jealous. His quicksilver eyes flashed with a brilliant gleam that excited her. Yes, she did want him to be jealous, so jealous he'd claim her forever as his own! Her heart would not settle for anything less!

"Well, to answer your question about me and Pierre, Captain Morrow, we are—"

"I'll answer that, Morrow," Renaud roared. "Mademoiselle Lamoureux is *my* lady, and yes, she is to be my wife! I think that settles that!" He placed the long pole he held in Morrow's palm and he grasped Charmaine's hand. There was no gentleness in his touch as he yanked her away with him.

She had no time to protest or do anything as he dragged her along the deck and down to their cabin, his awesome silence making her tremble. How untamed and wild his fury could be!

Panting from trying to keep up with his long strides and vexed because the heel of her shoe had caught in the hemline of her dress, tearing it, Charmaine was in a foul mood by the time they'd reached their quarters and he'd slammed the door. The imposing figure he made as he stood standing with his long, muscled legs slightly apart didn't intimidate her. She glared back at him with as much intensity and fire as he displayed.

"You amaze me, Pierre Renaud! You truly do! It's news to me that I am to be your wife!" She whirled around and began to pace, churning with resentment that he'd assumed so much, especially about something as precious and dear as a marriage proposal. "Maybe I'm old-fashioned, perhaps even a little prudish, but I've always thought the lady is asked if her answer is yes or no before an engagement is announced."

"Oh, for God's sakes, Charmaine! What is this all about— this dramatic scene?"

"A simple matter of courtesy, Pierre! A matter of respect, which I feel you sometimes sorely neglect." Her head was held high and she'd never looked more appealing to him. He knew what she meant, and there was truth to what she'd said. Young as she might be, he realized she had a good deal of wisdom and pride.

"I bow to you, my fair *mademoiselle*. I concede that you are right." But his tone sounded too light-hearted for Charmaine, who could not look inside his heart and know that he found her utterly enchanting as she stood there so fired with fury.

His words only ignited her determination to show him she would not be treated like a child, and she decided to shock him. In a chilling voice she announced, "Perhaps, Pierre Renaud . . . perhaps I don't wish to be your wife. Have you thought of that?" She turned quickly away from his all-knowing eyes.

If it had been her intention to stun him, she had assuredly done so. And she'd wounded his fierce male ego. For those reasons, he sat, frozen with disbelief, staring at her cold, harsh eyes and wondering what had happened to the blue fire they possessed.

His pride now demanded that he be as cold and cruel as she so when he finally spoke, no bitterly cold winter wind had ever chilled her more. His voice was low, but full of meaning. "Believe me, I'll never, never be so presumptuous again! You can depend on that!"

He rose from the chair on which he'd been sitting and walked out of the cabin. Charmaine did not see him for the rest of that night.

For long, lonely hours she lay alone with no one to comfort her, and she'd cried all the tears a woman can cry. Pride is often painful, but hers had cost her dearly. The only consolation she could find in this whole miserable night was she had as much right to her pride as he had to his.

Was it true that love conquered all? Charmaine clung to that hope, for it was all she had. If only he loved her as she loved him, things would work out.

Pride could be bent, and she was willing to bend if he would. But she would be damned if she'd do all the bending!

Chapter 44

The impasse they'd gotten into had left Charmaine and Pierre with frayed nerves. They were ill at ease when they were around each other, not knowing how to act. Charmaine would have preferred to argue it all out and then make up, but he'd been ridiculously polite.

With so much tension engulfing her, she was herself short-tempered, even with Tasha. When she snapped out sharp remarks, she detested herself a few minutes later. She wondered if she blamed Tasha for giving her advice she'd followed. It had not worked for Charmaine.

Poor Tasha did not know what was going on between the couple, but she was aware that they were at odds since her encounter with Pierre.

She'd been making her way across the keel boat to take some food to Jacques when the young Frenchman had come in her direction. When she'd greeted him in her usually friendly fashion and had said that he looked very tired, he'd given a weak smile.

"I am and I'll be glad when we get off this boat."

"Oh, I think we all will now, Pierre. I know Charmaine will be more than ready," Tasha remarked casually, not expecting Renaud's reaction.

"Oh, I think she's eager to be rid of me."

"Rid of you? What are you talking about? You've been working too hard, I think." His words made no sense to Tasha for she knew how Charmaine felt.

Shrugging his shoulders, Pierre forced a crooked grin, then he patted Tasha's shoulder. "Sure, that's probably what it is. A little rest will cure what ails me. See you later, Tasha." He ambled off, leaving Tasha to stare after him.

She'd talk to Charmaine, she decided, find out just what all this was about. Renaud could not be any wearier than her husband, for Jacques had matched him hour for hour at the poles and the ropes.

But when she found Charmaine in her cabin and questioned her, the young woman was reluctant to confide in her friend. That pained Tasha tremendously. From the moment they'd met, they had enjoyed a warm friendship and now there was a barrier between them. Tasha did not know how to break it down.

When Charmaine whirled around there were misty tears in her blue eyes, and Tasha knew her little friend was in despair. Charmaine's long lashes fluttered as she began to speak. "Please, Tasha—I've no desire to discuss this with you! It concerns me and Pierre. I will say only this and then I'd like to be alone. What has worked for you and Jacques can't work for me and Pierre."

What does she mean? Tasha wondered. She pondered Charmaine's statement for the rest of the day, and in the evening, even when her beloved Jacques returned to their quarters, she did not have to mention that her heart was heavy and she was preoccupied. As tired as he was, Jacques sensed that his bride was worried about something.

Knowing the black mood of his friend Renaud, he rather suspected they were both concerned about their friends, and when he prodded her to tell him what was weighing so heavily on her mind, her comments came as no shock.

At first, he attempted to cajole her. "Tasha, *ma petite,* they are two very volatile people. They are not as easygoing as we are. Explosions are bound to happen more often, *oui?*"

"What you say is true, Jacques, but I fear that they will take this too far and there will be no going back. That would be horrible. You know and I know that they love one another. It is a good love they have. Pierre would kill for her and she would surely die for him. This I know, Jacques."

Tasha is so loyal, Jacques thought. But then, so was he. He went to her and took her in his arms. He liked holding her like this. To some it might seem crazy, but it was as exhilarating to him as the times they made love. He brushed a straying slip of hair away from her face and kissed her cheek tenderly. "Tasha, *chérie,* I agree. But in the end, they must find their heart's desire as we found ours. We can't do it for them. Pierre is a stubborn man, and prideful. Charmaine is proud too. She will not bow to him even though she loves him. Pierre has to accept that if he wants her badly enough. It is as simple as that! *N'est-ce pas?* A man like Pierre has had many ladies, yet the very thing in Charmaine that held his interest he cannot abide now. She has a free spirit and she won't succumb to his will."

Tasha raised her black eyes to her husband and they were filled with admiration. "Jacques Bernay, you are so smart. Do you know what? I'm glad we were older when we met, not foolish children like those two or else we could have had the same heartaches they're having."

"That is true. I never thought of it that way. You are smart too, my Tasha! There is an advantage to being older, now that I think about it." He laughed. He told himself once again how lucky he was to have met Tasha Weer.

His husky body welled with love, and he felt himself fortunate to have a woman who thought he was so grand. She made up for the privileges his illegitimacy had deprived him of. He really didn't envy his pampered half brother, Pierre. Mon Dieu, he would not wish to trade places with him. He had what he wanted.

He bent his head and whispered, *"Je t'aime."*

371

A teasing, wicked look gleamed in Tasha's black eyes. "Jacques Bernay, you wicked Frenchman! You say these things I don't understand, knowing full well I'm not French like you and Renaud and Charmaine! Someday, I shall surprise you!" She stretched the full length of her tiny body and stood on tiptoe so she could press her lips to his. "Whatever you said sounded intriguing, though. You beguile me with your charm. So the answer is yes!"

They laughed as Jacques picked her up in his strong arms, and the problems of Charmaine and Pierre were forgotten.

Rains pelted the delta along the Mississippi River, and the planters sowed no seed for the ground was too muddy. Cat Morrow had left behind the forest and woods as his keel boat had floated northward of Memphis, inching nearer and nearer to the Missouri Territory. The land was cleared and flat now, and farming was the prime livelihood in this countryside, not the logging industry.

Pierre had found the barges and the pirogues he'd seen in Memphis fascinating. This strange, primitive country was never dull. There was now no doubt in his mind that he would remain here. He had no desire to return to France, regardless of what his father's plans for him were. He knew he wanted to live and seek adventure in this country where everything was new and amazing. It whetted his curiosity and challenged his daring spirit. If he could only tame that little vixen he adored so very much, he would share his life with her. No other woman would do, only Charmaine Lamoureux!

By God, he would do it! I must do it, he told himself, so my destiny can be fulfilled!

His ego did not permit him to believe that she did not love him. Whatever female whimsy she was indulging in right now he would break down, he promised himself. When they arrived at his uncle's, he'd seek the support of his dear Tante

Genevieve who had adored him before she and Charles had left France to come to this strange land. Pierre knew she was a lady of fire and spirit, much like his adorable Charmaine.

Morrow had been most enlightening as to what he could expect when he arrived at his destination. It was a thriving trading post, a frontier river town filled with traders, gamblers, boatmen, and hunters. They were English, Spanish, French, Indian, and Negro.

One little bit of information Morrow had told him made him wish he'd had the foresight of his friend Bernay: the priest and the preacher only visited New Madrid occasionally. It was the same with the judge and the attorney.

What that golden-haired minx couldn't seem to get through her head was that no priest could bind him to her more tightly than she had. Forever, his heart was hers. Forever, she'd be a part of him. He could not be free of her if he wanted to. Without Charmaine, he felt he had no reason to live and breathe!

Renaud was thinking more and more that this venture he'd been sent on was intended to enlighten him. Old Étienne knew damned well he'd never learn such things in Cherbourg. Most of Morrow's boatmen were of French descent, and the St. Louis Creoles, he'd learned, were chosen by keel boat captains in preference to the French Canadians. He'd felt right at home the minute he'd boarded Morrow's boat and he'd heard the man in his buckskin garb yell out his orders in French. *"Levez les perches,"* he'd called to the men working the long poles and they'd immediately lifted them out of the water. Since that first day he'd become very acquainted with those poles and with the hundreds of feet of rope it took to navigate this seventy-foot craft.

This morning it seemed they were moving very slowly, but that wasn't hard to understand for rain pelted the men walking along the shore and guiding the boat upstream. The water was too deep to cordelle the boat so the six oars on either side were being used. There was only a gentle breeze so the square sail with its hundred square feet of canvas was no advantage. Morrow had told him that they'd be lucky if they made twenty miles today.

Renaud had learned a valuable lesson where the elements were concerned. No matter how smart a man might think he was, he was never clever enough to outsmart nature.

Hell, this trip had been humbling in more than one way. As clever and cunning as he'd once thought himself, he wasn't shrewd enough to figure out one little French belle.

Being able to admit this, he asked himself if Étienne had been aware of this and had wanted to strengthen his character. Well, Pierre knew he was a stronger person, and he'd certainly been humbled by Charmaine!

His private musings came to an abrupt halt when a skiff rowed up to Cat's boat and the man aboard it announced he was Sheriff Shelby from Memphis. He said he wished to come aboard to question the pilot in charge.

When Cat granted his request and declared himself in charge, Pierre quickly concealed himself behind the outside of the cargo compartment of the keel boat.

Straining to see if he could hear what the men were discussing with Morrow, Pierre wondered if they were looking for him in connection with the murder of Henri Gervais back in New Orleans, but he could make out only muffled voices, no distinct words. The two men accompanying the sheriff kept glancing around the keel boat while the lawman queried Cat. Time seemed endless as Renaud watched them, but he could only wait and hope.

Every muscle in his body was taut, and his heart pounded erratically. The palms of his hands were beaded with sweat now, but the trio lingered on the boat. Most inopportunely, Charmaine appeared on deck and he instinctively yanked her into the secluded area where he stood.

Her rosebud lips opened as if to protest, but he muzzled her. He had no time to be gentle, and he could not worry that she did not understand. "Shut up! I'll explain later!" he

374

muttered, his gray eyes urging her to obey him.

His strong hands held her in a viselike grip, her bosom pressed against his chest. As their eyes locked, his hand was still covering her lips. "It's the sheriff out of Memphis," he whispered in her ear. Her long lashes fluttered nervously, telling him she understood, so he took his hand from her lips and rested it against her cheek. They stood close together, saying nothing, and in that awesome period they forgot any differences they had felt. They were united. Mutual concern bound them. That horrible episode in New Orleans was haunting them. Nonetheless, their proximity sparked the fire of desire.

Blue sapphire eyes told Pierre she wanted him, and his caressing hands let Charmaine know he wanted her. They wanted very much to make love.

But their building rapture faded when the trio of lawmen left the keel boat and Cat Morrow stood alone, waving farewell to them as they boarded their skiff.

Pierre's insatiable curiosity made him release her. "Stay here, *petite amie*. I must talk to Cat. I'll come back as soon as I find out what that was all about." He turned to leave her, but halted for one second to give her a flashing, teasing grin and to tell her, "I promise I won't be long, *chérie*. Wait for me . . . please!"

She readily returned his smile. After feeling the divine warmth of the body she'd hungered for all these long nights, she didn't have to be asked to wait. *Mon Dieu!*

Tasha's theory had put her through torment. She was weak, she supposed. The nights of pleasure she'd denied herself were not worth it. Without Pierre, life meant nothing!

Her romantic, reckless heart cried out to her to take this day—this night. Who could say what would happen in the future?

She stood there and she waited, though she sneaked a peek at the two men who were talking. Pierre had his back turned to her so she could not tell what expression was on his face, but the bronzed face of Cat Morrow was creased with broad, friendly grin. That was enough to tell Charmaine she and Pierre had nothing to fear. She heaved a deep sigh of relief.

Now her heart pounded with anticipation for she hoped to spend the rest of the afternoon with Pierre. She waited eagerly for him to return. There was a twinkle in her blue sapphire eyes of hers, and a cunning smile lit her lovely face. The wanton in her had great expectations of the hours ahead.

As Pierre's magnificent male body turned in her direction, his muscles rippling, she knew he was feeling just as she was. His face was relaxed and he was smiling smugly. Ah, this was going to be a grand afternoon, she just knew it!

And it was!

Chapter 45

The sheriff and his men weren't hunting him, Pierre had learned from his talk with Cat Morrow. So when he joined Charmaine he was light-hearted.

"Ah, *chérie,* it is nothing to concern ourselves about. Our unsavory past has not caught up with us yet." He took her arm and drew her along with him. Then he let out a roar of laughter.

"I could feel insulted by such a remark, though I'm glad you included yourself. But how would they possibly know about what happened back in New Orleans, Pierre?"

"My sweet thing, I'm learning more and more how news travels back and forth on this river. When you stop to think about it, from the minute you and I hit these American shores we left a trail behind us. Savannah was the first city we had to get out of in a hurry because of Bedlow. Then we left New Orleans in haste because of Henri Gervais. That could have happened on the keel boat, but Farrell disappeared instead. I must bear in mind that your charms tend to be fatal *ma petite amie!*"

"Well, you look very much alive to me. I don't seem to have that effect on you," she retorted. "I didn't invite the trouble which has dogged my footsteps since I left Jersey."

Pierre noticed what he thought was a faraway look in her

blue eyes, and compassion welled up in him. He bent down to plant a gentle kiss on her cheek. "An invitation is necessary, Charmaine, not when a woman looks like you. Your beauty lures men, as honey draws bees."

Her eyes locked with his. His face had no teasing grin on it now, and the words he spoke rang with sincerity and feeling. Her response came from her own heart and was just as sincere. "I love you, Pierre. If we could always be as we are now, it would be wonderful."

"But that's not the way life is, Charmaine. We're both far too independent and free spirited not to have our differences. You must realize that. But the love that binds us will always draw us together; you must know that too." He put his arm around her as they approached their cabin, and he ushered her through the door ahead of him, closing and locking it behind him. He was going to try to heal the wound festering between them the last few days. He wanted to present this lovable Charmaine to his aunt and uncle when they disembarked at New Madrid, not a sullen, pouting little vixen.

They stood silently in the middle of the cabin. It was as if each waited for the other to break the ghostly silence which seemed to permeate the small area. They were an amusing study. Pierre was a paragon of a man, handsome and virile yet ill at ease before this petite maiden whose head did not reach his broad shoulders. Charmaine was just as unsure of herself, yet every fiber in her small body cried out to him to claim her. Though she'd dared not admit it, silently she was pleading with him to make her wait no longer. A voice in Renaud urged him not to waste these precious moments— moments that might never come again. So, bracing himself for a denial, he took a step toward her.

"You didn't answer me a moment ago, Charmaine. Am I to take it that you don't feel our love binds us together?"

It was not her nature to play the foolish games some ladies enjoyed but candidness had yielded her nothing. In a soft, calm voice she replied, "I wonder, Renaud, if love has many meanings. I guess in my simple way I'm trying to say that what I feel for you is completely different from what you feel for me."

She sat down on the bed, and he looked at her bowed head, glossy and golden, as she casually removed her slippers and tossed them aside. How wonderfully childlike she was; yet all women were when they were rapturously engaged in making love. He asked himself a question he'd never expected to entertain where any woman was concerned. Where or how was he failing her? That he was, was obvious.

In that brief, fleeting moment, he looked deeper into himself and he wondered if men weren't such egotistical bastards they assumed far too much where their lady loves were concerned. Perhaps he had been guilty of that.

He strolled slowly over to the bed and sat down beside her. "What is it you wish of me, Charmaine? You tell me. Perhaps this crazy Frenchman is thick headed, eh?" He gave her a mellow smile, but there was nothing teasing or light-hearted about it. He was in earnest.

"I want only one thing, Pierre, and that is all I've ever wanted since our night on the beach in Jersey. I want your love—all your love. You see, it is very simple for me, not complicated at all!"

He pulled her into his arms and pressed her against him. Then his lips found hers.

The minute his arms had drawn her to him, Charmaine felt serenity engulf her, that and the overwhelming pleasure his touch always provided. She dared not pull away. As tempestuous as their love had always been, Pierre was her anchor—her security. In his strong, powerful arms, she always felt safe.

Her sweet lips were like nectar to Pierre, and his head whirled with desire. The taste intoxicated him and he craved to indulge himself more. His lips trailed down to the rosy tip of her luscious breast to sample the nectar he'd find there.

379

She moaned as his mouth and tongue caressed her, and he sought to intertwine himself with her to feel the satiny softness of her flesh pressed against him. As he sensed the heat of her desire, liquid fire shot through him, igniting his very essence. He knew her feelings were as intense, for she undulated and arched beneath him. Dear God, she was a thing of wonder, a delight!

They moved together, in perfect harmony, the beat of passion's music becoming faster and faster. His male throbbed as he carried her to the heights of pleasure—to ecstasy. Then he gave to sweet release and they drifted together, their passion momentarily spent.

Outside their cabin, the sun was still high in the sky, but inside the lovers knew moonlight ecstasy as on the first night they'd made love, the night that had bound them to one another.

Having recaptured this special bliss they'd hungered for, they lay in one another's arms, not daring to let go for fear of losing the magic they'd rediscovered.

They needed no food or wine. They needed only one another! Their bodies and their souls had become one. Both knew it.

They dwelt in a lovers' paradise as Morrow's keel boat traveled ever closer to New Madrid.

Only the bright sunlight beaming through the small porthole and the shouts of the crew announcing that New Madrid was in sight brought Renaud back to reality and he leaped out of the bed.

Charmaine, still heavy with sleep, struggled to sit up, mumbling in her dazed state, "What . . . what are you saying . . . New Madrid? We're there?"

"Yes, *ma petite,* we're there! I suggest you get your pretty derrière out of that bed or you might be left on this keel boat to go on to St. Louis." He grinned down at her.

A twinkle of mischief in her eyes, she stretched sensually so the sheet outlined her body. "But then you'd be denied the pleasure of my . . . uh company. Would you want that, Pierre?" she taunted.

He threw back his head and roared with laughter. She is an enchanting little witch and she knows it, he thought.

"Sometimes, a man must make a sacrifice, but no, you wicked little vixen, I'd not let you get away from me. Now, I might just carry you off the boat in your chemise if you don't hurry up and do as I said." He took hold of the sheet, and giving it one mighty yank, he left her lying there nude.

She'd not gone to the trouble of putting her nightgown back on after they'd made love, and Pierre had forgotten that so he was more startled than she. The look on his face brought a ripple of giggles from Charmaine.

"Something wrong, Pierre?"

As she gazed boldly up at him he was embarrassed for a moment, but only a moment. He realized he must look like a schoolboy ogling his first nude lady, and he knew the power this slip of a woman had over him. Had she become more aware of it? he wondered.

Pretending a coolness he was hardly feeling, he turned his back on her loveliness and shrugged his broad shoulders as he remarked, "I'll leave you to get dressed while I go talk to Jacques. I must tell him something." Actually he had to remove himself from the tantalizing sight of her before he surrendered to his urgent desire for her.

As he marched out of the cabin door, Charmaine moved to the side of the bed and hastily began to gather up her clothing so she could get dressed. It dawned on her the time she'd dreaded was at hand. She'd soon be meeting some of Pierre's family. That prodded her to get busy with her toilette.

When Pierre ventured back into the cabin, he was amazed at how much she'd accomplished in such a short spell of time. She was putting the final touches to her hair. Her jacket and cape lay across the bed, along with the blue velvet reticule he'd purchased for her back in Savannah.

He let his eyes dance admiringly over her before saying, "You look mighty fetching, Mademoiselle Lamoureux."

A pleased smile came to her lips. "I have to make a good impression on your aunt and uncle, don't I?"

"You've no need to impress anyone but me, *ma petite,* and you've already done that."

His words meant more to her than he could possibly know, for at that moment when she was filled with uncertainty. She was about to ask him what he intended to tell his aunt and uncle once they'd arrived at their home in New Madrid, but he anxiously insisted, "Come, let's join our friends. They're already up on deck. Prepare yourself. New Madrid is not the size of New Orleans or Memphis. You may not like it, Charmaine."

She noted the serious look on his handsome face, the concern in his gray, searching eyes. "We'll not know that until we get there, will we? Perhaps, you won't like it either, Pierre?"

"Well, we'll find out very soon now." His hand held her arm as he assisted her up to the deck of the keel boat. The sun was shining brightly and the smell of springtime was in the air. As he guided her across the deck to join their friends, Pierre thought these were good omens for the beginning of a new life in this strange new country.

PART IV

New Madrid

Missouri Territory

Chapter 46

A gentle breeze whipped Charmaine's long skirt as she stood on the keel boat and gazed at the banks of the river. A vast array of tall, green pines flourished on either side, as yet, she'd seen no sign of a settlement.

She leaned over to whisper to Tasha, "Are you as curious as I am about this place—New Madrid? Pierre has already informed me it will be nothing like New Orleans."

"Of course I am. I have a good feeling about it. I feel this might be where Jacques and I will live for many years to come." It was very hard for Tasha not to tell Charmaine that New Madrid would probably be the place where her first child was born. She was almost certain she was pregnant.

"I still have not seen anything to indicate there is a town nearby," Charmaine said, as she strained to see farther down the river.

"We will as soon as we make the next turn to the east, Jacques told me awhile ago. Look, Charmaine—straight ahead. That bend must be the one Jacques was talking about."

"Yes, I see it." It seemed to Charmaine that the keel boat was picking up speed. Maybe the crew was working harder now that a village was directly ahead.

In a short while the seventy-foot boat veered around the

bend and the woods, which had been so dense and thick, thinned out. The river was suddenly busy with priogues, crudely carved out of long cypress trunks. Log cabins dotted the banks of the river and people could be seen moving about.

Jacques and Pierre had ambled across to talk to one of the French crewmen so Charmaine and Tasha stood alone. They didn't hear the keel boat captain saunter up behind them until he addressed Charmaine, who was startled by his deep, bass voice. "Well, Miss Lamoureux, you ready to greet New Madrid?"

Charmaine turned swiftly to see Cat standing behind her. "Oh, Captain Morrow! I didn't hear you come up. I guess I'm as ready as I'll ever be."

There was a warm glint in his dark eyes as he looked into her brilliant blue ones. "Don't know if New Madrid is ready for you. Never been such a lovely lady as you landing there, I'd wager."

Tasha heard his declaration and was grateful that Renaud was some distance away for Morrow's demeanor was far too familiar and bold. He was a striking man in his rugged way, Tasha had to admit. She wondered how Charmaine was going to respond.

"You're very kind, but you'd better not wager anything for you could be a loser, Captain."

They joined each other in laughter. Cat Morrow's impulsive remarks were something he'd restrained for the whole trip, and now that he had a chance to just stand by her side one more time without the possessive Renaud being around, he'd given in to his desire to express his admiration.

He figured this was probably going to be the last time he'd ever see her, but he knew her lovely oval face would haunt him as he roamed up and down the vast Mississippi. He wanted to absorb each delicate feature so on long lonely nights he could sip his whiskey and envision her glowing beauty.

The threat of Renaud would not have stopped him from

having a farewell chat with her on this last day. He'd decided to do it the night before. Luckily for all concerned, Renaud had wandered away for a moment.

Although Renaud was not there to threaten him, Cat Morrow suddenly noticed that Tasha Weer's piercing black eyes were focused on him. Something reflected in them made him wonder if she saw through him. He had her pegged as a very perceptive little lady, and she was a few years older than Charmaine Lamoureux.

"Well, ladies, I just wanted you to know that it's been my pleasure to have you aboard my boat all the way from New Orleans," Cat told them, a more formal air about him now.

"Why, thank you, Captain Morrow. I'm sure Charmaine feels as I do when I say we thank you for your consideration during the long journey," Tasha declared.

"Why yes, Captain Morrow, I feel exactly as Tasha does, I've learned so much about the country we've gone through from your interesting stories about it," Charmaine said graciously.

"My pleasure, ma'am, and now I've got to leave, for the wharf's in view and I'll be needed." Cat bowed gallantly. Renaud and Bernay were sauntering back toward their ladies anyway, so his brief interlude was over. It wasn't much for a man like Cat to cherish. He usually expected and got more from a lady who attracted his roving eye. He'd stolen kisses from many sweet lips and he'd taken numerous women to bed, but with Charmaine Lamoureux he'd not be able to claim so much as a kiss.

To be infatuated with a woman when there was no hope of fulfillment was a little insane, Cat knew. Hell, he was no starry-eyed youth. He'd bummed around a long time.

As he yelled orders to the men unloading the cargo for New Madrid he forgot the golden-haired Charmaine. He didn't think of her until he watched the Renaud entourage leave his keel boat after all their farewells were said.

Cat Morrow took off his faded blue cap and ran his long

fingers through his thick jet-black hair, an amused grin on his face as he thought about what he'd done as he'd stood by Charmaine Lamoureux on deck. He'd slipped a tiny amulet into the reticule hanging over her wrist. He'd done it on impulse. He did hope the tiny amulet would keep her from harm, and if the truth were known, he did believe, as his Indian mother had, that the amulet could ward off evil.

Would she realize he was the one who'd put it there? He'd never know.

Two or three days passed before Charmaine discovered the strange little talisman of beads and feather, along with a tiny ivory fang. From the minute she'd left the keel boat to step on the ground, a whirlwind of activity had consumed her time. She'd never seen so many friendly people as she'd already encountered in this small village. The tobacco-chewing driver Renaud had hired to get them to his uncle's home talked and acted as if he'd known them all his life.

"Son of a gun, so you be Mister Charles' nephew. Here all the way from France, you say? Well, I'll be danged!" He'd been quick to tell them he was Ray Waters and before they arrived at Pierre's uncle's home he'd told them his whole life's story.

A palisade surrounded the property, and when Charmaine wondered why such a high fence was necessary, Waters quickly explained it used to be a measure of defense when a band of Indians attacked. "Ain't no cause now to be scared, ma'am, 'cause we ain't had no trouble like that in a long time here in New Madrid."

"That's good to know." Charmaine sighed.

"Mister Charles took this place over after that there fence was put up, and this here log cabin's sure been added on to many times since your uncle and his dear wife came to live here, I can tell you, son," Waters had informed them.

A short time later, when Charmaine met Genevieve and

388

Charles Renaud she realized she'd had nothing to fear. Genevieve reminded her of her Aunt Simone, though she was a few years younger and not quite so plump, and despite his dignified air Charles Renaud was very gracious and friendly. It was obvious they both adored their nephew as they embraced and greeted Pierre, speaking their native language. Charmaine noticed the confused look on poor Tasha's face and so did Genevieve Renaud. Graciously, she inquired of Tasha, "You are from England, is that not right?"

Upon hearing her own language being spoken, Tasha replied, "Yes, Madame Renaud. But I can assure you I'll get busy learning my husband's language." Everyone exploded with laughter then, and Genevieve assured her she'd be delighted to be her tutor.

Charles told Pierre how the meager log blockhouse had been expanded into the comfortable home it now was.

"I confess, it is nothing to compare to your father's fine mansion in Cherbourg or his grand château," he said, "but I am not like Étienne. I never needed as much as he desired, and Genevieve felt the same. So we came to this primitive country and now we consider it home. We never want to leave it. Perhaps you will feel the same, though you may miss what you had in Cherbourg so much you'll want to get back. We never did!" His dark, penetrating eyes darted in Charmaine's direction for one fleeting moment. Already, Charles was forming an opinion about the beautiful lady accompanying his nephew. He recalled his nephew's reckless reputation in Cherbourg, but he knew this golden-haired girl was no courtesan. He'd known too many such women in his young randy days to be fooled. No, this young lady was not that sort. He decided to leave the assignment of rooms in the hands of his beloved wife for he trusted her discretion completely.

Genevieve did not disappoint him. She assigned a bedroom to Monsieur and Madame Jacques Bernay. Then she personally took charge of Charmaine after she sweetly said to Charles, "I think you know the bedroom our dear Pierre would enjoy, *oui?*"

Charles obligingly played along with her cunning plan. Since the Bernays had excused themselves and had been escorted to their room by one of the Renaud servants, as Genevieve was preparing to take Charmaine out of the parlor, Charles suggested he and Pierre indulge in a nightcap of brandy—French, no less. In that always gracious manner of his which Pierre found it hard to find fault with, Charles calmly remarked, "We shall toast the future, my nephew."

All Pierre could do was smile as he watched his aunt take his lady away to a room he was not to share. He was disgruntled, but he had to accept it. He was under their roof, and he was well aware this house was run according to Charles' rules.

Genevieve could hardly hide her amused smile when she saw the utter dismay on Pierre's face, and she was reminded of the boy she'd adored when he was a sapling back in Cherbourg, before she and Charles had left France.

Given to first impressions, Genevieve had already made up her mind about Charmaine Lamoureux. Under her roof, she would not allow her nephew to sorely use this lovely creature without marrying her. She refused to put her stamp of approval on such an arrangement. Pierre must conduct himself properly here.

As she guided Charmaine to her quarters, across the hall from Genevieve's own bedroom, Madame Renaud remarked, "Your name is as lovely as you are. I want you to look upon our home as yours as long as you are here."

"I thank you so very much, Madame Renaud, I truly do, for you've been very kind and you've made me feel welcome from the moment I walked through your front door."

"Ah, *chérie,* you are! Truly! I wish you would call me Tante Genevieve as Pierre does. That would give me great pleasure, Charmaine. You see, I have no lovely niece and I never shall have one. I had no brothers or sisters, you see?" Something very sad was reflected in Genevieve Renaud's eyes, and it dawned on Charmaine that Pierre had mentioned that she and Charles had never had any children.

"It would surely give me pleasure as well." She embraced the smiling lady beside her, and that gesture endeared her to Genevieve, who was a warm, loving person. Madame Renaud now felt she knew all she needed to know about this young lady Pierre had brought to their home. If he did not know what a blessing and a jewel he had, she would certainly enlighten him, she promised herself.

"I love your home, Tante Genevieve, everything about it. It's so cozy and warm, and it has such a rustic look." Her blue eyes danced around the room. Rich, vivid colors brought the dark wood walls and the plank flooring alive. The massive furniture would have looked dismal had it not been lightened by bright pillows and rugs and an urn of dried flowers. The spreading branches of the green-leafed fern on the high oak stand next to the north window added a touch of life to the room.

"I—I hope you will like it here, Charmaine. But I must warn you it is rather primitive for one so beautiful and so very young. There isn't much to excite the young in a place like New Madrid."

"Not like New Orleans?" Charmaine asked, a twinkle of mischief in her eyes.

"*Ah, oui!* This is certainly not New Orleans." Genevieve laughed, recalling the time she'd spent in that flamboyant city.

"Well, I've seen New Orleans, and I don't know that I'd care to live there. You see, Tante Genevieve, I was a farm girl on the isle of Jersey. After my parents died, I was sent from France to live on that isle with my aunt."

"I want to hear more about this, but not tonight. You must rest after your journey. Besides, we'll have lots of time to talk. Come, give your new aunt a kiss and then I'll let you get your rest."

"All right," Charmaine said, giving her a sweet smile. After the two women embraced and Genevieve took her leave, Charmaine wandered around the room to explore her new surroundings. She looked out the windows into the night. Moonlight outlined the grounds below and the high palisade enclosing them. A little later she blew out the candle and dimmed the lamp. The tied-back curtains allowed the room to be lit by moonlight, and she liked the feeling of openness that created. Although Pierre was not by her side, she felt secure in this new place.

As she lay in the massive bed alone, she wondered why. The answer did not come, because her long lashes fluttered and became heavy with sleep.

She knew a contentment she'd not felt for a long, long time, except in Pierre's encircling arms.

She gave herself up to it!

Chapter 47

Pierre was not content, however. Frustration was his lot, for his Tante Genevieve had kept an eye on him since they'd arrived. She'd appointed herself Charmaine's protectress on that first evening, and it seemed she and his uncle were in league on keeping him and Charmaine apart. They'd damned sure managed to do it too.

Days had extended into weeks and soon the entire spring season had gone by. Pierre spent the days with his uncle, and when darkness drove them home in the evening, he ate dinner and then collapsed on his lonely bed with no female warmth to give him sweet release. He was beginning to wonder if his aunt and uncle were conspiring with his father, and he sometimes wondered if Charmaine had joined forces with his aunt and uncle.

It vexed him that she did not seem to mind that she was never alone with him. Damn the little minx, she seemed serenely happy! Obviously, she wasn't aching with hunger as he was, wanting to lie with him and have him love her. At night when he was in his room alone this gnawed at him. He thought about Jacques and Tasha lying in one another's arms down the long hallway, and he envied them. The long day's work was actually exciting to Pierre and that time passed quickly, but he wanted to come back at night to the sweet bounty of Charmaine.

Actually, this untamed country was a challenge, and Pierre was eager to explore more and more of it. But, *mon Dieu,* he wanted the woman he loved to be with him at night, enclosed in his arms. Stolen little kisses merely whetted his hot-blooded appetite and left him wanting.

Jacques Bernay was the smart one. He wished he'd been as smart when they were in New Orleans. If he'd used his head he'd have hightailed it to a parish priest to marry his lovely Charmaine. Observing her these last few weeks in New Madrid, he knew beyond a shadow of a doubt that this was the place for them, not back in France.

Was it his imagination that in the bright sunlight her hair looked more golden? Her lovely face was completely flawless, though he rarely saw her with a bonnet or hat atop her head, and he loved to see her spun-gold tresses hanging long and free, instead of swept up in a sophisticated hairdo. Even the simple muslin frocks she wore were more appealing to him than silks and satins. But she could wear a fancy gown like a royal princess, and when they were married he'd lavish fancy gowns and jewels on her so when they traveled to some faraway place she could enjoy the luxuries she deserved. But she was nature's child, and seeing her in this setting, he knew it. She would never be completely tamed and that was her attraction. Never would he want to break that spirit of hers! Never would he want her to change!

His expert eye also told him that here, in New Madrid, she had discarded the undergarments she used to wear and their absence made her sensuous body more exciting to him. Furthermore her low necklines seemed to be overflowing with her full breasts.

Either he was a man fevered with desire for his lady or one forced to dwell with only nightly fantasies, but he was certainly ready to plunge into frenzied madness.

For this land, this countryside, made things thrive and grow. He'd noticed the same was true of Jacques' wee wife, Tasha. Unless he was having wild imaginings, she was putting on weight, was broader in the hip and fuller in the bosom. It never entered Renaud's mind that she was expecting Bernay's child.

Bernay had not bragged to his friend about his being a father before the year was out because he realized Renaud's situation in his uncle's home. The rules had been laid down that first night. In fact, Jacques had been completely surprised that Renaud had not defied them. Pierre usually lived by no one's rules but his own.

It had been Tasha who'd urged Jacques to say nothing to Pierre, even though she'd told Charmaine. She'd dejectedly said to Bernay, "If only a priest or preacher would come through the territory, I know Pierre would welcome the chance to make her his wife. Madame Renaud says that judges and lawyers travel together to make the circuit every so often, but weeks and weeks pass before they appear again."

"I know, *ma petite*. Renaud is a man ready to explode. He has a terrible case of frayed nerves. He is feeling the full impact of loneliness, and he won't last much longer, I can tell you. His snapping temper is not easy to deal with. I feel for him. I would feel the same if I were denied you, my Tasha."

"Oh Jacques, aren't we lucky?"

"The luckiest, and no one knows that more than I."

Pierre Renaud felt that luck was finally coming his way on the sunny afternoon he came out of the woods to find his golden-haired lady sitting on the ground and leaning against a fallen log. With her was one of the children from the village, and it seemed to Pierre, from what he could overhear of their conversation as he approached, that Charmaine was soothing the little girl because her pet puppy was dying. Seeing the child in her arms had a strange effect on Pierre. It mellowed and warmed him, and for the first time he imagined her with a babe in her arms. Dear God, no child could have a more beautiful mother!

The very thought shook him. He, a father. Charmaine, a

mother! He'd never thought of any woman as the mother of his child. Charmaine Lamoureux had certainly intertwined herself in his life—his destiny. He knew this most assuredly on this late spring day.

He made no effort to interfere with the two he watched until the curly-haired girl scampered off and Charmaine was alone. Only then did he move toward her, and when she heard the heavy strides of his booted feet, she knew instinctively what was on his mind. The silver fire in his eyes told her everything she needed to know. To say the very sight of him didn't excite her would have been a lie. He was a tantalizing sight! She wanted his lips to capture hers, his strong arms to press her against his broad chest.

If he thought for one minute she did not wanted him, he was crazy. But she also wanted to stay in the favor with his aunt and uncle so she'd tried to please Genevieve in every possible way. It was a strange thing the instant warmth—perhaps she could have called it love—she felt for the lady she called Tante Genevieve, but she saw her as the mother she'd lost. It had been different with Aunt Simone; Charmaine could not explain it. The feeling was just there, as with so many things in life. More and more, she was realizing that some things had no explanation—they just were! It was so with her boundless love for Pierre Renaud. It was there and she knew it would never change. It was endless!

Just before he came up to her, he bent down to pluck a wildflower blooming in a cluster of six. He took only one blossom, then he walked over and sat down beside her. With a featherlike touch, he tucked the blossom over her ear after sweeping her long hair back. *"Ma petite amie,* I've missed you," his husky voice whispered. It was so laced with emotion she could not possibly doubt his words.

"And I have been lonely too, Pierre," she confessed.

He was like a boy being rewarded. His handsome face creased in a delighted smile. "God, come here! Come into my arm, *chérie!* Let me hold you—love you—as I've ached to do."

Eagerly, she went to him and felt the sweet comfort of his arms. She never wanted to leave the magic circle they provided. Each sighed in the flush of feeling the other's body. She expected him to kiss her, but when she felt herself being lifted up in his arms, she realized he was carrying her away from the spot where she'd been sitting.

"Pierre, where are we—"

"A place, *ma petite*, where we can have a little privacy. A wonderful spot I've discovered." He walked at a fast pace in and out of the many trees, bobbing and weaving to keep from brushing his head against the low-hanging branches. She made no protest, but her eyes devoured his handsome, tanned face as he carried her through the forest. It took her breath away just to be so intimately close to him. When his eyes darted down to gaze at her for a fleeting moment, a searing fire raced through her. He gave her a fast, flashing grin, making her tingle with wild sensations she'd not experienced in weeks.

God, she'd missed him and the rapture of his love. Nothing mattered to her at this moment but the ecstasy only Pierre could give her. What Genevieve or Charles Renaud thought about her meant nothing, in the least at this moment.

To her amazement, when Pierre came to a halt, they were directly in front of a cave, and she was reminded of the cove where they'd first made love. Instead of sand, there was the earth, and sprouting sprigs of grass grew here. The rhythm of an incoming tide was replaced by the lapping of the river about a hundred feet away. None of this really mattered though, for the magic was Pierre. She shared the feeling reflected in his eyes.

"You like my little spot, *chérie?*" he asked, as he placed her within the cozy seclusion of the cave.

"I think it is perfect. Why, I could shut my eyes and swear we were back in Jersey." She broke out in a soft little lilting chime of laughter.

"*Ah, oui.*" Pierre recalled the rendezvous she remembered

with such pleasure. "Close your eyes, *chérie*. Close your eyes and we will go back again. This time—thank God—I don't have to give you that fleeting moment of pain. Only pleasure, *ma petite!* Only pleasure!" His voice was husky with mounting desire. Too many nights had passed, and he had a need to satisfy the terrible ache in his groin. Now she was with him—alone. No one would tell them they could not be together as they yearned to be. She did want him, he knew it, and that only heightened his desire to bury himself in the circle of her velvet flesh, to feel the hot liquid fire of her.

She did as he requested and closed her eyes. Then he gazed at the long lashes inviting him to come to her, to give her what she, too, desired. It took him only a short time to bare himself for he was an impatient man, driven by passion. He never intended to endure such lonely agony again, for Charmaine was his world.

The moment his strong male body touched hers, her need soared to amazing heights. She gasped as his powerful thrust filled her; then she called out his name. "Pierre, my love! Pierre! Yes!"

Nothing could have pleased him more than the sweet agony in her voice, for he knew she'd been hurting as he had. His hands moved to cup her full breasts so he might kiss and caress one and then the other. He held one and let his lips and tongue tantalize the tip until she undulated her soft body. When she arched wildly upward he released her breast and sought her lips so he could bury himself deeper in the velvety softness of her as she urged him to do.

He moaned with pleasure, and though he wanted to linger longer in her his body quaked. Unable to delay his ultimate release, he gave way to it.

Now he knew what that night on a Jersey beach had initiated. He knew why his restless heart would not allow him to forget the golden-haired girl he'd deflowered in the cove. He could never have forgotten her. She was meant to be a part of his life, of his destiny!

Chapter 48

The two lovers left their cozy bower of bliss very reluctantly, but their brief interlude convinced Renaud that he'd not deny himself and Charmaine these golden moments together.

He'd let his aunt think they were abiding by her rules for as long as it was necessary, but nothing could stop them from having a secret rendezvous now and then.

He proposed this to Charmaine before they parted company, suggesting she leave first and he follow a short time later.

Charmaine's heart swelled with happiness when Pierre declared, "No priest or preacher saying a few words is going to bind me to you more than my feeling for you. You're mine and I'm yours. So why should we be miserable just because we aren't man and wife. We will be. You must know that."

"I know, Pierre, but your Tante Genevieve would disapprove. I don't want her and your Uncle Charles to think I'm a trollop. It matters very much what she thinks of me. I want her respect because I respect her."

"Well, that's my point. She need not know, yet we can be together as we yearn to be. The truth is, my Tante Genevieve adores you. Her eagle eye is for me. She doesn't trust me around you. No, Charmaine, you don't have to concern yourself about the impression you've made on the Renaud family."

His winning charm convinced her that there would be no harm in his plan, and the sweet persuasion of his lips made her eagerly agree to meet him whenever it could be arranged.

After a long, lingering kiss, he released her so she could pretend she'd merely taken a walk in the woods on this sunny day. When he was certain she was well ahead of him, he left the cave, veering back to the left so he'd come out into the clearing from a different direction.

In the following days of summer, they played their little game, meeting at what came to be called "their cave." Charmaine felt no guilt over the arrangement. She now felt Pierre's logic was right and wise. They were not offending anyone, but they no longer felt such aching loneliness.

The time passed swiftly but it did not dawn on Charmaine that no minister or priest had traveled through the territory until summer faded into autumn and there was a noticeable rounding to her friend Tasha's belly. Charmaine suddenly recalled that Tasha had told her the birth would be in winter.

The more Tasha's pregnancy advanced, the more Genevieve became the mother hen with her. It was of great concern to Tasha since this was her first baby that she'd have the services of a doctor, but Genevieve assured her that in New Madrid, there were at least four good ladies who served as midwives.

"Our one poor doctor could not possibly handle all the births because he travels to many settlements nearby. Poor man is killing himself as it is. Such a dedicated, hard-working young gentleman, he is. But you have nothing to worry about when your time comes, I assure you."

Genevieve's motherly, consoling manner eased Tasha's concern. But Charmaine suddenly experienced some anxiety. What if she suddenly became pregnant? Then all of Pierre's clever planning would not keep her from being in an embarrassing mess.

When she left Tasha and Madame Renaud, she could not get her mind off of this disturbing thought. Why had she ignored the chance she was taking each time she lay in her lover's arms? Each time she began to think she'd become smarter, she was jolted into realizing she was very naïve.

Renaud probably hasn't thought of that possibility, she angrily mused. Well, she'd point it out to him the next time they were alone!

She walked aimlessly along the path that took her to the bank of the river. It was a peaceful spot, where she liked to stand and just gaze out over the water. On this day the current was lazy, and the occasional bubble at the surface told her there were fish for the catching. When a mocking bird's trill broke the silence she noticed three brilliant red cardinals up on the branch of a tree. Then a young eagle perched in the branch of a dead cypress caught her eye. Its feathers were mottled, brown and black with a sprinkling of white. Pierre's Uncle Charles had told her that eagles wintered in the area around New Madrid. They were interesting birds, arrogant and impressive birds. The sinking sun filtered through the thick growth of trees edging the banks of the river, and fluffy white clouds drifted above her, reminding her of cotton or giant balls of white down. This was beautiful country, she had to admit. Jersey, with its fields of wildflowers and green meadows had nothing on this primitive part of the world. These woods, where oaks and cottonwoods flourished provided game for the table and it was delectable, she could attest to that.

France had always beckoned her to come back, but she knew she could not return to what once was. Always, there was change, and the sweet memories she cherished were all she had for nothing would be the same.

Charmaine stood, deep in thought. She knew without doubt that she could be happy the rest of her days as long as she could share her life with Pierre Renaud. He had said he wished to share his life with her, yet he had done nothing to confirm his vow.

Why, he could walk away from her anytime he wished to and she would be left with nothing to show for her love and devotion. Only an aching heart . . . and perhaps a baby!

At first, the sound that came to her ears was muffled. As her eyes scanned the river ahead of her, she saw nothing. Then she made out a carved-out log, a boat the people of this region called a pirogue. She did not know why the man in the boat was yelling frantically at her until he stood up and waved exuberantly. As she strained her eyes to observe the man more closely, she realized who was paddling the pirogue. He was like this countryside, untamed, wild, and wonderful!

What is he doing in the priogue? she wondered. Cat Morrow is the pilot of a keel boat. He never missed a stroke when he'd stood up and waved frantically at her. Charmaine sensed that the sight of her was as big a surprise to him as it was to her.

That fleeting glimpse of him brought back certain moments they'd shared on the trek up the Mississippi River. That man in buckskins with the piercing black eyes! That man whose mother had been a beautiful Indian maiden and whose father had raised him in the woods that ran up and down the banks of the Mississippi River. He'd been a hunter, a trapper, and a scout before becoming captain of his own keel boat.

Yes, she had to admit there was something very sensual about that rawboned, rugged man in the tight-fitting buckskin pants. While she'd never dared admit it even to herself, from the first moment she'd gazed into those all-knowing black eyes of Morrow's, something had captured her interest. Today, she stood on the bank of this remote place and asked herself what it was. She did not know, nor could she answer herself honestly.

Charmaine was a creature given to fantasy, so she knew at some time she would realize what it was all about.

Sometime, somewhere, that half-breed—Morrow—was going to enter her life again.

But more important things dominated her thoughts now.

Strange phenomena were invading the territory around New Madrid and those with perceptive natures, like Genevieve Renaud, experienced a sense of foreboding. She could not shake the feeling as she went about her usual routine. Charles never had a cold, but suddenly he was in bed with one. Her adorable little lap dog was so nervous and fractious even Genevieve's soothing hands could not comfort her.

And she was not pleased with herself. She was impatient, chiding herself that she could find no contentment in the evenings as she usually did from sitting by her fireplace and knitting.

Genevieve found some solace in the fact that her half-breed Indian servant confirmed that her feelings were the same.

"Are you telling me, Morning Star, that you're as upset as I am?" Genevieve asked.

"Oh, yes, ma'am. I can't tell you why, but yes!"

Perhaps, their religions and gods were different, but Genevieve respected Morning Star's beliefs and she valued her wisdom. Who was to say whose Gods were the most powerful? In truth, Genevieve had realized as she'd grown older and wiser, there was not much difference in any of the higher powers. Faith was the secret ingredient!

It had upset Genevieve when Charles had told her he'd let Pierre go alone on the mission to Boone's Lick Road to check on the prospect of salt. The up country along the Missouri River was reported to be rich in salt springs, though the iron Étienne had expected him to find in the Missouri Territory had not been present in any great amount. A fair supply of pig iron was to be had, but that was

403

not what the wealthy Étienne Renaud had had in mind. Genevieve knew Charles loved this country. He did not have his brother's greed, and neither he nor Genevieve had any desire to return to Cherbourg.

Just before Pierre had arrived with his friends, Charles had made the acquaintance of Nathan Boone and he'd learned that he and his brother Daniel had been making a killing on salt. He'd told Charles that the Indians had such respect for their father that they let them pursue their lucrative salt trading in peace.

"The old man seems to inspire fear in them, so we work the St. Charles area, Renaud," Nathan had said. "I'd not tell everyone this, but I know you and your good wife have done so much good for the territory around New Madrid. That's what I want for this country and that's what my father has instilled in me and Daniel. You're not a greedy bastard who'd ruin the land or the streams."

Charles had appreciated young Nathan's praise. It was true that he would never abuse the land or the streams. That was done by men with no foresight! He credited himself with more intelligence than that!

But he knew he must insist that Pierre carry out the mission. He could not now go on for his cold and fever had confined him to his bed. The motivation was partly selfish on Charles' part for he knew if he could prove to Étienne that the salt industry was lucrative, Renaud funds would keep pouring into the Missouri Territory. This great country had captured Charles Renaud's heart. He loved it, and he was truly amazed that so many of their countrymen were here.

But something had lain heavy on Charles' heart since Pierre's arrival in New Madrid, though he'd kept it from his beloved Genevieve. Oh, Pierre was most assuredly the son of Étienne and his stunningly beautiful wife. But Charles saw in Pierre a young man who was not exactly what Étienne would have wanted as an only son. Pierre had the romantic, impulsive nature of his mother. It seemed to overpower his need for wealth and position, the driving obsessions of Étienne for as long as Charles could remember.

Charles Renaud reflected that before Étienne's prestigious marriage to Pierre's mother, there had been another young maiden in his life—a young girl with the striking beauty of Charmaine Lamoureux. But for Étienne's insatiable greed and ambition, Charles figured he'd have married that girl who had adored him.

The first night Charles had met Jacques Bernay the man's voice and mannerisms had reminded him of his brother. Bernay even looked exactly as Étienne had at that age of his life.

In his heart, Charles knew Jacques had to be Étienne's son and his own nephew. He was certain of it.

Charles, being a romantic, sentimental gentleman, questioned whether Étienne's wealth had made up for the other things he'd sacrificed. But then, men felt differently about life and what they wanted out of it, Charles realized.

As he settled down in his bed to await Pierre, who'd been summoned to his room, Charles thanked God he'd found a woman like his Genevieve, and he hoped his nephew would be as lucky.

Charmaine reminded him of the younger Genevieve, so full of life and spirit. This was where she and Pierre belonged, not in that superficial Cherbourg. He and Genevieve had found the life there shallow and meaningless!

He wanted the young couple to stay right here in New Madrid! This was why he intended to put Pierre at the helm of the Renaud power in the new world.

He prayed his nephew would accept that responsibility.

Chapter 49

While he could still feel the sweet warmth of the kisses he'd enjoyed only a few hours ago, Pierre was disturbed by Charmaine's mention of the fact that she could get pregnant just like Tasha. In that case, what would he do? she had asked. He couldn't answer that for her or himself. He would love her even more, he supposed.

Hell, he had to confess he'd not thought about it until now. That wasn't to say he had not thought about the sons he'd have after they were married.

Had he only imagined it or was she restrained and moody all the time they were in the cave? Were her kisses not as responsive and eager?

Later, as they dined, with the exception of Uncle Charles who was confined to his bed, it seemed Charmaine rarely glanced his way, and when she did let her eyes turn in his direction, their blue fire didn't flash so brilliantly with love.

If his Tante Genevieve had not mentioned that Charles wished to speak to him directly after dinner, he would have invited Charmaine to take a stroll with him. Instead, when he left the table Charmaine was involved in conversation with his aunt, and Jacques and Tasha excused themselves to go for a stroll as he'd liked to have done with Charmaine. But he was very much occupied with his own private thoughts as he ambled down the dark hall to oblige his uncle. Charles bid him enter as he rapped on the door.

"Come in, Pierre. Come in! Miserable way to spend one's time—lying uselessly in a bed. Pour yourself a brandy and one for me too," Charles urged, pointing to the bottle sitting on the long chest that stood against the dark paneled wall.

"Are you sure Tante Genevieve won't have my head?" Pierre teased, a grin on his tanned face.

"What's better than brandy for a sore throat and a cold, eh? No Frenchman would dare question that." Charles chuckled. As he looked at his nephew, he was struck by the thought that he'd have given anything to have had such a fine-looking son. There'd been a very distinct change in Pierre since he'd arrived in New Madrid. While he'd had a magnificent physique when he'd arrived, it seemed the muscles in his strong arms bulged more under the fine white linen shirt he had on this evening.

"Well, I will agree with you on that, Uncle Charles, but I don't know about Tante Genevieve's remedy. She's still of the opinion she can take me over her lap and spank me as she did when I was a child."

Charles chuckled again, then he had a siege of coughing. "That would prove to be a hell of a job for the little lady. Too many years have gone by, and you've grown too big for that. It's a fine man you've become, Pierre, and I'm proud of you. I'm glad you and your friend Jacques came to our part of the country. Have a seat here by the bed for we must talk tonight."

It was soon clear to Pierre that Charles did not want to delay the trip to the upper country on the Missouri River to check out the salt springs supposedly flourishing there.

"You can do it without me, especially with the half-breed scout I'd already lined up to guide us. Take Bernay if you'd like, for I think he's a good man to have around. I've been very impressed with him as well as you."

Pierre had assumed that the trip would be postponed until

408

Charles was ready to go along, but his uncle told him they must make haste or they could lose precious land that might be claimed as Renaud land. Pierre agreed.

"When do you want me to leave, Uncle Charles?" Pierre asked.

"White Wolf has been ready and raring to go for the last two days, but I got sick. Tonight you go to his little shack at the outskirt of the town. The house I took you to two weeks ago?"

"Yes, I remember." That shanty can hardly be called a house, Pierre thought. It was more like a lean-to, and only the earth served as a floor.

"Good. Tell him you are to take my place and he is to take his orders from you. Now, my boy, I might as well tell you that White Wolf has a way about him as you will see for yourself. He really takes orders from no one."

Pierre grinned, because he recalled the tall, massive man with hawklike features and dark skin. His arrogance equaled that of any French nobleman. He took no quarter from any man, white or red. Pierre figured him to be in his late fifties, but he knew why Charles had picked him. White Wolf was the best scout around New Madrid.

"Leave tomorrow, if White Wolf is ready, and I think he will be. It will be in the interest of the Renaud family to get started."

Pierre said he intended to go to White Wolf's shack that night, but even as he did so he knew he'd break his aunt's rules by going to Charmaine for he must speak to her before leaving on a trip which could mean weeks away from New Madrid.

Within moments he moved down the darkened hallway cautiously and quietly. When he stood at a spot from which he could gaze into the parlor without being seen, he paused long enough to be certain Tante Genevieve was working at her needlepoint and to note that she sat all alone, which gave him a ray of hope that he could find Charmaine in her bedroom.

He slipped around the corner and mounted the stairway unobserved. Only when he was halfway up, did he heave a relaxed sigh. When he came to Charmaine's door, he did not knock. He turned the knob and opened it, entering unceremoniously.

Charmaine stood before him in her chemise, surprise on her face. "Pierre!" she shrieked.

"Shut up for God's sakes! Do you want to tell everyone in the house?" he barked.

"What do you expect of me? I'm human and you said nothing of this visit." Her eyes blazed with the fire he adored. He'd never understand why he found her as exciting when she was angry as he did when she was impassioned with desire.

"I know, *ma petite amie,* but I had to see you tonight. I just had to!"

Something in his eyes insisted she not be angry and impatient, that he was not just being frivolous and carefree. She made no effort to cover herself, though she knew standing there in her chemise she was exposed.

He walked toward her like a man in a trance, his silver-gray eyes fixed on her breasts and then on the tantalizing curve of her hips. He knew well the pleasure awaiting him between those satiny thighs.

"I could not leave without seeing you, Charmaine," he told her in a low, husky voice and he saw shocked surprise in the deep blue eyes.

"You're leaving here . . . New Madrid?" Her lovely face paled and her lips trembled.

He rushed to her, and taking her hands in his, he guided them around his back and pressed her firmly against the front of him. When Charmaine felt his desire she gazed upward into his eyes and saw the passion blazing in them.

"I'm going up the Missouri River to check the salt springs for Uncle Charles. He wants me to see if they're really there, so I can claim them in the name of Renaud. I want to do that for us, Charmaine. Do you understand what I'm saying, *ma petite?* I want to carve a place for us in this country."

"You have no desire to go back, back to France?" Charmaine asked.

"Not if you'd be happy here. I find this country challenging, and it whets my curiosity. I rather suspected you were feeling the same way. Oh, I know few ladies would find it so, but you are different, Charmaine. It is the thing that drew me to you, held me to you." His lips claimed hers before she had a chance to answer him. He drank their sweet nectar in a long kiss, letting his tongue tease and tantalize her.

As his hands explored the satiny softness of her flesh, she made sounds that told him he was pleasuring her. That was what he yearned to do. Her movements told him she craved his caresses, and his desire mounted. When blazing fire shone from her blue-sapphire eyes, he unlaced the bodice of her chemise so her lovely, jutting breasts would be free for him to fondle.

Effortlessly, Charmaine removed her undergarments. Pierre was now nude too, and his flesh seared hers as his thighs encircled her. His hands cupped her round, firm hips, pressing them closer to him.

The feeling of his hardened maleness made her heart pound wildly, and Pierre sensed this as he guided her back toward the bed, eager to fill her with his love.

He sank down on the bed's softness and drew her down with him to impale her. Such passion engulfed him he found hard to restrain himself, and she made sweet sounds of rapture.

He whispered of his deep feelings for her, wanting her to know how he felt, wanting to give her what he'd never given any woman before—himself. He must prove how he felt about her. It was most important to him.

"I love it when we make love like this, *chérie . . .* love it!"

411

he moaned huskily.

"I love it too," she gasped. She was out of control, unashamed and uncaring.

Together they swirled to passion's loftiest heights; then she collapsed atop Pierre. His lips pressed against her damp cheek as her body lay over his, and he, too, was breathless. He didn't utter words of love but he was sure she knew how he felt.

They'd reached a new plateau in their lovemaking. Both lovers were aware of that as he held her over him, wanting to absorb her warmth, to let the liquid fire of her velvet flesh envelop him. Dear God, he wished this night would never end!

The moonlight seemed to be focused directly on her thick golden hair, and he knew then what she'd always be to him. In the sublime quiet, he gave her a title. From this time forward, she would always be his moonlight goddess!

Whenever he gazed upon a full moon up in the night sky, he would recall this glorious night of ecstasy!

Chapter 50

Languidness engulfed Charmaine as she finally sank down at Pierre's side, and her hand came to rest on his broad chest. She could feel the pounding of his heart, still racing from the impact of their lovemaking. She smiled and purred contentedly.

Soon, he would have to leave her and return to his own bedroom, but she wished he could stay there by her side. How very lucky Tasha was to have her man with her every night!

Pierre was reluctant to go, and he dreaded telling her how soon he'd be leaving on the trip he'd mentioned earlier. He did not know how long he and White Wolf would be on the trip up the river. Since it was his decision to make about taking Jacques, he was inclined not to ask Bernay to come with him. Not that he didn't want him along, but he felt Tasha might need him before they could return.

As devilish hard as it was, Renaud willed his body to obey even though his heart did not wish to yield. Softly, he murmured in Charmaine's ear, "You must know I do this under protest. But I must go, *chérie.*" He flung his long legs over the edge of the bed and planted his feet on the floor.

Until he was dressed and ready to go out the door, Pierre hesitated to tell her it was only a matter of a few hours before he'd be departing.

Though he was amazed by her silence when he did inform her of that, he could not interpret her mood in the darkness. Her voice gave no hint as to what was going on inside her tousled head when she inquired, "How long will you be gone, Pierre?"

"I can't say, Charmaine. I really can't. But I shall miss you, that I do know."

"And I shall miss you. Stay safe." She lifted her lips to him and he kissed her tenderly but not too long. He didn't dare!

She watched him move to the door and out into the hall. Already she was lonely, and the dark bedroom seemed even darker. Funny, she mused, the moon in the night sky had shifted so that the room was no longer washed with silver moonbeams. The magic was gone and so was the ecstasy, at least until Pierre returned.

Dawn was breaking before her long-lashed eyelids finally closed in sleep. But as late as the hour was and as weary as she felt, her sleep was a restless one. Her dreams were so troublesome and unpleasant she finally sat up in the bed for fear they would start all over again. She knew it was because Pierre was leaving on this trip up the Missouri.

She could sit there in the bed and reason that no river would ever separate them, but in her dreams she saw a vast span of water and Pierre was on one side while she was on the other. She cried out to him frantically, but futility was etched on his face, and pain, as if he felt helpless and knew not what to do.

The swiftly rushing river seemed to be coming over its banks to attack her and muddy, brown slime soiled her beautiful satin slippers. She screamed a protest at the surging water, but like some devil thing, it did not heed her command. Then she started to back up, and she and Pierre were farther and farther apart.

She could still see across the river, could make out the frenzied look on Pierre's face. He was pleading with her to stay where she was, but she could not. She could not allow that filthy mud to cover her slippers.

She sat up in bed, her dream so real it had awakened her.

While Charmaine did not consider herself a superstitious person, she knew this particular dream held a meaning for her and Pierre.

It was a warning . . . a foreboding which she was not wise enough to figure out!

The old half-breed, White Wolf would have agreed with Charmaine Lamoureux, and he would have listened if she'd related her dream to him. There would have been no smirk or amused smile on his hawklike, bronze face. The truth was White Wolf had observed her from afar and while they'd never met, his instincts told him this maiden was as beautiful within as she was without.

White Wolf had his own rules for measuring a man or a woman. With uncanny senses he had only to look into the eyes of an individual, and he could see good or evil. There was no in-between for him.

So it had been the first time he'd met Charles Renaud. In him, he'd seen a good man, kind and generous, with not an ounce of greed. Perhaps, if he'd gazed into Étienne Renaud's eyes, he would not have felt the same.

Now, when he opened the door of his shack to find Étienne's son standing in the shadowy moonlight at this late night hour, White Wolf saw a formidable figure of a man, and he was impressed. Pierre's quicksilver eyes scrutinized White Wolf as fiercely as the half-breed's eyes took his measure. Then White Wolf invited him into his humble shack and for a few moments, he maintained a cool reserve with the young Frenchman.

But after they'd talked for almost an hour that reserve had mellowed without the old scout realizing it. He was confessing to Pierre, "I'd do just about anything Charles

Renaud asked of me. Your uncle—he is a brave man with a good heart! He does not seek to abuse the land or the streams like so many who come here from across the ocean. This I admire. He and his kindhearted wife give and care so much for the people of the territory."

Pierre gave him a friendly, understanding smile. He found that easy to believe. "Uncle Charles would value your esteem, White Wolf. He says you are a man of honor, one he respects."

"This fills White Wolf's heart with much joy. You see, young Renaud, your aunt took me into her house and she soiled her hands with my blood when I was wounded. She wanted only to help me. Her hands . . . they had a healing power. Her hands and their good works saved me. Oh yes, I have great feeling for your aunt and uncle. I will never forget the caring, kind eyes of Genevieve Renaud."

Once again, Pierre gave the man an understanding smile and a nod of his head. White Wolf was of a mind to speak and Pierre allowed him to do so.

"There is a village up from New Madrid and it is called Ste. Genevieve. Many Frenchmen have settled there. I, White Wolf, like to think it was named for your dear, generous aunt."

"Ste. Genevieve, eh? I would like to visit it sometime, White Wolf. Would you take me there?" Pierre asked the half-breed Indian scout.

"Of course, we will go in that direction at dawn if you can be ready. White Wolf is ready now." He grinned challengingly at Pierre and his dark, all-knowing eyes flashed. Pierre got the distinct impression that he'd better measure up to this Indian's demands or he'd be found lacking.

Yet Renaud sensed that White Wolf liked him as he liked the old Indian. It was an instant, impulsive thing, something words could not describe but it was there. He and the scout knew it.

Pierre extended his huge hand and White Wolf took it.

There was strength in their viselike grips and their eyes locked.

"At dawn, we'll go to the upper country—Boone's Lick Road, they call it. My Indian brothers will not bother us, young Renaud. They leave Nathan or Daniel Boone alone for they respect them. They are men of their word . . . they have honor. You are a man of honor. I see it in your eyes, and I feel it in your handshake," White Wolf told him.

There was an arrogant, assured tone to Pierre's voice as he replied to White Wolf, but his words forever endeared him to the scout. "Then we understand one another, White Wolf. We are brothers. I put my faith and trust in you, as Uncle Charles has told me to do. But I'm glad we had this meeting since he can not go. I'll see you at dawn's first light, White Wolf."

"Dawn's first light," White Wolf replied. He watched the tall, powerfully built young man go down the path and mount his horse. He shared the secret thoughts of Charles Renaud as he watched Pierre ride off. This was the son Charles should have had.

A shroud of fog hung over the river and a snapping chill was in the air as dawn broke over New Madrid. White Wolf observed the busy pace of the squirrels gathering their supplies for the winter and he knew that autumn was passing. Pierre Renaud proved to be a man of his word. When he arrived at the dawn's first light White Wolf was glad to see that he, too, traveled light as he approached the small fishing pier where White Wolf awaited him in his pirogue. The half-breed's boat was made from a giant cottonwood tree. He'd scooped out the trunk and axed the sides smooth in the shape of a canoe.

Renaud realized that they could supply themselves along the way so he had not brought excess weight along. That enhanced White Wolf's opinion of him. He had Pierre pegged right, White Wolf thought to himself, a broad smile on his dark face.

He liked Renaud's attitude as he flung his long legs into the pirogue and suggested, "To the upper country, White Wolf and those salt springs."

"Yes, young Renaud!" With a pleased smile on his face, White Wolf put the pirogue in action. The going would be easy and effortless for a while, but soon their plowing up the Missouri River would become tedious and slow for they would be moving against the current instead of with it.

Pierre gazed back toward New Madrid only once, and his thoughts were about his beautiful Charmaine. He hated to leave her, but he could not deny that he was excited about this venture with White Wolf. He was eager to see the places they would be traveling to.

That first day on the river was a revelation to Renaud. He marveled at White Wolf's skill in maneuvering the pirogue away from sand bars and the hidden snags. While they surged upward in the river the old half-breed told him tales of the territory. He told Pierre about the sons of Daniel Boone, Nathan and Daniel, and how they'd become the chief salt makers around St. Charles. No Indians would dare to bother the sons of such a great warrior as their father, White Wolf declared. The Boone name inspired fear as well as respect.

What Pierre found fascinating was the simple method used to make the salt for which there was apparently much demand in this part of the country.

"You know that big black kettle like your Tante Genevieve has?" White Wolf asked.

"Yes, I know."

"Well, those are filled with brine from the salt springs and they are boiled and boiled until all the liquid evaporates to leave only the grainy salt. That, young Renaud, is how we get the precious salt!"

Astounded by the simplicity of this operation, Pierre

gasped. *"Mon Dieu,* and that is all there is to it?"

"That is all!"

"It seems so simple. I guess I was expecting it to be more complicated, like mining of ore, and more tedious," Pierre told him, recalling his father's tales about the iron industry.

"The making of salt is very simple. The difficult part is finding the precious springs which give forth the salt. Once they are found and claimed the rest is easy. Those springs are not found everywhere, only in special spots."

"Then you and I will find some special spots, White Wolf," Pierre said playfully.

"But of course, *mon ami,"* White Wolf replied, letting Pierre know he considered him his friend. It was White Wolf's tribute to him and Pierre Renaud appreciated it.

A glint of silver came to Pierre's eyes and he had a crooked grin on his fine-chiseled face as he suggested to the old half-breed, "I suspect I'm going to be much wiser by the time I come back down this river with you, White Wolf."

The old Indian liked that remark, and he liked what the much younger man was trying to convey to him. He was truly honored by such praise from a man of Pierre's stature. He had figured him right and that made White Wolf a little smug.

He cocked his head and his thick mane of snowy hair fell to the side. His dark eyes twinkled with friendly warmth and he pointed a long, slender finger in a dramatic gesture as he spoke. "Ah, young Renaud, I assure you will be wiser. I, White Wolf, will see to that!"

They both broke into gusts of laughter, knowing that a camaraderie was shared by them. What they could not know on that particular day was how long it would last.

At least, Renaud didn't!

White Wolf already knew he was not to see the next summer for he had had a vision!

Chapter 51

Whatever it was with White Wolf, premonition or superstition, he was driven by an insatiable need to pass the wisdom he'd accumulated on to Renaud. He didn't try to understand it, but he followed that impulse as they made their journey up the Missouri River toward Boone's Lick and the salt springs.

He told Pierre of the healing herbs to be found in the woods and of the warning the creatures of the woods gave forth. These were far more dependable than mere mortal senses. He spoke of the winds and of what they foretold about the weather and of the ways the wild creatures of the forest would help a man.

Pierre was awed, almost hypnotized, by this man who was so knowledgeable. He'd never known anyone like White Wolf.

The nights they spent around their campfire were never dull, for each night, White Wolf had a new and different revelation for Pierre.

One night Pierre was taken by surprise and humbled when White Wolf took from a leather pouch an amulet, which he hung around the young man's neck. It was a panther's tooth, crude but impressive.

"It will keep you from harm, young Renaud, and it will

save your beautiful lady—the one I've named Moonbeam."

Pierre was speechless for he'd had no inkling White Wolf knew Charmaine. When he finally recovered his voice, Pierre stammered, "You speak . . . of Charmaine . . . the lady I love, White Wolf?"

"That is the one. Hair like the golden sunshine and eyes like the rare gems these eyes only saw once. But I named her Moonbeam and I shall not tell you why . . . not yet."

Pierre chuckled. "White Wolf, you tax me sorely at times. Is there a puzzle I must figure out?"

"It is good to stretch yourself, young Renaud. There is where all wisdom lies . . . just waiting. But few do. So sad too."

"Charmaine would adore you, and I think she'd rather like the name you've given her. Moonbeam . . . yes, she'd like it."

"I pay her a high compliment. We will meet someday, young Renaud." White Wolf's manner was so assured Pierre did not doubt him for a minute.

The half-breed watched his young Frenchman mouth the title over and over as though he were trying to digest it. Pierre knew White Wolf well enough by now to realize he had a very specific reason for giving that name to Charmaine. Logically one would associate her golden hair with the sun instead of the moon. Pierre asked the old scout, "Tell me, White Wolf, how did you happen to come up with the name of Moonbeam for my lovely Charmaine, eh? I'd be interested in knowing."

"Have you ever gazed on a golden autumn moon . . . some call it a harvest moon?"

Pierre's quick mind immediately knew then why he'd thought of the moon and not the sun. "I have and they are big and golden."

"True and your lovely lady has such a golden crown of hair when I first saw her I saw an autumn moon, so magnificent and gold. Then from afar, I see the radiant look on her face when she smiles and I am reminded of the splendor of a moonbeam shining brightly on a dark night. The light of a bright, shining moon has been like a beacon to men throughout the ages, guiding them along their way. Did not her spellbinding beauty beckon you to her, young Renaud?"

This sly old wolf is so clever, Pierre thought to himself and an amused grin came to his face. "White Wolf, you're too smart for me to try to fool! Of course, she did just that. She bewitched me from the first moment I laid eyes on her. She's remained a fever in my blood ever since. No other woman has effected me as Charmaine Lamoureux has. I don't mind admitting it to you."

"Consider yourself a lucky man, Renaud, a very lucky man. Few have what you have. I was one of those lucky ones. Life's not been the same since she went away one winter's day . . . so swiftly. But we will be together someday and I will once again have that great joy she gave to me." What White Wolf did not say was that it would be soon and he was anticipating each day that passed, knowing it meant he'd be with her.

This was a special man, Pierre realized. He knew he'd probably never meet the equal of White Wolf. Within the Indian was the wisdom of the ages, yet he made it sound so very simple and uncomplicated. That is true wisdom, Pierre thought.

And he possessed a kind and gentle heart, for Pierre had watched him work at mending a fallen bird's broken wing. Yet he'd shown no fear when they'd encountered a bobcat a few days ago on the banks of the river.

His impressive voice had the qualities of any great orator Pierre had ever listened to in the great halls of France. It was powerful, persuasive, and dramatically compelling.

Now as he spoke about the woman Renaud loved in such glowing terms and with such thorough understanding of her, Pierre was convinced the old scout might just be more than a mere mortal.

"You are a poet, White Wolf, among many other things, I think," Renaud told him.

"No, my young friend, I am a man who's taken the time to observe the life around me and I've been curious enough to investigate the wonders of the world I've lived in. Anyone who'll take the time can do it. Dare to seek out and explore. I can tell you that it will amaze you what you shall find. Try it and soon you will see that I speak the truth. I promise you will not be disappointed. Your young eyes will behold wonders you'll not believe."

Renaud could not understand what the white-haired half-breed was speaking about at that moment for White Wolf was only trying to prepare him for the future, to encourage him to dare to do what few tried. Somehow, he sensed that Pierre Renaud was of that rare breed who did dare. Their number was small.

But the look on Pierre Renaud's face was enough to stir a feeling of exaltation in White Wolf because he knew his words were being absorbed and carefully weighed.

The solemn concentration etched on Renaud's face was exactly what White Wolf would have hoped to see. He was glad because he'd become very attached to this young man these last few days. By the time their days had stretched into weeks, White Wolf had found in Pierre Renaud the son he'd never had, and so he sought to give him all he would have given to a son. His worldly goods were meager, but his knowledge of the woods and streams was vast. He became a tutor as they traveled the river and camped on its banks.

Pierre was feeling mixed emotions by the time eight weeks had gone by since he and White Wolf had left New Madrid. There were times he felt he could no longer stand to be so far away from the little village where Charmaine awaited him. But the days usually went by quickly for there was always so much to learn from White Wolf.

Two weeks later, they came upon the salt springs they'd gone to find and a claim was made in the name of Renaud. According to his word, White Wolf then took great delight in showing Pierre through the little settlement of Ste. Genevieve, and there he intended to buy the supplies they would need to travel back down the river.

"We'll go much faster now than we did fighting the current upstream, I can tell you," White Wolf assured Renaud.

With this in mind, the old Indian instructed Renaud to buy supplies at a local village store after they'd explored the small community. Pierre would liked to have purchased some little gift for Charmaine but nothing seemed worthy of her.

As they walked away from the village toward the riverbank, sacks of supplies slung over their shoulders, the eagle eyes of White Wolf picked out something in the knee-high grass, an object which he thought would make the perfect gift for the lovely lady waiting back in New Madrid. He rather suspected she would like it more than an expensive gift.

A poor little pup huddled in the tall grass. It had obviously been separated from its mother and the rest of the litter. Compassion swelled in the guide for he sensed the creature's fright from the way it trembled.

Trailing slightly behind Renaud who was leading the way, he bent down and picked the pup up in one hand. It was a round ball of white fluff and White Wolf could tell it had not been without nourishment too long. The mere warming touch of White Wolf's weathered wrinkled hand seemed to soothe the tiny animal, and the scout smiled as black eyes stared up at him and a button-black nose sniffed his fingers. In the next second the pup's tongue was licking his finger. White Wolf smiled, understanding its gratitude.

Careful scrutiny of the pup assured him this was a fine dog and worthy of Renaud's lady, he called out to his companion.

"I have a gift for our lady, Moonbeam. What do you think, Renaud?"

Pierre turned to see the strange little fuzzy creature White Wolf held easily in the palm of one of his huge hands. When he realized what the scout had in his possession, he wondered where he'd gotten it?

A slow, easy grin creased his face for he realized Charmaine would melt with love for the tiny pup. No exquisite piece of jewelry or fine silk gown would excite her as much as this tiny little fluff ball.

"I think you are right, White Wolf. I think she'd love it."

Cocky with conceit, White Wolf declared, "I know so." He clutched the pup closer to his chest, almost possessively now that he had Renaud's approval.

Pierre started striding along the path to the riverbank again, a smile still etched on his face, and he knew that White Wolf was matching his pace.

When they'd reached the bank of the river where the pirogue was situated and they were preparing to load their supplies into the boat to leave, Pierre turned to the scout. "I thank you for the gift you found for my lady, White Wolf. I gratefully accept it for Charmaine, and I also insist this little imp be named White Wolf. You would not mind that, would you?" Renaud watched the old man's face and saw emotion suddenly engulfing it.

He did not answer Pierre directly. Instead, he placed the pup in a secure spot in the pirogue before he positioned himself at his station; then he casually remarked, "Come on, White Wolf, we are going home!"

His black eyes twinkled with a glint of mischief as they locked with Pierre's gray ones, and both men grinned.

No words were spoken. They were not needed.

It was a heartwarming moment shared by the two of them; the old half-breed guide and the young French aristocrat.

Like so many inspiring times he'd shared with White Wolf, Pierre knew he'd cherish the memory of it.

Mon Dieu, he'd be forever grateful he'd made this journey to the New World! Marvelous vistas had opened up to him. He wouldn't have missed this adventure for anything.

Well . . . almost anything! But Charmaine was really a part of this fascinating place.

Chapter 52

Back in New Madrid, Charles Renaud was finding it hard to conceal his torment. He feared that something might have gone wrong, for he'd expected Pierre and White Wolf back by now. It was already more than a week longer than he'd projected the trip would take them and yet, he reasoned his nephew could not have had a better guide than White Wolf. Of course, White Wolf was no longer young, and one unexpected happening along that river could spell disaster.

It was especially hard to pretend around Genevieve or Charmaine for Charles wasn't good at masking his feelings or lying. Regardless of feigned casualness about all the weeks the pair had been gone, both ladies were worried, and Charmaine became more depressed as each new day came and went without any sign of White Wolf's pirogue.

Privately, Tasha was ever so thankful that Jacques had not been asked to go along. She'd met one of the ladies who served the village as a midwife, and the woman had taken one look at her and then announced, "It won't be long now, my dear. Your baby's dropped since the last time I was here at Mrs. Renaud's only two weeks ago. You just send for me whenever it starts and I'll come running." The woman's manner and her kind-looking face assured Tasha that she would be in good, caring hands since there was no doctor to call on.

Before the matronly Rose Adams bid Tasha goodbye she predicted a birth in less than two more weeks. Tasha knew how utterly desolate she would have been if Jacques hadn't been here with her. Like Genevieve, she felt sorry for Charmaine. These last two weeks watching she'd moped around the house or wandered down by the river, looking upstream as if searching for some sign of Pierre.

When she or Genevieve had tried to spark some enthusiasm about the approaching holiday season, Charmaine had remained unmoved. Oh, she forced herself to laugh when the rest of them found something amusing and she made herself join their quilting circle. But her lovely eyes had a faraway look and she didn't follow their conversation.

Almost daily, she sought solitude by walking along the river, and Tasha suspected that she often lay there on the grassy carpet weeping with loneliness for Pierre.

This was true, for Charmaine had a deep fear that Pierre would never return and this horrible thought had plagued her for weeks.

One afternoon as she lay on the ground sobbing out her sorrow, Jacques Bernay chanced to come upon her. For a moment, he hesitated to make his presence known, but compassion urged him to go to her and sink down on the ground beside her.

She looked so tiny and helpless he took her in his stout, muscular arms to console her. "Charmaine, it is going to be all right. Pierre is too big a rascal to let harm come to him." Bernay was also talking to himself for he was sorry he had not insisted on going along with White Wolf and Renaud. His extra hands and eyes could have served them, but he'd appreciated Renaud's flat refusal to take him. Knowing his friend was considering Tasha heightened his loyalty to Pierre.

As the two of them, he and Charmaine, sat together on the grass, his arms enfolding her, he reminded himself that he had Tasha to consider right then and he released Charmaine. There had been a time when her glorious beauty had had a devastating effect on him, and he dared not flirt with such temptations.

At least, she was not sobbing so hard when she looked up at him and thanked him for being so understanding. "I don't mean to be a cry baby, but I just love him so and I'm afraid something has happened to him."

"There's nothing wrong, *ma petite,* with worrying about someone you love," Jacques said, patting her shoulders.

She stroked away the mist remaining gathered there in those deep blue eyes, then flipped her long hair back away from her face. Sitting up straighter and looking directly into Jacques' eyes, she declared, "Well, I know his Uncle Charles is far more concerned than he's pretending to be. I heard Tante Genevieve remarking to her husband the other evening when they didn't know I could hear them that White Wolf might be the best of scouts around these parts, but he is not young enough to be of much assistance if trouble arises. Oh, Jacques, I'd have felt much better if you'd been along."

Her words pained him, but he knew she meant them as a form of flattery. He respected her too much to try to lie to her so he sighed dejectedly. "I wish I was with him too, Charmaine. I wish to hell I'd gone."

The forlorn look on Jacques' solemn face made her realize she was not the only one concerned about Pierre. Thinking that her remarks might have hurt Bernay, she now tried to rectify her mistake. "But, Jacques, I know your obligation is to Tasha."

Jacques gave her a slow, easy smile, but he knew what he was going to propose to Charles Renaud. Renaud and White Wolf could be traveling in only one direction. He didn't know what Charles would think, but he wanted to go upstream to see if he could learn anything about White Wolf and Renaud.

Jacques was of the opinion that Charles might just

volunteer to accompany him. The months he'd spent at New Madrid, under the same roof with Charles Renaud and his good wife Genevieve, had been a rewarding experience, and he felt the greatest esteem and respect for this couple. He was convinced that Charles was completely different from his older brother Étienne. Charles was a man with a gentle heart. He was not cold and unfeeling like Étienne. Somehow, Bernay felt that if Charles Renaud had fathered him he wouldn't have been a bastard.

When he bid Charmaine farewell to go on his way, he had one thing on his mind, seeking out Charles Renaud. As for leaving Tasha alone for a few days, he had no qualms about that, not with the capable Genevieve at hand and with Charmaine to care for her. Tasha would not be neglected. Besides, his best friend and half brother needed him!

Charles Renaud was receptive when Jacques told him what he'd like to do.

His lost his dignified manner and took on a boyish enthusiasm as he stood up from his desk to ask, "Is the morning too early for you, young man? I can be ready if you can."

An amused grin lit up Bernay's face for he'd rather suspected that Charles would want to go along. "I'll be ready, sir! Bright and early. With that in mind I guess I better not waste anymore time for I've some things to get done."

"Yes, I'd say you've got the rest of what's left of this afternoon and evening well filled. So have I." Charles chuckled. He was thinking about Genevieve's reaction when he told her what he and Bernay were plotting. It beat the hell out of being here twiddling his thumbs and wondering about his nephew. They'd run into Renaud and White Wolf coming downstream or they'd hear some news of them. That white-haired old half-breed and his fine-looking nephew were not a pair to be ignored or swallowed up in the wooded countryside.

Those two would well be remembered by anyone who'd

observed them. Of that, Charles was certain. Morning couldn't come soon enough to please Charles Renaud.

Those sentiments were shared by his nephew Pierre as he and White Wolf sat at their campsite on their last night away from New Madrid. There were fewer hours of sunlight on their return trip. The days grew shorter and darkness lingered longer. White Wolf had remarked about it, telling Renaud if the sun had stayed high for another hour or so, they could have arrived in New Madrid this very night.

Knowing his guide fairly well by now, Pierre figured they'd reach the Renaud house before anyone was up, even his early rising Tante Genevieve.

This being the last evening spent with his friend, White Wolf, Renaud had enjoyed it. Once again, he'd heard one of the scout's marvelous tales; then they'd eaten a hearty meal as they'd sat by the crackling campfire. Little White Wolf had scampered around them, and he'd eaten so much his little belly bulged. Finally, he lay near them, contentedly chewing on a leather strap Renaud had offered him.

Pierre was a man of high spirits. The trip was an experience he knew he'd always remember. He'd learned much from the old half-breed, and he knew there would be times when he'd apply the sage wisdom of White Wolf to his life.

He'd done what he'd set out to do for his uncle. He'd laid a claim to the salt deposits. That was satisfying and exhilarating.

What a marvelous holiday season it would be at the Renaud's residence, and what better time was there to have a wedding? Pierre could not wait to inform Charmaine, as well as his aunt, that he'd had the good luck to meet a priest, Father Cabot at the last settlement at which he and White Wolf had stopped. The father was to be in New Madrid no later than the twentieth of December.

431

Now there were to be no more delays. He and Charmaine would be married. What a perfect way to start off the new year.

He was content as he lay under the starlit sky, the white pup sleeping by his side. His handsome face wore a pleased expression as he dreamed about the future he'd share with his beautiful Charmaine in the year of 1812 which would begin soon after their marriage.

In fact, he was a young man so engrossed with his many plans he found it hard to accept the rumors being carried up and down the river that the English were still stirring up trouble and encouraging the Indians to join their cause. Some rivermen actually thought English invading forces would come up the river on their powerful navy vessels. That had to be mere speculation, Pierre thought.

It all seemed so impossible to Pierre in these remote forests. Battles and destruction were not real in woods that echoed with scampering sounds of lively little wild creatures. Would enemy frigates invade this flowing stream full of fish which provided such tasty meals? And who would dare disturb the majestic eagles who built their nest in the cypress trees, or the exquisite blue heron that swooped down to get a fish to fill his belly.

Suddenly, Pierre realized he'd unknowingly absorbed old White Wolf's way of thinking. He marveled at it and he was tremendously pleased.

God's creations . . . all of them . . . these marvels of the woods . . . the land . . . and the streams. Man could not do this! Man's power had its limitations, Pierre thoughtfully mused, and God help man should he ever forget it!

He patted the white fluff ball lying beside him, glad to be taking this tiny pup back to Charmaine. It was the dearest gift he could have brought her, and the look in those gorgeous blue eyes would surely tell him so when he presented Little White Wolf to her. White Wolf would grow along with them. He'd share their life. Yes, he was the perfect gift for his lady!

Renaud's sleep had been a deep one, and his dreams had been of the lady he loved. But when the first rays of light hit his eyes he was suddenly alert and he sat up on his bedroll. The air was oppressive, and he immediately noticed that White Wolf's manner had changed. He was already busily preparing their morning meal as if he was in a hurry to be gone from this place. Somehow, that spurred Pierre to get his gear together and load it into the pirogue.

Was their mood rubbing off on little White Wolf? The pup seemed fractious. He had not eaten what the scout had put in a tin for him, and this was not his usual behavior.

White Wolf sat silently, as if he were meditating, staring at the sky above which was a lovely shade of azure blue dotted by a few balls of cottony clouds. But there was a heavy feeling to the air, and Pierre could not quite describe the aroma wafting to his nostrils. The closest thing he could relate it to was sulphur.

After they put out their campfire and were preparing to board White Wolf's pirogue, the scout asked Pierre a puzzling question, "You wear the amulet I gave you, young Renaud?"

A quizzical look was on the young Frenchman's face as he replied in a faltering voice, "I . . . I wear it, White Wolf. I have since the day you gave it to me."

"Good! Do not take it off for any reason, you promise me?"

"I promise, White Wolf. But will you tell me why you say this?" Pierre clutched the tiny pup securely in his arms.

"I wish I could. I just know it is for your own good, my young friend. We both have a need to get to New Madrid, do we not?"

The intensity of White Wolf's eyes made Pierre do as he'd requested and not delay for one second. Whatever it was . . . this foreboding the old Indian had was enough to convince Pierre of the necessity to be with the woman

433

he loved.

An hour or an hour and a half and they'd be back in New Madrid, old White Wolf had told him. All the way down the river the same ominous pall hung over the river like a shroud. Never had he and White Wolf been so silent when they were together.

The same uncanny atmosphere hovered over New Madrid. Charles woke to find it difficult to breathe and he blamed it on the miserable cold he'd suffered. But Jacques Bernay did not know why there was a heaviness in his chest.

Tasha had tossed and turned all night, and he'd blamed that on the announcement of his plan to go upstream to investigate Pierre's long-overdue return. To think he'd distressed her was upsetting to Jacques for she carried his child—his first child!

For a multitude of reasons, Charles and Jacques did not leave the house to go down to the pier to load their gear in the pirogue at the hour when they'd planned to do so.

The sun had been up for an hour or more when the two men finally walked down the path leading to the riverbank and to the small wharf where their pirogue was secured.

Back in the house, Tasha lay abed, but sleep escaped her. Genevieve used up her nervous energy in bustling around her house. This day had started badly, and she could not explain why but it did not feel right. She wished her beloved Charles was not starting up the river in a boat. She was a lady whose instinct always guided her. Today, it was not good!

Charmaine had not slept all night long because when Jacques and Charles had announced their plans last night, she'd known she'd not been having foolish fears. The men were concerned too. That was enough to convince her she'd been right all along.

Her night was spent praying. She even placed the mysterious amulet she'd found in her reticule after they'd

434

arrived in New Madrid around her neck. She wracked her brain to try to remember who could have possibly put it there. In a strange way, the amulet was a thing of beauty, and if it did possess powers, she hoped to call on them. Before the night was over and dawn broke, she certainly would as best as she knew how. All she desired was that Pierre lived and was safe!

As if a lightning bolt suddenly struck her, she knew who had placed such an object in her reticule. Only one person could have done it, the keel boat pilot, Cat Morrow. He had stood close to her just before they'd disembarked here at New Madrid. Why he would have sought to give her such a gift, she could not figure out. Nonetheless, she tied it around her neck for good luck, much as Pierre had tied White Wolf's amulet around his neck.

Whatever mystic powers the amulet possessed, and Charmaine could not explain them, when she got out of bed, she felt lighter in spirit as if a heavy burden had been taken from her. She dressed, giving special attention to her toilette, and for the first time in weeks she took the time to dab jasmine water at her throat and behind her ears.

As she descended the stairs, a feeling of peace flowed over her. She knew not why but suddenly she was radiant and glowing and all Genevieve had to do was gaze up at her as she gracefully descended the steps to know it. Genevieve could not figure this out, why this was so.

She looked at the young lady she'd known for many weeks now—months to be exact! She was spellbound for a moment before she finally spoke. "Charmaine . . . Charmaine, I've never seen you look more beautiful! You must have rested well last night, *oui?*"

In a calm, cool tone, a divine smile on her rosebud lips, Charmaine confessed, "I don't think I slept a wink, Tante Genevieve, but for some reason I cannot explain, I feel wonderful! Is that not madness?"

For once in her life, Genevieve Renaud was dumbfounded. She only prayed this sweet girl had reason to feel so wonderful.

An hour later, Madame Renaud and Charmaine would know why she felt so wonderful. An hour later, the mystery would be unveiled.

Pierre had returned to New Madrid! White Wolf's pirogue had made the last bend in the river and it was heading toward the wharf where Charles and Jacques were about to board their own pirogue to go in search of the long overdue pair.

Pierre's heart beat with the wild excitement at the thought of seeing his beautiful Charmaine after so many weeks.

He was coming home!

Chapter 53

Just before White Wolf's pirogue was spotted making its way down the stream, Charles had quizzed his much younger comrade, "Is it just me, Jacques, or is there a foul, unusual smell in the air this morning?"

The two were making their way down the path toward the riverbank to board their boat. "You are right, *mon ami*. But I can't tell you what odor it reminds me of. My sweet Tasha was having a miserable time this morning which made me feel bad about leaving her. How does one order one's loyalties, Monsieur Renaud? I love my wife more than anything in this world, but I also feel compelled to find out what happened to my best friend."

Charles gave him an easy, understanding smile. He knew now why he liked this young man so much. Bernay was a man of principle. His nephew was very lucky to have such a good friend.

They were just starting to walk onto the plank wharf when Charles heard a roar of delight erupt from the young man behind him. Startled, he jerked around to see Jacques Bernay leap into the air and wave madly upstream. Charles quickly turned about and he saw a glorious sight, his old friend, White Wolf, and his nephew Pierre plowing through the waters with a pirogue.

Pierre was all right and no harm had come to him. Charles chided himself for ever having thought that old Indian would have allowed anything to go wrong. What a marvelous holiday season this would be, the older Renaud thought. He gave no thought to whether Pierre had been lucky enough to lay claim to any salt springs which would enhance the Renaud fortune as his older brother would have done.

The only thing that mattered to Charles was that Pierre was just fine. This was the vast difference in the two Renaud brothers.

By now, Charles was waving along with Jacques Bernay. White Wolf and Pierre were returning with their own response. There were broad smiles on both their faces and it was obvious that Pierre was going to be the bearer of good news. Charles knew then that he'd been successful in his mission.

By the time the pirogue neared the wharf, the four men were able to call back and forth. When an excited feminine voice broke into their exchange, the men turned to see a vision of loveliness rush through the knee-high grass and down the narrow path.

Pierre would forever remember Charmaine running like a wood nymph, her spun-gold mane of hair flying wild and free. The lovely radiant face gleamed with happiness, and her sensuous figure was enough to fire any man with wild desire. Her soft cotton blouse was tucked inside her dark challis skirt, and rounded mounds of her breasts jutted the material as she ran swiftly to the wharf. Pierre wondered if she'd taken the time to put on her undergarments before rushing out of the house. He selfishly hoped she hadn't, for he was going to remove them very soon anyway.

The less she had on the sooner he'd get to see and adore her satiny flesh. He'd yearned to caress her so many weeks now. Suddenly, the mere thought of loving her made him swell with longing, and he was aware of an agonizing ache in his groin. He'd been hungry for her love for too many weeks.

438

"Pierre! Pierre!" Charmaine cried out, overjoyed to see him again when she had wondered if she'd ever be with him again. She ran as fast as she could down to the riverbank, already anticipating the feeling of his strong arms.

The men now standing around Pierre, as though they did not wanting to delay this reunion between the two young lovers, moved back to clear the path for the approach of Charmaine. All were having their private thoughts about the love she must be feeling, and Pierre's pleased, flushed face told them all they needed to know of how he was feeling. He rushed toward her as swiftly as she had been all the way down the path.

When they finally embraced and Pierre swung his petite lady up in his arms so that her feet were well off the ground, the three men watched them with broad, amused smiles on their faces, feeling like intruders on this private moment!

White Wolf patted the pup nestled in the huge pouchlike pocket of his vest made of raccoon hides. There was no doubt in his mind that this young creature would be loved. The lovely Moonbeam had a capacity for loving. She was a lady of deep passion and spirit. The old Indian was pleased to think that his namesake would have such a fine home.

White Wolf was now certain he knew the hour which would be his last on earth. He'd seen it last night in the campfire. It was eleven or so. Just before the midnight hour he would be joined with his beloved. That would be White Wolf's long-awaited rapture! But he did wish to meet the lovely Moonbeam just once, so he lingered on the wharf.

Patiently, he waited with little White Wolf. Finally, Renaud released the beautiful lady and led her toward the trio on the wharf. His face was the face of a man who owned the world, and in White Wolf's mind he surely had the love and devotion of such a jewel of a lady. No amount of gold or silver could buy that!

White Wolf's all-knowing eyes measured Charmaine as she strolled along by Renaud's side. She was so petite,

439

almost fragile looking, but there was nothing fragile about her—not with the blue fire he saw in her eyes. Her golden head was held high and proud. He liked that! And her body moved with grace, slowly but assuredly! She was a true princess . . . a goddess!

White Wolf would venture to guess that she would enjoy the trill of a bird in the woods or the particular color of a wildflower. Maybe, she would pass an hour just gazing at the flowing current of the river, deep in thoughtful meditation. The rustling breeze in the tall trees would be refreshing to a lady like this.

But her ultimate ecstasy would be found on the night of the full moon, White Wolf mused. Her first child would be conceived on such a night and their nights of sensual rapture would always occur when the moon was full and golden.

When he finally looked into her radiant face, White Wolf was impressed by the honesty reflected in her blue-amethyst eyes. They looked straight into his. He noticed how her thick lashes fluttered and her eyes twinkled as she measured him.

"My good friend, White Wolf, Charmaine. White Wolf this is my lovely lady, Charmaine," Pierre was saying. Charmaine extended her dainty hand to the half-breed scout and his rough, weathered hand took hers almost cautiously as though he felt he would scratch such delicate flesh. But he admired tremendously the warmth and the sincerity he felt in her clasp, the strength.

"My great pleasure to meet you, White Wolf. I'm . . . I'm glad it was you with Pierre on this trip up the great Missouri River. I've heard nothing but praise for the one called White Wolf.

White Wolf gave her a gracious bow and smiled. She saw in his classic face a rare dignity and a handsomeness she could not have described.

"It is my great pleasure to meet you for I've a confession to make. I've heard nothing but praise of a lady called Charmaine. I hope you'll not think me too bold if I tell you

I've another name for you, for I mean it in the most honorable way."

Wide-eyed with curiosity and that certain air of naïve innocence which had always intrigued Pierre, she insisted on knowing what White Wolf meant. "Please, White Wolf, please tell me what you've named me?"

"I call you Moonbeam." He waited anxiously, dark eyes searching her face for a reaction. Somehow, it was most important that she approve. When he saw a glowing smile appear, he heaved a deep sigh of relief and pleasure.

He appreciated the fact that she had absorbed the name a few seconds before reacting, for that told him she had weighed the truth of its meaning. Ah yes, he liked very much the lady Renaud had chosen to be his woman!

With eyes warm with delight, Charmaine softly voiced her gratitude, "It is a beautiful name and you pay me a great honor. I thank you from the bottom of my heart." She extended her hand for a friendly handshake.

White Wolf felt this was the right time to present her with the gift he had in his pocket, however, and he pulled out the ball of white fluff wriggling there. He placed the lovable little pup in her hand and said, "For you, Moonbeam. This is little White Wolf . . . so named by your man, young Renaud."

Charmaine was overwhelmed with emotion and she could not restrain the tears welling up in her eyes. She looked over at Pierre and then back to White Wolf. Nothing could have pleased her more. She was speechless, but she did not need to say anything to White Wolf or Pierre. The spellbound look on her beautiful face was enough for both of them. She was pleased. That was all they wanted.

When they parted to go their separate ways, White Wolf knew he'd never see young Renaud again in this lifetime. The lady he'd named Moonbeam, he wasn't sure about. That part of his vision was not clear to him.

He watched her go along the path toward the Renaud house, the little pup snuggled against her cheek, and he saw

441

Renaud's strong arm snake around her waist as his eyes devoured her.

White Wolf turned with the bend of the road to go toward his shack for there were things he still had to put in order. At least, Renaud had the amulet around his neck and Moonbeam had her little White Wolf.

The oppressive air and the smell of sulphur Charles had picked up earlier were forgotten in the overwhelming joy over Pierre's return. Of course, Charles was pleased that the Renaud's had laid claim to acres of land for the exploration of salt. Pierre had done well!

This was certainly enough to prompt a gala celebration in the log-cabin dwelling of Charles and Genevieve Renaud on the night of December 16, 1811. Mountains of food were prepared and their neighbors were invited to their home. The local musicians brought their fiddles and banjos to provide lively music for the evening's dancing.

Charles brought out the wine he'd held back for a special occasion and Genevieve wore her best silk gown and the cherished jewelry she'd not worn since their last trip downstream to New Orleans.

Poor Tasha tried to tell herself that she felt better than she actually did so she would not dampen the evening for her dear, sweet Jacques, whose mood was so high and carefree. The truth was she had not seen such a fun-loving Jacques Bernay before, and she did not want to do anything to dull his pleasure. He'd never been more alive or exciting since she'd first met him aboard the packet.

Never had Pierre felt so frustrated for he'd not had one moment alone with Charmaine. Dear God, it was almost more than he could endure! She looked more enchanting than she had with that pup in her arms, but from the moment they'd entered the house they'd been smothered by attention. And so it had been all the rest of the day.

While he was delighted that she was overjoyed by the gift of the puppy, he was also envious of the loving caresses that little beast was receiving while he'd had nothing but a welcoming kiss. It hardly seemed fair to the disgruntled Pierre.

With people gathering for such a festive occasion, it would be dawn before the celebration broke up. That seemed like an eternity to Pierre for it was still early in the evening. His eyes devoured Charmaine's luscious curves. She'd worn her pale blue silk gown to celebrate his homecoming. Long golden curls hung down her back, but she'd pulled back the sides of her hair with jeweled, pearl combs and she wore her pearldrop earrings. She was a bewitching vision in blue.

He'd not seen her so exquisitely dressed since they'd left New Orleans. Dear God, it taxed a man sorely to be so heated with passion!

Once when he'd glanced in Bernay's direction he'd seen an amused look on his friend's face. That lucky bastard, Pierre thought to himself.

Meanwhile, Charmaine was trying to mask her own amusement for she sensed Pierre's impatience and she was well aware that they'd had no privacy since he'd stepped foot on the riverbank. Had it not been that she had the adorable little White Wolf to occupy her, she would probably have been as tense as he was. The darling little ball of white fluff had lain on her bed as she'd taken her bath and attended to her toilette before Genevieve's gala festivities began.

It had come as a surprise that Genevieve had managed to put such an affair together in one afternoon, but she had only to look around to see the reality of her achievement. What else could anyone want for a marvelous gathering? Charmaine concluded. Congenial people, laughing and frolicking together as they enjoyed good food and fine wine, and lively music to add to the gaiety of the evening.

All these people obviously adored their host and hostess, Charmaine could see that. She also noticed that Jacques

Bernay was having himself a grand time this evening. Tasha was trying desperately to pretend she was, but Charmaine knew from talking to her yesterday that the heaviness she was feeling as the baby dropped was tiring her.

Tasha had told Charmaine that she was afraid the infant was going to be a huge one. "A robust little boy like his dad, I'm sure. The kicking is too strong for a sweet, little girl. I jump out of bed at night sometimes, I'll swear."

Charmaine had laughed light-heartedly. Her friend's shape was almost grotesque, so tiny except for her enormous protruding stomach!

"And I suppose you have a boy's name picked out?" Charmaine asked Tasha.

"Oh, most assuredly! Our son will be called Pierre Étienne Bernay." She smiled sweetly at her little golden-haired friend. "You know how much Jacques thinks of Pierre, Charmaine—always has from what he's told me."

"Pierre will be thrilled, I'm sure," Charmaine declared.

Suddenly Charmaine felt the searing heat of Pierre's nearness directly behind her. So overpowering was the essence of him, she slowly turned to gaze upon his handsome face.

"*Ma belle . . . ma petite amie!* You are so ravishingly beautiful tonight you take my breath away." He bent low to whisper in her ear, "If I can't hold you in my arms soon, I swear I'll surely die!"

She could not suppress a soft gust of laughter for he looked almost like a little boy pleading for his way. "We cannot allow that, *mon cher.*"

"Don't taunt me! I am so tempted I could ravage you right here in Tante Genevieve's parlor." His black brows arched boldly and challenged her to believe what he said.

"To taunt you, Pierre, would be taunting myself. Have you not thought of that?" Her teasing blue eyes had a glint in them as bold and flirtatious as that of any French coquette.

"Then after we dance this one dance, you go upstairs for

your cape and meet me at the back of the house so we can slip away from this crowd and go to our spot." He immediately took her into his arms to whirl her onto the floor as the music started to play. With his strong arms holding her like this, Charmaine did not need to be persuaded to do his bidding.

Their eyes made love as they danced around the room and no words were spoken. The special movements of Pierre's hands spoke for him. Like rushing waters overflowing a riverbank, the liquid fire of passion shot through her.

She was as anxious as he was for the music to stop so she could dash upstairs to get her cape and slip out of the house.

The instant the last chord of music was played by the fiddlers, she gave Pierre a smile and turned to go. Then he knew that she was as eager as he was to get to the sublime seclusion of their cave.

Discreetly, he moved through the crowd. He wanted no delays or conversation for he felt he'd wasted enough time already on idle chatter and socializing.

The quiet of the starlit night lit by a full moon was welcomed by Pierre. He moved anxiously around the corner of the house to where his lady love would be joining him. He was most impatient!

There was something magical and marvelous about the sight of her rushing toward him, her deep blue cape flowing out behind her. They could have been children on a lark so eagerly did they hurry away. Their hearts were light and gay and they were consumed by their urgent desire!

Chapter 54

Their lips were hungry and greedy and so were their eager, exploring hands and bodies. It had been an eternity since last they'd touched each other's flesh. Flushed with love and desire, neither could control that furious need that overwhelmed them once they'd arrived at the cave.

Pierre was a man impatient to bury himself deep within the velvet softness of the woman he loved. He needed desperately to feel the warmth that only she could give him. Yet, he did not want to rush this moment in paradise for he wanted to savor it to the fullest. But when her warm, eager body arched sensuously against him he would have had to be more than mortal to resist the furious surge of his male body.

Hastily, he straddled her and buried himself deep within the folds of her satiny flesh. She moaned with pleasure as he filled her, and this only heightened his desire. As strong willed as he was, he could not master the mounting urgency consuming him. He cursed the fact that he could not as a mighty tremor jarred him with its impact. He'd never experienced such intensity before. He heard Charmaine gasp breathlessly as her body gave way to a wild undulation, and he huskily whispered words of love. The untamed joy he'd just experienced was new to Pierre. He'd thought he'd known it at other times with his ravishing Charmaine, but never had there been a time such as this. It was surely a rare night.

His heart had blended with hers long ago, but on this night Pierre knew his soul—his life—had fused with hers. For as long as he lived he would love her!

Inside the cozy confines of their cave, they were not aware that there was no starlit sky nor was there moonlight. It was cloudy.

As they lay enclosed in each other's arms, their legs still entwined, Pierre heard the rumble of thunder. He found that hard to believe, recalling the clearness of the night, as they'd rushed across the grounds and down to the riverbank.

He was then startled by a mighty jolt, like the quake which had jarred his own body. Charmaine started up, a frightened look in her blue eyes.

"Mon Dieu, Pierre! What . . . what was that?" Her body trembled with fear of the unknown. Sitting there in stunned silence she heard a dog howling mournfully in the night.

For once, Pierre was dumbfounded. He had no answer for her. But he did have a suspicion of what that rumbling and rolling sensation had been. If he told her, would she panic?

"Get your clothes on, *ma petite.* I think we'd better get out of this cave." He felt a dusting of dirt sprinkle the top of his head. Quickly and silently, she obeyed him, putting on her garments as Pierre moved to the entrance of the cave. The blackness of the sky was awesome for now there was no bright moon, not even a twinkling star. Everything had changed so quickly.

He was overcome by a fierce foreboding, and for some strange reason, his hand went to the amulet, as if he needed the touch of it to sustain him. He turned back to check on Charmaine. She was flinging her cape around her shoulders as she came toward him. Something was urging her to get out of the cave as soon as possible.

His hand clasped hers tightly, and she sensed his concern as they dashed out of the narrow opening. They were barely fifty feet away from their little bower when a giant rolling motion of the earth made Charmaine lose her footing. The ground trembled beneath her hands as she struggled to rise. With Pierre's help, she finally managed to stand up.

He asked if she was all right, but she had no time to reply for the earth and boulders were crashing directly behind them. When they turned in the direction of the horrible rumbling, they saw that the entrance to their cave was no more, and the incline above it was cascading down toward the riverbank.

Charmaine screamed out, for she suddenly realized that a second more in the cavern and they would have been imprisoned there forever. Pierre pulled her closer to his side and put an arm around her waist, hoping to calm her fears. Then they ran, veering to escape the falling trees for the shaking earth dropped them, like so much kindling. Pierre's eyes strained to see some kind of guiding light ahead, but there was none, though by now, the lights of his uncle's house should have been glowing brightly.

His heart pounded wildly and he didn't want to admit that what he feared had really happened. In that fleeting moment as he pondered about why he could see no light in the direction in which his uncle's home should be situated, he glanced to the north and there he saw a giant flame of fire mounting high into the sky.

He said nothing to Charmaine, but continued to guide her nearer to the clearing and out of the woods. She'd never known there could be such a hellish horror as this, and she pulled her hood up over her head in hopes of blocking out the pounding roar invading her ears.

Now they were about to emerge into the clearing, and she thanked God for that. No longer did they have to dodge the crashing, falling trees!

But she was to face a startling new horror when they made their way into the grassy clearing. Abruptly, there was a strange sound below them. Pierre stood, stretching out his strong arm full length. His hand still held hers, but she was looking down into a crevice for the ground had cracked and separated them, though their hands were still clasped.

"Jump, *ma petite!* Quick! It's getting wider!" he impatiently insisted.

Uncertain she could manage such a leap, she hesitated until Pierre angrily yelled, "Damn it, Charmaine, do as I say. My hand is slipping!"

She stretched her petite body as far as she could and leaped over the deepening fissure in the ground. She'd never imagined she'd see anything so utterly grotesque as that.

When they finally came to the dark grounds of the Renaud home, it was dark. A ghostly quiet now surrounded them, but that quiet was shortlived for just as they entered the gate to go up the walkway a second wave of tremors made the earth billow like the waves of an angry ocean. Pierre enclosed her in his arms, as tightly and securely as he could. But his ears heard the screams of frightened people somewhere close by. Moans of pain mingled with them in that night so black with doom. With this second shock strange sharp streaks of lightning split the sky.

The land around the New Madrid countryside was sliding into the Mississippi River. With this second, devastating wave, the whole graveyard of New Madrid slipped into the waters, but the darkness spared Pierre and Charmaine that sight.

When Pierre encountered his dazed aunt and uncle wandering around the corner of the house, he thanked God. He had to know of the others though—Jacques and Tasha.

He leaned down to murmur in Tante Geneviève's ear, "Tante Geneviève, can you understand what I'm saying? I want you and Uncle Charles to keep Charmaine here with you. I'm going inside to look for Jacques and Tasha." His searching eyes darted anxiously from his aunt to his uncle as he measured just which one of them was more attuned with what was going on around them. He really wasn't sure.

Her voice was slow and hesitating, but her eyes told him Genevieve was aware of what he was saying. "You go, Pierre. Charmaine will be right here with us when you return, my dear. Please go . . . see about Tasha and her husband."

Pierre now felt that Genevieve was in far more control than Charles. He saw the stark disbelief in his uncle's eyes as the man stood like a zombie by the side of his wife. To Charmaine, he whispered, "Help Tante Genevieve, if you can. I think Uncle Charles is in a state of shock. I'll hurry back just as soon as I can, *ma petite.*"

She gazed up into his face and he saw the fear in her blue eyes as she urged, "Do hurry back, Pierre. I don't feel safe without you close to me. But I pray you find our friends unharmed." She raised her lips for a kiss; she needed his reassuring touch so desperately right then.

"You can be assured I'll hurry. Stand by that big tree over there. It's so bloody dark I want to be able to spot you easily when I return. Take them over there and just wait for me. I hope to be back quickly." He rewarded himself with one more kiss before quickly disappearing into the darkness, but he heard Charmaine's soft voice urging his aunt and uncle over to the giant oak as he scurried away. Thank God, she was still in control of herself.

Parts of his uncle's house were intact, as far as he could tell in the darkness. Some of the lamps or candleholders had been jarred off the tables, and the back of the house was totally destroyed. There he found himself looking down into a valley, which had been, an hour ago, his dear aunt's cherished herb and flower garden.

He left this area of the house and turned to go down the long hallway, intending to mount the stairs in the hope of finding Jacques and Tasha. He encountered a few of the guests, who were roaming aimlessly about, as dazed as his aunt and uncle seemed to be. He paused to ask them about Monsieur and Madame Bernay, but no one had seen Jacques and his wife.

He dashed up the stairway, taking the steps three at a time, and it was only when he reached the second landing that he noticed the stairs had pulled away from the wall. Dear God, what total devastation an earthquake could wreak. He'd heard about them but he'd never imagined such a powerful force!

He called out to Jacques, but got no response, nor did flinging open the doors of each room reveal the Bernays. Consumed with concern for Bernay and Tasha, he gave no thought to little White Wolf who'd been sequestered in Charmaine's bedroom.

He had no idea where Jacques and Tasha could be, but he saw no point in searching the second landing further. It was obvious they were not on it. He was convinced of that.

As he started down the steps, his curiosity drove him to observe more carefully the havoc this powerful force had inflicted on his uncle's house.

Halfway down the winding stairway, he felt the telltale quiver begin again and he now knew what was about to come. He hastened to return to Charmaine.

She felt that Pierre had been gone forever, but she waited in silence with his aunt and uncle, who seemed struck speechless. She did not even try to encourage them to talk.

When she suddenly heard a muffled whimpering out there in the dark, she left the Renauds to investigate, and to her delight, she found a scared puppy trying to dig into the ground, his fuzzy white body rippling with spasms of sheer fright. As she picked up the poor little creature, compassion flooded through her. Putting his head close to her cheek, she tried to soothe him as best she could. "You're all right now, White Wolf. Everything is just fine!"

Her warmth and the comforting effect of her hands did calm the pup, and for the first time since the earthquake had started, Charmaine had a reason to smile. Holding the warm little body close to her, she stood by the lilac bush for a moment, enjoying the feeling of the puppy.

As White Wolf pressed close to her bosom, she had an ominous feeling, and just as she was about to move back to the spot where she'd left Charles and Genevieve, there was a deafening subterranean explosion. Like Pierre, Charmaine now knew the significance of what it meant. She clutched little White Wolf tighter to her and started to move as quickly as she could back to the place where Pierre had told her to wait—back with Charles and Genevieve.

A second can be an eternity, she suddenly realized. When she'd strayed around the corner of the house and headed toward the lilac bush, it had seemed such a short distance to go but now, it seemed very far.

Upon hearing a sharp crackling sound, Charmaine gasped, "Oh, dear God, no! No!" she screamed.

She froze in the spot where she stood and her eyes looked downward into what seemed like a unfathomless pit.

Not only did this chasm divide her from Charles and Genevieve, it separated her from Pierre. His extended hand could not reach this far, she dejectedly realized.

Hopeless and helpless, she reluctantly accepted her dilemma. She had to. Harsh truth was staring her straight in the face.

She heard a deep voice calling out to her across the deep gap, and she looked up to see the grief-stricken face of the man she adored. Pierre was staring at her and crying out to her. "Charmaine! Dear God Almighty!"

The frantic, desperate look on his face wrung her heart, and she forgot her own fears for that fleeting moment. All she could say was, "I love you, Pierre. I love you, *mon cher.*"

She stood there, holding the puppy in her arms, alone in this holocaust. The only important thing at this moment was crying out her love for him.

"I'll find you, *ma petite amie!* I swear—if it takes me a lifetime. I'll find you, Charmaine," he vowed across the great distance separating them.

The arrogant young Frenchman had not cried since he

was a youth but this night he was so humbled and devastated by his helplessness, he cared not that tears cascaded down his cheeks.

How long they stood there just looking across the gap dividing them, neither of them knew. But Charmaine did know Renaud loved her for she'd heard the pain in his voice and that eased her torment.

She did not see his tears, but the tenderness in his voice was enough to give her faith that he would find her. Dear God, she had to believe he would! Without that ray of hope, she could not have gone on.

Pierre would find her!

He'd always rescued her when danger stared her in the face—in Savannah and in New Orleans. She had to believe that he could do the same here in New Madrid.

Chapter 55

Jacques and Tasha were standing some thirty or forty feet behind Pierre, observing with disbelief what their eyes were seeing. They felt numb and helpless. Tears flowed down Tasha's face as she strained to see across the gorge that separated them from her golden-haired friend who stood on the other side clutching the little white pup in her arms. Jacques had a pain in his gut, he felt such compassion for the man whose broad shoulders were bowed in total desolation. All Pierre's power and strength could not help him at this moment, nor could his vast wealth or being the heir of Étienne Renaud.

When he left Tasha's side and started to walk to Pierre, his wife understood why he was leaving her. Giving him a nod of her head, she urged, "Yes Jacques . . . go to him. God knows, he needs you now. I'm . . . I'm all right." But she wasn't. Already her labor pains had started.

Jacques went to his half brother and he put an arm around Pierre's shoulders. The young Renaud turned to see Jacques standing beside him, but he didn't try to hide the tears flowing down his tanned cheeks. Jacques gave him a comradely hug as any caring brother would have done. *"Mon ami,* we will get our little Charmaine back. I will help you. I will!"

"Oh God, Jacques, there might as well be an ocean

dividing us. I couldn't—I can't—believe the huge chasm my eyes have seen this night."

Neither could Jacques but he knew the two would not be united tonight. Pierre was, like so many others, in a state of shock.

"Come, *mon ami*. Let us go back to the house, gather our forces, and put our heads together over how we should go about helping Charmaine. We can't span that huge gap so we must go around it, *oui?*"

Pierre merely nodded his head for he knew that Bernay spoke the truth. He allowed Jacques to guide him, and they joined Tasha. The three of them consoled one another in silence by holding onto each other all the way back to Charles Renaud's house.

The house had been spared as far as damage was concerned, except for the grounds at the back. Jacques Bernay placed himself in charge of the dazed group, for Pierre was consumed with grief and Charles Renaud was fighting to keep his sanity. Jacques marveled at the amazing courage of the two women, Tasha and Genevieve.

As yet, Tasha had not told him what she suspected. But Genevieve knew and had already begun to assemble the things they would need to see the baby born. She was going to be the midwife at the birthing. It would be born before this night ended, Genevieve suspected. This horrible night!

Jacques found a bottle of brandy, and he urged Charles and Pierre to take generous sips of the amber liquid, although a night's sleep was probably the best tonic they could have. When the dawn came and they could actually see what had happened to the countryside, then Pierre could start on his quest to find Charmaine, Jacques reasoned. In the darkness, it would be too treacherous to seek out a trail. One could fall into a pit where the earth had cracked. Jacques hoped Pierre would wait until dawn to start out.

Because Pierre was in a state of shock and because Jacques so readily filled his glass with brandy, Renaud was finally numbed by the liquor. And Charles slept peacefully too, unaware of the additional tremors that shook the earth in the next few hours.

Poor Jacques wanted to drink himself into a stupor but feeling responsible for those he loved so dearly, he did not give way to the urge. Instead he savored the warmth of the brandy until he was assured that Pierre was drunk enough to sleep until dawn's first light.

Only then did he turn his attention to what the two ladies were doing. They were far busier than he'd been. Genevieve had helped Tasha into a clean nightgown and had gotten her into a comfortable bed. She'd then located a leather strap for her to bite on and another to tie to the bedpost that Tasha could pull on when the pains insisted she bear down with all her might. Although a doctor or midwife would not have done so, Genevieve poured two generous glasses of her favorite sherry and offered them to Tasha. She believed they would help her relax, which would help under the circumstances of this miserable night.

"This bébé will be a miracle, Tasha. We will do fine. You will see!" She tried to encourage the younger woman who was having her first child under such terrible conditions. More than ever, she admired this little black-haired lady with the piercing black eyes who looked up at her with such trust.

The excruciating pain stabbed at Tasha, making her stammer as she tried to reply to the kindhearted Genevieve, but she managed to say, "I . . . I wanted a son so much until tonight, Madame Renaud. Now, I pray it will be a girl. Because it is a miracle that we are all alive, I pray I'll have a daughter so I can name her Charmaine Genevieve Bernay."

A smile came to Genevieve's face and she sighed softly. *"Charmant, ma petite Tasha!* I . . . I am most humbled by the honor you pay me."

At this moment Jacques entered the room and discovered just what the two ladies had been doing while he'd been so occupied downstairs. Without a moment's hesitation he took up his station by the side of Tasha's bed so he might hold her hand and rub her aching, throbbing back. She needed no leather strap to grip now for Jacques gave her his strong hand to hold on to each time those stabbing pains struck.

His lips caressed her damp cheek when he wasn't applying a cool wet cloth to her face and forehead. Jacques would not know until much later what a consolation this was to Tasha. It meant everything to her that he sought to share the moment of their child's birth with her. Never would she cherish any moment more!

His strength permeated her, easing the frightening feeling engulfing her, and Genevieve marveled at the strength of this young man who was so tender and so caring. Every husband should be as Jacques Bernay, she privately mused.

Time was not measured this night in New Madrid. But had it been noted, Tasha's delivery of her first born would have been found to be remarkably swift. Perhaps it was the love surrounding her with Jacques and Genevieve by her side, or maybe it was her utter faith that neither of them would allow anything to go wrong. But eight hours after her pains had started, she gave birth to a daughter. For a newborn babe the infant had an abundant mane of black hair.

Tasha's prayer had, indeed, been answered for she had the daughter she'd yearned to have. When Genevieve handed her the baby wrapped in a soft blanket, tears ran down her cheeks for she thought about the holocaust she'd lived through to enjoy this beautiful moment.

Little Charmaine Genevieve Bernay was surely the most beautiful baby she'd ever laid eyes on, Madame Renaud would have sworn, and never had she witnessed two happier people than Jacques and Tasha Bernay as they gazed on their firstborn.

Last night was not doomsday, as most would surely think, Genevieve concluded. No, it was a new beginning! Somehow, she knew when the sun came up in the morning, their world would not be laden with gloom and despair.

It would be a new day, a new beginning. Whatever was lost or destroyed could be replaced and rebuilt. We'll start all over again, she told herself. That thought lifted her spirits, and she began to anticipate the dawn. I must give courage to my beloved Charles, she thought, as she left the little family alone to go to her own bedroom and sleep so she might greet the new day.

The next day all the citizens of New Madrid did not feel as exuberant as Genevieve Renaud. They moved like people in a trance, leaving their devastated village with their bundles of possessions over their shoulders. Like vagabonds, they marched aimlessly over the countryside, caring not in which direction they were going, only that they were going away from the hell they'd endured. Still tremors shook the earth under their feet and where there had been land and farms there were now massive holes and gaps. Much farmland was flooded with water, and the fertile river land was covered with inches of salt.

The true miracle was none of the people had been lost though many cattle had been killed. One of the settlers had been devoured by a gaping hole, but someone nearby had quickly pulled him to safety. That was a miracle!

But the environment was not spared this night of December 16, 1811. The currents of the mighty Mississippi River changed course, and the snags and bends of the river were altered. The most capable pilot or captain could not cope with these changes, and Cat Morrow was no exception. His keel boat was well beyond the village of New Madrid when the mighty quake hit. The ropes securing it snapped and suddenly the current was surging in an opposite direction. Cat knew no mortal could do battle with these odds, so he only tried to survive.

Luckily, he did and he later found himself on the riverbank, his buckskins drenched. He knew not what had happened to his crew or to his seventy-foot keel boat. At this point, he didn't care.

All his years of living and all the tales his father had told him had not prepared him for this subterranean phenomena. As he wandered along the riverbank, wet as a drowned rat, he thought of the beautiful Charmaine Lamoureux. He hoped she'd been wearing that amulet around her pretty throat. New Madrid had to have felt the brunt of all this, he knew. He strode down the grassy banks of the river in the direction of that settlement.

That lovely Charmaine with her golden hair and her sapphire blue eyes seemed to be the object of three men's thoughts this horrible night: Pierre Renaud's, of course; Captain Morrow's as he struggled to make his way back to New Madrid; and White Wolf's.

The old Indian thought of her and of his friend Renaud as the earth began to tremble around ten that evening. At the same moment, White Wolf knew that this was how he would go to his beloved. He made no move to leave his shack when the mighty quake struck. He felt the swaying motion of the earth which made the walls buckle and when the crude structure collapsed around him and one of the rough-hewn timbers pinned him beneath it, he knew his moment had come. Fighter that he'd always been, he did not try to release himself or resist his destiny. But he was not then aware of a wandering young maiden clutching to her breast a small white puppy. Aimlessly, she walked toward the shack she'd spotted when a bright beam of light had beckoned only moments before.

But just as she approached it, another tremor occurred and a part of the shack crumbled. She heard White Wolf moan sharply as the cypress support fell across his chest, and she rushed forward, hoping to be able to help whoever was injured. She had no inkling that the occupant of the shack was White Wolf, Renaud's old friend and guide.

One glance at the massive width of the timber pinning him told her it was futile to think she could lift it off the old half-breed's chest. She looked down at him, a desolate, helpless expression on her lovely face. White Wolf saw gemlike tears drop from her eyes and he wanted to console and comfort her. She was feeling deep pain. She cared!

He found it difficult to talk, but he drew on the power within him for he had to ease her pain. What nicer parting gift could he have as he left this earth than the tears of this lovely young lady whose gold hair fell down to touch him as he left to meet the woman he had loved so dearly in the past. His woman would have liked Charmaine Lamoureux.

"Moonbeam, please don't cry for me. I am happy for I go to meet a lady as beautiful as you and I love her very much. It was written long ago to be this way. I am just happy I am able to tell you goodbye. I am happy you and little White Wolf came now. My wish was granted."

"Oh, White Wolf!" Charmaine moaned. As she bent down to kiss his cheek, his eyes closed slowly and she knew he was dying.

But he muttered a parting remark, "I am truly happy, Moonbeam. Believe me!" When she looked at his face, she could not doubt that he was. His classic features were serene. He was at peace.

But she was not. She flung herself across him and gave way to the uncontrollable urge to cry. She sobbed, "White Wolf, I love you and I hardly knew you."

She and little White Wolf were lying in an exhausted sleep by the dead half-breed when Cat Morrow happened to come on the scene. Instantly, he recognized Charmaine's golden tresses, though he couldn't see her lovely face.

But how did she happen to be here at this old half-breed's shack and where was her protector Renaud with his scrutinizing eagle eyes?

Had this night of terror separated them? If ever he'd seen a

461

lost soul Charmaine Lamoureux was just that. He had an overwhelming desire to run to her and take her in his arms as he'd yearned to do so many times.

But he did not. He walked deliberately toward her. Alone, without the overpowering presence of Pierre Renaud, she might just turn to him.

Chapter 56

When Charmaine first felt Cat's hand on her shoulder, she instantly assumed Pierre had found her and she jumped up, ready to cry out his name. But it was not Pierre staring down at her; it was the rugged Captain Morrow.

In a stammering voice, she greeted him, "Captain . . . Captain Morrow!"

Cat sank down to the ground beside her, and his eyes danced over her admiringly. Dear God, she had to be the most beautiful woman in the whole, wide world!

"Surprised to see me? I sure didn't mean to alarm you. But I just had to know that you weren't injured, ma'am."

"By the grace of God, Captain Morrow. You could say I am one of the lucky ones, I guess." By now little White Wolf had roused and was wriggling in her arms. She gave him his freedom, and he went to relieve himself after his long sleep at his mistress' side.

"After what I've seen as I've come up the riverbank I'd say we've both been lucky, ma'am. I've never seen the likes of this in all my life. Lost everything I've worked a lifetime for . . . my boat is gone . . . splintered."

"Oh, I'm terribly sorry, Captain Morrow." Charmaine's blue eyes were soft and mellow.

"Hey, I'm just damned happy to be alive and breathing.

Tell you something, after I peered down those pits back there and I thought about being swallowed up in one of those holes, losing a boat isn't anything." He went on to tell her how he'd been going upstream to St. Louis when suddenly the currents on the river became erratic. Suddenly, islands in the river had mysteriously disappeared before his eyes.

"Hell, I thought I could navigate this river blindfolded if I had to, but not last night. Walking along the riverbank, it was like I was walking over a strange countryside."

"It's a night I'll have nightmares about for the rest of my life," Charmaine declared. Perhaps, this wasn't Pierre, but the mere fact that someone was with her gave her a certain amount of comfort. It was nice to have Captain Cat Morrow at her side.

She told him how she'd happened to be at White Wolf's shack and he smiled. "He was something, wasn't he? Everyone up and down this river knew White Wolf. Some thought him to be a strange fellow, but he could certainly spout a lot of wisdom if you listened to that old Indian."

By now the little white pup had jumped back up into Charmaine's lap and he lay curled up in the folds of Charmaine's skirt. Her dress hardly resembled the gorgeous pale blue gown she'd worn the night before to the festive party. That seemed like a lifetime ago, but it was only the night before.

The hemline was fringed with jagged splits, for it had caught on numerous branches when she and Pierre had rushed in and out among the trees as they'd tried to get back to the house from the cave. And the material was smudged with dirt from her many falls on the ground when the earth had shaken with such fury she could not stay on her feet.

Her lovely face was dirty too, and her dainty hands were scratched. Dried blood stained her satiny skin and Cat noticed that she was pale. Concern mounted in him.

"Let me see if there's the makings for some coffee in the remains of this cabin, and you have some cuts that need tending to, ma'am. I'll see that our old friend here gets a proper burying."

Charmaine nodded her approval, but when she tried to get up her legs were like jelly, there was a horrible stabbing pain in her gut, and weariness engulfed her.

Cat did not ask her permission, he just picked her up, the pup in her arms, and carried her across the ruins of the shack. Once they were out of the sun, he placed her, with the puppy, on White Wolf's bunk.

"Now, you just stretch out and rest awhile and I'll see what we can salvage. I'm thinking you could use a little food, ma'am." There was a gentleness in this man in buckskin garb, Charmaine realized. Perhaps, he did not have the charm of Pierre Renaud, but he was good and kind.

She did as he requested, and when she lay down on the bed White Wolf fitted himself to the curve of her body. Sleep immediately came to her for she felt safe in Cat Morrow's presence.

Hours passed and Charmaine was unaware that Morrow had buried White Wolf in the little flower garden south of his shack. He'd then banked the fireplace with a pile of seasoned oak logs and a crackling, glowing fire was now burning. The cabin wall that had splintered had been covered with a length of canvas to keep out the chill of the winter evening.

He'd braved the cold waters of the river to cleanse himself after attending to White Wolf's burial. Then he'd gotten a big kettle of water boiling. It hung on the hook over the fire.

Luckily, he found an abundant supply of food in White Wolf's cupboard, along with a basket of apples, and some flour and meal. He'd found sacks of potatoes and beans, and a side of bacon. The old Indian guide had obviously had a hearty feast before devastation struck New Madrid for Cat found the remains of a pan of cornbread wrapped in a cloth, some fine cured ham, and a chunk of cheese.

Cat was starved so he'd sliced himself a generous portion of the ham as Charmaine lay sleeping. But the smell of the

465

ham and cheese wafted to the nose of the pup for he immediately left Charmaine's cozy warmth to go to Cat.

"Oh, I'm suddenly your good buddy, huh? Hungry as hell aren't you, you little rascal." Cat laughed and handed the pup a hefty hunk of cheese and a slice of the ham.

The pup ate it all with zest, and his tail wagged delightedly. When he had finished, he looked up at Cat, his black eyes expectant. Morrow didn't disappoint him.

In fact, Cat fed him until he was no longer hungry, and little White Wolf showed his gratefulness by licking Cat's hand.

The tall, lean man moved around the cabin, trying to put things in order so the sleeping beauty could be more comfortable, and the pup followed him. Cat had a friend!

The delicious aroma of the brewing coffee was sheer ambrosia, and to add to that pleasure, Cat found White Wolf's pipe and pouch of pungent tobacco.

Puffing on the pipe and savoring a steaming cup of coffee, he watched the flames in the fireplace dancing, their shades brilliant gold and rust. The pup was curled at his feet absorbing the heat of the fireplace, and it was hard to believe the devastation just outside the little shack.

Cat really didn't care what the future held for him, though he had nothing left. Tonight, he was happier than he'd been in a long, long time. He was content and peaceful. His eyes darted from time to time to the golden-haired miss sleeping across the room.

When she awoke, he'd have a very tasty meal ready for her, and it pleased him to be able to provide all this for her. Cat knew he'd take care of Charmaine as long as she needed him, but he knew Renaud would soon come. Until that day, though, Cat intended to savor his precious moments with Charmaine Lamoureux. Fate had placed them together, and Cat did not care why. It had happened!

When Charmaine's thick lashes finally fluttered open and she saw him sitting across the cabin, smoking contentedly, he looked completely different from the man she'd remembered as the pilot of a keel boat. This backwoods man was attractive. His tall, lean body and broad shoulders exuded force and strength.

As she lay there silently for a moment, watching him pull on the pipe, she noticed his fine high cheekbones, so bronzed and tan. She recalled that she'd thought it was due to his being out in the sun so much aboard his boat, but Renaud had said Morrow had told him his mother had been an Indian maiden. So that contributed to the darkness of his skin.

She'd always known it had to be Cat Morrow who'd slipped the amulet in her reticule the day they'd disembarked here in New Madrid. Perhaps she'd finally be able to satisfy her curiosity about that.

She'd not found the amulet until a few days later, she recalled. She'd been reluctant to mention it to Pierre. Knowing he'd be furious it had seemed pointless to do so. No man could be sweeter than her amorous, handsome Pierre, but no man could be more unbearable when he was in one of those black moods of his.

Perhaps that was how it was when one felt so strongly about another. Indeed, Pierre had told her he'd never met such a hot-tempered vixen.

Her hands reached around the crook of her body to seek out little White Wolf, but he was not to be found. She glanced down the length of her body, but he was not there. So she raised up in the bed, and found him sprawled at Cat's feet. She smiled for the first time in many, long hours. The rest had done her a world of good.

A tempting smell greeted her, making her aware of how ravenously hungry she was. At this moment she let Cat know she was awake. "Hello."

When he turned and saw her sitting up in the bunk and smiling, his heart began to pound wildly. He returned her smile with one of his own. "Hello to you, Charmaine." He grinned. Unconsciously, he had addressed her in the casual, informal way he'd dared not do before. Maybe, it was because he'd been absorbed in his intimate thoughts about her.

"I hope you feel like eating. We can thank our old friend White Wolf for having a pantry full of supplies. I am not the greatest cook in the world, but I think you'll find I'm not bad either," he boasted.

"It smells utterly delicious, and I am famished!" Charmaine got up from the bunk, needing no urging to test his skills with the pots and pans. Looking around White Wolf's cabin, she did not have to be told just how busy he'd been while she'd slept.

A fire glowed in the open fireplace, kettles of food simmered, and she smelled brewing coffee. The crude little square table was set up with a plate of ham, a crock of butter, and a chunk of cheese. A tin held a few pieces of cornbread.

She noticed the huge strip of canvas hung to keep out the night breeze. While it fluttered slightly in and out, it blocked out a lot of the chill, and the blazing fire made the shack comfortable.

"I see you've made a friend of White Wolf." She grinned.

"Oh, he was easy to win over. I just filled his little belly with some ham and cheese. I think he's so full he can't move now." Cat laughed. Then he urged Charmaine to have a seat at the table, and he poured her a cup of the coffee.

Together, they ate their first meal together. This was to be the first of many meals they would share in the days and nights to follow.

They passed a pleasant evening together, one Charmaine would never forget. She realized the keel-boat captain had many virtues she'd failed to see in those weeks she'd been on his boat. It seemed only natural and right as they dined by the candlelight in old White Wolf's cabin to call him Cat as he'd called her Charmaine.

In the cozy enclosure of White Wolf's cabin, the

468

devastated countryside was blocked out. They knew nothing of the wandering bands of people fleeing through the countryside. Some were befuddled and dazed, not knowing where they roamed. Others were hellbent on getting as far away from New Madrid as they could. Wagons filled with their hastily packed possessions rolled to the south and the north of the settlement, some of the drivers so panic-filled they wrecked the rigs before they'd traveled the first five miles out of the settlement.

Some people refused to stay in their houses even though they did not leave New Madrid, and they set up tents or wigwams for shelter.

The true impact of the disaster was not learned until a survey of the countryside told the people of New Madrid that crops had been ruined and many cattle killed. Forests had been leveled and fertile land had been covered by layers of sand. The poor creatures of the woods were as disoriented as the people. The birds seemed to have forgotten how to fly or trill their songs.

The first three days after the quake Cat Morrow and Charmaine were isolated in White Wolf's cabin and they seemed to be untouched by all this. White Wolf's shack sat back in the woods not far from the riverbank and just off the main country road. To get to the shack, one followed a narrow lane lined by a grove of tall cottonwood trees.

Cat saw the supplies dwindling in the pantry, however, and there was no place to obtain more from what a young drifter had told him. The mercantile store in New Madrid was in ruins, and boats carrying goods upstream were no longer coming to New Madrid, those going downstream had lost their cargoes or been wrecked or had hit a sandbar not there before the mighty quake.

Cat decided there was only one thing to do, get out of this madness and secure a boat if he could. He'd get the beautiful Charmaine away from here—a long way away!

When the aftershocks had hit, she'd rushed to him and

dear God Almighty, it was heaven to hold her in his strong arms! But hold her was all he'd done, though that was certainly not what he wanted. He wanted more—a lot more!

He wanted to kiss her sweet, trembling lips, to fondle her tempting breasts, and he wanted to bury himself deep within her and whisper in her ear that he worshiped her. He'd adored her since she'd walked down that wharf on Renaud's arm that day in New Orleans. Yes, by God, every fiber in his body dared him to take her, but he didn't. He was probably the biggest fool he knew!

The truth was, he'd never expected to have had this much time alone in the little paradise of White Wolf's cabin. He'd expected Pierre Renaud to be slamming through the cabin door with the devil's fury blazing on his face. But he hadn't and Cat was pleasantly surprised.

There could only be one answer to that, Cat Morrow figured. That vast gorge Charmaine had told him about must have cracked the earth for many, many miles in both directions.

But Cat was a half-breed too, like old White Wolf, and he believed a lot of the Indian lore and legends. He had a foreboding that the danger was not over yet.

Last night when he couldn't sleep he'd walked outside the cabin to smoke old White Wolf's pipe. He'd sat on the step in the darkness and he'd heard a nocturnal bird over in one of the old oak trees. The sound caught his attention and held it. His eyes finally spotted the white and gray plumage of the owl perched on a low-hanging branch. He was filled with an eerie, uncanny feeling—and then he knew why.

The shrill screech of the bird continued, and it flew boldly to perch closer to the cabin, as if he was stubbornly dispatching its message before leaving.

That's when Cat Morrow knew old White Wolf was warning them to leave his cabin and New Madrid.

He must get Charmaine away, somewhere up the river where she would be safe.

Chapter 57

Vapor and fog shrouded the riverbanks as well as the countryside, giving them an uncanny aura. It was like everything else around New Madrid right now, Pierre Renaud thought, as he rode the huge dapple-gray stallion. With one hand he reined his steed and with the other he guided the pack horse following behind him.

He'd never existed in a time or place so totally consumed by melancholy. The torment of wondering about Charmaine's welfare was enough to drive him crazy, but he'd left his uncle's house almost reluctantly.

Dear, sweet Tante Genevieve had insisted he not delay his departure any longer, and he could not deny he was anxious to be on his way. Nonetheless, it pained him to leave his aunt with so much responsibility. Uncle Charles was not himself, though he should have been coming back to the realm of reality. Still, his friend Jacques was there to stand in for him.

Every mile he covered, he saw more evidence of the devastation of the fateful night they'd just lived through. Being alive was a miracle, he realized. As long as there was life there was hope to build on.

The gorge that had divided him from Charmaine had looked like a bottomless pit when he'd gazed down into it the next morning, and he'd been stunned to see the vast width of the crack. He'd followed the gorge after he'd left his uncle's home, but there had seemed to be no end to it, no narrowing that would allow him to cross.

When he'd come to the first roaming band he'd met, he'd questioned them about a young lady with golden hair, but all they'd just mumbled were negatives.

He had to conclude that they were all either in a trance or they'd actually not seen her. As he continued to question one of the men who seemed to be a little more alert than some of the other poor dazed souls, he was told they were from a settlement called Little Prairie, not from New Madrid. That told him the earthquake had affected quite an area. What he could not know was that it was even more far reaching than he thought.

He urged his stallion on, trying to ignore the dense vapors that flowed upward out of the monster cracks. Where was she, his beautiful Charmaine? Had she joined some group of people who were fleeing?

For her own safety, he prayed she was with a crowd and not alone in this devastated countryside. Pierre had nothing to do but think as he rode along, and he envisioned some people becoming savage when supplies ran low or were exhausted.

He rode for hours without finding a way to breach that gap and cross to the other side. But he was obsessed with his quest, so he did not notice the setting sun or the fact that he'd not eaten all day. Only the deepening darkness jarred him into realizing he must stop to make camp. Yet, he fought the urge to do so, for he wanted to keep going until he found the woman he loved.

Patience had never been one of his virtues, and it most assuredly wasn't now.

Pierre could not know it this first night out, but his patience was going to be even more sorely tested before he had a hope of finding his lovely lady. This night was going to be one of many in which he searched the countryside which was in chaos.

But after he'd spent seven long days and nights without any clue to Charmaine's whereabouts coming to light, he found himself more willing to accept that his search was not going to be as simple as he'd anticipated. Circumstances were demanding more of Pierre Renaud then he'd ever imagined himself willing to give. He now knew more than ever before the overwhelming love he felt for Charmaine, the only woman he'd sacrifice this much for!

Each time the aftershocks struck, he thought of her and prayed she wasn't too afraid. He hoped some kindly woman was near to comfort her. His sleep would have not been so peaceful had he known it was Cat Morrow's arms who were soothing her fears, but Pierre's body was so tired from long hours in the saddle when he lay in his bedroll at night and the shocks made the earth quiver, he just lay there until the tremors stopped.

One night as one of the more jarring shocks hit, he was roused from sleep before the quaking began by the annoying hooting of an old owl on a branch overhead. The despicable old bastard seemed hellbent on keeping him awake, Pierre decided.

At one point, he was tempted to get his rifle and take aim at the pesty devil. Then a strange thing happened and Pierre was stunned for a moment. The owl swooped down from the overhanging branch to sit arrogantly on the ground less than twenty feet away from Pierre's bedroll. The old owl just sat and stared at him. And Pierre had the strangest feeling that he saw old White Wolf in that owl's face. It shook him! It shook him to the core of his being.

He sat there and muttered to himself in the awesome quiet of the night. "What is it, you old devil? What is it you're telling me?"

He got no answer and the owl flew away. Pierre was left to wonder if he was losing his sanity. He lay quietly, gazing up at the starlit sky and meditating thoughtfully for a long, long time. He didn't know how long he lay there staring up at the night sky, but one thing was made very clear to him before he closed his weary eyes in sleep; tomorrow he would find that narrow trail and get across to the other side.

That was enough to satisfy Renaud. To get to the other side was all he asked for now. He knew he'd find Charmaine. She was there, he knew that! He'd find her.

Fate would not deny them now!

The second of the severe quakes destined to hit the New Madrid area struck in the third week of January, but Cat Morrow had made his decision to leave long before that. The week following that horrible night of December sixteenth had robbed him of all his worldly possessions, but the irony of it all was he was with the lady he'd dreamed of and idolized for so long. The week of paradise they'd shared in the old half-breed's cabin would forever be treasured by him, but after the night when the old owl had haunted him, Cat knew what he must do.

He managed to find a canoe, and he scrounged around the nearby area to collect enough supplies to see them safely to a place down the river.

He didn't like playing tricks on Charmaine, but to get her to leave White Wolf's cabin he felt the ends justified the means he used. A heavy burden of worry was lifted off Cat's chest when he loaded her and little White Wolf into the canoe with their meager belongings and supplies. Once he started paddling downstream, he felt blissfully light of heart, and he flashed a warm grin at Charmaine.

"We're leaving this miserable place, Charmaine. I want you safe. Hey, I think little White Wolf is tickled. Look, his tail's going."

She let her eyes dart down to the adorable little ball of white fluff. "He does seem excited, doesn't he?" Her soft laugh gladdened Cat's heart.

The sun gleamed down on them and the water shimmered. He saw a great blue heron perched on a cypress tree, floating in the river. With this splendor all around them his eyes met hers.

Charmaine was feeling emotions she couldn't even explain to herself at this moment. She voiced them in her usual straightforward way. "I . . . I shall be forever grateful to you, Cat. I don't know how I'd have made it without you."

His face was mellow with feeling. To know she felt this way about him was the nicest reward Morrow could receive. He stammered like an embarrassed youth as he replied, "Ah, Charmaine . . . I . . . I gave so little."

A radiant fire came to her eyes and he remembered her spirited air when she was aboard his keel boat exhibited itself. She sat up straight then. "Cat Morrow, you gave me my life, I'd say! You took care of me. I could not have survived without you!"

She could not have known that her words had made Cat's chest swell. She had fed his hope that he could win and woo her.

"You are a woman worth saving, Charmaine Lamoureux, and as far as taking care of you, I can't imagine a greater pleasure or honor for any man."

She said nothing, responding only with a warm smile. She dared not speak right then. She needed time to gather her thoughts for she suddenly realized that she was seeing sparks of desire in Cat's eyes.

That made her ill at ease. During the days and nights they'd spent at White Wolf's cabin, she'd taken so freely of his generosity and protection. And, God knows, she'd welcomed the comfort of his arms when the aftershocks had frightened her. Yet, he'd asked nothing of her, demanded nothing of her!

But their relationship had changed. On this bright sunshiny day of winter she knew it. She had no one to blame but herself, for she'd agreed to come with him and she'd not even asked Cat where they were going when she stepped into that canoe with him. Charmaine chided herself for being as naïve and stupid as she'd been back on the isle of Jersey. Her affair with the handsome Pierre, the episodes in Savannah and New Orleans had apparently taught her nothing. She was still a simple little French farm girl!

She must be fair with Cat Morrow. He deserved that much from her for she dare not let him think for one minute that her heart could ever belong to him. Pierre had stolen her heart long ago. Her love for him was strong and all-consuming. She must impress that on Cat!

Perhaps, it was long overdue that she tell him this. In a voice filled with tender warmth, she said, "Cat, I know I've not been myself a lot of the time since we've started down the river today, but I'm feeling better now. I must get back to my . . . my friends. I've come with you, not even asking where we're headed, yet I've suddenly realized that I've been very thoughtless."

Her lovely eyes searched his face and Cat was stunned for a moment by her sudden change of her mood. But he was a perceptive man so he weighed her words before he sought to answer her. He tried desperately to hide his displeasure about what she was trying to tell him. He also tried his darndest to reflect his usual carefree, easygoing nature when he finally remarked, "I just couldn't get any provisions as you know, Charmaine. We had to get out of there and go downstream in the hope of finding a safe place for you. Hell, I could manage for myself."

"Oh, Cat, I know you're concerned for me and I will forever be grateful."

His face took on a sober look and his firm muscular body tensed. "Look, Charmaine . . . I gave Renaud ample time to find you . . . us. There's no way a man, not even Renaud, could span the gap left by the quake. From all I've learned from the drifting bands of people it extends for miles and miles. I'm not trying to steal you away from Renaud or abduct you before he can get to you."

Her long lashes fluttered as she realized she'd insulted him, which was not her intention. "Oh, Cat, I didn't mean that at all. I just don't want to go so far away that I can't get word back to my friends. Pierre, of course, but there is also Tasha and the Renauds, Charles and Genevieve."

Cat had known many ladies and he'd bedded a fair share of the women living along the river. He knew he was not an ugly man. Oh, he didn't dress in fancy attire like Renaud, nor was he educated, but he did have a virile appeal which excited the ladies. Now this lady did something to him no other woman had ever done.

His eyes devoured her as she sat there, her long thick lashes fluttering, looking as innocent as a child. Damn! He couldn't be angry with her. His groin ached with a wild desire to possess her, and his gut churned with outrage and frustration but when he spoke his voice was casual and calm. "Honey, thank your lucky stars you're with an old keel-boat captain who knows every place up and down this river. Everyone up and down this river knows Charles Renaud so I can send word back by any of the river people we chance to meet, and we will meet them. Trust me, Charmaine. I may not be much, but I'm the best you've got right now."

Her eyes could have been exquisite blue sapphires from the Orient, they were so radiant and bright. "You are the best, Cat Morrow! I trust you. I leave everything in your capable hands, all right?"

"All right, Mademoiselle Lamoureux! I assure you I'll take the best of care of you." What he didn't say was he would unrelentingly try to win her, for Cat could be patient. If he was patient enough to wait for the memories of Renaud to fade, she would see how much he loved her. She would yield herself to him when he showered her with devotion.

Cat was a man blinded by his love for Charmaine, otherwise his instincts would have been more keen. His senses would have smelled the rain in the atmosphere, and his eyes would have noticed the gathering clouds. Like a bad omen of the things to come, a torrent of rain exploded over the river. Sharp flashes of lightning broke in the sky ahead of them, and the rumbling of thunder echoed along with the flashing lightning.

Cat knew they had to seek refuge away from the river; raindrops were already pelting them. He paddled the canoe as hastily as his strong arms could toward the bank. If he had his bearings right, there was a cabin not too far away that belonged to a friend of his.

By the time they reached the shore and Cat secured the canoe, the thunder and lightning were overhead. He guided Charmaine up the embankment and saw the little cabin. Cat felt gods were on his side for the first time in days.

"Come on, Charmaine!" he urged, for the rain was coming down in sheets. Already her golden hair was limp and he was drenched to the skin.

Despite all that was happening to them, he heard her giggle light-heartedly and he turned to see a twinkle in her bright blue eyes as they scampered, like two children, to the small shack.

He grinned and pulled her closer to him. While he did not say it, his heart cried out his love for her!

Chapter 58

Rain fell on the New Madrid area Charmaine and Cat Morrow had left hours earlier. But the melancholy which had settled over most of her neighbors and friends did not dispirit Genevieve Renaud. Her stubborn determination was her salvation. She would not look on the future as hopeless. This was not doomsday!

Genevieve's other source of courage was Jacques Bernay. She wondered how they would have made it without Jacques. No son could have shown more devotion to her beloved Charles. She could thank him for the improvement in her husband in the week since Pierre had left on his quest to find Charmaine. *Mon Dieu,* he has to find her, Genevieve thought to herself! Charmaine could not be lost to them, especially to Pierre.

The rain had started late in the day but it had continued throughout the evening, right through their evening meal and the clearing of the dishes.

Genevieve had insisted that Tasha attend to her precious bébé. "After all, little Charmaine Genevieve deserves the best," she said. "I'll manage quite nicely down here. I'll make Jacques put on an apron and help me."

Tasha did not have to be coaxed to do as Genevieve requested for she had not regained her strength after her daughter was born. She blamed that on the quake and her concern over Charmaine's well-being. No one was prepared to meet and endure such stressful times as these, so Tasha didn't fault herself, nor did she consider herself weak. She knew she wasn't!

Jacques did put on one of Genevieve's white aprons and he helped her with the dishes after he'd seen Charles to his bedroom and put him in bed.

While he and Genevieve busily worked around the kitchen together, he remarked, "Charles is better! I'm certain of it!"

A glowing smile came to Genevieve's face, and it gladdened Jacques for he knew what this remarkable lady had endured. "I think you're right, Jacques. Everything is going to be just fine, *oui?*"

"Oui, Madame Renaud!"

"I have a wonderful idea. When we finish in here we will go into the parlor and enjoy a glass of wine together. I've something to say to you."

This is exactly what they did when Genevieve's kitchen was cleaned and the dishes were all put away. She had been so grateful that the pantry and storerooms were so amply filled and that there was wine in the cellar. She applauded Charles this foresight.

When the two of them were comfortably settled in the parlor, Genevieve poured Jacques a glass of her favorite wine, and she poured herself a most generous portion.

She felt it the right time to pay this fine young man the tribute he deserved and she sought to do so. "Jacques, I don't know what I would have done without you. If I had a son, I would have hoped he'd have been just like you, Jacques Bernay."

He was visibly effected, which impressed Genevieve Renaud, and he was honored because he knew of no lady who was more genuine and honest. Jacques shook his curly head and smiled, then his eyes finally met hers, those all-knowing eyes that seemed to search one's soul.

"You make me feel so humble, Madame Renaud. I thank you from the bottom of my heart. I can't say I've not had a mother, but you and my mother have a lot of things in common. She was wonderful! But I can say I'd like to have had a father like Charles . . . Uncle Charles."

Her eyes had an hypnotic effect on him and Jacques felt the power in this matronly lady. "You could have been Charles's son, but I would wager all I have that you are Etienne's son. You see, my dear young man, I knew Étienne as well as my Charles when they were young men in Cherbourg. My Charles was the serious one, but Étienne was a rogue. He was utterly heartless where the ladies were concerned. That is why I decided to become Charmaine's protectress. I feared Pierre would be like his father. I was determined he would not use her solely, not under my roof."

"Ah, no madame . . . no. I would swear he loves her! You see, I was privy to his encounter with her on the isle of Jersey. I can tell you he was smitten the minute he saw her."

Genevieve smiled at Jacques. "Ah, I know this now, Jacques. I observed his torment—his hell—after that horrible night he was separated from her. He is not Étienne and I thank God for that! But I must get back to what we were speaking about. I'll be the first to admit I've an insatiable curiosity, my Jacques Bernay." She laughed gustily and focused her eyes on him, daring him to deny the truth. Quite candidly, she insisted on knowing, "You are Étienne's son, aren't you? *Mon Dieu,* you have to be, for you are the image of him at your age! It could not be otherwise, this I know. I was Charles's wife at the time."

He could not have lied to this forceful lady and he saw no need to. "I am Étienne's son—his bastard son, Madame Renaud."

"But that makes you no less his son, Jacques Bernay, and somehow I feel you know this. I feel you are a very secure man, although you class yourself as a bastard. May I ask you, does Pierre know you are his half-brother?"

481

"No, madame, he does not. But it is funny, from our first meeting on the isle of Guernsey, I knew there was something binding us together. Is that crazy? Ah, perhaps, it is, but it is true. I swear to you!" It amazed him how easily he could talk to her, and it astonished him that her expression did not change or her eyes so much as blink when he'd confessed to being Étienne's son. He had to know why and he asked her.

She gave a soft little laugh, "It just came as no surprise, Jacques. The day you arrived I came to that conclusion after I'd been around you during the evening. Your mannerisms are so like Étienne's."

"Does Monsieur Renaud have as perceptive a pair of eyes as yours, madame?" Jacques gave her one of his crooked grins.

"Ah, yes, Jacques. We discussed you on numerous occasions," she confessed. "We share the same feelings about you. We feel you are as much our nephew as Pierre." She reached out to pat his hand affectionately.

"Bless you, madame. That means the world to me."

"It would mean the world to us if you would call us by our proper titles, *oui?*" she teased him light-heartedly.

He bent forward to plant a kiss on her cheek and declare, "So it shall be, Tante Genevieve."

The hooting old owl's visit left Pierre with a strange feeling until he walked down to the riverbank at dawn to wash his face in the stream. There he caught the sight of a majestic eagle perched on a branch just above him. He'd heard the Indians believed sighting an eagle was a sign of good luck and he needed all the luck he could get!

By the time he had his gear gathered and hoisted onto his pack horse, his spirits lifted and his faith was restored. When he urged his stallion into motion he followed his instincts as to which direction to travel on this particular morning.

By midday, he began to think he had taken the wrong trail

482

to find a crossing to the other side. But a couple of hours later, he was overjoyed and amply rewarded by the sight of the earth coming together. It was the end of the horrible crack. The countryside ahead of him not marred. He spurred the stallion to go faster.

By sunset, he'd been given his first clue that Charmaine had been spotted in this vicinity. He was elated when a fellow by the name of Nat Cooper, a trapper, said, "Yeah, as a matter of fact I did see the pretty young lady you're asking about. Guess there couldn't be too many gals with such hair. No sir! Most likely that's the one you're a'huntin', Mister."

But when Pierre pressed him for more details, his exuberance diminished. "That old rascal Morrow and her took a canoe and headed downstream. That was a couple of days ago I'd say."

Pierre grimaced, "A couple of days . . . you sure?"

"Sure as I can be, mister. Yeah, it was about that."

Pierre hastily thanked him and then headed downriver. Every muscle in his strong body grew taut at the thought of her being alone with Morrow. If the bastard laid a hand on her, Renaud swore he'd kill him. Thinking of them together filled him with firing rage.

Each mile added to his frustration for he could only cover so much ground and it was impossible to narrow the distance between him and the woman he loved. That she was with the roguish boat captain was even more disturbing.

Picking his way through the woods and trying to avoid the low-hanging branches and the tangle of underbrush slowed him down, but following the bends and curves of the river along a high rise of ground gave him a view of the stream below and every time his searching eyes caught sight of a boat or canoe going up or down the stream, he strained for a sign of a golden-haired passenger.

The woods were no longer as ravaged by splintered trees, but the sun was sinking far faster than Pierre would have wished. Twilight had come and there was no sight of

Charmaine. But he vowed he would not let dejection and depression overpower him. He'd just continue on until he found her.

A dusky haze was gathering around him by now, and as a cool breeze whistled above him, he slammed his hat tighter over his head. To try to push on after dark would be more than risky, it would be foolhardy. Still, he wanted to do just that.

Suddenly, he pulled up sharply on the reins of his horse. Below him, on the bluff, a canoe was tied up. But he saw no one on the bank of the river.

Did he dare hope that this could be Cat Morrow's canoe? He braced himself not wanting to be to hopeful. There were hundreds of such canoes on the river. After all, they were the primary means of transportation. This was no time for foolish fancy, Pierre cautioned himself as he urged the horse forward.

But his nostrils picked up the aroma of smoke, and in the dappled moonlight shining through the tall sycamore trees, he saw the circling haze of a campfire or from a nearby cabin. Pierre spurred his horse in the sides to move in that direction. There was an awesome quietness in the woods now that darkness had settled in. The only sound coming to Pierre's ears was rushing of water as it traveled over the huge boulders there in the stream below the cliff.

As he approached the old lean-to, Pierre's heart beat wildly with expectation and wonder. He imagined all sorts of things. What would he do if he bolted through that door and found Charmaine nestled in Morrow's arms. Dear God, the thought sickened him and it made fury mount in him at the same time!

Whatever or whoever was inside, he would soon find out. Dismounting from his stallion, he stopped short upon hearing a sound behind him. He turned slowly to look back and he spotted a shadowy creature moving amidst the trees

His keen eyes searched the darkness, and his ears strained to hear any giveaway sounds. He heard it . . . a hiss! Pierre knew it must be a bobcat, but he found that unusual for White Wolf had told him they usually stayed deeper in the woods.

He stood for a moment, not moving on toward the door. Again, the hiss came and Pierre reached for his rifle for these were ornery animals and tough, White Wolf had told him that. Smaller than their close cousin, the lynx, they made up for their size in cunning and courage. So Pierre used caution as he moved furtively, his gray eyes watching the shadows for any movement.

As he slammed through the door of the shack, the encounter outside the door enhanced the fierce look on his face, and his silver gray eyes blazed like those of the wild animal out there in the woods. He was a ferocious figure of a man.

Cat Morrow was no fool, though he considered himself a rugged man and a brave one. Hell, he could not compete with this bastard glaring down at him with fire in his eyes. Since he could not move swiftly with his foot swathed in bandages, he flippantly greeted Renaud, "Well, you finally got here."

Pierre's eyes were too busy searching every corner of the meager dwelling to answer him. No golden-haired loveliness greeted his eyes to see.

"Where is she, Cat? God damn it, I'm in no mood for idle matter. Where is Charmaine?" His eyes pierced Cat with the same untamed fierceness of the bobcat outside the cabin door.

"I wish I knew, Renaud, and that's the damned truth. She came downstream with me two days ago. I got my foot hurt taking a fall down one of those cliffs in the dark when I was hunting her after I found her missing. I'm a useless son of a bitch and have been since then or I'd be out hunting her right now." Cat was talking fast and furious, hoping he'd get it all said before the irate Renaud aimed his rifle at him and pulled the trigger.

But Pierre was not about to destroy the only source o information he had on Charmaine's whereabouts. He wa far too smart for that.

Cat figured he'd won himself some time. "Pour yourself glass of whiskey and I'll help you all I'm able," he said.

Pierre sauntered over to the old oak table where a bottle o whiskey sat, along with a glass. From the looks of Cat's foo and leg, it would appear he did speak the truth about hi injury.

Cat allowed Pierre to take a couple of drinks before h dared to tell him about the days and nights he'd shared wit Charmaine at White Wolf's cabin. In his own crude way Cat Morrow was as shrewd and clever as Pierre Renaud Actually these men secretly admired one another for tha very reason, and it had sparked the camaraderie they' shared on Cat's keel boat on that long trip from New Orlean to New Madrid. Cat figured he needed to mention two thing to Renaud immediately and he did.

"I came upon Charmaine at White Wolf's cabin. She an that pup were there with the old dead guide, Renaud." Cat eyes watched Renaud mellow with emotion. He said nothin for a moment and then he took a generous drink of Cat whiskey.

"Old White Wolf dead! Damn!"

"Yeah. Charmaine was dazed with shock and I tended t her as best as I knew how. Now, you can believe what yo like, but I tell you, as one man to another, I was neve anything but a friend during the time we stayed there. M reason for getting her away from the area was the panic I sav in her face everytime a new shock hit. And we'd run out o supplies at White Wolf's."

"Go ahead, Cat. You'll find me a reasonable man. I ca

cept your story so far," Renaud said, letting his eyes lock
ith Cat's. Renaud was convinced that the keel boat captain
as not lying.

"A downpour hit the river and I was forced to get us to
ore or I'd have been farther away from that hellish hole of
place. Thought I'd seen about everything there was to see
ocking around and going up and down this river, but God
ows, I hadn't."

"I'll agree with you on that but I don't understand why, if
harmaine arrived here with you, she's mysteriously gone?"

"Well, it drove me crazy, I can tell you. We got ourselves
y from the downpour and ate a little food from the stuff I'd
ought in my pack. I made myself a pallet and she bedded
wn on that miserable old cot over there in the corner—she
d that little pup. I woke up the next morning and she
asn't in the shack. Hell, I jumped up and rushed down by
e riverbank, figuring she'd gone down there to wash up.
n sure she did cause I saw her footprints in the damp
ound from the rains."

"I don't need to ask if you checked the woods. I'm sure you
d."

"I checked her footprints into the woods all that first day
d into the night. That's what happened to this," he pointed
wn to his foot. "I managed to drag myself back here to the
ack and this is where I've been stuck since. Hell, what else
uld I do?"

"Not a hell of a lot, Cat. But I have something to go on and
at's more than I've had in many days and nights."

They suddenly became two in league for a common cause.
t insisted that Renaud take the time to share some of his
od before he started out into the night, and Pierre accepted
t's meager fare to give him the strength for the long night
faced.

Then, without further ado, he bid Cat adieu and Cat
shed him well.

487

"I'll find her! I must find her, Cat!" Renaud said in a tone of voice that convinced Morrow he would do just that.

Cat smiled and waved to the Frenchman. Now he understood why he'd never had a chance to win the heart of the lovely Charmaine.

She had the love and devotion of Pierre Renaud.

Chapter 59

The last two days had been an eternity for Charmaine Lamoureux, and the only consolation she'd had was the little white fluff of a pup she'd held almost constantly in her arms. But curious little White Wolf was the cause of the dilemma she found herself at that early morning hour when she'd decided to go down to the river to refresh herself while Cat lay asleep in the old shack.

She'd taken little White Wolf with her so he could stretch his legs while she washed in the stream. She felt so marvelous after splashing the cooling water on her face, her attention had gone across the river and she'd watched the blue heron dipping down into the water to get himself a fish as he perched on a fallen cypress tree. When she'd turned around there was no sight of little White Wolf, and frantically, she'd scampered through the thick underbrush and the dense forest calling out to him. Fearing that he was lost, she took no notice of the direction in which she was heading through the woods.

"White Wolf, you little imp . . . where are you?" she muttered, knowing the pup's tiny legs could not carry him that far ahead of her. It never entered her mind to think about her own welfare or that she was in danger in these woods where wild animals roamed. All Charmaine was thinking about was the adorable little pup, White Wolf had presented to her. During her seemingly endless separation from Pierre, she'd bestowed on him the caresses she could not give her love. She, in turn, had received from the little puppy the affection Pierre could not give to her.

Some might think that crazy, but to Charmaine it was very real. It had surely kept her sane to think this way. But she went much farther away from the cabin and Cat Morrow than she realized. When she was about to drop from exhaustion and dissolve into a river of tears, she spotted White Wolf. His long, thick fur was tangled in the underbrush and he was unable to move. He looked up at her with his large black eyes, pleading with her to help him out of his own dilemma.

She laughed delightedly. "Oh, you little devil, I ought to let you squirm. You've been a naughty boy." She freed him and got a grateful lick of his tongue. "You charming rogue! You remind me of another whose winning ways always got me into trouble."

She was as powerless to resist the pup's charms as she was when Pierre turned his sensuous gray eyes on her. She sat down on the ground, the pup clutched in her arms, and thought of Pierre. She yearned so for the sight of his handsome face.

How long she sat there she did not know. But when she did decide she'd best get back to the cabin where she'd left Cat Morrow sleeping, she had no inkling that two hours had passed. By this time, Cat awakened and had set out to hunt her.

Charmaine walked and walked, but she could find no sight of the lean-to. At first, she fought the panic churning within her and it worked. Hunger forced her to pick some of the wild berries she found along the trail, and she quenched her thirst down at the stream. Her eyes searched for some sign of Cat's canoe, but she couldn't spot it.

It seemed she'd walked forever, and her legs felt like jelly.

Exhausted, she sank to the ground to rest. As the warm sunshine beamed down on her, she gave way to her weariness as her frustrated brain tried to sort out which way she should go.

Lethargy washed over her and she gave way to it. Little White Wolf was content to snuggle in her encircling arms as she lay back on the grassy carpet, listening to a mocking bird's trill. She thought of her mother, Uncle Angus, and Aunt Simone. Why, she lamented, had so much happened to her?

She silently moaned that everything had gone so wrong with her life. "Oh, *Maman* . . . if only you'd not died," she heard herself whisper out loud.

Had she never had to leave France and go to live with Aunt Simone and Uncle Angus, then the distasteful incident with her dear Johnny would never have happened. There would have been no reason for her to have crossed that vast ocean to come to this strange country in the first place.

"Oh, *Maman* . . . I'm so afraid! I'm so alone!" she cried out softly and held the tiny puppy tighter.

Mon Dieu, how she'd liked to feel the warm comfort of her gentle, loving mother's arms. Instead, she tried to absorb the warmth of little White Wolf.

Fear and the exhaustion took their toll and finally Charmaine slept. When she woke up a new panic seized her. A shroud of darkness surrounded her.

"Oh, God! White Wolf, it's night and we're stuck in these woods and I know not what to do." But the pup didn't seem to be disturbed. His tail wagged excitedly.

"Oh, you little mutt. I wish I could be you." She smiled down on him. There was never a time in her life that she remembered being so hungry, and she knew this little pup must be as starved. She wondered what Cat must be thinking, and she thought about what they'd eaten that first night. Right now, that seemed like a feast!

To get her mind off food, she rose up from the ground and

started to stroll toward the river. It was then she noticed the magnificent golden moon above her. Dear God, I need its magic this night, she mused! Then she recalled the ecstasy of the moonlight there on the cliffs of Jersey and the fulfilling rapture of Pierre's love. Somehow, it lightened the burden pressing down so hard on her at this moment.

She found a spot where she could feel the full glowing radiance of that same moon this night. She sat there on the side of the bluff of the river, that muddy Mississippi River. Tonight, she was going to give in to her fancy and pretend it was the English Channel. These bluffs would be her favorite cliffs above the bay back on the isle of Jersey. Tonight, she was going to give way to foolish whimsy for if she didn't, Charmaine didn't know if she could retain her sanity.

Scared and hungry, she felt giddy and so light-headed she didn't trust herself to take care of little White Wolf. She could not fail him now that she'd found him. She would not give way to this madness which kept trying to conquer her!

She prayed fervently that Pierre would come to her. Had he ever failed her before? In Savannah, he had saved her from that awful Chauncey Bedlow and had whisked her away to New Orleans. In New Orleans, he'd come just in the nick of time to rescue her from that despicable villain, Henri Gervais. How could she possibly doubt that he would not come to her now when she needed him more than ever?

She knew why there was a glimmer of doubt this time, for she was disappointed that Pierre had not come to her all that long, endless time when she'd stayed with Cat Morrow at White Wolf's cabin. Dear Lord, how she'd anticipated his arrival and it had never come!

It was strange and exciting, this feeling consuming his tense, male body as he urged his stallion along the winding riverbank. He knew instinctively that he was going to find her before this night ended. Call it fate or destiny, but he churned with anticipation!

492

If life dared to cheat him of this, Pierre did not know whether life would hold any meaning for him. If he was not to share his days and his nights with his golden-haired Charmaine, he could not accept another woman as some men did. Oh, his physical needs could always be sated, but he was a man who wanted more than that! He'd enjoyed his follies since the age of sixteen. He was mature enough now to want far more than that, and he had found it in Charmaine Lamoureux. So no one else would do!

If he had to search to the ends of the earth, he was willing to do that gladly. She would be worth it, he well knew!

He'd been riding now for over two hours since he'd left Cat Morrow back at that crude shack and by now, the bright full moon above him was easily guiding him along a trail in the dense forest. He welcomed it for he could make better time. His senses were not enough. He knew he would have been smarter to wait for the dawn. But when he guided the stallion around the bend of the trail, his gray eyes caught that unforgettable sight of long, flowing spun-gold tresses cascading down the back of the goddess he saw sitting on the bluff by the river. She was looking across the wide stream below her. In her dainty hands, she held the little ball of white fur that his old friend White Wolf had given to her. Pierre knew now somehow that the old half-breed had known he was to die soon. She held the little dog lovingly, and he thought to himself that someday she would hold their son or daughter that way. *Mon Dieu,* he pulsed with an eagerness for it to be soon. He wanted a son or a daughter! His and Charmaine's!

She sat so frozen and stiff, he observed. He knew the trauma she'd endured. How should he approach her, he wondered? Then he smiled, deciding that he'd do as he had done that night on the isle of Jersey when he'd stood blocking her in the narrow passageway. So he dismounted and tied the reins of his horse to one of the slender saplings.

He'd never seen a more beautiful silhouette. Funny, but it

493

seemed right and proper that he should find her again on a moonlit night such as this. Had he not first encountered her on such a night at a most unlikely time and place?

Ah, yes, it had to have been written in the stars that they should meet and love one another. It could have been no other way.

He moved toward her, every fiber in his male body alert and alive. All that mattered to him at this moment was that she was alive. He knew not what she'd suffered or what he might be faced with, but he'd meet that challenge and conquer it.

He was standing directly behind her when she turned to look up at him. Those glorious blue sapphire eyes of hers were fathomless in that first moment.

"*Ma petite amie,* I've found you—found you at last," he murmured in that husky deep voice of his. He sank down to the earth to enclose her in his arms, and as she came to him eagerly he swelled with overwhelming desire.

"*Ah, chérie ... ma chérie ...* I searched so long for you," he sighed, cherishing the sweet feel of her against him. She clung to him as if her very life depended on it.

Neither of them gave any thought to little White Wolf who crawled off her lap to lie by her side.

The silvery moonbeams were already spinning their magic spell as Pierre's sensuous lips captured hers in the kiss he'd yearned for so long.

"*Je t'aime,*" he whispered in her ear, and she responded with her own words of endearment in his ear. "Ah, yes, Pierre ... love me ... love me as only you can!" Her body arched eagerly against him. The hunger she felt now was not for food, but his love.

Dear God, he wanted to fill her with that! Never did he want her to lack his love! His lips sought to pleasure her as well as himself as he explored the lovely velvet valleys and mounds of her satiny flesh. His passion was heightened as her hands sought him, anxiously touching and caressing.

494

He moaned with delight, and prided himself on the expertise he'd exhibited in swiftly ridding them of their clothing. The reward of feeling her flushed, supple flesh was sheer rapture. He was no god though, and he could not resist being the mere mortal he was, so he eagerly sought to bury himself between her silken thighs. He wanted them to encircle him and press him closer to her.

"Oh, God, Pierre . . . God!" she moaned, feeling the same flaming pleasure as he when his flesh caressed her.

It had been so long since sparks of love had blazed into passion, their desire was almost out of control.

They allowed themselves to soar up to the heavens and the moon. Ecstasy was theirs in its golden rays. They surrendered to it!

Only later, as they lay quiet and exhausted, did Charmaine think about little White Wolf and she suddenly freed herself from Pierre's encircling arms. But he quickly calmed her by saying, *"Ah, cherie* . . . lie down. He is here right beside me, licking my ear, but I cannot say he excited me like you do."

She lay back down as Pierre had asked her to do, then sighed. "Isn't he adorable?"

"Oui, he is adorable and as wily as the old wolf who gave him to you, I'm thinking. That old wolf was guiding me all the way on my long search for you."

"You really think that, Pierre?" she asked.

"Of course, I do. Remember he named you Moonbeam so I had only to follow the beams of the moon tonight to find you, *ma petite.*"

She lay there thoughtfully for a moment without speaking. Now Charmaine knew she need never return to France to know her heart's desire as she'd believed when she'd sat on the cliffs at Jersey. All she needed to have her heart's desire was her handsome Pierre.

She snuggled close to him, flinging her satiny thigh sensuously against his. "Pierre, *mon cher,* will you always make love to me on the nights of a full moon?"

He gave her his devious grin. Aware beyond a shadow of doubt that she'd bewitched him, he was fired anew with overwhelming desire to make love to her.

"*Ma petite*, I vow to make love to you on every night of the full moon."

Moonlight ecstasy was theirs!